THE SON SHE LOST

Mommy—

Jenna sniffled and sobbed some more. Movement caught her eye and she raised her head. The murky hallway was fractured through the tears in her eyes, but she saw a small figure standing at the other end. It was very small, no more than three feet tall, wearing a little jacket with a hood that covered its head. It stood unmoving, well back from the pool of dim illumination cast by the single overhead light, a mere shape, facing her.

She stopped crying, stopped breathing for a long moment as she stared at the blurry figure. She wiped one eye, then the other, and blinked rapidly several times until her vision cleared.

The shadowy silhouette of a hooded child stood at the other end of the hallway, still and silent.

Jenna thought of Josh looking at her that last time, his puffy eyes so intense.

Mommy—

Her voice was throaty and broken. "Juh…Josh? Is that you? Josh?"

The dark little figure spread its stubby arms wide and began to hurry jauntily toward her. But it did not make a sound—no footsteps on the hardwood floor, no happy child's cry, only silence….

HIGH PRAISE FOR RAY GARTON!

THE LOVELIEST DEAD

RAY GARTON

LEISURE BOOKS **NEW YORK CITY**

For my wife, and my life,
Dawn

A LEISURE BOOK®

January 2006

Published by

Dorchester Publishing Co., Inc.
200 Madison Avenue
New York, NY 10016

ISBN 0-8439-5648-8

The name "Leisure Books" and the stylized "L" with design are trademarks of Dorchester Publishing Co., Inc.

Printed in the United States of America.

Visit us on the web at www.dorchesterpub.com.

ACKNOWLEDGMENTS

I'd like to thank those who gave me assistance and support during the writing of this novel. My wife, Dawn, Scott Sandin, Derek Sandin, Brian Hodges, Susan Colliflower, Della Clavere, my nephew Billy Tuschen, my brother-in-law Bill Blair, Jen Orosel, Bobby Mooney, TC, all my friends at the Shocklines Board, the Message Board of the Damned, and the Red Light District, my editor Don D'Auria, and my agent Richard Curtis.

How shall the burial rite be read?
The solemn song be sung?
The requiem for the loveliest dead,
That ever died so young?

—From "A Paean"
Edgar Allan Poe

PROLOGUE

Saturday, November 18, 2001

Dawn was just beginning to break when Jenna woke to the sound of Josh crying in his room. He was trying to be quiet, but the apartment was small, and Jenna had become a much lighter sleeper than usual lately. She got up quietly so she wouldn't disturb David, but he turned over anyway and lifted his head.

"Whasmatter?" he said, facing her with closed eyes.

"Josh is crying," she said, and David's eyes opened.

She crossed the hall to the boys' bedroom. Seven-year-old Miles was asleep in his bed. Josh sat leaning forward on the edge of his bed in his blue Bugs Bunny pajamas, head held in his small hands, blond hair spiky. It was an unnatural posture for a four-year-old boy—the posture of someone whose head throbbed.

Jenna went to Josh's bed and sat beside him, put an arm around him. "Oh, baby, is your head hurting again?" she whispered.

He sniffled as he nodded once.

1

"Why didn't you wake me, sweetheart?" It was not the first time she had awakened to find Josh up with a headache. He seemed to think it wasn't important enough to wake her, and it broke Jenna's heart.

David stepped into the room, tying the belt of his gray terry-cloth robe. "How's my buddy?"

Josh did not look up.

Jenna whispered to David, "Could you get his pills from the medicine cabinet? He's got another headache." To Josh, she said, "Come on, get up on Mommy's lap." She reached for the glass of water on his bedstand as he got on her lap and leaned into the crook of her arm. David quickly returned with the orange bottle of pills, removed the cap, and shook one into Jenna's palm. "Okay, honey, I want you to swallow a pill for me, okay?"

Josh slowly lifted his head and looked at her with puffy, barely open eyes. He opened his mouth and flattened his tongue, where she carefully placed the pill.

"A couple big swallows, now." Jenna put the glass to his lips, tilted it back. For a moment, his gulps were the only sound in the room besides Miles's gentle snoring. When he was done, she handed the glass to David, who put it back on the bedstand with the pill bottle. She put her arms around Josh and rocked him as she said, "Honey, you've got to wake me up as soon as your head starts to hurt, okay? I *want* you to, so I can give you your pill. The sooner you take it, the better it works. Okay?"

He said nothing, but she knew he was not asleep.

Jenna quietly hummed Brahms's "Lullaby" as she stroked Josh's back. After a couple minutes passed, she looked up at David, who stood silently beside her with his arms folded across his broad chest. "We've got to get a second opinion," she whispered.

David spread his arms, then let them drop at his sides.

"I know we do, but I don't know how. We can't afford the opinion we're getting."

"If I have to get on my hands and knees and *beg* another doctor to take a look at Josh, I will. I mean, how long do these damned pills have to not work before Dr. Peters *admits* they're not working?"

"If we manage to get a new doctor, there's no way we could afford to pay for all those tests again."

"Even if we could afford it, I wouldn't make him go through them again. The new doctor will just have to look at the results of the first tests. Those things scared the hell out of him, those big noisy machines."

Jenna brushed a strand of her long blond hair from her face and put her cheek against the side of Josh's head. He felt warm against her, limp in her arms.

Jenna and David had not been sleeping well. She was twenty-seven and David was twenty-eight, but constant worry and lack of sleep since Josh's headaches began had added lines to their faces. The last three hours had made up the best sleep Jenna had gotten in as many nights. Her pale face was splotchy and puffy, her blue eyes half closed as she gently rocked Josh in her arms.

"Are you feeling any better, sweetheart?" she whispered.

After a moment, Josh said, "Uh-uh." His voice was a moist croak. "Worse."

Looking up at David again, Jenna said, "I don't know why I even bother giving him those pills. I just don't know . . . what else to do." She felt like crying, but she was too tired.

Still rocking Josh, Jenna hummed the lullaby again. She glanced up at David and saw he had his arms folded over his chest again and shifted his weight from one foot to the other. His angular face looked sleepy and his thick, curly, chocolate-brown hair was wildly mussed on one side and flat on the other, but his muscles were tense and he was agitated. His sleepiness could not hide the concern in his eyes. Jenna wanted to hold him, too, but she kept both arms around Josh.

The boy startled her by sitting up suddenly and looking directly into her eyes. He frowned, but it was not an upset frown, or even a painful one. It was thoughtful, and a little frightened. She stopped rocking.

Josh said, "Mommy—"

It was the way he always said it when he had something important to tell her. Jenna recognized the tone immediately. But he did not continue.

"Yes, honey," she said.

Clenching his eyes shut, Josh opened his mouth and screamed so loudly that Jenna's ears rang. A dog barked outside. The scream stopped after what seemed a deafening eternity, and his body became stiff in her arms across her lap.

Jenna said, "Josh? *Josh!*"

David knelt in front of her and put an arm around Josh's shoulders.

Miles sat up in bed, clutched the blankets in his fists, and looked over at his brother.

Josh's body fell limp again. His head flopped backward and his eyes opened. The glow of dawn was coming through the window above his bed, and in the soft light, Jenna saw the pupil of Josh's left eye suddenly dilate, but only the left.

She screamed, "He's stopped breathing!"

"No!" David said, his hand on Josh's chest. "He's breathing, but it's very weak. I'll call an ambulance." He rushed out of the room, and his bare feet thumped through the small apartment.

Sobbing, Jenna pulled him to her and began rocking

him again. In her mind, all she could see was that single pupil dilating over and over. She did not know what it meant, but knew it could not be good.

Miles did not move, just sat in bed gripping the blankets in white-knuckled fists.

"C'mon, honey, c'mon, Josh," Jenna said between sobs. "Hang on, Josh, hang on. Tell me what you were going to say. What were you going to tell Mommy, sweetheart? Huh? What was it? C'mon, tell Mommy, tell me what—"

A shudder passed through Josh's small body and a gurgle rattled in his throat.

Jenna performed CPR on her son until the ambulance arrived and a paramedic took over, but Josh never recovered. He was pronounced dead at 7:48 A.M.

Hardly a day had passed since without Jenna Kellar wondering, at least once, what Josh had been about to say to her.

CHAPTER ONE

"Okay, sit down," Jenna said. "Nobody leaves until you've had breakfast."

The kitchen smelled of eggs, bacon, waffles, and coffee—it was their first real breakfast in the new house. For the first few days, before Jenna had been able to stock the kitchen, they'd been having cold cereal and Pop-Tarts. She finished setting the table in the breakfast nook, where her mother, Martha, had already settled in with a cup of coffee. The nook had a green-house window with a broad sill, where Martha had set her radio, which played George Gershwin's "Rhapsody in Blue" on a tinny AM big-band station.

Jenna suspected the breakfast nook would become one of her favorite spots in the house. A built-in bench with blue vinyl-upholstered cushions on the seats and backs went around the table on three sides. The cushions needed re-upholstering, but it was cozy. The window looked out over the backyard and through the

6

pines, Douglas firs, and redwoods to the ocean beyond. The view was obscured by gray morning fog.

"Smells good, Mom," Miles said. "Morning, Grandma."

"Hi, kiddo," Martha said with a smile. She scooted over on the bench and patted the spot beside her. "Come sit next to Grandma."

Miles sat down and poured a glass of orange juice for himself. He had his father's wavy brown hair and square face. Jenna knew it was her imagination, but he seemed to get taller every day.

Jenna stood at the stove in a baggy red sweatshirt and blue sweatpants, with her long, honey-blond hair pulled back in a ponytail. She scooped scrambled eggs onto one half of a platter, the other half of which held freshly cooked bacon. David came up behind her, put his hands on her shoulders, and kissed the back of her head.

"Morning, honey," he said.

She put the platter down, turned around and smiled, kissed him on the mouth. "Good morning."

He looked weary and preoccupied. She knew he was already worrying about a new day of job-hunting. So far he'd had no luck, but he had been unable to devote much time to it because they'd been so busy moving in. This would be his first full day of applying at garages in Eureka and the surrounding area.

"I've made a big breakfast," she said.

"I'm not really hungry."

She poured him a cup of coffee. "Come on, you've got to eat something before you start pounding the pavement. Sit." She handed him the cup of coffee and the platter of eggs and bacon.

David took the platter and coffee to the table and seated himself. "Good morning, Grandma," he said.

David always called Martha Grandma. "Hey, Tiger," he said to Miles. "Ready for your third day at school? Wait . . . this *is* Wednesday, isn't it?"

"Yep," Miles said. "I guess I'm ready for it."

"Have you made any friends yet?"

"I met a guy named Todd Haney who says he's got a big collection of Spider-Man comic books. He said I could come over and see 'em."

"Then you'll have to do that."

As Jenna brought a platter of waffles to the table, Miles looked up and said, "Could I, Mom?"

"Could you what?"

"Go over to Todd's house after school and see his Spider-Man comics?"

"Well, I think it'd be a good idea if we met Todd first before you start going home with him after school."

"Mom's right," David said. "Why don't you bring him over here?"

"Hey," Jenna said, "I'm not so sure I'm ready for extra kids around here yet."

Miles said, "What if Todd's mom wants to meet *me* before she lets him come over *here?*"

Jenna, David, and Martha laughed.

Miles smiled sheepishly, uncertain why they were so amused.

"You're a smart kid," David said.

Jenna poured herself a cup of coffee and took a seat at the table. As they began to fill their plates, she said, "We'll do it someday soon, okay, Miles?"

"Okay," he said.

"Today," Jenna said, "I'd like to paint the kitchen cupboards with that paint we found in the garage last night."

"If you wait for the weekend, I can do it," David said.

8

"No, I don't mind. In fact, I want to, I think it'll be fun."

They fell silent as they ate their breakfast. The music on the radio stopped for a news break.

"By the way, Mom," Jenna said, "I heard your radio in the middle of the night last night. Do you think you could keep the volume a little lower? The music woke me up."

"Music? I wasn't listening to music last night," Martha said. "I was listening to talk shows. But I turned it off a little after twelve, and it wasn't loud enough for you to hear upstairs, I'm sure." Martha had the downstairs bedroom. Since her stroke, she had trouble keeping her balance at times and occasionally had bouts of dizziness. They all thought it best that she not have to tackle the stairs.

Jenna frowned as she chewed a bite of bacon. "Well, I know I heard music. I got up and went to the bathroom, and by the time I came out, it had stopped." She turned to Miles. "Were you listening to the radio last night?"

"Nope."

"Maybe you dreamed it," David said with a smirk.

Still frowning, Jenna said, "No. No, I definitely . . . well . . . I could've sworn I heard music. Maybe . . . I don't know. Maybe I did dream it." Her frown dissolved and they said no more as they ate their breakfast.

It was not a new house, by any means, but it was new to the Kellars. It was a rather boxy four-bedroom, two-bathroom house with a flat roof, fully furnished, that stood two stories tall on ten thickly wooded acres in northern California's Humboldt County. It had a large square yard, and a two-car garage branched off from the house on the north side. It was a tired-looking gray with white trim, its paint peeling, the shingled roof in need of repair. The yard, surrounded by a tall, rusted Cyclone fence, was overrun with weeds. Shrubbery along the fence and around the house had gone wild, and ivy had crawled up the sides of the house like eager tendrils trying to pull it down into the ground.

Two clotheslines sagged between a couple of rusted metal poles in the backyard. An old rusted children's swing set and slide stood nearby, both crawling with ivy. Inside, the house was equipped with central air and heat, but it would be a while before the Kellars could afford to use it. There was a fireplace in the living room and an enormous stack of chopped wood beneath an awning behind the garage.

The acreage was surrounded by a tall barbed-wire fence on three sides, with a cliff facing the ocean in back. The graveled driveway came off Starfish Drive through a long aluminum gate and went straight through the woods about half a mile to the house. A trail behind the house led to the cliff a couple hundred feet away, where a rickety wooden staircase zigzagged down the cliff face to the rocky, isolated beach below, known as Starfish Cove. The stairs were old and decayed and treacherous, and David had told Miles to stay away from them.

The house and yard needed work, but the Kellars did not mind. All the paperwork was out of the way and it was theirs, free and clear, left to Jenna by the father she never knew. Even with the yearly property taxes, it was a big improvement on the small apartment they had been renting about a hundred and sixty miles east of there in Redding.

After Josh died, everything had seemed to go sour for David and Jenna. David's medical insurance at work had covered very little of the battery of tests Josh had gone through, and the bills had drained what little savings they had. A few months after Josh's death, David, an auto mechanic, had lost his job when the owner of the garage where he worked had died and the place had closed, and he had been unable to find full-time work ever since.

Their little apartment had gotten smaller about eighteen months later when Martha had suffered a mild stroke and had come to live with them. Along with her monthly Social Security check and some savings, Martha had her retirement money from her many years working for Pacific Bell in Redding, and she was eager to help out as much as she could. She had aided them in paying off some, though not all, of the medical bills, and she helped with bills and groceries.

As old and run-down as the house was, it was a new start for the Kellars. It was just outside the city limits of Eureka, where David hoped to have better luck finding employment than he'd had in Redding. But most of all, it was a home of their very own. It belonged to them completely, warts and all.

Some time ago, someone had stripped all the paint from the wooden cupboards on both sides of the kitchen, then had neglected to repaint them. By eleven o'clock, the cupboards on the southern side of the kitchen were drying a soft creamy white, and Jenna, still in her sweats, was at work on the cupboards opposite them. The counter was covered with newspapers, and as she painted, she stood on a green folding stepladder.

Martha sat in the breakfast nook reading the *Global Inquisitor* while Glenn Miller's "String of Pearls" played on her radio and tendrils of steam rose from a mug of green tea. Martha read all the tabloids every week, but the *Inquisitor* was her favorite.

The sky outside was dark with gunmetal-gray clouds.

A strong wind had come up and whistled around the corners of the house. The rusty chains of the swings on the old set in the backyard screeched and rattled as they blew in the wind.

"A UFO landed in the middle of a park in Oslo, Norway," Martha said, "and aliens came out and took a little boy off the monkey bars, hauled him into the flying saucer, and flew away."

Jenna smiled and shook her head without turning away from her painting. "Mom, don't you think if that really happened, it would be on the news?"

"Oh, I don't know. Maybe not." Martha turned a page and adjusted her glasses. Her silver hair was short and curly. Her cane stood against the wall beside the breakfast nook's bench. "They're too busy with who's screwin' who in Hollywood and Washington. They're not much different than the tabloids, you know."

"Well, I won't argue with that."

"The Binghams cleared another house."

"The who?"

"Arthur and Mavis Bingham, the occult investigators. Remember? I've told you about them before. They cleared another house possessed by demons. In Connecticut this time."

Jenna dipped her brush in the can of paint on the counter. "Do they do yards? Maybe they could clear all the weeds and ivy outside."

Martha laughed.

"How's your bedroom coming along?" Jenna asked. "Have you got all your things unpacked and put away?"

"I've unpacked everything but my photo albums and jewelry. That's a big room. Even with all my junk, it's going to look half empty."

"I promise to get those boxes out of there soon," Jenna said. "But like you said, it's a big room, and I needed someplace to put that stuff until I can unpack it."

"No problem," she said. She took a sip of her tea and turned another page.

After a set of commercials on the radio, Doris Day sang "Sentimental Journey."

"I hope Miles is doing okay at school," Jenna said.

"Oh, our Miles always does well at school. Hasn't he always gotten good grades?"

"That's not what I mean. Yes, he's a great student, a lot better than I ever was."

"You did well in school, Jenna."

"But it was always such a struggle for me. I really had to work at it. It seems to come naturally for Miles. He's very smart. No, I mean I hope he's making friends. He's so shy."

"He said this morning he'd made a friend."

"He said he'd met a boy—that's not the same thing. He never complains about anything, he keeps everything inside." *Josh was the same way*, she thought as she dipped the brush again.

Mommy—

"Last year," Jenna said, "there was a boy at school who picked on him every day. Miles didn't say a word about it. I only found out because one day after school he went to his bedroom as usual, and I took a snack to him, but his door was locked. He never locks his door. He didn't want to open it at first, but I insisted, and when he let me in, I saw that he'd been crying."

"Crying? Miles?"

"I almost had a heart attack when I saw the tears on his cheeks, because . . . well, I just . . ." Jenna said nothing for a moment. When she'd seen the tears on Miles's cheeks, panic had exploded inside her, because ever since Josh had died, she'd been living with the palpitating fear that something might happen to her only remaining son. But she said none of that. "It took me a while, but I finally got it out of him. He told me about that bully, and it made me so angry. Miles didn't want me to do anything about it, and I promised him I wouldn't, but that was a little white lie, because I called his teacher and told her about it. Apparently, she intervened somehow. I asked him about it a week later and he said things were okay, that the boy was leaving him alone." She sighed. "Children can be so cruel to each other."

"Speaking of children," Martha said, "there are about half a dozen of them in the backyard right now playing on the slide and swing set."

Jenna stopped painting and looked over at the breakfast nook. Martha was leaning to her left, craning her neck to peer out the breakfast-nook window. "What?"

"A bunch of boys. There's, let's see—one, two, three . . . five of them."

"It's not even noon yet, they should be in school."

"Well, they're not." Still looking out the window, Martha sipped her tea. "You know, you really should chase them off, Jenna. If one of them hurts himself in your yard, his parents are likely to sue you. Everybody's suing everybody these days."

The house was in such a remote location and so far off the main road, it seemed unlikely that a bunch of little boys would be playing in the yard. But Martha was obviously watching *something*.

Frowning, Jenna placed the brush across the top of the paint can and carefully climbed down off the stepladder. She walked over to the breakfast nook and slid onto the bench opposite Martha.

"Oh!" Martha said softly, her back suddenly stiff.

Jenna looked out the window. The backyard was

empty. The two swings twisted and swayed in the wind. She looked across the table at her mother.

"There are no kids out there now, Mom."

Martha's eyes were wide behind her large, silver-framed glasses as her head turned slowly from the window to face Jenna. "They disappeared."

Jenna looked out the window again. They hadn't had time to climb over the Cyclone fence, which would have been difficult, so there was only one direction the boys could have gone. "Did they head for the front yard?"

"They disappeared into the ground."

Jenna looked at her again, this time with a wrinkled brow, and a chill passed over her shoulders.

Martha's eyes lowered to her cup of tea. She looked as if she were about to cry.

"Are . . . are you all right, Mom?"

She said nothing for a moment, did not even move.

Martha had become much more forgetful since the stroke. She lost her train of thought during conversations and forgot what she was saying. She did silly little things, like searching for her glasses while they were on her face, or remembering conversations or events that had never taken place. But this was the most drastic thing that had happened so far—that Jenna was aware of, anyway.

"Mom, have you taken all your pills today?"

Martha slowly raised her head to look at Jenna. "You think I made it up?"

"No, I didn't say that."

"Then you think I imagined it."

"I didn't say—"

"They were out there. One had a green knit cap on his head, and another wore a red plaid jacket and . . . and they just . . . disappeared into the ground."

Jenna nodded and started to say that, yes, she believed her—but she knew her voice would give her away, that she would not sound convincing, because, of course, she did not believe her. So she said nothing. Instead, she scooted out from behind the table and went around to the other side, put an arm around Martha's shoulders, and hugged her.

"You didn't answer me," Jenna said. "Have you taken all your pills?"

After a moment, Martha said, "What time is it?"

Jenna looked at the clock on the microwave oven. "Almost eleven-thirty."

"Okay, I . . . I do need to take a couple pills. I'm glad you reminded me. I think I'll do that now, and then . . . maybe I'll lie down for a little while."

"All right. I'll fix lunch around one. How do soup and sandwiches sound?"

Martha nodded. "Good. That sounds good."

Jenna stepped back and watched Martha get up and shuffle out of the kitchen with her cane. When she heard the bedroom door close down the hall from the kitchen, Jenna sat down in Martha's place at the table for a moment and stared out the window.

Martha's stroke had frightened Jenna. She had not been ready for another death so soon after Josh's. She knew she would *never* be ready for the death of her mother. They had always been close. But as much as it hurt her to think it, she would prefer a quick death for Martha to the slow, lingering fate of something like Alzheimer's disease. She wondered if that possibly could be the cause of such a hallucination.

Before the move, Martha's doctor in Redding, Dr. Evan Reasor, had recommended a doctor in Eureka, Dr. Blanche Wenders. He had written a letter of referral for Martha and sent it along with her medical records.

Jenna decided to call Dr. Wenders's office that day and make an appointment. She thought Dr. Wenders should be told about Martha's hallucination.

As "Take the 'A' Train" began to play on the radio, Jenna went back to her painting.

Jenna was lying naked in bed, reading a paperback novel, when David came into the bedroom in his robe and slippers. He shed the gray robe and tossed it onto the foot of the bed, kicked off the slippers, and slid naked beneath the covers. He propped himself up on his side, facing her, and put a hand on her belly.

After two children, Jenna's belly wasn't as flat as it used to be. But aside from the fleshy pouch over her abdomen, she had managed to keep her figure mostly intact. Her curves were perhaps a little curvier than they used to be, but that was all. It helped to have good genes—at sixty-nine, her mother was still a slender woman.

Jenna closed the book and put it on the bedstand, then turned out the lamp, leaving the room dark. Turning to David, she brushed her hair back from her face—she had just brushed it and it was soft and feathery—and kissed him on the mouth. He tasted of toothpaste and Listerine.

"Hey, you did a terrific job in the kitchen today," David said as he lay back on the bed. "It looks great."

"Thank you, sir." Jenna nestled against him, stretched a long leg over both of his, and put a hand on his chest. He was tall and strong, fit except for a paunch he'd developed from eating Martha's baking. Jenna felt safe in the crook of his strong arm.

"Now, how about doing the outside of the house?"

She laughed and tweaked his nipple, then rubbed her

17

fingers through the thin tuft of hair on his chest. "Very funny. You know, we really need to do something about the light out in the hall. It's way too dark out there."

"I know. Just add it to the long list of things we need to do."

"Is Miles settled?"

"He's already asleep. I think watching that monster movie on TV tonight excited him so much, it wore him out."

"I wish you wouldn't let him watch movies like that."

"Oh, c'mon. I watched them when I was his age, and I turned out okay."

"Oh, you think so?"

"They scared the hell out of me back then, but that was what made them fun. I think Grandma even enjoyed it."

"Well, nobody ever accused Mom of having good taste."

They leaned close and spoke just above a whisper. Their apartment back in Redding had been so small, the only time they had any privacy together was when they were in bed, and it was then that they whispered about their day and whatever was on their minds. They had plenty of opportunities to talk alone now that they were in a large house, but they had not been there long enough to break the old habit.

"Speaking of Mom," Jenna said. She told David about Martha's hallucination that morning. "I called Dr. Wenders's office today and made an appointment. If it hadn't been for that letter of referral Dr. Reasor sent, we would've had to wait months, but I pressed it and managed to get her in two weeks from Friday."

"Why wait? Call Dr. Reasor and tell him what happened. He's a lot more familiar with her than this new doctor will be. He might have something to say about it."

Jenna rolled her eyes. "Why didn't I think of that? I was so busy worrying . . ."

"I wouldn't worry too much. Remember, she had a stroke. It was a year and a half ago, but still, that's a sucker punch to the brain."

"True."

"Call Dr. Reasor tomorrow, but for now, don't worry about it, okay?"

"Okay. What about you? Didn't you have any luck at all today?"

He shrugged one shoulder. "One possibility. A garage in Eureka. The guy said he might need some part-time help, but he won't know for sure for another week or so."

"Well, that's a possibility, at least."

"I went everywhere in Eureka today. Tomorrow I'm going to try Fortuna and Arcata."

He was trying to conceal his discouragement, but Jenna could hear it in his voice, and knew if the lights were on she would see it in his eyes. It made her chest ache. She tilted her head up and kissed him again.

"Don't let it get you down, okay?" she said. "Something will turn up."

"It better, or I may end up working in the food-service industry."

"Hey, if nothing else, you can freelance, like you did back home."

"Back home?"

She laughed. "Yeah, what am I saying? This is home now."

They lay in silence for a while, Jenna stroking his chest as he lightly brushed a hand over her hair.

"You know, we haven't made love in this house yet," David whispered.

"We've been too wiped out from moving in."

"I'm up for it if you are."

She smiled. "We don't even have to be quiet anymore—there's nobody on the other side of the wall."

"Is that a yes?"

She rolled over on top of him. "Only if you don't make me paint the house."

CHAPTER TWO

Lily. Wednesday, 2:19 P.M.

The Reading Room in the back of The Crystal Well bookstore in the northern California town of Mt. Shasta was not for reading books. It was where forty-three-year-old Lily Rourke, the store's owner, conducted psychic readings.

In the doorway that led into the Reading Room, Lily had hung a curtain of multicolored beads that clacked and chittered whenever someone walked through them. It was a small room, with a round table in the center and two carved mahogany chairs, each with burgundy velvet-upholstered cushions, facing each other on opposite sides. The room was painted hunter green, with plush burgundy carpet. On the wall were a few framed pictures of Victorian-era séances that Lily had cut out of some old books. A brass floor lamp topped by a burgundy shade with beaded fringe stood in one corner, giving off a muted glow. Candles flickered on a sideboard, and incense in a small marble holder gave the room a sandalwood scent.

At five feet, five inches tall, Lily weighed 304 pounds. She wore a black silk broomstick skirt with a red rose print, a matching red silk blouse, and black pumps. Her dark-blond hair was short, in a pageboy cut. She sat at the table in the Reading Room with one of her regular clients, Maggie Rydell. Lily's arms rested on the table-top and her plump hands gently held both of Maggie's small, slender ones. A votive candle glowed in a plain glass holder between them.

"Things are going better with Rupert," Lily said.

Maggie smiled and nodded. "Yes, they are."

"That's good, I'm glad. Whatever you're doing, it's working, because I sense that his eyes aren't wandering like they were before."

Maggie sighed with relief.

"The kids, though . . . you might want to keep a close eye on them for a while. Have . . ." Lily frowned. "Have you hired a new babysitter? Tina? No . . . Dina, right?"

Maggie's smile melted away and she suddenly looked concerned. "Yes, Dina. We hired her a couple weeks ago. She was recommended to us by friends."

"Get rid of her."

"Why? I mean, what's wrong with her? Has she hurt the kids?"

"No, no, nothing like that. I just sense . . . neglect. A lack of safety. She's not very good at what she does, that's all. You can do better."

"Okay, we won't use her anymore. But we've already used her twice. Did anything happen to the kids while we were—"

"No, no, I'm not getting that. But don't use her anymore. And you might want to say the same to the friends who recommended her."

"What about my dad?"

Lily closed her eyes a moment and creases appeared in her forehead. She tried never to let anything show on her face when she was giving a reading. Sometimes it was more difficult than others, and this was one of those times. She opened her eyes.

"He's not doing well," Lily said.

"No, he's not."

Lily closed her eyes again and took a moment to decide how to respond.

"And to be honest," Maggie said, "we don't expect him to get better this time. So . . . well, I mean, if you've got bad news . . . I can take it."

Lily opened her eyes and said, "Well, you know I don't like giving bad news, but . . . you should prepare yourself for the worst."

Maggie's shoulders sagged and she sighed. "We already have. He's in pretty bad shape. I expected you to say that. I just . . . well, I thought it couldn't hurt to ask."

"He's had a good long life, Maggie. You shouldn't—"

Lily saw faint flashes of electric blue in the periphery of her vision on both sides, and she caught a whiff of bananas. A burst of adrenaline coursed through her and she dropped Maggie's hands as if they suddenly had become unbearably hot. She scooted her chair back from the table and pressed the heels of her hands to her closed eyes for a moment, hoping the flashing and the smell would go away.

"Are you all right?" Maggie asked. When she got no response, she spoke more urgently. "Lily, is something wrong?"

23

The electric-blue flashing continued, even with her eyes closed, and the smell of bananas grew stronger.

"Lily, what's the matter? Do you want me to call someone?"

It stopped as abruptly as it had begun. Lily opened her eyes again. Sometimes it happened that way—the flashing and the smell would come and then stop, and nothing would follow. She blinked her eyes a few times, then looked at Maggie, who was staring at her with concern.

"I'm sorry," Lily said. "I . . . I don't feel so good all of a sudden."

"Can I get something for you?"

"No, I think it's passing. Just give me a few seconds to—"

The flashing started again and the smell of bananas filled her nostrils. Lily felt all the strength drain rapidly from her body, felt herself slide off the chair. She lost all awareness of Maggie and the room around her before she hit the floor.

Floating in silent darkness.

A distant scream grows louder. No, not a scream, but a metallic screech. Light flickers in the darkness, a strobe effect. She sees glimpses of a children's swing set and a slide. Both are dark with rust and covered with wild tangles of ivy. The swing's chains screech and chitter as they sway. The swing set and slide flicker out. The screeching stops.

Floating in dark silence, until—

Another sound, garbled, as if under water. It is music—a delicate, twinkling tune, as if from a music box. It's vaguely familiar, but off key, warped.

A filthy old teddy bear appears. It has only one round black eye. A dark ribbon is tied in a bow around its neck. Stuffing dangles out of its filthy chest and abdomen.

24

The bear disappears. The distorted music stops. Lost again in the darkness.

A voice, whispered but throaty and gruff. It is unfamiliar, but fills her with terror. "Be a good puppy. C'mon over here and be a good puppy."

She wants to scream but has no voice, no breath, no heartbeat.

The darkness is driven away by blinding daylight. She sees an enormous, gray, two-story house from a distorted angle, as if she is an ant on the ground looking up at it. Ivy clings to the towering walls. A dark, bulking figure rises menacingly before her, blocks her view of the house. It's a fat man wearing a cowboy hat, and he fills her with dread. She wants to flee but has nowhere to go.

"Come here and be a good puppy, now."

Suddenly, she is falling through darkness. As she plummets, the voice fades.

"Be a good puppy . . . a good puppy . . . good puppy . . ."

Lily opened her eyes to look up into the faces of her only employee, Claudia McNeil, and her client, Maggie Rydell. They looked panicky. A dull ache behind Lily's eyes grew worse with each throb, and her mouth felt cottony.

"You didn't call an ambulance, did you?" Lily asked as she rubbed her eyes.

Claudia said, "Should I?"

"No, no. How long was I out?" She licked her dry lips and groaned quietly.

"Not long," Claudia said. "Maybe twenty or thirty seconds."

"Can we get you something?" Maggie asked.

"Maybe some water."

Claudia shot to her feet and hurried away.

"How do you feel?" Maggie said.

"I'm fine. Just a little headache. No, wait. Make that a splitting headache."

"I have some Tylenol in my purse."

"That's okay, I've got something in my medicine cabinet." Lily rolled onto her side and slowly got to her knees. She leaned a hand on the chair and stood with effort, but swayed dizzily and immediately sat down. Maggie stood beside her. "Sorry, Maggie. We didn't get very far. This one's on the house."

"Are you kidding? What you told me about the babysitter alone was worth it. I'll pay the regular fee."

Claudia returned with a glass of ice water. Lily took a few sips as Claudia stood, hands on her hips, looking concerned. Claudia was twenty-eight, skinny, with short red hair, full and shaggy. She stood a couple inches taller than Lily and wore a light blue cashmere-blend sweater, a pair of jeans, and sneakers.

"Can you handle things, Claudia?" Lily asked. "I think I should go lie down for a little while."

"Sure, no problem, Lily, I'll be fine." She looked worried. "Are you sure you don't want to see a doctor or something?"

"No, I'm okay. I just need a nap, is all. I'll be fine. See you later, Maggie."

Lily stood and waited to make sure the room wasn't going to tilt again. She patted her hair, then smiled wearily. The beads clacked as she passed through them. She crossed the rear of the store, went through the stockroom and into her kitchen in the back. She went down the hall to the bathroom with her glass of ice water and got a Vicodin from her cabinet. The pills had been there since she'd had her wisdom teeth pulled seven months before—she'd taken only a couple back then. After swallowing it, she went to her bedroom, put the glass of water on her bedstand, and got a spiral-bound notebook from a drawer in her dresser, found a pen, and sat down on the edge of the bed. She jotted down a few notes about the vision, then put the notebook and pen on the bedstand. She stretched out on the bed with a long sigh.

As she lay on her back and stared at the ceiling of her bedroom, Lily's hands trembled. She realized she was afraid. She could still hear, in her mind, the warped, garbled music and the gruffly whispered voice from her vision. Lily was afraid, because she knew there would be more. Visions like that did not happen only once. They returned with increasing frequency and in greater detail, and they did not go away until she figured out what they meant, what they were trying to tell her. It did not end there, either. Once she figured the vision out, she had to *do* something about it.

Lily Rourke had been psychic all her life. She could not remember a time when her mind did not show her things she did not want to see, tell her things she did not want to know.

She had been born and raised in the small northern California town of Cottonwood, seventy-five miles south of Mt. Shasta. She had a brother, Charles, five years her senior, whom she heard from every year at Christmas and on her birthday. Her father, dead for a dozen years now, had been a plumber, her mother a kindergarten teacher. None of them had understood her—Lily had scarcely understood herself early in life—but her mother was the only one who'd tried. As a child, Lily preferred solitude—being around people only filled her mind with confusing, sometimes frightening, images and thoughts. As a result, school had been a daily nightmare for her from the beginning. She had no trouble with her studies—she was an exceptionally bright, intelligent student—but she had difficulty concentrating on them when she was being mentally bombarded from all directions. Socially, she was an outcast by choice. She preferred to be alone with a book and a snack. Reading had been her favorite activity and food her only friend. Her weight had gone up early on and had never come down again.

Lily's mother had died of breast cancer when Lily was eleven years old, leaving her a stranger in the house with her father and Charles. She had become even more withdrawn then. Outside of school, which she cut whenever the opportunity arose, the only place she had gone with any regularity was the small Cottonwood Library, where, at the age of twelve, she'd met the best friend she'd ever had.

The new head librarian, Annabelle Youngblood, was a tall, graceful, fifty-three-year-old widow with streaks of silver in her short black hair and a pair of jeweled reading glasses she wore on a chain around her neck. When Lily walked into the library on Mrs. Youngblood's first day, the woman immediately turned to her and watched her closely wherever she went. After a few minutes of the librarian carefully watching her every move, Lily began to feel very self-conscious—more so than usual, because she always felt self-conscious—so she went to the back of the library where the woman could not see her. On that day, as on every day for eight months, she'd looked for books on psychic phenomena.

By then, Lily had begun to understand that not only was she different from others, she had some strange ability that allowed her to know things she could not possibly know. She had been confused by the thoughts and images that plagued her until she saw her mother's funeral the year before—she'd seen it weeks before her mother had been diagnosed with cancer. By the time it had been found, the cancer had spread and become inoperable, and Lily's mother had died only months after being diagnosed. When the funeral took place, it was exactly as Lily had seen it in her mind, with her mother lying in an open casket at the front of the funeral chapel. Lily had never been in the funeral chapel before, but she had seen it in vivid detail in her mind months before. She even had heard the organ playing the exact same music it had played at the funeral. That was when she began to suspect that maybe she wasn't crazy as she'd always suspected. She had worked her way through most of the library's books on psychic phenomena, with only four left that she had not yet read.

That day in the library, as she looked through one of the books, a hand came to rest on Lily's shoulder from behind, and she almost jumped out of her skin. She dropped the book she was holding and spun around to find the librarian standing behind her, smiling.

"Hello, Lily," she said. "I'm Mrs. Youngblood. I think you and I have something in common."

"We . . . do? How did you know my name?"

"You know, I might be able to help you even more than those books."

Mrs. Youngblood invited Lily over to her house that evening to make cookies. Lily did not have to ask permission from her father. Since she spent all her time in her bedroom reading anyway, he did not even notice she was gone. She climbed out her bedroom window and rode her bike over to Mrs. Youngblood's house, eager to hear what the woman had to say.

As they made cookies that evening, Mrs. Youngblood had explained that she'd been just as frightened and mystified as Lily when she was that age. She had not understood her abilities, had not known how to deal with them. Just as Lily had been doing, Mrs. Youngblood had read up on psychic phenomena. Everything she'd learned about her abilities she'd learned on her own.

"But it would have been so much easier," she said, "if someone else who had the gift had shared her knowledge of it with me. And that's what I want to do for you."

Until then, Lily had been unable to walk through a room full of people without being deluged with dizzying psychic input that made no sense to her. Over the next four years, Mrs. Youngblood taught her how to turn down the volume of that input, how to deflect the incoming information so she could think clearly and concentrate on her school work. She taught Lily how to sift through all the thoughts and images and single out specific information, how to make sense of it. Most of all, she made Lily understand that there was nothing *wrong* with her, that she was not crazy. She simply had been born with a gift that few shared. Mrs. Youngblood always referred to it as a "gift."

"A lot of people *claim* to have the gift," Mrs. Youngblood told her one evening. "Most of them are frauds. Those who really do have it tend to keep it to themselves, because it can't be used as easily as those frauds claim to use it. You can't pick and choose the information you get so easily—what comes, comes. If you know what you're doing, you can make sense of it, but not always. While you can manipulate the gift, you can never completely control it. For instance, you can't go to Las Vegas and make a fortune with it, or use it to play the horses at the tracks. Sometimes, no matter how well you try to block them, things will come through. Sometimes these things will be so powerful, so overwhelming, they will make you physically ill. And when you have visions like that, you'll find you have to act on them."

"What do you mean, act on them?" Lily had asked.

"The gift comes with a certain responsibility, Lily. You may receive information that could help someone, perhaps save someone from harm or even death. When that happens, you are obligated to act on that information. At least, that's the way I see it. Have you gotten any religion in your life, Lily?"

"We used to go to the Methodist church every Sunday when Mom was alive."

"Well, I am of the opinion that this is a gift from God, and God does not give gifts without reason or purpose. There will be times when you *must* use this gift to help others, whether you want to or not."

Lily did not fully understand what Mrs. Youngblood meant until years later.

When Lily was fourteen, Mrs. Youngblood introduced her to a friend named Dolores Reeder, a plump, gray-haired woman in her early sixties who dressed flamboyantly and wore a lot of clattering jewelry. Mrs. Reeder and her husband, Clay, owned a metaphysical bookstore, The Crystal Well, in the town of Mt. Shasta. The Reeders had a lifelong interest in the paranormal, and while neither of them shared Mrs. Youngblood's gift, they were aware of it. With Lily's permission, Mrs. Youngblood told Mrs. Reeder how strong Lily's gift was, that it was the most powerful she had ever encountered, even stronger than her own.

The summer after Lily graduated from high school, Mrs. Youngblood moved to Colorado to be near her daughter and grandchildren. Mrs. Youngblood knew how unhappy Lily was at home. By then, Charles was working with their father in his plumbing business, but he still lived at home. Lily's father and brother, while unaware of her gift, knew there was something odd about her and no longer even tried to hide their discomfort around her. They made no effort to understand her, and sometimes Lily even sensed they were a little afraid of her. Lily had a job at a bookstore. She had no idea what she wanted to do with her life, although she had a deep interest in writing, but she knew she did not want to go to college right after graduating—she needed a break, some time to herself. Before leaving Cottonwood, Mrs. Youngblood suggested Lily move up to Mt. Shasta and work at The Crystal Well for a while. She had already discussed it with the Reeders, and they offered to let Lily live in the apartment behind their bookstore, once occupied by their niece, who had married and moved out three years before. Lily eagerly accepted the opportunity to get out of Cottonwood and out of her smothering, uncomfortable house.

She settled into the apartment in back of the bookstore and approached her new job with great enthusiasm. The Reeders were not very organized, but after a few months, Lily had things running so efficiently that Mrs. Reeder expressed regret that she had not come to work there much sooner.

Fourteen months after moving to Mt. Shasta, Lily was on her knees putting some new books on a low shelf when she began to see flashes of electric blue in the periphery of her vision and was overwhelmed by the smell of bananas. She stood and looked around, expecting to see that someone had come in with a bag of groceries, including a bunch of ripe bananas, but no one had entered the store. The flashing grew worse, and Lily went to the register, where Mrs. Reeder was poring over that day's edition of the *Redding Record Searchlight*. Mrs. Reeder said Lily didn't look well and told her to sit down. But before Lily could get to a chair, she blacked out and fell to the floor.

She opened her eyes less than a minute later, frightened by what she had seen: an unusual bloodstained knife that had glowed with an odd light. She tried unsuccessfully to describe it to Mrs. Reeder, who gave her a pad and pen and told her to draw it. The knife appeared to have two handles—like a pair of scissors, but without the finger loops—and a single narrow blade. Mrs. Reeder said she'd never seen anything like it. The vision made no sense to Lily, and that evening, she called Mrs. Youngblood in Colorado and told her about it.

"The knife wasn't at all familiar to you?" Mrs. Youngblood said.

"No, I've never seen a knife like that before in my life."

"And you say you smelled bananas?"

"Yes. Is that normal?"

"There is no such thing as normal. Prior to a powerful vision, some people will smell roses, or burnt toast. My ears start ringing before it happens."

"It's happened to you?"

"Only a few times. But enough for me to know it will happen to you again."

"Again? Why?"

"Because you don't understand what you've seen. It will keep happening until you understand its significance and can do something about it."

"*Do* something about it? But what am I supposed to do?"

"I don't know. That's what you're going to have to figure out. Remember when I told you the gift comes with responsibility?"

"Yes."

"Well, significant visions like this usually require something from you. Don't worry, you'll figure it out. When you do, you'll know what to do. And even if you're not sure, you'll figure something out. I have faith in you. You should, too."

The vision occurred again later that same week, even more vivid than before. This time, Lily saw a narrow, serpentlike dragon intricately carved into each of the handles. The third vision was the worst, because Lily saw the knife's blade sink to the hilt between two bare female breasts, not once, but again and again, eighteen times, and each bloody stab was accompanied by a horrible scream. She also noticed three initials crudely carved near the very bottom of one of the handles: O.J.B.

"Maybe it's got something to do with the stabbings in Redding," Mrs. Reeder said.

"Stabbings?" Lily said. "What stabbings?"

Mrs. Reeder showed her an article in the *Record Searchlight*. Four young women ranging in age from nineteen to twenty-four had been brutally stabbed to death in the past seven months. Forensics had determined the shape of the blade used in each murder, but other than that, the article said the police had no leads. The next day, during her lunch break, Lily was listening to the news on the radio when she heard that a fifth stabbing victim had been found that morning, a twenty-year-old nursing student. She had been stabbed eighteen times in the chest and abdomen.

It was then that Lily understood what Mrs. Youngblood had meant. As difficult as it may be to explain to the police, she felt obligated to tell them what she had seen in her vision. There was a chance that a detailed description of the knife could help their investigation.

So Mrs. Reeder drove her down to Redding, about an hour south of Mt. Shasta. On the way, Lily told her that she did not want to draw any attention to herself—she was afraid the press would turn her into a freak show. When they arrived at the police station in Redding, Mrs. Reeder would not let her say a word until she had explained to the detective that Lily was a gifted psychic who wanted no recognition for what she was about to tell them. She insisted that if the information was useful to them, they were to respect Lily's privacy and keep her out of the press. Lily drew for the detective a detailed picture of the knife she had seen, including the carved dragons and the initials on the handle.

It turned out that the knife Lily had seen in her visions was a Filipino butterfly knife, or balisong. According to forensic evidence, the shape of the blade matched the one that had been used in all five murders. The police went to every store in the Redding area that sold exotic knives. The proprietor of a small knife shop remembered seeing a Filipino butterfly knife about eight or nine months earlier—a man had brought it in to have one of the broken handles repaired. The proprietor specifically remembered the carved dragons and the three initials on the handle. The customer had paid his bill with a credit card. A search of the store's records uncovered the man's name and address, and the police went to his house to question him. When they knocked on the front door, he ran out the back to escape but was apprehended just a block away. A warrant was obtained to search his house, and police found jewelry owned by all five of the victims—trophies from the killings—and the Filipino butterfly knife. The murderer's name was Oliver Jackson Burke. At a press conference, the police attributed their apprehension of the killer to an anonymous tip.

* * *

The Vicodin was starting to kick in, and the headache left over from the vision began to recede. Lily sat up on the edge of her bed and opened her bedstand drawer. Inside was a half-empty package of Oreo cookies. She plucked one of the cookies up and popped it into her mouth.

During the two weeks she'd had the visions of the butterfly knife, Lily had become quite ill. She'd been unable to sleep, lost her appetite to persistent nausea, and even had dropped several pounds. She hoped that did not happen again.

God knows I could stand to lose some weight now, she thought as she chewed the cookie. She washed it down with a few swallows of ice water. She took a deep breath and clenched her fists to stop the stubborn trembling in her hands. She knew the best thing to do was get back to work and not dwell on it. It would return soon enough, with more details, more information. She could try to figure out what it meant then. Lily left her bedroom and went back out front to the store.

CHAPTER THREE

Thursday, 10:33 A.M.

On Thursday morning, Jenna and Martha went for a drive around Eureka and made note of the locations of various stores, the mall, the hospital. It was a gray, rainy day and the chilly air smelled of the sea. They stopped at Humboldt State University in Arcata and walked leisurely around the campus as Jenna tacked cards to bulletin boards offering her editorial and typing services to students to make a little extra money.

Jenna had majored in education in college, with plans to teach grammar school, but her heart had never been in it, not really. She had met David and her plans had changed. But she was an excellent editor and typist, and when their financial troubles had begun in Redding, she had offered her services for reasonable prices to students at Shasta College and had made a surprising amount of money as a result. There seemed to be no shortage of students looking for help and willing to pay for it.

Back at the house, Martha went to her bedroom to take a nap, and Jenna called Dr. Reasor's office in Redding. She told the receptionist, Kristen, that it was very important she talk to Dr. Reasor as soon as possible. She briefly explained what had happened the day before and expressed her concern. The receptionist took Jenna's number and said the doctor would get back to her as soon as he could, probably during his lunch break.

While she waited, Jenna got a hammer, a Phillips screwdriver, and a package of hollow-wall anchors and went upstairs to the bedroom. She carried a couple boxes of framed family photos out into the hallway.

The upstairs hallway was papered in off-white, which had yellowed over the years, with an ugly repeating weeping willow pattern. Jenna hoped to get rid of it someday. The hallway was, to Jenna's taste, too narrow, but worse than that, it had only one overhead light, which made it too dark. With bare walls, it looked long and bleak.

She knelt beside the boxes and began placing the photos gently on the hardwood floor. She looked at each one as she removed it from the box, squinting as her eyes adjusted to the hallway's poor light, and separated the ones she wanted to hang in the hallway from those she would hang elsewhere. Jenna had a dozen framed photos in two stacks on the floor when she pulled another from the box and froze.

Jenna slowly moved off her knees to a sitting position on the floor, legs crossed, as she stared at the picture. A knot tightened in the pit of her stomach and tears stung her eyes. She remembered the day well.

In the picture, she and David were seated on the bench of a picnic table with the remains of a KFC meal spread out on it. Their backs were to the table, the Sacramento River behind them in the distance, the sky a clear, brilliant blue. They were in Caldwell Park in Redding. Josh sat between them holding a string with a red-and-silver Mylar balloon attached that read, "HAPPY BIRTHDAY!" All three of them wore colorful paper party hats, and David held a colorful whistle in his hand. It was Josh's second birthday. His cake—chocolate with white frosting, orange and green dinosaurs on top, from the Costco bakery—was on the table and had not been cut yet. A candle in the shape of a two stood unlit in the center of the cake. Josh was grinning happily. He had her blond hair and his father's big deep-brown eyes, her crooked smile and his father's straight nose.

Miles had been a wailer when he was a baby, but Josh had been so quiet—Jenna remembered getting up repeatedly at night just to make sure he was still breathing. And she remembered that early morning when he had stopped breathing in her arms.

Mommy—

Although she tried to hold it back, a sob wrenched its way out of Jenna as she put the picture on the "elsewhere" stack. Taking a deep breath, she took another framed photo from the box, this one of Josh staring in awe at a neighbor's kitten in the yard in front of their old apartment building.

Three years sounded like a good piece of time, but as she looked at the picture, it seemed like no time at all. The years dissolved and Jenna felt as if she had just lost Josh all over again. She continued to sob as she took another photo from the box.

Josh grinned at her from the back of a pony at the Shasta District Fair. It was the last picture taken of him before the headaches got so bad that he didn't go out much anymore.

Mommy—

Jenna sniffled and sobbed some more. Movement caught her eye and she raised her head. The murky hallway was fractured through the tears in her eyes, but she saw a small figure standing at the other end. It was very small, no more than three feet tall, wearing a little jacket with a hood that covered its head. It stood unmoving, well back from the pool of dim illumination cast by the single overhead light, a mere shape, facing her.

She stopped crying, stopped breathing for a long moment as she stared at the blurry figure. With the knuckle of her left index finger, she wiped one eye, then the other, and blinked rapidly several times until her vision cleared.

The shadowy silhouette of a hooded child stood at the other end of the hallway, still and silent.

Jenna thought of Josh looking at her that last time, his puffy eyes so intense.

Mommy—

Her voice was throaty and broken. "Juh . . . Josh? Is that you? Josh?"

The dark little figure spread its stubby arms wide and began to hurry jauntily toward her. But it did not make a sound—no footsteps on the hardwood floor, no happy child's cry, only silence.

The telephone chirped and so startled Jenna that she tossed the picture into the air and yelped as her head jerked around toward the open bedroom doorway. The picture crashed onto the "elsewhere" stack and the glass in the frame shattered.

When Jenna looked down the hallway again, the small figure was gone. She stared at the spot where it had stood a heartbeat ago as the telephone continued to trill a second and third time, her lips parted, teary eyes wide. Her heart pounded so hard, she felt it in her fingertips.

There was a child standing there, Jenna thought. *A toddler. Just now. I couldn't have imagined that. Could I?*

Mommy—

She realized the answering machine was about to pick up and it was probably Dr. Reasor returning her call. Clearing her throat, she got to her feet, hurried into the bedroom, and picked up the cordless receiver.

"Hel— Um, hello?"

"Jenna? Dr. Reasor calling."

"Dr. Reasor, um . . . thank you for calling. I, uh . . . I was just, uh . . ." She cleared her throat and sniffled.

"Is everything okay?"

She cleared her throat again and assured him that yes, everything was okay, as she tried to collect her thoughts. She told him what had happened the day before with Martha.

"Is that normal?" she asked. "I mean, should I be concerned that she, uh . . . well, that she's seeing things?"

"Are you positive she was seeing things? Is it possible there *were* some kids in the yard?"

"I didn't see any, and I couldn't get past the fact that she said they disappeared into the ground. I've been worried about it ever since. I didn't know if it could be a side effect of the stroke, or if maybe . . . well, I was worried about the possibility of something like Alzheimer's disease."

"Well, even if she were in the early stages of Alzheimer's—and I have no reason to believe that she is—hallucinations would not be a part of that. Early Alzheimer's would include memory loss, maybe mild disorientation, but not hallucinations. Was she wearing her glasses?"

"Yes."

"When was the last time she had her eyes checked?"

"You know, I hadn't thought of that. It's been . . . well, a while."

"It's possible she saw some children in the yard, and from her point of view—and if, say, her glasses need a new prescription—it might have looked to her like they disappeared into the ground when they took off."

"Yes, I guess that's possible." She glanced at the bedroom's open door.

"You're a worrier, Jenna," Dr. Reasor said with a smile in his voice. "Have you made an appointment with Dr. Wenders?"

"Yes."

"Okay, take her to see Dr. Wenders, but make an appointment with an eye doctor as well, okay? Just in case. Tell Dr. Wenders what you told me and see what she has to say. If there's any reason to be concerned, I'm confident she'll pick up on it. She's a very good doctor."

"Thank you so much, Dr. Reasor. I feel kind of silly now. I'm sorry to have bothered you."

"No bother. Give your mom my best."

After replacing the cordless phone on its base, Jenna hurried to the bedroom door. The hallway was still empty. No one stood at the other end. She leaned her shoulder against the doorjamb and began to cry again.

Jenna had never been a believer in the supernatural and was not even a religious person. Her mother had never once taken her to church or Sunday school when she was little, and on the few occasions when friends had asked Jenna to attend with them, her mother had always said no. Although she never expressed any dislike toward them, Martha did not trust churchgoing people.

She sometimes said, "Anybody who smiles that much is up to something." For Jenna, God had always been something other people believed in.

When Josh died, she had been irritated whenever someone told her that he had gone to a better place, that he was in Heaven, even though she knew they had the best of intentions. To Jenna, dead was dead, and her baby had died, had ceased to be—that was bad enough without believing he'd gone to some faraway place where she could not reach him without dying herself. Had she believed that, Jenna would not have hesitated to end her own life to get to Josh's side as soon as possible. She had not given an afterlife so much as a moment's consideration when Josh died. To do so would have been to go insane.

Jenna went to the two boxes on the hallway floor and knelt beside them. She picked up the picture of Josh on the pony at the fair. He grinned from behind a web of cracks in the glass, where Jenna's tears shattered as they dropped from her eyes. She was frightened by the thoughts she was having so suddenly, thoughts foreign to her. She did not have the strength to resist them, though, and that was even worse.

Helpless against it, Jenna surrendered to the possibility that her dead son had tried to communicate with her just minutes ago.

By one o'clock, the rain had stopped, and so had the roller coaster of thoughts in Jenna's mind. For about half an hour as she hung pictures, she had driven herself nearly crazy thinking about what she had seen. But her heartbeat gradually calmed as she reminded herself of her state of mind at that moment, and the fact that she'd been crying and had tears in her eyes, and of the bad light in the hallway. By the time she put a frozen pizza in the oven for lunch, she had calmed herself down. It helped that she'd sneaked one of Martha's Xanaxes.

Although the possibility lingered in her mind that some essence of her dead son had reached out to her for a moment, she decided to keep it to herself for the time being. It was not because she was afraid of how David would react—she knew *exactly* how he would react. There had been silence between them for months after Josh's death. They had been afraid to speak, unable to trust their own voices. The silence finally ended one night while Jenna and David were in bed, staring into the darkness instead of sleeping. David had suddenly released an agonizing wail and curled up in a ball beside her. They'd spent most of that night holding each other and crying. But even once they were talking again, their wounds remained open just beneath the surface, raw and ready to bleed again. They had not healed. Jenna knew they never would, not entirely. She knew if she simply mentioned Josh's name to David, she would be prodding at that wound.

If Jenna were certain that Josh had tried to communicate with her, she would have gotten into the car, gone out, and hunted David down to tell him about it without wasting a second. But she was not certain of what she had, or had not, seen—whether she had seen a small figure at the end of the hallway, or had wanted, perhaps even needed, to see one. It would rip David open to bring it up, so she would not. Not just yet. She would wait. For what, she was not sure. But she would wait.

When Miles got home from school, he went to his bedroom to do his homework so he could spend the rest of the afternoon and evening playing outside and watching television. David got home shortly before four o'clock, and Jenna knew as soon as she saw him that he had not found a job. He came into the kitchen, where she was preparing a stew for dinner.

"One possibility," he said. "At a garage in Fortuna, there's a guy retiring next month, and so far, they don't have a replacement. I filled out an application and spent a while talking to the manager. I'm the first one to apply for the job. The manager's a good guy—we hit it off."

"That's *great*," Jenna said. "It sounds very promising."

"I'm not holding my breath."

"But don't dismiss it, either. You got along with him, nobody else has applied. It sounds good to me."

A smile broke through David's long face. "Are you baking something?"

"Mom's baking a cake for dessert."

Sitting at the breakfast nook, Martha looked up from one of her tabloids and smiled. "Chocolate," she said.

David's smile grew even larger. "Hey, Grandma's chocolate cake. Well, the day's not a total loss, then."

After dinner, David went to the store and picked up a few lightbulbs. When he got back, he took the stepladder upstairs and put a brighter bulb in the hallway's overhead light. They watched television for a while, then Jenna told Miles to go upstairs and get ready for bed. A few minutes later, she went up to his room.

She kissed Miles goodnight and, as she went out, left the bedroom door open about a foot. A cat-shaped night-light plugged into a low outlet in the hallway outside the door sent a soft glow spilling into his bedroom through the opening.

"Goodnight, honey," she said.

" 'Night, Mom."

* * *

Miles propped himself up on both arms in bed, in the dark, wide awake. He was not sure what had awakened him, but he had the impression someone had come into his bedroom.

The wind blew outside and sent a spatter of rain against the windowpane. Miles could hear the distant surf crashing against the rocks at the foot of the cliff behind the house. His bed was against the wall across from the door, and there were two bare windows just above it. The ivy on the outside wall of the house whispered secretly every time the wind blew. Maybe that was it—the strange new sounds of the night had awakened him, sounds it would take a while to get used to, that was all. And the room was new, the bed, everything. Even the things he had brought with him from Redding took on new shapes in the dark—the toy dinosaurs on the shelves, the stuffed King Kong huddled in the corner, the lamp and books crouching on the desk.

But something was not right. He could feel it.

"Come on, be a good puppy." The whispered voice was rough, and it came from within Miles's bedroom. "C'mon over here and be a good puppy."

Miles made a small, strangled sound in his throat just before it closed. His elbows locked at his sides and he was paralyzed by fear. His eyes moved to the spot in the room from which the voice had come—over by the shelf with the dinosaurs on it, but low, near the floor. Miles's eyes dropped and he saw a figure in the dark—round shoulders and a large, oddly shaped head. The figure rose slowly up out of the floor, a black shape within the darkness, out of reach of the hallway nightlight's glow. Arms took shape at the round sides of the fat figure as it rose, large and hulking.

46

"Gitcher butt over here, y'fuckin' puppy."

Miles was not aware of the exact moment when he was finally able to scream; he only knew he was screaming.

The overhead light flashed on after what seemed an eternity. The room filled with light and Dad and Mom were beside him, sleepy but frantic. Mom's arms were around him, and he was able to stop screaming.

Mom glanced up at Dad. "David, what did I tell you about those movies?" She pressed her cheek to Miles's head. "No more horror movies."

Even as Mom hugged him, Miles's eyes held on the spot where, just seconds before, he had seen the figure of what had appeared to be a fat man wearing something on his head rising up out of the floor.

"There was a man in here!" Miles said.

Mom backed away suddenly and frowned down at him. "What?"

"There was a man in here just a minute ago!"

She looked up at Dad, who frowned at her.

Dad said, "What man?"

"He was coming up out of the floor."

They both rolled their eyes.

"See what I mean?" Mom said. "No more monster movies, period." She smiled at him and kissed his cheek, then put her hand on his chest and gently pressed him back toward his pillow.

Miles moved away from her hand and sat up. "No! I don't want to go back to bed! He'll be back!" He did not know why, but he had no doubt of this. There had been a purposefulness to the man's voice that suggested he was not yet finished with Miles. "He called me a puppy!"

Mom laughed. "He called you a *puppy?* Well, that's kind of sweet, isn't it?"

"Not the way he said it. Can I come sleep with you? I don't want to sleep in here."

Mom sighed and looked up at Dad.

After a moment, Dad said, "Okay, but don't get used to it. This is a one-time deal, okay? No more after this."

He bobbed his head up and down with vigor. "Okay. Okay."

Miles lay between them with his eyes wide open and stared into the dark long after they were both asleep. They thought he had a nightmare—they didn't even have to say it out loud, it was an accepted fact. But he knew he had not been dreaming. He kept his eyes open until he finally dozed off a couple hours later. Miles no longer trusted the dark.

CHAPTER FOUR

Friday, 1:38 P.M.

The next day, Jenna spent the afternoon working on the living room. It was dark and dreary, and she hoped someday to be able to redecorate and brighten it up. It had been decorated last, she guessed, sometime in the seventies.

There was a rust-colored shag carpet that hadn't been vacuumed in a long time, and matching drapes on the picture window behind the large Mediterranean-style couch upholstered in brown crushed velvet. A matching coffee table stood in front of the couch with a center-piece of wax fruit that was gray with dust. The couch was flanked by two matching end tables, and on each stood a hideous lamp with a cream-colored, chimney shade and a light in the fat round base of amber glass. There was an old wooden straight-back chair with a brown cushion tied to the seat and back. The brown vinyl-upholstered recliner had seen better days—David said it was comfortable, but tears in the upholstery

49

made it an eyesore. Another end table stood beside the recliner, with another matching ugly lamp on it.

First, Jenna threw the wax fruit in the garbage. She dusted everything and vacuumed the carpet. She put a tan-and-cream afghan Martha had crocheted over the back of the couch. On the mantel over the fireplace, which had been bare when they moved in, she set out a collection of handblown glass animals that had belonged to her grandmother. She found it odd that there were no photographs in the house—none on the walls in the living room or hallways, none on the mantel. She set out a few of their own framed pictures on top of the entertainment center, a black cabinet that held the television, VCR, DVD player, and an old stereo that included a turntable, all of which had been there when they arrived. Among the photographs, she set out a collection of ceramic elves she'd had since she was a girl. There were already a couple hooks in the ceiling just in front of the picture window, over the couch—no doubt the chains of a swag lamp once had hung from them—and she hung a potted philodendron from each one.

A shelving unit built into the wall beside the entertainment center held a large collection of hardcover Reader's Digest Condensed Books and a few dozen paperbacks, mostly westerns and science fiction novels. An impressive collection of Roseville pottery was lined up on the shelves in front of the rows of books. There were several old magazines—*Modern Maturity*, *People*, *Popular Mechanics*—inside the coffee table, and they joined the wax fruit in the garbage.

David came home looking as dejected as he had the day before. This time, he didn't even have any leads. Over dinner Jenna tried to cheer him up by making plans for the weekend.

"Why don't you and Miles work on cleaning out the

garage so we can actually park the car and pickup in there?" she said.

"Well, I guess you *did* paint the cupboards and hang pictures," David said. "I suppose I should do *some*-thing." He turned to Miles. "What do you say, Tiger. Want to clean out the garage with me tomorrow?"

"Yeah, sure."

"Might mean a couple trips to the dump," David said.

"Really? Cool!"

"If I can find the dump."

After dinner, Jenna went to the kitchen to clean up while everyone else went to the living room. As she stacked the dishes in the dishwasher, she could hear them laughing with a studio audience at something on television.

She heard something else. Leaning forward with a plate in her hand, she froze, cocked her head, and listened. She dropped the plate and it clattered against others as it fell into its slot in the rack.

It was the music she'd heard in the early hours of Wednesday morning, the music she had thought was coming from Martha's radio downstairs. But now it sounded nothing like music from a radio, and more like that of a music box.

Jenna stood up straight and turned toward the music—toward the laundry room, which opened off the kitchen near the back door. She crossed the kitchen slowly. The closer she got to the laundry room, the louder and clearer the music sounded. She hurried the last few steps and flipped on the light as she stepped inside.

It was Brahms's "Lullaby." That was why it had sounded so familiar when she'd heard it Wednesday morning, probably half asleep. It was the song she had hummed to Josh just before he'd—

Mommy—

The memory made her chest grow cold, her fingertips numb. She thought of the hooded toddler that had stood at the end of the upstairs hallway the day before. In her mind, she returned to that brief but explosive certainty she'd experienced that Josh had tried to communicate with her.

Hold it, Jenna thought. *What mother hasn't hummed Brahms's "Lullaby" to her baby? I used to hum that tune to both the boys;* all *mothers sing that to their babies.*

She barely had time to think that much, though, because she was too busy focusing on the fact that she was *hearing* it. And it was coming from behind the basement door.

She reached out and turned the basement door's shaky old metal knob. The door was warped and she had to tug on it a couple times before it jerked open. She stepped into the doorway and looked down into the dark.

There were two bare bulbs hanging over the narrow, steep wooden staircase that led down to the basement. Jenna had not been down there yet. She didn't like the look of the exposed bulbs—she'd had a fear of electricity ever since a string of Christmas-tree lights had shocked her mother and knocked her across the living room when Jenna was seven.

She reached in with her left hand and flipped the light switch. The bulbs came on only for an instant before throwing sparks and going dark with a couple dull pops. She gasped and stumbled backward.

But the twinkling music continued to play down in the basement.

Jenna stepped out of the laundry room and turned right. A long black Mag-Lite flashlight stood facedown, like a sentry, beside the back door. She picked it up and ducked back into the laundry room. She clicked the flashlight on, aimed the beam down the stairs, and made her way down.

The music was much closer, clearer. Jenna stopped on the stairs and turned the light past the wooden railing to her right, down into the basement.

The beam fell on the toddler in the hooded jacket standing in front of a pile of old damp, decaying cardboard boxes. In the light, Jenna saw that the jacket was navy blue. The child's face was swallowed up in the shadow of the hood. He was hugging to his chest a brown teddy bear with a bright blue ribbon around its neck. The music was coming from the teddy bear, she was sure of it.

She remembered that Josh had had a teddy bear. Martha had given it to him for his first birthday. But it had plush black and white fur and had not played music.

Jenna tried to keep the flashlight trained on the child, but the beam shook with each step down. She lost the child and stopped again, sent the beam to the left through the dark.

She found him again on the other side of the basement, still holding the bear. She did not move, did not even breathe for a moment. Her eyes teared up and her heart pounded hard against her ribs. She took in a breath.

"Josh?" Her voice broke and she cleared her throat. "Josh? Is that you?"

The hood moved slightly.

Jenna stepped slowly down the stairs, keeping the light on the child. But he was gone. She gasped and stopped again, searched with the light.

The child was standing in the center of the basement, still holding the musical teddy bear, which continued to play its tune.

"Josh? Please hold still. Hold still for Mommy, okay?"

Two-thirds of the way down the stairs, she missed a step. Jenna screamed as she tumbled the rest of the way down. She landed on her back on the dirt floor with her feet up on the stairs, but she had not let go of the flashlight.

Footsteps thundered overhead. David appeared in the basement doorway. He was joined seconds later by Miles.

"Oh, my God, Jenna!" David raced down the stairs.

"No, it's all right," she said as she sat up. "I'm fine. I'm not hurt. Help me up." She reached her left hand up and David pulled her to her feet. She looked up the stairs at Miles, who was on his way down. "No, honey, why don't you go watch TV with Grandma. I'm fine, really, I'm not hurt at all. I just tripped near the bottom, is all."

Miles stood on the stairs a moment, reluctant to go. "Okay," he said. He turned and went back up the stairs as Martha appeared in the doorway.

"What the hell happened?" she said.

"I'm fine, Mom. I just tripped and scared myself, that's all."

"Well, you scared the crap out of us, too." She left the doorway.

Jenna sniffled and wiped her eyes with a knuckle.

When David realized she was crying, he gripped her shoulders. "You *are* hurt!"

"No, I'm not, I was crying before I fell."

"Why?"

Jenna turned away from him and held the long, heavy flashlight in both hands. She passed it slowly through the basement, over the boxes and crates stacked against the cinder-block walls.

"You're not going to believe me," she said, just as a sob escaped her.

He turned to her and put a hand on her back. "What's wrong?"

She recognized the tone of his voice—he was a little irritated. Jenna turned to him and clutched his arm. The glow of the Mag-Lite oozed up over his face. "Honey, you're going to think I'm crazy, but . . . Josh . . . was just here."

The features of his face relaxed for a moment, then tensed into a painful mask as his eyes slowly widened. *"What?"*

Jenna glanced up at the doorway to make sure it was empty. She didn't want Miles or her mother to hear, not yet. She turned to David again and whispered rapidly, "This is the second time it's happened. I saw him upstairs in the hallway yesterday. He just stood there at the end of the hall, watching me. And then he started to run toward me, but the phone rang and I turned away, and he disappeared. And just now, up in the kitchen, I heard music, and it was the same music I—"

"What are you *saying*?" His voice was loud, but quavered. "Are you hearing what you're saying, Jenna?"

She placed her hand flat against his chest, over the blue sweatshirt he wore. "I know, honey, I know, but wait, just listen to me. It was the music I said I heard Wednesday morning. Remember, when I said I heard music in the middle of the night? It was Brahms's "Lullaby," honey—remember how I used to hum that to him all the time? And to Miles, both of them. And I was humming it to Josh when he . . . just before he . . . before we lost him. And down here, he was holding a teddy bear. Remember how much he loved his teddy—"

"*Every* kid loves his teddy bear, Jenna!" David said. It sounded as much like a plea as a declaration.

She closed her eyes a moment and nodded as she took a deep breath, tried to calm herself down. "You're right. I know how this sounds. But listen to me, David—if it wasn't Josh, then I'm crazy, because I saw him. I *saw* him. Does . . . does that mean I'm crazy, David? Does it?" Cold fear gripped her, and she quaked with sobs.

David took her in his arms. The light was smothered between them. "You're not crazy. I know you're not crazy. Don't think that."

"But I saw him."

"I see him, too." David took a trembling breath. "You think I don't see him?"

"But . . . I saw him in the hallway."

"He disappeared, didn't he?"

After a moment, Jenna nodded against his chest.

"And he disappeared down here, too, didn't he? I mean, if he were here, he'd still be here, right? He'd be here right now, wouldn't he?"

"I know, I know, it doesn't make any sense, all I know is—"

He held her upper arms gently as he pushed her a few inches back and looked at her. "I'm saying it makes *perfect* sense, Jenna. I've been thinking about it because I see him, too. And I think it's because we've moved to a new place, and we couldn't bring him with us. So we're missing him even more than usual. Have you had that feeling?"

A fresh round of sobs came when Jenna realized she *had* been feeling that way, but had been unaware—or unwilling to be aware of it—until now.

He held her to him again. "That's all it is, honey. We're just missing him all over again."

Jenna stood there and cried on his shirt for a long time. After a while, she became quiet. They turned and started up the stairs, Jenna first.

"Be careful, okay?" David said.

Jenna looked up at the dead bulbs. "Those bulbs must be old. They blew out as soon as I turned them on."

"I'll have to replace them. I'm gonna have to come down here and clean up this mess sooner or later anyway. Might as well have light."

She stopped on the stairs and looked over her shoulder at him. "Will you do it tomorrow?"

"Look, I'd rather you just didn't come down here, okay? Miles, either. I'm afraid you're going to fall from the *top* of these stairs, and then you'll—"

"Do it tomorrow. Please?"

He smiled. "You and your electricity thing. Okay. I'll do it tomorrow." Outside the laundry room, he put the Mag-Lite back in its place beside the back door.

Jenna woke at 2:41 with a full bladder. David snored beside her. Wind blew the rain against the windowpane above the headboard. She got up and shivered in the cold, slipped on David's robe, and padded barefoot out of the bedroom. She went down the hall to the bathroom and relieved herself. When she stepped into the hallway again, she stopped and listened.

She could hear David snoring in the bedroom, the wind and rain outside, but nothing else. The house was silent.

She noticed Miles's bedroom door was closed, which was odd. She and David always left his door open about a foot—Miles preferred it that way, always had. Light streamed out from under the closed door.

Jenna went to his door and opened it a crack. Miles was sound asleep in his bed with the overhead light on.

"Damned horror movies," she whispered. She reached in, turned the light off, and left the door open several inches before going back to bed.

* * *

Miles opened his eyes in the dark and was immediately wide awake. Was it because he'd heard the voice? Or was it only because one of his parents had noticed his door was closed and his light was on, and had turned it off? He'd closed the door hoping they wouldn't notice his overhead light was on, but apparently someone had, and had left him in the dark.

He was prepared. He reached beneath his pillow and removed a small Mag-Lite penlight. It had been in his Christmas stocking last year. He twisted the head to turn it on and trained it on the light switch beside the cracked-open door. He sat up on the edge of his bed and almost stood, but waited a moment. The digital clock on his bedstand, shaped like a flying saucer, read 3:04.

Had he heard the voice? He waited several seconds but heard nothing. He looked over at the area by the shelf where he'd seen the fat man coming up through the floor once before, and he was tempted to follow with the powerful penlight. But he could not do it. He hadn't heard anything, but that didn't mean there was nothing there, and if there *was*, Miles wasn't sure he wanted to see it.

He turned to the light switch again, focused all his attention on it. He stood and started walking toward it. He was so afraid, he had trouble moving his legs.

Miles wondered if the fat man could come up through the floor anywhere in the room. He wondered what it would be like if the man were suddenly to come up right under his feet, if his head were to rise beneath the oval rug on the hardwood floor beside his bed. Or would he come through the rug? Would he come straight up through the rug and into Miles? The thought only made him feel worse.

He was halfway to the light switch when the rough, whispered voice said, "Where you goin'? Get over here and be a good puppy, now."

With his arm outstretched, hand reaching for the light switch, Miles turned his head toward the voice. He tripped over his own feet and fell flat on the floor. The penlight slipped from his hand and rolled away.

"C'mon, y'fuckin' puppy," the voice said.

Miles saw movement in the darkness to his right, over by the shelves. As he scrambled to his feet, he screamed. He didn't want to, but could not help himself. His hand found the light switch and flipped it up.

The room filled with light as the floor creaked down the hall in his parents' bedroom. They spoke to each other as their footsteps drew nearer.

Turning, Miles saw nothing by the shelves, not even a sign that anything had been there.

Whatever it is, he thought, *it doesn't like the light.*

Mom and Dad came into the room and squinted against the light.

"What's going on?" Dad said.

Miles was breathless when he said, "He was here again! That man!"

Mom sighed.

Dad said, "Miles, you can't keep doing this. You're just having bad dreams."

"It's not a dream. I heard his voice. He keeps calling me a puppy."

"Two nights in a row from one stupid movie," Mom said.

Miles looked up at them and pleaded, "Can I come sleep with you again?"

Dad shook his head. "No, I told you, that was a one-time deal. You're a little old for this, aren't you, Miles? Come on, now, Tiger, get back into bed."

"But you can't turn the light out," Miles said.

"I got up earlier," Mom said, "and his door was closed and the overhead light was on in here."

"How about this." Dad shuffled over to the desk and turned on the squat lamp that stood on its corner. "We'll leave that one on, okay? Will that do for now?"

"Do I have to go back to bed?" Miles said.

Mom said, "It's after three o'clock in the morning."

"But it's the weekend, there's no school. Couldn't I stay up and watch TV for a while?"

Dad's voice was firm. "No. Now go back to bed. You can leave that lamp on, but—" He went to the door and turned off the overhead light. "Not that one. And leave the door all the way open, if you want. Okay?" Dad scooped Miles up in his arms and carried him to the bed. He spotted the penlight on the floor, put Miles down on the bed, and picked it up, handed it to him. Miles twisted the head of the penlight to turn it off, then slipped it under his pillow.

Dad frowned for a moment, turned to Mom, and said, "Go back to bed, honey, I'll be there in a second."

Mom kissed the top of Miles's head. "Go back to sleep, sweetheart." Then she turned and left the room.

Dad sat down on the edge of the bed. "You keep that light under your pillow?"

Miles nodded. "He only comes in the dark. He doesn't like the light."

"Come on, Tiger. It's only a dream. There's no man coming to your room. Okay?"

To say yes would be dishonest, but to disagree with Dad would only drag it out.

"You know that, right?" Dad said. "It's just a bad dream."

Finally, Miles nodded once. It was no dream, but there was no point arguing.

"Okay, big guy." He kissed Miles's cheek. "We've got work to do today, so we're both going to need all the sleep we can get." He stood and left the room, leaving the door wide open.

The lamp on the desk was not quite bright enough to illuminate that section of the room where the voice had come from, where Miles had seen the fat man. He lay awake, staring at the spot for a long time. He started nodding off now and then, but jerked awake each time, eyes suddenly wide, watching. Miles finally dozed off as the first light of dawn began to seep through the windows.

CHAPTER FIVE

Saturday, 9:17 A.M.

The next morning was gray and drizzly. Jenna made buttermilk pancakes for breakfast. David was relieved that he did not have to go out job-hunting again. There were probably plenty of garages open on Saturday, but he needed the break. He was discouraged by his failure to find work, and it nagged at him.

He was also bothered by the incident in the basement the previous evening. He had never seen Jenna in such a state. She was usually so levelheaded, so unflaggingly reasonable about everything. But she had been convinced she'd seen Josh in the basement. It disturbed David. He was not a believer in things supernatural—but neither was Jenna, and the fact that she believed she was seeing Josh's spirit, that he was somehow trying to contact her, was troubling.

David and his older brother, Jerry, and younger sister, Karen, had been raised in Redding, where their parents had found religion when David was eight. Life had changed suddenly after that. Their parents stopped letting them watch television and read Bible stories to them instead of fairy tales and adventure stories. They went to Sunday school and church every week and prayer meetings on Wednesday nights. Worst of all was the constant prayer. His parents seemed to pray at the drop of a hat—first thing in the morning, before bed at night, before they left the house for any reason, and before each meal—and David and Jerry and Karen were expected to bow their heads and close their eyes and be still. Suddenly, they had to memorize Bible verses and learn Bible trivia and color in Bible coloring books. Dad, a successful landscaper, and Mom, an office manager at a veterinary clinic, even changed the way they talked—suddenly, their conversations were peppered with phrases like "God willing" and "Praise Jesus" and "I felt the Holy Spirit." David didn't like the sound of that—*Holy Spirit*. He was skeptical of its existence, doubted anyone who said they "felt" it, and he would believe people were "moved" by it when he saw it happen with his own eyes (he'd imagined the Holy Spirit "moving" people by picking them up off the floor and levitating them around the room). When David asked his mother why they were doing everything differently, she had said, "Because we live for Jesus now, honey. Only people who live for Jesus go to Heaven, and you want to go to Heaven, don't you?" David did not want to go to Heaven if it was going to be filled with the kind of people his parents had become.

Jerry and Karen had grown into good churchgoing Christians, but David had fought it every step of the way, becoming the family's sinful black sheep. He could not imagine that the creator of the universe, the creator of all living things, of life itself, required people to drop what they were doing and pray to Him every few hours, and to behave in a certain way so He wouldn't throw them into a fiery pit, and to pass judgment on other people according to what *they* believed, or did not believe, about the creator. He came to the conclusion that there could not possibly be a God at all, because if there were and He saw what had been done on earth in His name, He would vaporize the planet in a heartbeat and start all over again.

David did not stay in touch with his family. He often missed having a family to stay in touch with—he knew they would not respond if he called or wrote. His brother and sister sent Christmas cards every year, but that was all. His dad had let him know he'd been written out of the will years ago. That meant very little, because Dad was leaving most of his money to the church, anyway.

After seeing what it had done to his family, David had spent his life steering clear of organized religion in any form. He saw no difference between people who believed in spirits and an afterlife and the religious fanatics who went door to door passing out their literature. They were all peddling the same thing—a better life after this one.

David believed this was the only life anybody ever got. The life he and Jenna had made for themselves had not gone very well the last few years, but they had clung to each other instead of a belief in some better life to come, or the idea that their suffering in this life would only enrich the next. They had found their strength in each other, and they had endured so far.

While he did not believe Jenna had seen anything like a ghost, he understood how she could think she'd seen Josh. The day before, while job-hunting in Arcata, David had to fight the urge to turn down a side street to follow a woman who'd been walking along the sidewalk with a little blond boy who looked, at first glance, exactly like Josh. It was not the first time something like that had happened since the move. He knew exactly how Jenna felt.

"Chatanooga Choo-Choo" played on Grandma's radio on the sill of the breakfast nook's greenhouse window. The four of them ate breakfast in silence. They all looked tired, but Grandma seemed to be especially sluggish.

"You feeling okay, Grandma?" David asked.

She shrugged. "Just tired. It's hard, you know . . . getting used to sleeping in a new place."

"Especially with our screamer, here," Jenna said as she reached over and messed up Miles's hair.

"I thought I heard something going on up there early this morning," Grandma said.

David said, "Miles just had a bad dream. Happens to everybody."

Miles did not look up from his pancakes as he ate.

After breakfast, David decided to change the lightbulbs over the basement stairway. As he picked up the long black Mag-Lite beside the back door and went into the laundry room, Miles joined him and asked, "Can I go down there with you, Dad?"

"No, not now. Not until we've got plenty of light down there, and even then, I don't want you going down these steps unless it's with me or your mom, understood?"

" 'Kay. Can I watch?"

"Sure. Hold the lightbulbs for me." He handed Miles a box of two bulbs.

Miles stood in the basement doorway as David went down the stairs. He went down into the basement to find something he could stand on to reach the bulbs. It was damp and smelled of mildew and moist earth. He was surprised how cold it was. It wasn't a large basement, and it was crammed full of junk.

"Another cleanup job," David muttered as he passed the flashlight beam around, searching.

Against a wall, he found a narrow wooden crate that looked like it was just the right height and size. He tried to lift the lid to see what was inside, but it was nailed shut. It was not very heavy, though, and it was sturdy enough. He picked it up and carried it two-thirds of the way up the stairs, bent down, and placed it on one of the steps. It fit perfectly. Standing a step above the crate, he tested it with one foot, then gripped the railing with one hand and stepped up on it. On the crate, he was able to reach the first bulb. He replaced the burnt-out bulbs in minutes. When he was done, he climbed back up the stairs and flipped the light switch.

The lights came on for an instant, then sent two small explosions of sparks into the air with a pop and went out again.

"Son of a bitch!" David said. He looked down at Miles. "You didn't hear me say that. It's not nice to talk that way, you know."

Miles laughed. "I know."

David sighed. "I wonder if it's a problem with the wiring." He went down the stairs with the flashlight in hand, stepped over the crate, then picked it up and carried it back down to the basement. He noticed again the drastic difference in temperature from the top of the stairs to the bottom. He tossed the crate down where he'd found it. It slammed against a stack of boxes and knocked them over.

"Damn," David muttered.

He started to turn and go back up when he heard music playing. He frowned. It was a slow, plinking, off-key rendition of Brahms's "Lullaby." He found the source of the music with the flashlight. A filthy old brown teddy bear with a dark ribbon around its neck lay on the floor near the fallen boxes. Stuffing dangled from a couple holes in the bear's torso and only one round black button-eye remained on its face. As the tune slowed down, footsteps clattered rapidly down the stairs.

"David! That's it! Do you hear it?"

He looked up at Jenna, who stopped near the bottom of the stairs. "Be careful," he said. "It's just a toy."

She came off the stairs and hurried to his side, looking down at the bear. As she swept it up off the floor and held it in both hands, the music wore down and stopped. She turned it over to find a key sticking out of the back. Jenna turned the key a couple times and the music continued. She turned the bear face up again.

"My God, David, this is the bear he was holding," Jenna whispered. "Except . . . it looked like new. It was clean and had both eyes, the ribbon was a bright blue, and the stuffing wasn't—"

David looked up at Miles in the doorway and said, "Go check on Grandma, Tiger, see how she's doing, okay?"

Miles sighed, knowing full well he was being gotten rid of again. He said, "Okay," and left.

"Jenna, it's just an old teddy bear that fell out of one of these boxes."

"Yes!" She looked up at him with round eyes, a few strands of her long blond hair dangling over her face. "That's why he was down here, for the teddy bear. He knew it was down here, and he just wanted to find it and play with it, probably because we don't have any of his toys here in—"

He snatched the bear from her hands and said angrily, "Jenna, will you *stop* it!"

She flinched, and the outer corners of her eyes crinkled.

Quietly, he said, "You're talking crazy." He tossed the teddy bear down on the fallen boxes. "He's gone, Jenna, and he's not coming back. You've got to stop this, because I can't take it, I really can't. Do you understand? I feel bad enough as it is. If you keep this up, you're gonna start to scare me, you know what I mean? We can't afford any counseling right now. And I really don't think we need it—I think we're pretty normal, under the circumstances. But if you keep this up, you're gonna tear me apart, okay? So please, you've got to—"

"I'm sorry." She put her arms around him. "I'm sorry. You're right."

He put an arm around her and they stood that way for a while. Then he said, "Come on, let's go upstairs. It's freezing down here."

"Aren't you going to change the bulbs?"

"I did. They blew out again as soon as I flipped the switch. I think there might be something wrong with the wiring."

Her tone was wary. "Something wrong with the wiring?"

"Yeah, but don't worry about it. We just won't come down here until we—"

"We'll have an electrician take a look at the wiring, then."

"We can't afford an—"

"Mom will pay for it."

Mom will pay for it. David was beginning to hate those words. He needed to find a job before he started hating Jenna for saying them.

"David, we don't know anything about electrical

wiring, and I'm going to be worried sick if I think there's an electrical problem in this house."

"All right, all right. Talk to your mother about it." He pushed her gently toward the stairs. "Go on. I'll be up in a minute."

Jenna hesitated, stepped around him, and went over to the teddy bear on the dirt floor. She bent down to pick it up. "I'd like to take this and—"

"No."

"But I just wanted to—"

"*No*. The bear stays down here with the rest of this junk. After I clean up the garage, I'm going to come down here and throw all this stuff out."

Jenna took one last look around in the dark, then went upstairs.

The breaker box was on the wall at the foot of the stairs. David opened it, turned the flashlight on it. It looked like a regular breaker box to him, but Jenna was right—he didn't know any more about electrical wiring than she did.

He turned and went to the center of the basement and aimed the light upward. There were exposed pipes overhead, and a chain dangled from a single light fixture hung from a cord without a bulb.

He passed the light over the mess once again. Of the boxes that had toppled, a couple had broken open. Some toys and old magazines had spilled out onto the floor. An old wooden high chair was leaning against a stack of boxes near the corner. Its wood was splintered in places and its black paint was peeling like dead skin. Part of one leg was missing. But there was something odd about it. David stepped over to the chair. Six black leather straps dangled from it, three on each side, three with buckles.

What kind of high chair has leather straps? he wondered.

He reached down and pulled the high chair away from the stacked boxes. Old cobwebs clung between it and the boxes.

David suddenly was overwhelmed by a deep feeling of growing horror. Like a current of electricity, it traveled up his arm from the chair itself and filled his entire body. Something about the chair felt so wrong, so corrupt, that he let it go, let it drop back against the boxes. He stumbled back a step, chest rising and falling with rapid breaths.

The basement's cold seemed to sink into his bones. The darkness around him appeared much darker, pressed in on him like a force.

A couple more notes tinkled out of the teddy bear.

David turned and hurried up the stairs, relieved to step into the light and relative warmth of the laundry room. Before closing the door, he looked down into the basement one more time. A shudder passed through him that he did not understand. He told himself that Jenna's fantasy that Josh had appeared to her in the basement the night before had gotten under his skin. That was all.

He was closing the basement door when he noticed an old surface bolt-lock on both the inside and outside, each about a foot above the doorknob. David slid the inside bolt back and forth in its track and was surprised by the smooth movement. He frowned at the locks, wondered why anyone would need to lock the basement door on either side.

David closed the door and left the laundry room. It was time to get to work on the garage.

Half an hour later, Jenna told David she had to do some grocery shopping, put on her coat, and left the house.

The truth was, she simply wanted to be alone.

Her mind had been racing ever since she'd seen the teddy bear in the basement. It was the same teddy bear she had seen the hooded toddler—*stop thinking of him that way*, she thought. *Admit it, you think it's Josh*—carrying in the basement the night before, and it had played the same music she'd heard twice and traced to the basement. Jenna was unable to rid herself of the nagging certainty that it was all somehow significant, but it was a significance she did not yet understand. That was why she wanted to be alone—to think.

David had been right, of course. Everything he'd said had made perfect sense. They were both thinking of Josh more than usual because they had moved to a new town, but their family was not intact. But even though she knew David had been right, she could not accept that she'd been wrong. No matter how reasonable David's argument, it did not explain away what she had seen. The teddy bear in the basement made her feel certain she'd seen *something*. But she still did not understand it.

Jenna pulled into the parking lot of the supermarket and parked the Toyota. She hadn't written up a shopping list, but could think of a few things she needed to pick up. Grocery shopping relaxed her, and she needed to do something that would make her feel normal, because she did not feel that way right now. She had not felt normal since seeing that small figure standing at the end of the upstairs hallway.

She pulled a shopping cart from the train of carts outside the store, wheeled it through the automatic doors, and began roaming the aisles. Her eyes scanned the shelves, but her mind was back in the dark, damp basement of their new house.

71

Ray Garton

If the small figure she had seen—first in the upstairs hallway, then in the basement—was Josh, why had he been carrying a teddy bear that was packed away with all the other junk down in the basement? It had been the same one, she had no doubt of that—the only difference was that the one Josh had carried had been like new, with shining black eyes, clean fur, and a bright blue ribbon around its neck. The one David had found—the very same teddy bear—was old, falling apart, missing an eye, and filthy.

Jenna stopped in front of a bank of shelves that held jars of pickles and scanned them slowly. She knew they were out of bread-and-butter pickles for sandwiches, and she thought vaguely that it might be nice to have a jar of dill pickles in the fridge as well. She took a large jar off a shelf, cradled it in her arm, and examined the label without focusing on it.

When she'd told David that Josh had come down to the basement because he liked the teddy bear, she'd been spouting the first explanation that had entered her mind. But it made perfect sense.

Jenna had held on to Josh's toys and clothes for those first few months after his death. She could not bear the thought of getting rid of them, or even moving them. But after the silence that had fallen over her family finally lifted, she and David agreed they had to get rid of Josh's things. To keep them would only worsen their pain. Every time they saw the tiny clothes Josh had worn and the toys he had played with, they would bleed inside. So they'd boxed everything up and taken it to the Salvation Army.

Josh had no toys left. There was nothing to play with in the house, nothing of his own. But somehow, he had discovered that teddy bear. Maybe through Josh's eyes, the teddy bear looked brand-new. Perhaps through

72

some interdimensional prism, he saw the bear as it had once been, and Jenna, in turn, saw a projection of that.

These are not my thoughts, Jenna thought as she stared, unseeing, at the label on the pickle jar. *I can't believe I'm thinking these things.*

At the same time, it all made a kind of gut-level sense that plucked at her soul. Even in the face of her own disbelief, she was asking herself questions that would have made her laugh coming from someone else. But she wanted answers, and she had none.

Jenna had been staring at the jar of dill pickles for a long time, oblivious of the supermarket employee who had spoken to her twice. When the woman touched her arm, Jenna was so startled, she cried out and dropped the pickle jar. It hit the floor with a flat crunch, and pickles, juice, and shards of glass went in all directions.

"Oh, shit," the woman said, quickly stepping back. She put a hand over her chest and looked at Jenna. "I'm sorry. I mean . . . oh, boy." She smiled.

Her name tag read "Kimberly." She was in her mid-thirties, plump and bosomy, with full, shiny black hair tied back in a ponytail. She wore the same uniform all the store's female employees wore: white blouse, red vest, and black pants.

"Are you okay?" Kimberly asked. "You aren't cut or anything, are you?"

Jenna realized she was crying, and became terribly embarrassed. She turned away from the woman and tried to make herself stop.

Kimberly said, "C'mon, let's get away from this mess." She took Jenna's elbow and steered her away from the spill. "You looked awfully interested in that pickle label, and you didn't hear me the first couple times I spoke to you, so I . . . I'm sorry, I didn't mean to scare you."

Jenna fought to stop her tears, but somehow that only made it worse.

Kimberly leaned close and lowered her voice. "Are you on something, honey?"

Jenna surprised herself by laughing. She shook her head as she got a tissue from her purse. "No, *no*. I'm sorry, my mind just wandered off and . . ." She dabbed at her eyes, blew her nose, stuffed the tissue back in her purse. "I'll pay for the pickles."

"Don't worry about the pickles. Sure you're okay?"

"No. I'm not. But I have to be. My husband and son and I, and my mother . . . we just moved here from Redding, so I don't really have time to not be okay."

"Oh? You're gonna love it here. I've been to Redding in the summertime, and it's like Indian summer in hell. It's much nicer here, I think. You renting or buying?"

"We're . . . inheriting. From my father."

"Oh? That's something you don't hear every day. My husband's in real estate. You inherited a whole house?"

Jenna nodded vaguely—her mind was already drifting off again, back down to the basement, to that musical teddy bear.

"Where is it?" Kimberly asked.

"I'm sorry—what did you say?"

"Where's the house? If you don't mind my asking."

"Off of Starfish Drive."

"Oh, it's very pretty over there. How do you like it?"

Tears welled up in Jenna's eyes, and she reached for another tissue. "How do I like the house?"

"Yeah. Are you all right?"

Jenna laughed again as she dabbed at her tears. "Like I said, no."

"How long have you been here?"

"We've been in the house a week," Jenna said, meeting Kimberly's eyes. "And I think I've seen my dead son twice."

Kimberly's smile collapsed and her eyebrows rose slowly. "I'm sorry?"

"You heard me." Another laugh. "Sounds crazy, huh? Tell me, you wouldn't happen to know where I might find . . . oh, I don't know, a psychic? A medium, maybe? I don't even know what I *need*. I don't know anything about this stuff—I don't even *believe* in it. At least . . . I've never believed in it before."

Kimberly's head tilted forward. "Are you serious?"

"Yeah. Can you believe it?"

"You said . . . you've seen your dead son?"

Jenna felt the heat of embarassment on her cheeks and throat. "Look, I'm really sorry about this mess." She stepped gingerly around the broken glass as she walked back over to the pickles. "I really was going to buy a couple of these."

"Don't worry about it—I'll get somebody to clean it up. You know, I've got three boys. Four, if you count my husband. I don't know what I'd do if I lost one of them. I'm sorry about your son."

"Please don't. You'll get me started again." She chose a jar of dills and another of bread-and-butter pickles and put them in her cart.

Tipping her head down again, Kimberly said, "But . . . you said you *saw* him?"

"I'm sorry, I was just babbling. I'm having a bad day, that's all."

"Yeah, sounds like a hell of a bad day. I don't know where you can find a psychic or a medium, but I'm getting off soon. I'd be happy to listen if you want to talk."

"Are you serious?"

Kimberly smiled. "You got a lot of friends around here?"

"I don't know a soul."

"I get off in about fifteen minutes. I'll meet you out front—we can go to the coffee shop a few doors down."

Kimberly went off to find someone to clean up the mess, and Jenna continued shopping. She could not believe she had just babbled those things to someone she'd just met. The woman probably thought she was crazy. At the same time, it might feel good to talk to someone, even a stranger—maybe especially a stranger.

The coffee shop a few doors down was tiny and sold overpriced coffees, sandwiches, and pastries. Jenna ordered a regular coffee, the cheapest thing on the menu.

Kimberly had biscotti with her cappuccino and waited patiently through small talk. Finally, when there was a brief pause in the conversation, she said, "How did your son die? If you don't mind my asking."

"Josh died of a cerebral aneurysm," Jenna said. "He'd been having headaches off and on for months, and after a bunch of tests, the doctor started treating him for migraines. Nothing showed up on the MRI, so . . ." She shrugged one shoulder. "It kind of made sense, because my mother has suffered from migraines all her life. I thought maybe they ran in the family. But . . . they weren't migraines."

"I'm so sorry."

Jenna was surprised that her eyes were dry. She was talking about it without crying. That was a first. She wondered if it was because she'd grown more convinced that she actually had heard from Josh.

Kimberly leaned forward at their small, round,

marble-topped table by the front window. "You said you saw him."

Slowly, Jenna told her about seeing the small figure in the upstairs hallway, and about hearing the music in the basement and seeing the child again down there.

"The blue jacket he wore," Kimberly said. "Was it a jacket that Josh owned?"

Jenna frowned down at her coffee as she thought about Josh's clothes. "He had a blue jacket, but . . . I don't remember it having a hood."

"I'm sorry, but I don't know anything about this sort of thing."

"Neither do I. But I can't think of any other explanation for it. I know what I saw, there's no doubt in my mind about that. But I keep wondering . . . well, if I really saw it, or if . . . if maybe I'm going crazy."

"I've always heard that people who are going crazy never wonder if they're going crazy. So I don't think you have anything to worry about."

Jenna smiled. "You mean, you believe me?"

Kimberly took a bite of her biscotti and washed it down with a sip of cappuccino. "One night when I was fourteen years old, about fifteen minutes after I'd gone to bed, when I was *just* about to fall asleep, my grandma came into my bedroom and kissed me, told me she loved me, and said good-bye. She turned and left my room and closed the door. I was wide awake then, so I had to go to sleep all over again, and I was lying there starting to drift off, when I realized that Grandma wasn't at our house, she was up in Crescent City with Grandpa in their house, so she *couldn't* have come in and kissed me goodnight. The next day, I found out Grandma had died the night before of a heart attack. About the time I went to bed."

Jenna sipped her coffee. "Did you ever tell anybody?"

Kimberly nodded. "I told Mom. She cried and hugged me. But she never said whether she believed me or not. I haven't told anyone since, but I've never doubted what I saw. I remember smelling Grandma's minty breath, her perfume. I felt her hand on my chest, her other hand on the top of my head. Even though she couldn't possibly have been there, she was there."

Jenna said, "If you'd told me that story a week ago, I would've smiled politely and tried to change the subject as quickly as possible. I wouldn't have believed you."

"Now?"

"Now . . . I don't know what I believe."

Kimberly smiled. "It was so easy when we were kids, wasn't it? We just believed whatever our parents told us. Then we grew up and found out they were desperately winging it."

"My mother winged it pretty well, and she did it all by herself."

"Your parents were divorced?"

Jenna shook her head. "They never married. Mom's never talked about him much, but I know he didn't want a family. She decided to keep me, but not him. Or maybe it was his decision—I don't know. He came back here, where he was from, and moved back in with his parents. He lived here with them until they died, then lived in the house alone for the rest of his life. He killed himself there about nine months ago."

"Did you ever meet him?"

"I talked to him on the phone once when I was nine. I thought maybe I'd like to meet him, get to know him. But he wasn't interested."

"He said no?"

"No, he said he'd meet me if I wanted, but he made it

clear there would be no relationship. So I figured . . . why bother?"

"Do you like the house?"

"It needs work. Unfortunately, so does David, my husband. I don't suppose you know of a garage that's desperate for a great mechanic, do you?"

"*We're* desperate for a great mechanic," Kimberly said, flattening a palm to her chest just above her generous breasts. "Ours retired last year. We had him for twelve years and we trusted him completely. We haven't been able to find a good car guy since."

Jenna smiled. "Then David's your man. Are you having problems?"

"There's something wrong with the Durango—it's idling fast. My Harry's a sweetheart, but he's about as handy as a clubfoot at a dance competition. He's a genius at real estate, but he doesn't know the first thing about cars. Do you think your husband would be willing to take a look at it for us? We'd pay the going rate." She reached down and removed a pen and a business card from her purse. She wrote on the back, then handed it over to Jenna. "Here's his card. That's our home number on the back. Talk to your husband, then call me this evening."

The card read simply, "Sand Dollar Realty," and below that, "Harry Gimble," with the address and phone number below his name. Jenna couldn't wait to tell David. It was only a single job, but he needed something, anything.

"Back at the store," Kimberly said, "you asked if I knew of any psychics or mediums. Were you serious?"

Jenna took a moment to ask herself that question—*was* she serious? She had always dismissed such people as frauds, sneered at their performances on television or radio talk shows. But if Josh was trying to reach her, if he had something to say to her, Jenna had no idea how to communicate with him. She knew nothing about talking to the dead.

Jenna said, "Why, do you know of any?"

Kimberly shook her head. "Nope. But if you're interested, I'm willing to help you find one."

"Really? How? Where?"

"Where else? The Internet."

CHAPTER SIX

Lily. Saturday, 2:26 P.M.

It had been a busy Saturday at The Crystal Well, but as soon as business slowed down a bit, Lily sent Claudia to get lunch. She came back from Ribisi's Deli with hot pastrami sandwiches and cream-of-broccoli soup.

"It smells so good," Claudia said, "I almost dug into it on the way back."

Lily thought Claudia McNeil could probably use more pastrami sandwiches in her diet. If she were any skinnier, she would look anorexic.

"Mr. Ribisi's hot pastrami sandwich is one of my many, many weaknesses," Lily said as she sat on one of the two stools behind the register, took the two bags from Claudia, and placed them on the countertop. She spread napkins out over the counter and set out the wrapped sandwiches and Styrofoam cups of soup. "And another is his cream-of-broccoli soup. What do I owe you?"

"My treat. You bought last time, remember?"

The door opened and two middle-aged women came into the store. Lily smiled and said hello. She recognized them immediately as tourists. One of them wore a white sweatshirt with a picture of Mt. Shasta on the front. They would browse for a while, but probably wouldn't buy anything. But just in case—

"Can I help you girls find anything?" Lily asked.

The woman in the sweatshirt said, "Do you have any books on the Lemurians?"

"They're right over here," Claudia said on her way out from behind the counter.

The Lemurians were one of the many legends surrounding Mt. Shasta—a mythical people believed by some to live inside the mountain. Others claimed the mountain was a regular landing spot for flying saucers. There were a lot of Bigfoot watchers in the area, too. The town of Mt. Shasta, nestled in the shadow of the great mountain, was a melting pot of New Age believers and alleged paranormal activity. The faithful came from around the world to bask in the mountain's energy and vibrations.

Lily believed none of it, but she provided her customers with a wide variety of it. Although it was a small town, The Crystal Well—which had been left to her by Mrs. Reeder when she died three years after her husband—was only one of four metaphysical book stores in Mt. Shasta. As a result, the store didn't exactly do a booming business. Several years before, Lily had decided, against her better judgment at first, to do psychic readings to supplement her income. She had done a good deal of writing as well—mostly short fiction—but so far she had submitted none of it, and shown it to no one. She was afraid of rejection, which she felt was inevitable.

By the time Claudia came back to the counter, Lily

had the sandwiches unwrapped and the lids off the soup cups. She closed her eyes and took a deep whiff of the sandwich before taking her first bite. The meat was tender, juicy, and aromatic, the pickles crisp. But as she chewed, the pastrami's rich aroma was overwhelmed by the smell of bananas, and the electric-blue flashing in the corners of her eyes made her sit up straight, suddenly more alert.

"What's the matter?" Claudia said.

Lily put the sandwich down and placed both hands flat on the counter. The banana smell grew stronger. She got off the stool and lowered herself to her hands and knees.

Frowning, Claudia said, "What are you *doing?*"

Lily lay facedown on the floor seconds before everything was swallowed up by darkness.

A sound in the darkness—the whispering ocean surf. The briny smell of the sea. The plinking music plays again, clearer this time—Brahms's "Lullaby" ringing as if from a music box.

Lily sees a key slowly turning, turning. It sticks out of the back of the filthy old teddy bear. The bear falls away and disappears in the darkness. The lullaby fades.

The house again, without the distortion this time. Its dull-gray paint peels as green ivy crawls rapidly up the walls, clutching at the house like the tentacles of some hungry underground beast. Then it all turns a deep shade of red, as if seen through tears of blood.

The voice of the fat man: "You gonna be a good puppy now?"

The house becomes a smear, blurs like a sidewalk chalk drawing in the rain. It transforms into something else—a face. An attractive woman with long blond hair and graceful cheekbones, mouth open wide, eyes filled with terror, scream-

ing without making a sound. The woman's face dissolves and becomes a man with a square jaw and curly brown hair, eyes wide with fear as he silently screams. Then a little boy's face, red from crying, filled with terror, his brown hair mussed and spiky, then an old woman's face, gaunt and pale, both of them screaming, eyes wide. The two faces merge into one blurry blob, then split again into two familiar faces—a man and a woman, both in their late sixties. The man has strong features, a broad, creased forehead, crew-cut white hair, large, prominent ears. The woman's face is kindly, with silver, blue-tinted hair in a high bouffant, pleasant eyes sparkling through large tortoiseshell-framed glasses, too much makeup. Their faces tremble and their mouths yawn open in soundless screams, then they disappear in a ball of fire. Another face emerges from the flames, and its charred red-black skin slides off the flaming skull.

Lily is falling again, spinning as she drops through the black nothingness in blind silence.

"Is she all right?"

"Shouldn't you call an ambulance or something?"

"No, I don't think so," Claudia said, but she sounded uncertain.

Lily slowly rolled onto her side.

Claudia was kneeling beside her. "Are you all right?"

"I'm fine." She looked up to see the two middle-aged tourist women peering over the counter at her. Each held a book to her chest. "Hi," she said with a half-hearted smile. She turned to Claudia. "Wait on our customers, Claudia. I'll be fine."

Sighing with frustration, Claudia stood and went to the register, rang up the women's purchases. By the time she was done, Lily was standing again, leaning heavily on the counter.

As soon as the women left the store, Claudia said,

"Are you going to tell me what's wrong? Have you seen a doctor?"

"I don't need a doctor." Lily was preoccupied. She was remembering the faces, particularly the last two before that flaming face. She had seen them before—the woman with her impossibly outdated bouffant of hair, the man with his big ears and stern eyes. Their names hovered just out of her reach. "Claudia, those two demon-busters—you know, the married couple." She closed her eyes and put a palm to her forehead. "Dammit, what are their names? They investigated that famous haunted house, the one they made the movie about, that turned out to be a hoax."

"You mean the Binghams?"

Lily snapped her fingers loudly and stomped a foot. "*That's* it! Bingham, Arthur and Mavis Bingham, right?"

"Yes. But what . . . Lily, are you okay?"

"I'm fine, Claudia."

"You were just lying unconscious on the floor—that's not *fine*."

"I wasn't unconscious. I was having a vision."

Claudia's expression softened. "Really?"

"Really. And I'll be having more."

"For how long? How often?"

"Depends on how long it takes me to figure out what they mean."

"What?"

"Do we have any books on the Binghams?"

Claudia shook her head. "No, you refused to carry them, remember? You said they were frauds."

"Of course they are. So are the authors of at least three-quarters of our inventory. We don't have *anything* on them?"

"No. But I saw a story about them in the *Inquisitor* recently."

85

"Would you do me a favor?" Lily said.

"Wait, *hold* it. Before I do anything, would you please sit down."

Lily sat on the stool, propped an elbow on the countertop.

"Now," Claudia said, "I want you to tell me, seriously . . . are you okay?"

Lily closed her eyes and rubbed them with thumb and finger. "Well, right now, I have a nasty headache. I need to take something for it. But other than that, I'm fine."

"So you really had . . . a vision?"

"I swear. Look, I'll explain it all when you get back."

"Where am I going?"

"To the grocery store to grab a copy of the *Inquisitor* for me. Then hit the other bookstores in town and get every book you can find on the Binghams."

The freckles on Claudia's pale forehead huddled in a frown. "Why?"

"I'll tell you when you get back. Use my credit card."

"Can I get you something for your head before I go?"

"Oh, that would be wonderful. In my bathroom medicine cabinet there's a bottle of Vicodin. I need one of those and a glass of water."

"Be right back."

Lily looked down at her sandwich with disappointment. The headache had destroyed her appetite. She wrapped it up again and put it back in the bag, replaced the lid on the cup of soup.

Claudia returned with the pill and a glass of water. Lily swallowed it, put the glass on the countertop. "I'm going to need a little extra help from you for a while."

"What do you mean?" Claudia said.

"These visions . . . I'm going to be having more of them. I never know when they'll hit, so I can't drive my car or do anything that would put myself or others in danger if I should black out suddenly."

"Has this happened before?"

"Yes, but it's been a while. The last time it happened was a couple years before I met you."

"Does it mean something . . . bad is going to happen?"

"I don't know. Whatever it means, somehow the Binghams are involved. They were screaming. There were other people, too, but I don't know who they are yet. I strongly suspect they live in a gray two-story house by the ocean with playground equipment in the backyard. Somewhere in the house, I think there's a teddy bear that plays music."

"They were screaming?"

"Bloody murder. Except I couldn't hear it."

"What are you looking for, exactly?" Claudia asked.

"If I knew, I wouldn't have to look."

"Will you be okay here by yourself while I'm out?"

She patted Claudia's arm. "Sure. It won't happen again this soon. But hurry back. I'm anxious to start digging."

CHAPTER SEVEN

Sunday, 7:12 A.M.

On Sunday morning, Jenna got out of bed without disturbing David and put on some sweats. Halfway down the stairs, she smelled coffee brewing. She found Martha sitting in the breakfast nook with a cup of coffee reading an old Sidney Sheldon paperback. Her radio was on the windowsill quietly playing big-band music.

"Morning," Martha said. "I made coffee."

"How long have you been up?" Jenna asked as she took a mug from the cupboard and filled it.

Martha shrugged. "A while."

Jenna sat opposite her. "Are you feeling all right?"

"Oh, sure, I'm fine. Just couldn't sleep. Looks like Miles couldn't, either. He's in the living room."

Frowning, Jenna got up and left the kitchen, went through the dining room to the living room. The television was on, tuned to The Cartoon Network with the volume low. Miles had pulled the afghan off the back of the couch and was curled up beneath it, his head on a throw pillow, sound asleep. Jenna wondered if he'd had another nightmare. She decided to let him sleep and returned to the kitchen.

"He hasn't gotten a good night's sleep since he watched that damned horror movie with you and David the other night," Jenna said.

"You sure that's all it is?"

"What do you mean?"

"I don't know. Maybe something's bothering him."

Jenna hoped nothing was wrong at school. She got up and started breakfast—scrambled eggs and cinnamon toast. Once the smell of the cooking eggs wafted through the house, she knew Miles and David would make their way to the kitchen.

Sure enough, Miles shuffled in wearing his pajamas about five minutes later.

"Why were you sleeping on the couch?" Jenna asked.

Miles's eyes were puffy with sleep as he scratched his head. He said nothing.

"Did you have another nightmare?"

He looked up at her and seemed to consider his answer. Finally, he nodded.

"Honey, you can't sleep on the couch with the TV on."

"Oh, why not," Martha said. It wasn't a question. She got up and shuffled over to Miles and gave him a hug. "You want some juice?"

He nodded again.

Martha got a glass from the cupboard, a carton of orange juice from the refrigerator, and poured. She handed him the glass and said, "Come sit with Grandma." They went to the breakfast nook together and sat at the table. Martha turned to Jenna, who stood

89

cooking at the stove. "If he's having nightmares, it'll pass. Maybe he sleeps better on the couch than he would in his bedroom."

"You're not helping, Mom."

"Oh, come on. You used to have nightmares when you were a little girl. I had to leave the lamp on in your bedroom. Sometimes you came in and slept with me, remember?"

A corner of Miles's mouth curled up as he turned to Jenna. "You did, Mom?"

Jenna sighed as she turned back to the eggs. "Yes, I did."

Miles grinned as Martha put an arm around him and said, "So don't feel bad, honey. Everybody goes through it."

David shuffled in wearing his robe, yawning. "Something smells good," he said as he poured a cup of coffee. He went to the table and sat across from Miles. "You ready to go back to work on the garage today, Tiger?"

Miles nodded.

Jenna said, "Don't forget, we're going over to see the Gimbles today."

"Oh, yeah, that's right. A Dodge Durango, huh?"

"Yep. It's idling fast or something."

"Well. A job's a job."

It was a gray, smoky day, but the rain had stopped. After breakfast, David and Miles worked a couple hours in the garage, which was now only half filled with junk. The day before, they had made two trips to a stinking landfill, and there was more to be hauled away: a couple rusted old bicycle frames, an old car battery, a broken trampoline, a rusted-out Weber Kettle barbecue, several garbage bags filled with empty Michelob beer cans that David planned to take to a recycling station, and more. They were ready to haul off another load when Jenna came out.

"Why don't you do that when we get back?" she said.

"You want to go now?" David said.

"Yeah, let's go before you hit the dump."

"Okay."

Jenna turned to Miles and said, "Stay here with Grandma, okay? Keep an eye on her for us?"

"Sure," Miles said.

David said, "First, I've got to clean up."

Kimberly and Harry Gimble lived in a gated community called Seacrest Estates, in a ranch-style house with an immaculately tended front yard. Harry Gimble was raking leaves in the yard when they arrived, and he put his rake down as they got out of the car. He stood a couple inches short of David's six feet, soft and doughy with a wreath of rust-colored hair surrounding his bald head. He wore a burgundy sweater over a yellow shirt, khaki pants, and sneakers.

"You must be the Kellars," he said with a wide smile. He pumped David's hand and said, "Harry Gimble, Sand Dollar Realty. I hear you're new in town."

David nodded, returning the smile. "We've been here a week."

Kimberly came out the front door and joined them. After a few minutes of small talk, she said, "Come on inside, Jenna, while these guys lift the hood on the Dodge."

She took Jenna through the living room, down the hall to the cheerful master bedroom decorated in cream and pale green. Kimberly knocked a pile of underwear and socks off a straight-back chair against the wall. "Look at this," she said. "It's bad enough I've got to clean up after three boys." She carried the chair over to the computer, set it next to the low, wheeled chair already positioned there.

Jenna sat in the straight-back. "I know what you mean," she said. "Miles cleans his room about every fourth or fifth time I tell him to. David's a little sloppy, but I let it pass because he's so good about taking the garbage out and helping me in the kitchen."

Kimberly said, "That's why I can only work part-time at the store. Harry does very well at real estate—we'd be okay if I didn't work. But the extra money is nice, you know? Full-time money would be even nicer, but I don't have *time*. This house would totally fall apart if I worked full-time. Nobody here would survive a week—they wouldn't know how. They would all die. It would be all over the news, and Rush Limbaugh and Dr. Laura would blame me because I wasn't home wiping their butts for them."

Jenna's laughter was quiet at first, but got louder as Kimberly went on. It felt good to laugh so hard, and she enjoyed the feeling while it lasted.

"I'm not kidding—they wouldn't survive their morning rituals without me," Kimberly said. She moved the mouse slightly over the pad on the desktop and opened her Internet browser, nodded her head toward the computer monitor. "There are a lot of local psychics on the Internet, a lot more than I expected to find. Mediums aren't as plentiful, but there are several. Some mediums call themselves 'channels,' and there are quite a few of those, too. But in the Humboldt County area, the most common are psychics. I did a little reading up on all of them, and I don't think a psychic is what you need. There are psychics who read the future, psychics who advise, and psychics who can help you find your lost dog. Some claim to have spirit guides—the spirits of dead people who give them information from the other side—but they don't talk to the dead, not the way you want to. For that, you need a physical medium. Or a channel. But the ones who call themselves channels tend to give off a New Agey vibe that really turns me off. Unless you're into that. Are you?"

Jenna frowned. "Into what?"

"All that New Age stuff. You know, crystals, aromatherapy, Shirley MacLaine, unicorn art."

"Definitely not."

"I'm not too sure about the mediums, either, but at least they don't give the impression they genuinely believe Yanni to be good music, you know what I mean?"

"I think so."

"So I bookmarked all the local mediums who have Web sites, and here—" She picked up a white sheet of paper off the desk and handed it over to Jenna. Printed on the page was a list of names, telephone numbers, and street addresses. "From the Yellow Pages, I made a list of the ones who don't." Kimberly clicked on the top of the list of bookmarks. "I've already looked at all these. Let's go through them, and I'll show you the ones I think smell bad. Like this first one."

A little animated naked man wearing a turban and sitting in the lotus position floated in the center of the screen, bobbing lightly in the virtual air, grinning. Above him arced the name ANTHONY WALL-COLE, and beneath him, MEDIUM TO THE STARS.

"First of all," Kimberly said, "if he's the medium to the stars, what the hell's he doing here? Secondly, look at his picture." She tapped her fingernail on the screen over the man's photograph in the corner. "If he really talked to dead people, they'd tell him how ridiculous he looks with that toupee on his head. And the stars—

Michael Landon, Princess Di, Bette Davis, Dudley Moore, Bill Bixby. It took me a minute to figure out they're all dead. He never worked for these people before they died—he claims to talk to them now that they're dead. *That's* what he means by 'Medium to the Stars.' Well, who's to say he doesn't talk to them, but what difference does that make? You don't need to talk to John Ritter, right? I think we can skip this guy."

Jenna said, "I agree. Who's next?"

"I'm gonna get some coffee first. You want some?" Kimberly stood.

"That sounds good. I'll come with you." As they went back through the house, she said, "How do you know so much about psychics and mediums?"

Kimberly laughed. "Are you kidding? I know *less* than nothing. Everything I told you I just picked up on the Internet last night. In fact, when I was growing up, I was taught to steer *way* clear of this stuff. My brother and I were both taught that it's all evil. We were raised Seventh-Day Adventists."

"Then why did you offer to help me?"

In the kitchen, Kimberly took her mug from the counter and got another from the cupboard, poured coffee into both, added cream to hers. "I said I was *raised* an Adventist, not that I still *am* one. Those stories scared me when I was a little girl, but I haven't been one of those in a long time. You take your coffee black, right?"

"Yes. If that's the way you were taught when you were young, then you must have been frightened when you realized it couldn't have been your grandmother who had come to your room—that it was something . . . evil?"

"Oh, no, not at all. I was already starting to think for myself by then. Before then, really. Some people have to learn to think outside the box; I had to learn to think outside the church, but I started early. When I learned that Grandma had died that night, I knew in my heart, without even having to debate it in my mind, that she had come to kiss me good-bye, in spite of all the things I'd been taught. Like I said, I smelled her breath. I could smell her perfume in the room after she left. She might not have been *there* there, but she was there."

Kimberly handed her the steaming mug, then they headed back to the bedroom.

"So this stuff doesn't bother you now?" Jenna said.

"No, I'm intrigued. I got the impression something was bothering you the first time I saw you, but I had no idea it would be so interesting. You seem much better today, by the way."

Jenna nodded. "I think it's because I'm doing something about it. I'm still blown away by the fact that I'm doing this. I mean, I've always laughed at those guys on TV who talk to people's dead relatives. And I've always thought the people who go to them are pathetic. But now *I'm* one of those pathetic people. If anyone who knows me ever finds out about this, I'll be so embarassed."

As they entered the bedroom, Kimberly said, "You're not pathetic and you shouldn't be embarassed. Spiritual paths take people in all kinds of directions, and if other people can't understand that, it's their problem, not yours. You want to talk embarrassing spiritual paths? Think of those Heaven's Gate guys who had themselves castrated, then ate poison so they could board the starship *Enterprise* in the tail of some comet—wherever they are, they *still* must be embarrassed about that."

Jenna nodded toward the monitor. "Could you e-mail all this information to me?"

"Sure, no problem. Look them over and decide who

you want to try. I don't go back to work till Wednesday, so that gives us a couple afternoons to check some out."

"Are you serious? You really want to do this with me?"

"Sure, why not? You've got me all interested now. And it seems like two of us will be less likely to get taken, you know what I mean? No offense, Jenna, but I've got a feeling I'll be a little less trusting than you."

Jenna nodded. "David says that, too. He says I look like I'd give a handout to Bill Gates. That's why homeless people approach me twice as often as they do everyone else I know. But really, I'm not all that trusting. Sometimes I actually feel guilty because I distrust people so much. But I keep it to myself, you know. It seems so . . . antisocial."

"I know exactly what you mean," Kimberly said. "Except I have a hard time keeping it to myself. But you've got some pretty emotional stuff wrapped up in this, Jenna. Some of these people are pretty good at what they do, and what most of them do is separate people from their money by manipulating their emotions. I can be an extra set of eyes. They might be able to catch you off guard, but it won't work with me."

"I hadn't thought of it that way. That's a good idea."

"Here's another one. Why don't you and David stay for lunch? I was gonna make a chicken salad. We can have sandwiches, and I think I've got some chips in the cupboard. We'll crack open some beers."

Jenna smiled. "Sounds good."

"Let's go back to the kitchen and I'll get to work on that chicken salad."

After Mom and Dad left, Miles had gone up to his room to finish some homework that was due Monday. But as he sat at his desk, he could not get his mind off the area of floor immediately behind him and to his left, where he had seen the man rising up in the dark. His awareness of it made the skin between his shoulder blades tingle until he could take it no longer and looked over his shoulder. He checked every few minutes after that, just to be sure. There was never anything there, but that did not ease his fears or calm his tension. Finally, unable to concentrate, he left his bedroom and went downstairs to the kitchen.

Grandma sat hunched over an open tabloid in the breakfast nook with a cup of something hot on the table. Big-band music played on her radio. Miles sat opposite her and waited for her to look up.

When Grandma spoke, she whispered. There was no particular reason for it, yet it always seemed perfectly natural to Miles whenever Grandma whispered, which she did now and then. "What's keeping you awake, Miles?" she said.

Miles did not have to say the same things to Grandma that he would normally say to his parents to keep peace. She made him feel, when it was just the two of them, that he could tell her anything, that he did not have to pretend about anything, and she always kept his secrets.

"Mom and Dad say I had a nightmare," he whispered back.

She looked at him without lifting her head from the open tabloid. "That's not what I asked you."

"I saw a man coming up out of the floor. A big fat man."

Outside, the wind blew and the swing's chains rattled and squeaked.

Grandma said, "How do you know it wasn't a nightmare?"

"Because I never woke up from it. I saw the man, and then I started screaming because I was so afraid, and

Mom and Dad came in and turned the light on. He was gone, but I was still awake. It wasn't a nightmare because I didn't wake up from it."

Grandma nodded once and turned a page. She looked at him again. "You know, sometimes we see things in those first few seconds after we wake up from a nightmare." She did not sound convinced by her own words.

He said, "I wasn't having a nightmare. I woke up all of a sudden, like I heard something, but I didn't know what. I listened for a while. And then I heard his voice. He called me a puppy. He said, 'You gonna be a good puppy?' Something like that. And then I saw him. Coming up through the floor in the dark. It looked like he was wearing some kind of hat, but I'm not sure because he was in the dark."

She nodded again and looked back down at the paper, but she did not turn another page. Miles watched her as she stared at the paper, sucked her lips between her teeth for a moment, and he decided she was thinking. Finally, she lifted her head and said, "Well, I don't sleep so well, either. I been getting up pretty early lately and haven't been able to go back to sleep. So next time you come downstairs, you check in here for me. Maybe we can play a game of checkers. That'll put you to sleep. Okay?"

He smiled. "Okay."

That evening, David got a phone call. The manager of one of the garages in Eureka where he had applied needed a part-time mechanic sooner than expected. He asked if David would be able to come in the next morning. Trying not to sound needy, he said sure, he'd be there.

"You did one job today, and then you got another,"

Jenna said as they got into bed that night, shortly after eleven. "At this rate, you'll be working full-time by Wednesday."

David laughed. "Harry Gimble's Dodge Durango wasn't exactly a job. It was just a disconnected vacuum tube—I fixed it in two minutes. I didn't even charge him. I bet he gets taken by crooked mechanics a lot. He doesn't know a *thing* about cars."

She cuddled up to him, thrilled that he'd finally gotten some work. She had already noticed a difference in his behavior since the phone call. His arm was more relaxed as he put it around her shoulders. "Do you like Harry?" she asked.

"He's okay. A little wrapped up in his work."

"He does talk shop a lot, doesn't he?"

"You seem to get along well with Kimberly," he said.

"Yeah, I do. I like her."

"That's good—I'm glad you're making friends. What were you guys doing on the computer?"

Jenna had hoped it would not come up, but now that it had, she found herself with nothing to say. She knew that telling him the truth was out of the question. His reaction in the basement had been angrier than she'd anticipated—if he knew she was shopping for mediums, he would probably blow his stack.

David did not get angry often, but when he did, it was ugly. He had never directed it at Jenna—he had always gotten angry about things outside his control, like his inability to get a job as a mechanic, or Josh's death. Jenna was afraid this would make him angry at her, and she did not want that.

She realized she was taking much too long to respond and said the first thing that popped into her head. "Shopping. We were shopping."

"What's wrong?"

"Nothing. Just . . . thinking. You know, Miles was bugging me about getting a dog again tonight. Now that you've got a job."

"It'll have to wait till I'm working full-time. He wants a big dog, and big dogs have big appetites."

"I explained that to him. He understands. He just wants a dog."

Neither of them said anything for a while. Jenna wondered if she and David were thinking about the same thing—about the fact that they had planned to pick up a golden retriever puppy the week Josh died. After that, the idea had faded away until Miles brought it up again.

David said, "Well, let's see where this job is going to go before we start—" He pulled his arm from under her and sat up in bed, back stiff. He cocked his head toward the large rectangular window above their headboard. The window looked out over the backyard. "Did you hear that?" he whispered.

"Hear what? I didn't—"

"Shh!"

Jenna sat up and listened. It was a still night. She heard the screech of the chains on the swing set outside. But there was no wind. And something else—a delicate sound that seemed to move around in the night outside: a child's laughter.

"That's coming from outside," David said as he got out of bed. He went to the closet and put on a pair of sweatpants. After slipping into a sweatshirt, he put on an old pair of running shoes and headed out of the room.

"Where are you going?" Jenna asked.

"Out to the backyard."

For a moment, she wondered if David had finally heard Josh. She was certain she'd heard, for just an instant, the laughter of a child, and apparently, so had David.

After he was gone, Jenna listened closely again. She heard nothing. She got on her knees facing the window over the bed. As she stared out the black rectangle of night, she made a mental note to find some curtains and start putting them up in the windows that had none, like this one. Naked, she leaned over the headboard and tried to look through her reflection, down at the back-yard.

Several seconds later, the bulb over the back porch came on and light oozed through the fog. Five small figures stood by the swing set and slide. Jenna could tell instinctively, by the way they stood, that they were all boys. They were little more than shadows in the mist, but it appeared that each boy stood with his head tilted back, looking up, directly at Jenna.

She gasped and pulled away from the window. She scrambled off the bed, grabbed David's gray robe, and put it on as she hurried barefoot down the hall.

Downstairs, David hurried past the living room, through the dining room to the kitchen, turning on lights as he went—he did not yet feel familiar enough with the house to rush through it in the dark.

There was a window in the top half of the back door with old, threadbare curtains on it, white with blue trim. David tugged a curtain aside with one hand as he flipped on the outside light with the other. He saw them standing there in the fog. Just standing there. None of them could have been any bigger than Miles. They stood motionless beyond the porch light's glow. Goose-flesh passed over the back of his neck. He bent down, grabbed the flashlight, and opened the door.

The light over the back porch went out with a pop

and a hail of sparks. David ducked reflexively and heard something from the fog—the whispers of terrified boys.

"He's coming."

"Go! Run!"

"He's *coming!*"

"I saw them!" Jenna hissed as she hurried into the kitchen behind him.

David quickly turned on the flashlight and went out on the concrete porch. It had old wooden railings on two sides, and four steps leading down to the left of the back door. He skipped the porch steps and hit the ground running. The flashlight beam softened to an amorphous glow in the fog, crept over the weeds that whispered under his feet. David stopped suddenly and swept the yard with the light, listened for the sound of the boys running. Five boys that age could not possibly run away silently. But he did not hear a sound, and they were not in the backyard.

Running along the side of the house, David listened beyond the sound of his own footfalls. He heard nothing. He passed the light all around but saw no sign of them. The front gate was closed, and he had not heard it open. He went to the fence and aimed the light out toward the woods that surrounded their house.

Although he had not heard them, the boys had somehow gotten out of the yard, which meant they were out there somewhere. There was a house a couple miles south of them on Starfish, although David and Jenna did not know the residents. He considered driving down there now and waking them up to ask if they had any kids. But he quickly rejected that idea for another.

He turned and hurried back along the side of the

house to the back door and into the kitchen. He picked up the telephone.

"Who are you calling?" Jenna asked.

"The police. Your mother wasn't seeing things."

CHAPTER EIGHT

Monday, 1:41 A.M.

Rosalind Hooper and Michael Caruso, deputies of the Humboldt County Sheriff's Department, showed up forty-five minutes after David called. They were both tall with dark hair, and looked almost as if they could be brother and sister.

Deputy Hooper said, "We would've gotten here sooner, but there have been a lot of traffic accidents tonight. The fog is pretty thick."

Deputy Caruso said, "It's thicker than—"

Deputy Hooper jabbed her elbow into his ribs while stifling a laugh. "Don't start now, okay? Just . . . not now." She turned to David and Jenna again and said, "You called about some kids in your yard?"

Jenna listened while David told them what he had seen. She interrupted him to describe the figures she'd seen through the window.

"They heard me coming and ran off," David said. "I heard them talking. You know, saying, 'Run, let's get outta here, he's coming,' that kind of thing. They were fast. I mean, they were just gone, they left the yard. Which means they're out there in the woods somewhere. They looked, at most, between five and maybe ten years old."

"And this is the second time they've been out here," Jenna said. "My mother saw them a few days ago."

"Are you positive they were the same kids?" Deputy Hooper said.

"No, not positive. But you could talk to her," Jenna said.

"Is that necessary right now?" David said. "I think the important thing is to find those kids."

Deputy Caruso said, "Did you recognize them? Were they neighbor kids?"

"No," David said. "We haven't met our neighbors yet."

"Did you see which direction they went?" Deputy Hooper asked.

"No, they were gone before I could catch up with them."

"So they could've just walked down to the road, right?" Deputy Hooper said.

Jenna could tell by the expression on David's face as he glanced at her that he hadn't considered that. "That's possible, yes."

"We didn't see them on the way in, but it took us a while to get over here, and we don't know which direction they went."

"Or if they took the road," David said. "They *could* be out in those woods."

"Don't worry," Deputy Caruso said, "we'll take a look around before we go. Tell me, you don't grow any corn around here, do you?"

David squinted at him. "What? Corn? No, why?"

"Ever see any of them *Children of the Corn* movies?"

Laughter exploded from Deputy Hooper, and she bent over a moment, then slapped Deputy Caruso on the shoulder. "Stop it," she said. "Not *now*."

Deputy Caruso shrugged his large shoulders and said, "Cornfields just give me the creeps, that's all I'm saying."

Deputy Hooper forced herself to stop laughing and said, "My partner here does some stand-up down at the Sand Bar."

Jenna and David looked at each other, then back at the deputies.

Deputy Hooper said, "You know, the place in Old Town? The comedy club?"

"We just moved here," Jenna said. "We barely know our way around yet."

"Anyway," Deputy Hooper said, "he tries his new material out on me. He's had me in stitches all night."

Deputy Caruso took his wallet from a back pocket and opened it. He removed two tickets and handed them to David. "Those're guest tickets. No cover charge and your first two drinks are on the house. Come on a Wednesday night—that's my night. It's just, you know, something to do with my days off."

"Thank you," David said. He put the tickets in the pocket of his sweatpants. "I appreciate that. But these kids—"

"Did they take anything?" Deputy Hooper asked. "Do any damage?"

David said, "I think they threw something at the back-porch light and knocked out the bulb."

She said, "Can we take a look?"

David nodded. "Sure, come on back."

Jenna walked beside David as they led the deputies past the stairs and down the short hall. They were entering the kitchen when a high, shrill scream sliced through the house.

Deputies Hooper and Caruso froze and tensed.

"It's our son," Jenna said as she made her way back toward the stairs. "He's been having nightmares."

She hurried up the stairs and found Miles standing in the hallway. He was pressed against the wall across from the bedroom door. He looked terrified.

"It's okay, Miles, I'm here," she said.

He wasn't crying, but his lower lip was unsteady. "I heard voices. What's going on down there?"

She hugged him, then gently led him back into his bedroom, where the overhead light was already on, as well as the lamp on the desk. "There were some kids in the yard, and we called the police. It's nothing—Dad was just worried about the kids because they were pretty young."

"I saw that man again. He was coming up through the floor like before, wearing some kind of hat. He talked to me again. He keeps calling me a puppy."

"Him again, huh?" She sat on the bed and pulled him down beside her. "That's just a nightmare, you know."

Miles sighed quietly but said nothing.

"Okay, you can leave the overhead light on if you just stay up here for now," Jenna said. "When we're finished down there, Dad and I will go back to bed, and if you're still awake, you can sleep on the couch in front of the TV if you want. How does that sound?"

"But I can leave the light on now?"

She nodded. "For now, yes."

"Okay."

Jenna tucked him back into bed and kissed him. She left the bedroom door wide open and both lights on when she went back downstairs.

David and the deputies were coming out of the

kitchen and back down the hall by the time Jenna rejoined them.

David looked at her with a puzzled frown. "The bulb in the back-porch light wasn't damaged," he said. "It just blew out, is all."

"Another one?" Jenna said. "I'm calling an electrician tomorrow."

"Yeah, that's what my ex-wife said," Deputy Caruso said. "First it was the electrician, then the cable guy, then the—"

Laughing again, Deputy Hooper elbowed him in the ribs a second time. She looked at Jenna and shook her head. "He just won't stop."

Jenna did not find it funny and did not smile. Neither did David.

"Okay, here's what we're going to do," Deputy Hooper said. "We'll take a look around, see if we can find these kids. But since no crime was committed and you can't describe them, there's not a lot we can do."

"I just want you to find them and make sure they're okay," David said. "They shouldn't be out there by themselves."

"Okay, we'll see if we can do that," she said. "In the meantime, if you see them again, call us, then let them know you mean no harm, you just want to know where they're from, and see if you can keep them here till we arrive."

David and Jenna stood on the front porch as the deputies made their way back to their patrol car. Deputy Caruso said something Jenna couldn't make out, and Deputy Hooper hooted with laughter.

"I called for police and they sent a comedian and his number-one fan," David said on the way up the stairs. In the hallway, he said, "Why is Miles's light on?"

Jenna explained she had left it on so Miles would stay

in his room while the police were there. She leaned into his open doorway. He was asleep in bed, so she turned off the overhead, leaving on the desk lamp. She couldn't wait to get to bed—she was exhausted.

David lay awake beside Jenna for a couple hours after she fell asleep. He'd expected to be worried about starting a new job the next day, but that was not it. He was listening for the laughter of young boys. Each time he started to doze off, something startled him awake, and he listened again, wondering if he'd heard it.

He did not hear it again that night, and finally drifted off to sleep at 4:24 A.M.

"Your son probably just wants to let you know he's all right," Mrs. Frangiapani said as she put a plate of lemon bars on the coffee table in front of Jenna and Kimberly. Next to the lemon bars was a plate of cupcakes, and next to that a bowl of candied walnuts, and they each had a cup of coffee. The squat, slightly hunched woman of about seventy, with an Italian accent slightly fainter than her mustache, had been getting up and bringing things from the kitchen since they'd arrived. "The cupcakes I made last night, but the lemon bars are from this morning, so be sure and have at least one of those before you go. Can I get you anything else?"

Jenna said, "No, thank you, Mrs. Frangiapani. Please, sit down and talk with us."

Kimberly had picked Jenna up in the almond-colored Durango SLT at nine that morning. Jenna was armed with a list of possible mediums, and they had visited each one. Mrs. Frangiapani, a psychic medium, wasn't on the list. They sat on the sofa in the small, doily-dappled living room of Mrs. Frangiapani's Victorian house in Ferndale.

"Well, I love to cook, and my Tony is usually here to eat all this," Mrs. Frangiapani said, "but he died last year. He was a podiatrist, my Tony, so what'd he do? He broke the big toe on his right foot. He was limping around here after we got back from the doctor and it was all bandaged up, and he fell in the bathroom, hit his head on the side of the tub. Went into a coma and never came out. So I've been eating all this stuff by myself, and I'm afraid I've put on some weight, but I'm too old to care." She sat down on the rolled arm of the sofa beside Jenna, reached down and took Jenna's left wrist in her hand.

At first, Jenna thought the old woman was taking her pulse, but she was simply holding her wrist lightly in her hand. "What are you doing?" Jenna asked.

"Look, angel," Mrs. Frangiapani said, "you don't need to worry about this right now, because there's something wrong at home. You having problems with your husband?"

"No, not at all."

"Well, *some*thing's wrong, and you should be taking care of that now, not this business with—"

"I'm seeing my dead son, that's what's wrong at home."

"*That's* the problem?" Mrs. Frangiapani said. "Well, for heaven's sake, that shouldn't be a problem. He's just waving at you like a child waves at a passing train."

Jenna watched the old woman, waiting for her to say more, but Mrs. Frangiapani had no more to say. Tears burned the back of Jenna's throat, and she swallowed a couple times before saying, "If I believe that, Mrs. Frangiapani, I'll go insane."

"Oh, a lot of people do, angel. That's why I'm telling you to forget about it. It's nice that it happened, but now it's time to let it go. It may never happen again, or it may happen the same time every day for the rest of your life, but either way, you can't obsess over it. Just let it go."

"No, that's not what I mean," Jenna said. "If I believed that Josh is conscious someplace where I can't reach him, it would drive me—"

"Oh, angel, it doesn't matter what you believe."

"But I've never believed in this sort of thing before."

Mrs. Frangiapani shrugged her round shoulders and said, "You didn't need to before. Now you don't have much choice, do you? Listen, sweetie, if I were like a lot of other mediums out there, I could come over and read your house and charge you by the room. But I wouldn't see or hear anything, because those communications, they're meant for you alone, Jenna. And if he really *is* trying to tell you something, then all you have to do is pay attention and see what he wants. Maybe there's something you can help him resolve."

Jenna said, "But how can I reach him?"

"He's pretty good at reaching you, isn't he? If he's got something to say, he'll say it." She turned to Kimberly, who was eating a lemon bar. "How many did you go to before me today?"

"You're the fourth," Kimberly said.

"And they all wanted money before they'd say a word, didn't they?"

Kimberly and Jenna nodded.

First, there was Mrs. Perez. She lived in a tiny house at the edge of the commercial district in Eureka. A giant hand with an eye in the center of the palm stood in front of her house with the words PSYCHIC READINGS at the bottom. Jenna and Kimberly had agreed that was a bad sign, but decided to go inside anyway. Mrs. Perez wanted fifty dollars just to listen to what they wanted. They left immediately.

Ada Brodky was a frail-looking woman with a cigarette-damaged voice and thick glasses in black frames. She appeared to be in her late fifties, although Jenna suspected she wasn't as old as she looked. A cigarette dangled from the corner of her mouth. Her sandy hair, lightening with gray, was pulled back tight and kept in a bun. She lived in an old mobile home on a small spot of land in Fortuna. Ada Brodky listened to Jenna for a few minutes, then put a nicotine-stained hand on her shoulder and said, "I charge two-fifty a sitting. They last anywheres from one to two hours, usually one. I work alone, no assistants, no tricks. If you got a poltergeist, you need to go see somebody else, 'cause I don't do poltergeists no more, not since I got a tooth knocked out by one. I'll be honest with you, dear, I'm not one of them vultures who'll make you come back again and again. I can take care of most things in one or two sittings. And if there's no contact—it happens sometimes—then you don't pay, that's my policy. Outside of that, I can't help you. You're a nice young lady, but I gotta make a buck, because as you can see, I'm not exactly livin' in luxury here."

Kimberly had turned for the door then, but Jenna touched her elbow and said, "No, wait." She turned to Ada Brodky and said, "You really think you might be able to contact my son in one sitting?"

"One or two, no more. If he's there."

Jenna thought she would have little trouble raising the money typing and editing college papers. She got Ada Brodky's card and slipped it into her purse.

Next, they saw Wayne Lapidus at the Humboldt County Institute of Paranormal Research. The institute occupied a single tiny office in a small building it shared with a refrigerator repairman, a key maker, a dry cleaner, and a Kinko's. Wayne Lapidus was a chubby man who appeared to be uncomfortable in his own skin, because he never stopped picking at his charcoal sweater or fidgeting in his chair as they spoke. He listened to Jenna for a while, then offered what he called an initial consultation. After that, he'd said, if he saw reason to investigate further, they could work out a schedule. Jenna asked how much all that would cost.

"Impossible to say. The consultation itself costs fifteen hundred."

Jenna and Kimberly had laughed. Jenna had explained she could not possibly pay that much and thanked him for his time.

"Hold on," Wayne Lapidus had said. "If you really need to talk to someone, I might be able to help you out. I know of someone who might talk to you for nothing."

He had given them Mrs. Frangiapani's phone number.

"Well, I'm retired now," Mrs. Frangiapani said as she got up off the arm of the sofa and turned to look down at them. "So I don't take money for it anymore. I'm not as young as I used to be, and it takes a lot out of me, talking to the dead. But I'm telling you, angel, you don't need a medium. You just need to go back home and pay attention to your . . . You've got a husband and a son, right?"

Jenna nodded and smiled. "How did you know?"

"Remember, I'm a *psychic* medium. I'm just not as sharp as I used to be. Things still come through, but not as strong anymore. Tony used to say my psychic vision needed glasses. But I'm getting enough on you to know you should go home and fix the problem there and stop worrying about this, because this is not a problem."

"But there is no problem at home," Jenna said.

Mrs. Frangiapani reached down again and took

Jenna's wrist in her hand. She frowned, and her lower lip protruded for a moment. "Does your son have a puppy?"

"No. But we've been talking about getting a dog."

"No, that's not it." Mrs. Frangiapani closed her eyes, shook her head once. "It's got nothing to do with a dog, it's just . . ." She opened her eyes and shook her head again. "I don't know, it didn't come through very strong." She released Jenna's wrist. "You say everything's okay with the husband?"

"Yes, everything's been fine. But . . . well, David wouldn't approve of this."

"Ah, he wouldn't approve of you coming to me about your son? So you've kept it a secret. Then you have a problem, angel, because secrets are always problems. You need to go home and talk to him and take care of your little boy. Something's bothering the boy, isn't it?"

"He's been having nightmares."

Mrs. Frangiapani cocked her head, birdlike, and frowned. "You sure they're nightmares?"

Jenna laughed. "That's what my mother said. You'd get along well with her—she likes to cook, too. Yes, they're nightmares." Her smile quickly dissolved. "Why?" A deep chill passed over her. "Is there something wrong with Miles?" she whispered.

"No, angel, what I'm trying to tell you is you got those two and yourself to worry about. Don't worry about the dead."

"So . . . you're not going to help me?"

"There's nothing I can do for you, don't you understand? You don't need help from me, your family needs help from you. You're still hurting from the loss of your son, you haven't gotten over that yet—do I have to draw you a picture, angel?"

Jenna felt almost as if she'd been slapped. It was not

very different from what David had told her—and again, it rang true.

"Listen," the old woman said, "I wouldn't be a bit surprised if my Tony came through the front door right now with his golf clubs, complaining about how his chiropractor friend cheats on the links, then disappeared like a cloud of smoke. It wouldn't surprise me because it happened a million times in life, but I'm not going to sit around waiting for it, because it'll probably never happen again."

"Or it may happen every day," Jenna said.

"You just never know. Which is another good reason to love the people in your life as much as you can while they're alive. And when they move on, you go on with your life and you don't dwell on it, because if you do, you go crazy. If it should happen that one of them pops up and says hello, you enjoy it, then let it go. You hear me? You let it go. Instead, you should be working on that problem at home. Now." She flattened her palms together and smiled. "I made a cheesecake last night. You can't leave without having a piece."

Later, having turned down Mrs. Frangiapani's cheesecake, Jenna and Kimberly went to Jack in the Box for lunch. They talked over Jumbo Jacks and curly fries.

Kimberly said, "I think I agree with everything Mrs. Frangiapani said."

"You're right. She made perfect sense. But believe it or not, I'm actually thinking of rounding up enough money to have Ada Brodky come over to the house for a . . . what did she call it? A sitting?"

"Why didn't you say so while we were there?" Kimberly said. "I'll spot you the two-fifty—I know you're good for it."

"You don't have to do that. I should be getting some

calls on those cards I posted. A few of those, and I can—"

"Don't be ridiculous. Look, if you want my advice, I'd say do what Mrs. Frangiapani said to do. I think it makes a lot of sense. But if you really want someone to come out to the house, you might as well do it and get it over with."

"That's very nice of you, Kimberly, but I don't like taking money from—"

"You're not taking, you're borrowing."

"Well . . . first I should find out when David is going to be working. I don't know his schedule yet, and I really don't want him to walk in and find a medium in the house trying to . . . well, you know." She sighed. "I'll think about it."

Kimberly dropped Jenna off at the house a few minutes before three in the afternoon. The day was misty and damp, and Jenna hugged herself as she went up the front walk and into the house. As she took off her coat and hung it on one of the wall hooks just inside the front door, she heard the cracking and popping of a fire in the fireplace. Jenna wondered if Martha had started it. She stepped into the living room to find David on one knee in front of the fire, stoking it, with an auto race on television. Jenna remembered that the garage was cleaned out and they were parking the Toyota and pickup truck in there now—she hadn't seen David's pickup parked out front and had assumed he hadn't gotten back yet.

"Hi," he said. "Where've you been?"

"Oh. When did you get home? I thought you were working today."

"No, today was just an orientation. I work tomorrow, Wednesday, and Thursday. And I have to be available to fill in for people."

"Oh." Jenna stood just inside the living room doorway, frozen in place. She had not expected David to be home yet, and had no idea what to tell him. She couldn't lie—he would be able to tell.

"Where'd you go today?" he asked.

"With Kimberly. We went out to lunch."

"What's the matter?"

"What do you mean?"

David stood and came to her, embraced her as he laughed. "You look like you just did something terrible."

So you've kept it a secret, Mrs. Frangiapani had said. *Then you have a problem, angel, because secrets are always problems.*

"Oh. Well, I didn't know you'd be home so early, so I didn't make any lunch, and I went out with Kimberly instead, so . . . I'm sorry."

"Honey, I'm not helpless—I fixed a sandwich. When does Miles get home?"

"He should be here any minute."

He gave her a kiss and whispered, "Got time for a quickie?"

"Oh, honey, not right now," Jenna said. "I'm sorry, but I feel really full from lunch. I had a big hamburger."

"Okay, later, then." He kissed her again, and she reached down and gave his ass a two-handed squeeze.

"How do you like work?" she asked.

"It's great. Nice layout, well-organized. Everybody seems like good people. I think I'll like it."

"I'm so happy you got it."

"You just want me out of the house so you can run off and shop and have girly lunches with your girlfriend."

Jenna laughed. "Is leftover stew for dinner all right with you?"

"Sounds good to me."

"Okay, then, I don't have to worry about dinner, so I

117

can focus on finding an electrician and making Mom an appointment with an eye doctor."

"I replaced the bulb on the back porch," David said. "It works fine now."

"I'm still calling an electrician. Enjoy your races." Jenna went into the kitchen to find the Yellow Pages.

David had thought of the boys in the backyard many times throughout the day. He wondered if Deputies Hooper and Caruso had found them, or any trace of them. Most of all, he wondered if they were all right.

They ate dinner in the living room, where it was warm. David found himself listening for something other than the television. But he wouldn't hear them in the living room, not if they were playing in the back-yard. He finished his bowl of stew and got up halfway through a rerun of *Friends*. "Delicious, honey," he said as he left Jenna, Miles, and Grandma in the living room.

David rinsed his bowl, put it in the sink, and went to the breakfast nook. He leaned his palms on the tabletop, looked out the window, and saw nothing but his own reflection over the darkness outside. He stayed there a moment, listening. A storm was blowing in and the chain swings chattered in the night like metal teeth. The branches of an elm tree in the back-yard scratched against the house. But he heard nothing else.

It was not until later that night, ten minutes after Jenna had fallen asleep in bed beside him, that he heard them again. The sound of their laughter was quickly whipped away by the wind, but he heard snatches of it fluttering through the night outside, the phantom laughs of little boys. He moved carefully to avoid disturbing Jenna as he got out of bed. He quickly put on his sweats and running shoes and left the bedroom without making a sound.

Miles's bedroom door was closed and the overhead light was on again. David ignored it for now. He moved slowly and carefully through the house because he did not want to turn on any lights. In the kitchen, he went to the back door and peered out the window. It was a dark night, but he could see movement in the yard.

David carefully unlocked and opened the back door a crack and listened. The ivy leaves in the yard gossiped quietly in the wind. The boys were laughing, but sounded as if they were trying to keep their voices low. It was secretive laughter. As he picked up the flashlight with his left hand, he used his right to carefully, silently open the back door all the way. He switched the Mag-Lite to his right hand, put his left on the light switch, and stepped out onto the porch. He could make out their figures over by the swing set and slide, but they weren't playing on the equipment. They appeared to be huddled together, whispering and laughing.

David turned on the porch light, but it was not bright enough to reach the boys. They fell silent as David clicked the flashlight on and sent the beam out toward them. They stood together between the slide and the swings. As bright as the beam was, it fell just short of reaching the boys, of revealing their faces.

"Don't worry, I don't want to hurt you," David said. "You're not in trouble or anything. I just . . . I want to know . . . What are you doing out this late by yourselves? Huh? Where are your parents?" He went down the concrete steps of the porch and advanced toward them, hoping to bring them into the light. But the five boys backed away together slowly and avoided the beam. "Where are you from? Do you live around here?"

David flinched when he heard a loud pop and the porch light went out behind him. "Dammit," he muttered.

"He's coming!" one of them hissed.

Another said, "Run!" and a third said, "Go!"

"No, wait," David said. He couldn't see the figures in the dark anymore. He swung the light around the yard. They were gone. "How the hell—"

David rounded the corner, went along the side of the house at a full run, and was in the front yard in seconds. The boys weren't there, either. The gate was closed, and he had not heard it open.

He decided to go all the way around the fence tomorrow and examine it. There had to be a hole in it somewhere—it was the only explanation for the boys' almost instantaneous escape.

I didn't hear them running, David thought as he walked back down the side of the house and into the backyard. *Why didn't I hear them running?*

"Fuckin' puppies," a voice said. It was the moist, roughly whispered voice of a man who sounded like he seldom felt the need to talk very loud. "Looks like we got some renegades there. Gonna have to take care of 'em."

David swept the flashlight in the direction of the voice, and the beam fell, for just a moment, on a man standing in the northwest corner of the backyard. The light stayed on just long enough for David to make out a pear-shaped man wearing a cowboy hat, a denim vest over a dirty white T-shirt, ratty old jeans, and cowboy boots. The vest was parted by the mound of his belly, which dangled sadly over the top of the sagging, beltless jeans. A melon slice of hairless, pale belly peeked out from beneath the strained T-shirt. The flashlight blinked out and David found himself in the cold, wet dark.

After flicking the button a few times, David smacked the heavy metal flashlight into the palm of his left hand. He had replaced the batteries just before they moved. He could not understand why it had gone out. The cold drizzle still sent chills over his back, but he felt a new chill, this one at the back of his neck, unrelated to the cold.

The sound of a match being lit just to his left was so close to David that he dropped the flashlight and took a quick step away from the sound. He turned to face the man, who remained in profile as he lit a cigar about two feet away, his cowboy hat tilted forward. He cupped a hand around the match's flame, which sent a dance of orange and yellow over his face. It revealed a large, pitted nose and an enormous second chin rough with stubble.

David felt his heartbeat in his throat. "Who are you? Where the hell did you come from?"

"Them renegade puppies . . . you gotta know how to handle 'em."

David winced when he got a whiff of the cigar and stepped back again. He was not fond of cigar odor of any kind, but this one was especially foul. It smelled like a combination of moldy leaves and rotting meat.

The man turned to face David. "You gotta know how to handle 'em," he said as he stepped forward once, twice.

David tried to dodge him, to move out of the way, and almost tripped on the flashlight. The fat man stepped into him as if he were a phone booth. David fell into the weeds, but quickly propped himself up on one elbow.

121

The cigar was no longer an odor, but a harsh, immediate taste inside his mouth, a burning in his lungs. It was vile . . . awful . . . pretty bad . . . an acquired taste.

I'm dreaming, David thought as everything turned black.

CHAPTER NINE

Tuesday, 2:58 A.M.

David found himself stacking boxes in the basement. His flashlight was working and he was putting the last box on the stack when he became conscious of his surroundings. As this happened, he was overwhelmed by the stomach-lurching sensation of something spiritually viscous extracting itself from his mind, from his soul. It left dribbling gobbets of itself behind as it ripped away from him like an overstrained membrane, and David's mind flashed with unspeakable images of children, someone's little boys, naked and sprawled. The images were bad enough, but there was something else, something unthinkable—they stirred deep in his gut the clinging ghost of a hungry, ugly desire, and David dropped the flashlight, fell to his hands and knees, and retched. He vomited to get rid of it, to get it out of him, and hoped it came up with the bile that foamed in the dirt.

The splintered old high chair with its six leather

straps fell flat on the dirt floor inches in front of him, and he cried out. He grabbed up the flashlight and clambered to his feet. He passed the beam all around the basement.

Why was I stacking boxes? he thought. *Was I putting something away? What am I doing down here?*

He realized he was down in the basement in the middle of the night—if it was still night; he had no idea what time it was—after . . . what? What had he been doing?

On his way up the stairs, he realized he had been walking in his sleep and dreaming. He hadn't done that since he was a kid. He shuffled down the hall with his eyes barely open, so tired he could feel himself nodding off as he walked. He left his sweats in a heap on the floor. He was so exhausted, he did not hear himself mutter under his breath as he got into bed, "Fuckin' puppies."

"It was like he was hungover," Jenna said. "I didn't think he was going to make it to work on time, I was really worried. I mean, it's his first day, you know?"

At the wheel of the Durango, Kimberly asked, "Did he do a little celebrating last night or something?"

"Oh, no. David's not a big drinker, and neither am I. In fact, we haven't had any beer or liquor in the house since we moved in. Even before that, back in our apartment in Redding. David was just really exhausted this morning. He said he didn't sleep well last night. Said he had a weird dream about digging around down in the basement. Probably just worried about the new job."

Jenna had called Ada Brodky and asked if she would come to her house for a sitting that day. "I'll provide the transportation, Mrs. Brodky," Jenna had said.

"It's not Mrs. I never married. I didn't see the point. You can call me Ada."

When they drove up to her trailer, Ada did not wait for them to get out of the Durango. She came out of the trailer wearing a long gray wool coat and carrying a dark green suitcase. A long, freshly lit cigarette poked from the corner of her mouth.

"I hope she didn't think I asked her to move in with us," Jenna said.

"Harry's gonna flip when he smells smoke in here," Kimberly said.

"Why don't you tell her to put it out?"

"I'm not sure she can. That's all right—let's just crack the windows and hope for the best."

Jenna got out of the SUV and greeted Ada, asked if she could help with the bag.

"Just put this in the back," Ada said as she handed the suitcase over to Jenna.

It was light and Jenna put it in the backseat, then got in with it, giving Ada the front seat.

"No offense," Ada said as Kimberly drove away from the trailer, "but I've always hated these damned things."

"What things?" Kimberly said as she pulled open the empty, pristine ashtray.

"These buses, or SUVs, or whatever you call 'em. They're so hard to get into and out of, and they're so damned *big*. I used to drive a little Volvo, and I'd hate to be on the road with these things. But I stopped driving a long time ago. I couldn't take the pressure no more. Too many cars, too many people. I take the bus everywhere now. A cab once in a while, on special occasions."

"Well, we have three kids," Kimberly said.

"Ah, kids. There's something I'm not sorry I never had."

Ada kept talking, but Jenna tuned her out. David was

at work, Miles at school, but she wondered how she was going to explain Ada and a sitting—whatever *that* was—to her mother.

By the time they got back to the house, Ada had complained about everything from the winter's effects on her joints to the quality of television news coverage. Jenna went into the house ahead of them to find Martha. The breakfast nook was empty, so she went to Martha's bedroom. The door was closed. "Mom?" she said. She opened the door a crack and looked in.

Martha was asleep on her neatly made bed beneath an afghan she had crocheted. Her clock radio was playing softly and the overhead light was on.

Everybody's trying to run our electric bill through the roof, Jenna thought as she turned off the light and silently pulled the door closed. She joined Kimberly and Ada in the living room. A slowly shifting cloud of smoke engulfed the top half of Ada's body.

"Where do you want to do this?" Jenna asked.

"Don't matter," Ada said. "If he's in the house, he'll hear me. You got something like a card table I could use to set up?"

Jenna hurried upstairs. The unused bedroom where they had hoped to keep only their books and the computer had become, like Martha's bedroom, a catchall for things that did not yet have a place or needed to be unpacked. The card table was in there, folded up and leaning against some still-unpacked boxes of books. Clutching the edge with both hands, she hurried back downstairs, wondering what else a sitting might involve. To make room, Jenna and Kimberly carried the coffee table into the dining room and put it up against the north wall. Then Jenna set the card table up in the center of the living room.

Ada had her suitcase open on the couch and was bent

over it. "There's all kindsa ways to communicate with the spirits. Some are better than others, but my favorite is always the board."

"The *board*?" Kimberly said. There was a slight note of alarm in her voice.

The cloud of smoke followed Ada from the suitcase to the card table, where she set an eighteen-and-a-half-by fourteen-inch rectangular board of quarter-inch-thick maple. A sun with a smiling face had been carved in the top left corner, a somber-profiled crescent moon in the top right. The signs of the zodiac were carved along the bottom. Across the center of the ornate board, two rows of the letters of the alphabet arced above the numbers zero through nine in a straight row, all carefully painted on. The word "Yes" had been painted next to the sun, and beside the moon, "No." At the bottom was the word "Good-bye." The Ouija board had been heavily varnished and was yellowed with age. The teardrop-shaped planchette was also of varnished maple, one-eighth of an inch thick, with three tiny felt-tipped legs beneath it.

Kimberly looked at Jenna with an expression of shock and . . . was that fear in her eyes? It softened quickly but did not quite go away.

"What's wrong?" Jenna said.

Kimberly smiled and shook her head, shrugged a shoulder. "When I was growing up, we were always told to stay away from these things."

Jenna frowned. "Really? Why?"

"You raised a Christian?" Ada asked.

Kimberly nodded. "Seventh-Day Adventist. When I was a kid, we were taught that they were evil and dangerous things, these boards, and that tampering with them could . . . well, it could completely ruin your life. I've never seen one before. It just . . . well . . ." She took a deep breath and let it out slowly. "It just gave me the creeps, that's all. I wasn't expecting it."

"That's common among Christians," Ada said. "I was raised Presbyterian, myself. Horror stories are told about the board. They scare the livin' crap outta their kids about 'em. Which I think is good, by the way, even though most of the stories are complete crap. People *should* stay away from the board, it's not something you futz around with if you don't know what you're doing. It *can* be dangerous."

"Wait," Jenna said. "So you're saying that this board you just brought into my house is . . . potentially dangerous?"

"Don't worry, honey. You wouldn't know it to look at me, but I know what I'm doing. Haven't lost a client yet." Ada took off her coat and tossed it onto the couch. Beneath it, she wore a black-and-white floral-print pantsuit. "We'll need three chairs at the table, positioned so we can hold hands."

Jenna got three old dented-up beige metal folding chairs from a cluttered narrow closet in the dining room, where she had found them the first day in the house. After setting up the chairs, she turned to Kimberly, who still stared warily at the Ouija board.

"Are you sure you're okay with this?" Jenna asked.

Kimberly smiled. "Yeah. But she's right. I heard horror stories about Ouija boards being evil. Really scary stuff."

"The board itself ain't evil," Ada said as she sat down at the table. "This one was made by my great-grandpa for my great-grandma. I come from a long line of mediums. Do you have an ashtray?"

"An ashtray," Jenna said. They'd found several filthy old ashtrays around the house—the first day, they'd opened all the windows to air out the odor of stale tobacco—and Jenna had washed them and put them in a kitchen cupboard. She got one and put it on the table by the Ouija board just in time to catch the skeletal finger of ash that dropped from Ada's cigarette. The cloud of smoke settled over the table.

Ada crushed the butt in the ashtray. "The board's just a tool. Like a computer. And you don't want somebody doesn't know what he's doin' pokin' around with it, is all."

Kimberly still did not take a seat at the card table. "I've always heard that once you use them . . . they leave things behind."

"They can't leave anything behind, honey, 'cause they don't come with anything attached. All they do is make it easier to communicate with what's already here in the first place. The board gives the spirits something to focus their energies on."

For a moment, Jenna wondered what she was doing. She couldn't believe someone had just said, "The board gives the spirits something to focus their energies on," and she wasn't at least rolling her eyes and smiling, trying to be polite enough not to laugh or ridicule. But she thought of that small figure standing at the end of the upstairs hallway, and of that same figure in the basement hugging a teddy bear.

Mommy—

Ada said, "The reason I only have to do this once or twice is most people watch me the first couple times, see how easy it is, and figure out they can do it themselves."

Jenna said, "But . . . I thought you just said people shouldn't do it on their own."

"I said people shouldn't operate a Ouija board unless they know what they're doing. But anybody can talk to the dead." She removed from a pocket a box of Marlboros and a zebra-print disposable butane lighter, lit up, then set them on the right corner of the table, the lighter on the box. "No secret to it, just talk, they'll hear you if they want to. Whether or not they're in the mood to listen, let alone reply, is what makes this a little like fishing. The difference is, a medium, which is what I am, can draw them out a lot easier and faster than most people. You can sit on your couch and talk to the ceiling all day long and maybe get nothing. I can get them to pay attention. It's a gift. You either got it or you don't."

Jenna said, "You do this for a living, Ada?"

"Never for a living. I worked at the Payless pharmacy in Eureka for almost thirty years before I retired early. I did this for a little extra money, and because I *could*. I mean, it's something I can do and not many other people seem to be so hot at, so why not help people out with it, huh? *And* make a little extra money? I mean, this is still America, right? Have they made it a crime to make a buck yet?"

"What if—" Kimberly said, but she stopped herself. She looked at Jenna, mouth open, as if she were not sure she wanted to continue.

"What if what, honey?" Ada said.

"What if they're not . . . spirits?"

"They tell *me* they're spirits. Who am I to argue? What do I know? What *else* would they be? Now, you two sit down at the table."

Kimberly still hesitated.

"You don't have to do this if you don't want to," Jenna said. "If it bothers you, Kimberly, I don't *want* you to do it."

Kimberly said, "Well, um . . ." Her round cheeks became rosy with embarrassment.

Ada looked up and said, "What I usually tell people like this at sittings is—give it a try, if you're uncomfortable with it, just leave. Nothing bad is going to happen to you either way. Trust me, if I thought something bad was going to happen to you, I wouldn't be sitting at the same table with you. I don't hang around when I know bad things're gonna happen—I'm just not that type, I don't have it in me."

Jenna said, "But if you don't *want* to, Kimberly—"

"No, that's okay. I'll give it a try. But you'll understand if I don't stick it out."

"Sure, honey," Ada said. "You feel free. Now sit down."

Jenna sat on the right side of Ada, Kimberly on the left. Ada produced a spiral-bound notebook with the cover folded all the way back, a pen attached to the binding, and placed it in front of Kimberly. "We'll hold hands for a while, but later, once things get started, you write down every letter the planchette points to." She reached over and patted Kimberly's hand. "Can you do that, hon? Because I'm gonna need Jenna to work on the board with both hands, okay?"

Kimberly said, "Yeah. Sure." But she did not sound confident.

"Now, at some point, I'm gonna need you both to put your fingertips on the planchette. Don't press on it. I want you to barely touch it, understand? I want your fingertips more off it than on." She turned to Kimberly again. "When you start writing, keep one hand on the planchette—can you do that, hon?"

"Yeah. Sure."

"When you feel the planchette move, don't take your hands away," Ada said.

"I'm sorry," Kimberly said, "but if that thing moves on its own, you two will have to figure out the writing problem yourselves."

Ada laughed, but it quickly turned into a series of coughs that required her to remove the cigarette from her lips for a moment.

"Do you want me to turn the lights out, or pull the shades?" Jenna asked.

"Oh, no," Ada said. "That's just in the movies. You get it dark in here, I can't read what they're trying to say. Now, first, we're just gonna hold hands here around the board for a while, and we're gonna close our eyes, and all we're gonna think about is little Josh." She reached out and took their hands. Jenna and Kimberly reached across the table and clasped hands behind the Ouija board. Ada lowered her voice near a whisper and spoke in the same gentle, almost reverent tone and with the same vaguely singsong cadence one might use when saying a familiar prayer. Her rough, cigarette voice softened. "We're gonna think about little Josh's spirit somewhere in this house, and we're gonna call him to us and he's gonna sense that, and eventually, he'll respond. Just concentrate your thoughts on Josh right now, on his spirit . . ."

Ada went on and on while Jenna tried to concentrate. It was difficult to do on top of dealing with the fact that she was actually *doing* this, and wondering what she would tell her mother if she were to walk in the room—or, even worse, what if David came home? That thought scrambled her mind like an egg and, for a moment, made her forget what she was supposed to be thinking about in the first place.

This is a séance, Jenna thought. *That's what a sitting is, it's a* séance. *I saw them do this on* Geraldo *one Halloween back in the eighties. What am I* doing *here?*

She started listening to Ada, followed the singsong rhythms with her mind, and each time Ada said Josh's name, Jenna felt a small pain deep in her chest. The séance seemed to melt away when the realization pierced her that she was trying to reach her dead son.

That's what you're doing here, she thought.

Mommy—

"We're just gonna keep thinking about Josh and focusing our thoughts and our energies together here, over this board, and we're gonna draw him to us . . ."

Jenna had no idea how long Ada had been rambling on when something in the air changed, but it had been a while. The temperature in the living room dropped noticeably and the air became charged with electricity. Jenna opened her eyes and found Kimberly staring at her wide-eyed, lips pressed together so hard they'd gone white—she sensed it, too.

"Okay," Ada said as she let go of their hands, "someone is with us."

"Someone?" Jenna whispered. "You're not sure if it's Josh?"

Ada peeled the filter tip from her lips and tapped the cigarette over the ashtray as she quietly said, "Remember what I said about this being a little like fishing? Now, put your fingertips lightly on the planchette, *very* lightly." She put the cigarette back in her mouth and placed her fingertips on the planchette's broad bottom edge.

Jenna gingerly touched her fingertips to the planchette's curved edge and suspended her hands above the board.

Kimberly reached out with both hands—Jenna noticed that her fingers were trembling—but pulled them back before she touched the planchette. "I'm sorry," she said. "I can't do it. I'll write down the letters for you, but . . . I just can't do it."

Jenna said, "It's okay, don't worry about it. Sure you want to stay for this?"

Kimberly took a moment to think about it. "I'll stay as long as I can, okay? That's the best I can do. But I can't put my hands on that thing."

"Don't worry about it, honey," Ada said, then turned to Jenna. "Now let's not waste time. They're here."

"They?" Jenna said.

"They, him, whatever. You never know who'll show up. Put your fingers on the planchette and keep concentrating on Josh, just think about Josh, keep your thoughts focused on Josh . . ." Ada was speaking with that lulling cadence again.

The planchette was cool beneath the pads of Jenna's fingertips, and she stared at it awhile as she tried to keep thinking about Josh, then closed her eyes. Her thoughts were shattered when the planchette budged forward—the varnished surface moved smoothly beneath her fingertips. Jenna's hands jerked reflexively away from the thin slice of wood when it moved, and she opened her eyes.

". . . keep our thoughts focused on Josh and your fingers on—" Ada opened her eyes. "Jenna, keep your fingers on the planchette, touch it lightly so it can move independent of your fingers. Don't push it with your fingertips, follow it with them."

Jenna forced her hands back down, placed her fingertips lightly on the smooth, varnished surface.

It budged forward again. This time, Jenna saw it move beneath her fingers and Ada's. She moved her hands along with it as the planchette inched up past the U to stop with its pointed end on the H. Ada said the letter out loud.

Kimberly sat frozen in her chair and stared openmouthed at the planchette.

Ada said, "Sweetheart, you're gonna have to get these letters down, 'cause I won't be able to remember 'em, okay? Now—H."

Eyes wide, Kimberly nodded, then wrote down the letter.

The planchette moved to the left in tiny little budges and stopped at the E. The next letter was L.

Hello, Jenna thought. *My baby's saying hello, he's saying—*

The next letter was P.

"Help," Kimberly said.

Ada's cigarette bobbed as she looked vaguely upward and said, "How can we help you, dear? That's what we're here for, just tell us."

Jenna feared her heart would explode—Josh needed *help*? How could she possibly help him? What good would all this do if she were only to learn he was in some kind of danger in a place where she could never reach him?

Jenna leaned toward Ada. "Ask him what's wrong. Why does he need help?"

Ada said, "You ask him, honey, he's right here with us."

Jenna looked over at Kimberly. The color had drained from her face. Her lower body was turned so her legs were at an angle, ready to shoot from the chair and run out of the room on short notice. Jenna sniffled, took a breath. "Josh, why do you need—"

The planchette moved again, this time to the center of the board. Then it slowly made its way back to the P, over to the U. Ada called out the letters and Kimberly wrote them down, until she had two words on the page: HELP PUPPEEZ.

"Puppies?" Ada muttered. "Do you have puppies?"

Jenna shook her head. "We have no pets."

Mrs. Frangiapani had asked if Miles had a puppy.

Jenna's eyes widened slightly. *He called me a puppy*, Miles had said of the man in his nightmare.

The planchette continued to move, but it hit the same letters three more times: HELP PUPPEEZ.

"What *about* the puppies?" Ada said. "You'll have to explain, because nobody here knows what you're talking about."

The planchette started to move again, but stopped when another drop in temperature occurred and the room became cold. Something happened that made Jenna feel vaguely nauseated—the air itself seemed to darken. A few things happened all at once.

One of the four lightbulbs in the overhead light went out with a pop and threw some sparks into the air, as did the bulb in the lamp on one of the sofa's end tables. At the same instant, a force like a large fist slammed down on the table and made it quake so hard it nearly collapsed. Jenna and Ada pulled away from the table. Kimberly scooted her chair backward as quickly as she could. The planchette cracked down the center and collapsed inward before being swept off the table. It missiled through the air straight for Kimberly and landed in her lap. Kimberly screamed and fell over backward in her chair.

"You got a poltergeist," Ada said as she stood.

As suddenly as it had changed, the air was fine again, the temperature normal.

"Jesus, oh Jesus," Kimberly whispered to herself as she got to her feet and hurried away from the table. She stood in the entryway near the front door, arms folded beneath her breasts. Bending at the waist, she bobbed up and down slightly as she whispered repeatedly, "Demons. Demons."

Jenna stood and hurried to Kimberly's side. "What did you say?"

"Demons."

"I don't understand. What demons?"

"I was raised to believe you don't go to Heaven when you die," Kimberly said. "Seventh-Day Adventists believe that won't happen until after the second coming of Christ, when the dead are all resurrected and everybody's judged and either thrown into the Lake of Fire or taken up to Heaven with Jesus. Until then, the dead are just . . . dead."

"Then how do they explain the spirits?" Ada said.

"They don't believe there *are* any spirits—only demons posing as the spirits of dead loved ones."

Ada wrinkled her nose and curled her upper lip. "Huh? Why?"

"It's one of Satan's most successful lies—that we live on after death, that we're immortal apart from God. It's a lie to trip us up and lead us away from the truth."

"Well," Ada said as she picked the board up off the card table, "the truth *here* is, you got a poltergeist."

Jenna said, "I'm sorry, Kimberly, but it's okay, everything's okay, those bulbs going out—that's our wiring, there's something wrong with our wiring. I'm serious— I've got an electrician coming tomorrow morning to take a look at it. Everything's fine."

Kimberly silently turned her head back and forth in disagreement as she calmed herself down.

Ada carried the board to the couch and dropped it into the open suitcase. "I don't do poltergeists."

"What's a poltergeist?" Jenna asked.

"A poltergeist is a spirit that could use a good asswhooping, if you ask me. You got a teenager in the house? A girl?"

"No, only our son. He's ten. Why?"

Shrugging, Ada said, "Poltergeist activity's usually associated with adolescent girls, but not always. A boy of ten—who knows? But you got a poltergeist." She took her notebook and pen from the card table, tossed them on top of the Ouija board, and closed and snapped the suitcase. "Poltergeists don't wanna talk, they wanna piss you off, and I just don't take any shit off 'em anymore. Let somebody younger screw around with the little bastards." She put on her coat, then stood with the suitcase at her side. She took what was left of her cigarette from her mouth and stubbed it out in the ashtray. "You can pay me now, and then I'd like to go home."

Jenna went to her and said, "I'm sorry about the planchette, Ada. I'll be happy to pay for it if—"

"Oh, don't be ridiculous, honey. That comes with the territory. How could you know you had a poltergeist?"

"But . . . how do we get rid of it?"

"That's why poltergeists are such a pain in the ass. There's not a whole lot you can do about 'em. They eventually go away. They never stay for long, but they're a real pain in the ass as long as they're around. You can't believe anything you see or hear in your own house as long as you got a poltergeist. It's like having a tantrum running loose in the house. And like I said, I don't do 'em. And not only don't I do 'em, I don't hang around in houses that have 'em, so you can pay me outside in the bus." Ada walked past Jenna, through the entryway, and out the front door.

With Kimberly's help, Jenna quickly put the table and chairs away and replaced the coffee table in the living room. Then they drove Ada home.

"I don't believe in ghosts," Kimberly said on the way back from dropping Ada off in front of her trailer. In spite of the rain, they drove with the windows rolled down to get the smell of Ada's cigarettes out of the SUV. As the woman had complained about everything under the sun, Jenna had watched Kimberly wiping tears from her eyes as she drove. Once Ada was gone,

Jenna had waited for Kimberly to speak. "I've never believed in them," she said. "That night I saw my grandma—I'm not sure what that was, but it wasn't a ghost. She didn't hang around and haunt me or anything. I don't believe in them."

"Neither have I," Jenna said. "Until now."

"Do you, now? Really? I mean . . . just all of a sudden?"

"I'm *so* sorry. I had no idea this would upset you so much."

Kimberly smiled, squeaked out a couple laughs. "Neither did I. I'm as surprised as you are. I haven't thought about this stuff in . . . well, in a lifetime. But seeing that board—and then when that planchette moved—I could tell neither of you was moving it, it was moving by *itself*—and that sudden crash—"

"I know, that was scary, wasn't it? All of this is kind of scary."

"Not only that, it might be . . . I think it might even be dangerous."

"Dangerous? How?"

"Well . . . just because Ada says you've got a poltergeist, or a ghost, or whatever, doesn't mean she's necessarily right. It could be . . . well, something *else*. Maybe something harmful."

"I didn't think you believed in that stuff anymore."

"I said I wasn't a Seventh-Day Adventist anymore. But I had that stuff drilled into me from a very young age. I guess it's hard to completely shake it. I'm sorry, Jenna, but that really shook me up. And it made me think. And all I'm saying is, *you* should think, too. I still think Mrs. Frangiapani was right—you should just leave this alone and focus your attention on your family."

"Ada says I have a poltergeist. You're saying I have—what, an *evil* spirit? A demon? Which is it?"

"I'm just saying you should *think* about it. You're new at this, remember. You said you didn't believe in *anything* before this. Well, some of us have had a little experience with beliefs, and I'm sure we'd all tell you the same thing—don't put all your eggs in one dogma."

Jenna chuckled.

"Hey," Kimberly said, perking up a little, "maybe that just pushed some of my old buttons back there, I don't know—seeing that Ouija board, and those lights going out like that . . ."

"I was telling the truth, Kimberly. That's happened a few times before in the house. An electrician is coming out in the morning to take a look at the wiring."

"Still, I saw that planchette move," Kimberly said. "And I saw it get crushed by . . . well, by *nothing*. I've never seen anything like that before in my life. The only way I know how to process it is through the filter of the religion I was raised with and trained in. So maybe I don't know what I'm talking about. But Ada's opinion is just that—an opinion. I want you to promise me, Jenna, please, promise me you'll at least keep an open mind. Maybe Ada's right and you've got a poltergeist, or maybe something *else* moved through your living room today. Something dangerous."

Jenna turned her eyes front and stared out past the sweeping wipers at the road ahead. *Something* had hit that table nearly hard enough to make it fall apart. It had broken the planchette and swept it through the air. There was *something* in the house. But until that moment, she had not considered the possibility that her family might be in any danger from it. The thought tied her stomach in knots.

CHAPTER TEN

Lily. Tuesday, 10:16 A.M.

While Jenna and Kimberly were picking up Ada that morning, Lily Rourke sat at her kitchen table in Mt. Shasta, sipped coffee, and read through the information Claudia had found on the Internet about the Binghams. Lily found searching the Internet tedious and frustrating, but Claudia was a wiz with her laptop. She had assembled a number of articles and links and e-mailed them to Lily. Along with that, Lily had skimmed through the books Claudia had brought her.

The computer took up much of the small round table. There was a desk in the spare bedroom where she would've had more room, but Lily preferred working in here where she caught some sunlight and the coffeepot was close. A cup of hot coffee stood beside her keyboard, and beside that, one of the cheese Danishes Claudia had brought to work with her, half-eaten on a napkin. Claudia was working the register up front, but

Lily hadn't heard a sound so there had been no business yet.

Since Saturday, Lily had learned more than she'd ever wanted to know about Arthur and Mavis Bingham. The problem was, she believed very little of it. It seemed the only people providing information about the Binghams were the Binghams themselves, or their students. Their "students" were anyone who had attended any of their many lectures at colleges and churches around the country, or had taken any of their classes in demonology, the dangers of witchcraft, the evil truth about the Ouija board, or half a dozen other subjects they taught at their Phoenix Society of Paranormal Research in Phoenix, Arizona.

Arthur and Mavis had been born and raised in small-town Wisconsin, where they were married in 1956. They left the cold winters behind six years later and moved to Phoenix, where they founded the society in 1962. Mavis was, according to their bio, a renowned clairvoyant whose abilities had been tested and well-documented at Arizona State University in Phoenix under the supervision of Dr. Melvin Roberts. That documentation, however, was not provided in any of the books or articles. Lily had made some phone calls to the university. An especially friendly and chatty woman in Records had told her that Dr. Roberts hadn't been there since 1969, when his Parapsychology Department was discontinued after an embarassing scandal. One of the three female students Dr. Roberts had been sleeping with at the time had found out about the other two and, as revenge, had revealed to the university's administration that Dr. Roberts had doctored the results of much of his research.

Lily noticed that the bios in later editions of the Binghams's books did not mention Dr. Roberts, but still claimed that Mavis's psychic abilities had been tested and documented by Arizona State University. But because the Parapsychology Department had been shut down nearly four decades earlier, there was no record of those tests, and no such documentation existed. Even if it did, it would be suspect because of Dr. Roberts's record of cooking his books.

By all accounts, the Binghams were very kind and grandparently, and expert storytellers. Lily had seen them on TV talk shows in the past and was familiar with their pleasant, folksy manner. But poring over their books reminded her of why she'd decided not to carry any of them in the store.

Early in their paranormal career, the Binghams had investigated haunted houses and claimed to send confused, earthbound spirits on their way. Then something changed in 1973. Suddenly, their investigations began to uncover demonic infestations. Instead of guiding the spirits of the dead to the next plane of existence, the Binghams, devout Catholics, started bringing in a priest to exorcise houses, and sometimes the residents. Instead of ghostly apparitions and eerie sounds, their books began to provide lurid descriptions of families being menaced by demons from Hell. In each case they investigated, people were being anally raped by Satan's minions. It happened so regularly that Lily began to wonder if the Binghams were projecting some of their own hang-ups onto their work.

Lily found it more than coincidental that in 1973 the movie *The Exorcist* was burning up the box office and demon possession was all the rage. It was obvious to her that the Binghams realized no one was interested in things that go bump in the night anymore, so they changed their act to keep up with the times. In doing so, they had become religious crusaders, and with each new book, they became more intolerant of other beliefs, and even of those who simply disagreed with them. That was why Lily had stopped carrying their books—it was one thing to update the act and still expect to be taken seriously, but the Binghams had become ultrareligious and used their beliefs as an excuse to behave hatefully toward others, and Lily would not condone that with commerce.

In 1975, the Binghams had hit it big with *The Loweryville Possession*. Their book told the story of a house in Kentucky that had been built on the site where a Satanic cult used to perform ritual human sacrifices (although how they knew that Lily was unable to determine). The house allegedly became possessed by demons as a result. The family that lived there was reportedly tormented by evil forces—the mother and teenage son were repeatedly anally raped by what the Binghams called "invisible demons"—until Arthur and Mavis became involved and brought in their priest, Father Malcolm, who exorcised the house. The book was a bestseller and became a financially, if not critically, successful movie that spawned a couple of sequels. It put the Binghams on the map.

In 1981, the family, no longer living in the same house, or in the same state—they had moved to Florida the year the movie was released—publicly admitted that the whole thing had been a hoax. They had made it all up to see if they could make any money. Although they hadn't gotten rich, they'd made a nice sum from the book and movie and had put their two children through college. When confronted with this, the Binghams had suggested that perhaps there was some mental illness in the family, because Arthur and Mavis had witnessed the exorcism and had felt the demonic power in the house themselves, so they *knew* it was real. The demonic activity had been so intense, they claimed, Arthur had suffered a heart attack. They still lectured about the Loweryville, Kentucky, investigation, and people still came to hear about it, twenty-two years after the family involved had publicly admitted it was a hoax.

None of the Binghams's earlier books had sold as well as *The Loweryville Possession*—one, *The Demon of Battle Creek*, was adapted into an awful made-for-cable movie that no one watched—but they maintained a popularity that baffled Lily. You couldn't throw a rock in the paranormal world without hitting the Binghams—they were everywhere, and their handprints were on everything. But they had plenty of detractors. The Binghams were not very popular in paranormal circles, because they continued to be intolerant of anyone who did not agree with them to the letter. Arthur and Mavis, backed by scripture and their Catholicism, were on the side of God, so disagreement with them meant disagreement with the Almighty, and they had no qualms about pointing that out.

The most critical article Claudia had found on the Binghams was not nearly as critical as it seemed to want to be. It was a piece called "Hunting Demons" on the Web site of the Southwestern Skeptical Society, written by Donald Penner. The article read as if it were unfinished, or severely truncated. It revealed little she didn't already know, but it had a lot of attitude, as if it were an exposé.

Lily browsed around the Web site and learned that Penner was also the site's administrator, the editor of the newsletter *The Southwest Skeptical*, and the society's president. The society was based in Tucson, where it had been arching a skeptical brow since 1976, but had members all over North America.

The contact information for the Southwestern Skeptical Society included a phone number. Lily could e-mail Donald Penner and wait for his response, but she preferred a conversation—she could get a lot from a person's voice.

Lily expected a receptionist, but the phone was answered by Penner himself. He sounded as if he'd been sleeping. She told him she owned a bookstore and was considering arranging a signing with Arthur and Mavis Bingham, but she wanted to know more about them first, and had read the article about them on the Southwestern Skeptical Society Web site.

"Oh, that," Penner said.

"It's a fine article, but I got the feeling it was incomplete. No offense, but—"

"Don't worry, none taken. In fact, that's very observant of you." He was soft-spoken and talked slowly. "That article caused a lot of trouble. Well, not the article you read, but the one I originally wrote. It *was* an exposé. But the Binghams filed a civil suit for libel. There really wasn't anything libelous in the article—I backed up every word I wrote with solid facts. But that wasn't the point of the suit. They just wanted to tie us up in court. They knew we couldn't afford it. We don't have the kind of money they do."

"They're wealthy, then?"

"They're very popular on the lecture circuit, and that's some fat money. Not to mention the royalties from their books and that awful movie."

"Which one?"

"Well, both of them, I guess."

"So you caved on the article?"

"Had to. I trimmed the article, they withdrew the suit. I've been railing on the Binghams for years, but nobody's listening. People enjoy their ghost stories."

"But they're not ghost stories anymore. They're all about sodomizing demons."

"Ever since *The Exorcist* came out."

Lily smiled. "You noticed that, too?"

"Yeah. All of a sudden, everybody's got horny demons in their woodwork."

"What was in your original article?"

Penner took a deep breath and let it out in a weary sigh. "Where do you want me to start?"

"Start at the beginning. How did they get into this stuff?"

"Arthur. He was booted out of the Army in 1953 on a Section 8—mental illness. Arthur's had a problem with that all his life, and all his life, he's had this obsession with ghosts. Ever since he was a little kid."

"What kind of mental illness?" Lily asked.

"Judging by the hospitals he's been in, I suspect some form of schizophrenia."

"How did they meet?"

"During one of Arthur's stays in a mental hospital," Penner said. "Mavis was doing some volunteer work for the church. There's some evidence that Mavis exhibited genuine psychic ability early in her life, but once she hooked up with Arthur, she became little more than a performer. Arthur looked her up after he got out of the hospital, and they hit it off. Apparently, Arthur witnessed something that convinced him Mavis was psychic, and suddenly, they were inseparable. They were both devout Catholics, and they both had an interest in the supernatural. They were married only a few months later."

"How romantic," Lily said. "When did they start their shtick?"

"Almost immediately. Fortunately, Mavis came from

money, because Arthur had a hard time holding down a job. They traveled around visiting houses that were reputedly haunted, and Mavis would *read* the house, then Arthur would draw it. Apparently, Arthur had taken up drawing during one of his hospital stays, and he started drawing these intricate pictures of houses that were said to be haunted."

"What did Mavis's reading prove?"

"She would declare the house haunted, then communicate with the spirits there. Pretty soon, they were popping up in all the paranormal circles and people were starting to notice them. Arthur's drawings were actually pretty good, and a small press publisher compiled them in a book, which had some success."

As she listened, Lily sipped her coffee and nibbled her Danish. She asked, "Were they so rigidly religious back then? Were they as harsh with people who disagreed with them as they are now?"

"They weren't important enough to disagree with yet. In fact, they've *never* been what you could call important in the field. They've made such a nuisance of themselves over the years, people are forced to have an opinion. But back then, they were nobody. They finally found a friend of a friend who was complaining of odd things happening in his house, and that became their first real case. Arthur wrote everything down, but he was terrible at it, so they found a writer. Have you read their books?"

"Some of them."

"Have you noticed anything about their writers?"

"Only that their names appear on the cover in very tiny letters beneath Arthur's and Mavis's."

"Yeah," Penner said, "the less attention drawn to the writers, the better for them. The authors of all their books have been low-rent horror novelists. There's one in particular—Joe Lockwood, who wrote *A Demonic Darkness*—who's happy to tell his Arthur and Mavis story to anyone who'll listen. The book was about a possessed teenager. Lockwood met with the family, but they couldn't keep their stories straight. He went to Arthur with the problem, and Arthur said, 'Oh, they're crazy. *All* the people who come to us are crazy. Why do you think they come to *us*? You write scary stories—just make it up and make it scary.' Lockwood has a piece about it on his Web site."

"And they haven't sued him?" Lily asked.

"I think they're afraid to. The guy's a hack, nobody knows him from Adam. If they sued him, suddenly he'd be getting a lot of attention that he isn't getting now. Lockwood says the family the Binghams were dealing with needed help, but the kind Arthur and Mavis couldn't provide. He saw evidence of alcoholism, drug use, possibly even abuse. But the Binghams weren't concerned about that, even when he tried to point it out to them. All they cared about was the book. And, of course, a possible movie deal. I talked to a few of the other writers who've worked with the Binghams, and it seems at least a few of the families they've dealt with have had similar problems—alcohol and drug abuse, possible child and/or spousal abuse. Vulnerable people who need professional help, not a couple of frauds like Arthur and Mavis."

Lily was not surprised to learn the cynical truth about the Binghams—she had always suspected it—but she was disturbed that they would prey on such troubled families. "What about that priest who hangs out with them?"

"Father Malcolm?" Penner laughed. "Malcolm

DiGenova. He's a piece of work. He was defrocked about twenty years ago. An embezzler and a convicted pedophile."

"Wow. I'm afraid to ask which one got him defrocked."

"Don't. I never figured out exactly how the Binghams hooked up with this guy, but it was sometime in the mid-seventies. Every time they find a new infestation of demons, Father Malcolm puts on his priest clothes and does his little exorcism show. It gives their books an ending and makes for nice tabloid photo ops."

"What does the Catholic church think of the Binghams and Father Malcolm?"

"They don't even *acknowledge* the Binghams, let alone condone what they do."

"Why hasn't anyone pointed out the truth about Father Malcolm?"

"Some have. Arthur and Mavis appeared on *Jenny Jones* in the late nineties with James Randi, the famous debunker. Randi pointed it out then, and Arthur stood up and challenged him to a fistfight. Security had to come up on the stage and physically put Arthur back in his chair. They've been on other radio and television talk shows, and every once in a while, someone tells the truth about him. But it never sticks. Like I said, people *want* to believe this stuff. Ever hear of the Fox sisters?"

"The founders of modern American spiritualism, weren't they?"

"The same. They lived in a farmhouse in Rochester, New York. Katherine was eleven and Margaret was thirteen in 1848 when they claimed to hear strange rapping sounds coming from a room in the house. They said it was the spirit of a murdered itinerant peddler who was rumored to have been buried in their basement. Pretty soon, people were coming from everywhere—I mean, from all over the *world*—to witness these rappings. The girls became famous and made a fortune traveling around America and England putting on their little rapping show."

"That much I remember," Lily said.

"Forty years later, they 'fessed up and admitted the whole thing was a hoax. At first, they used an apple on a string to make the rapping sounds—they'd thump it against a wall by pulling on the string. Later, they realized they could produce the sounds by popping the joints of their big toes." He chuckled. "Then they went on an 'exposure tour' to show everybody how they'd done it, and for the second time, people flocked to see them perform. Even after they admitted they were frauds, people *still* came to see the Fox sisters make their rapping sounds. People love this stuff. They don't want to know the truth—they prefer the lie."

"That's pretty cynical, don't you think?"

"Nope. You want to be the least popular person at the magic show? Tell everybody how the magician does his tricks. Trust me."

"How did you manage to uncover all this stuff on the Binghams?" Lily asked.

"I studied journalism in college. That's what I planned to do with my life. How I ended up here is anybody's guess."

"How *did* you end up there?"

"I sort of inherited it. My grandpa started it back in the seventies—inspired, in fact, by the Binghams. Then my uncle took it over in the eighties. Somehow, I got myself wrapped up in it. I enjoy it, to be honest. It's pretty sleepy around here most of the time, but it's okay."

"If you don't mind being the least popular person at the magic show."

He chuckled. "Yeah, well, there's that."

A couple minutes later, Lily finished the Danish. She thought of the horribly burned face she'd seen in her vision and wondered what it meant. Something bad was going to happen soon, and it would involve the Binghams. But she still did not know what, when, or where it would take place.

CHAPTER ELEVEN

Tuesday, 3:09 P.M.

That afternoon, Jenna got a phone call from a young woman named Avril Lauter. She was a college student with a paper that needed to be typed and printed up, and she wanted to bring it to Jenna first thing tomorrow morning.

It had started slow back in Redding, Jenna remembered, but after half a dozen customers had been satisfied, word got around that she was reliable and reasonable, and business had picked up. Jenna was confident the same thing would happen here, and it would start with Avril Lauter.

She expected David to be in a good mood when he got home from work, but he was tired and preoccupied. He had not been home five minutes when he asked her to call the Sheriff's Department and ask for Hooper or Caruso and find out if they ever found those kids.

"I'd do it," he said with an apologetic smile, "but you're a lot better on the phone with people than I am."

Jenna looked up the number and called. She managed to catch Deputy Hooper at the station, and learned that the children had not been found.

Deputy Hooper said, "I'm sure they're fine. If something had happened to them, we would've heard about it by now. But if they come back, don't hesitate to call us."

Jenna found David sitting in his recliner in the living room, frowning at the television as he thumbed the remote. She told him what Deputy Hooper had said. "You're still worried about those kids, aren't you?" she said.

"They were here again last night. After you went to sleep."

"They were? Why didn't you wake me? Did you talk to them?"

"No, they took off."

"The same kids?"

"Yeah, they were the same ones." He sighed. "I walked all the way around the fence when I got home and didn't find any openings. They *have* to be going through the gate. I'm going to put a padlock on it."

"I think there are a couple new ones in the toolbox, still in their blister packs."

He put the remote on the arm of the chair and stood. "I'll go look."

Half an hour later, the gate in the Cyclone fence was firmly locked with a large Schlage padlock. David seemed distracted the rest of the evening. They ate dinner in the living room in front of the television, as usual. Jenna was able to get David to talk about his day at work a little while they ate, but he soon became preoccupied again. After dinner, he dozed in the recliner.

Jenna cleaned up in the kitchen, then went looking

for Miles. He wasn't in the living room with David and Martha, so she went upstairs and found him at the computer operating a joystick, playing a game on the Internet. She took a stack of shoe boxes off a chair, put it beside Miles, and seated herself.

"Is all your homework done?"

"Yep. I did it right after school."

"Good for you. How's school going?"

"Fine."

"Really? Just fine? It's not fantastic, or wonderful?"

"It's fine. Really." He smiled at her briefly before turning back to the monitor.

"Are you making friends? I mean, besides Todd Haney?"

"Todd's okay. He's kinda weird."

Jenna reached out and turned his chair so he was facing her. "Hey, I want to talk about your nightmare. I don't like it that you're having trouble sleeping."

"I'm only having trouble sleeping in my bedroom in the dark," he said, as if it were all quite simple.

"Tell me about this nightmare."

Miles looked into her eyes a moment, then cocked his head—he seemed to come to some decision. "I see a big fat man coming up through the floor of my bedroom with some kinda hat on his head."

"And what does this man do?"

"He just talks to me."

"What does he say?"

Miles lowered his voice to a growl. " 'You gonna be a good puppy? Be a good puppy and come on over here.' Stuff like that."

Jenna's stomach did a fast-elevator flip when she heard the malice in Miles's impersonation. "What does he look like?"

155

"I can't get a good look at him because he never finishes coming up out of the floor. As soon as I turn on the light, he disappears. He doesn't like the light."

"Ah. So that's why you want the overhead light on."

Miles nodded.

"Well, if you haven't gotten a good look at him, how do you know it's a fat man?"

Miles frowned. " 'Cause that's what he is. I can tell."

"Do you think he's going to hurt you?"

"I know he will, if he ever gets to me. I can tell by the way he talks to me that he wants to do bad things to me."

"How tall is this man?"

"I don't know, because he never comes all the way up."

"How high does he get?"

"I don't know, maybe . . . this high?" he said uncertainly as he held his hand out approximately forty inches off the floor.

Jenna could not tell Miles that she had been trying to communicate with Josh, or that she was certain Josh had been trying to communicate with her. She found it all very confusing, and she was a grown woman—how would a ten-year-old boy take it? But she wondered if Josh was trying to get through to Miles as well? She remembered the message from the Ouija board—HELP PUPPEEZ. The figure in Miles's room kept calling him a puppy, and its height was about the same as the toddler she had been seeing. Could there be some connection? Could Miles be misinterpreting something from Josh?

She said, "I bet if you look at it closer next time, you'll see it's not that at all. You'll find that it's something much more interesting. Maybe even something pleasant."

Miles returned her smile and nodded once, but he said nothing. An awkward silence fell between them. Jenna stood, bent down, and kissed him on the head.

"If you promise not to abuse the privilege, you can go downstairs and turn on the television if it helps you to sleep," she said. "But you have to *try* to sleep in your bed every night, okay? And this only lasts as long as you keep having this nightmare. Is that a deal? You won't milk this like a monkey with a coconut, will you?"

Miles laughed, then shook his head. "No, I won't. Thanks, Mom."

"I'll put a blanket and pillow down there for you. And promise me you'll look closer next time, just to make sure, all right?"

"I promise. I don't *want* to, but I will. For you."

She hugged him, kissed his cheek, then started out of the room. She stopped in the doorway, turned to him. "Is anything else bothering you, honey? Anything at all?"

"No."

"You'd tell me if there was, wouldn't you?"

He nodded. "Sure."

"Okay. Go ahead and play a little longer. Then it's bedtime."

Downstairs, Jenna sat on the couch with Martha and watched television for a while. Fortunately, Martha had heard nothing earlier that day while Ada was there—apparently, she'd slept through the whole thing. Jenna was relieved that she did not have to explain herself to anyone.

While they watched television, both David and Martha nodded off for a minute or so, then jerked awake, only to do it again.

Am I the only person in this house who's sleeping well? Jenna wondered.

157

When they finally went to bed, David's feet were dragging on the floor. He let his clothes drop where he stood. Jenna picked them up, took them to the bathroom, and put them in the hamper while he crawled into bed. By the time she joined him, David was already asleep. She turned out the lights, curled up beside him, and wondered what tomorrow would bring. The question did not keep her awake long.

David was down in the kitchen by 12:49 A.M. He had awakened suddenly to the sound of the boys' laughter outside in the backyard. After putting on his sweats and running shoes, he'd come down to the kitchen without turning on any lights. He stood at the back door, pulled the curtain aside with a finger, and looked out the window. He could see nothing in the dark.

The gentle patter of rain falling outside was occasionally interrupted by the shriek of the swing's rusted chains and the boys' playful laughter.

They had to climb over the fence, he thought. It was the only remaining possibility.

He unlocked the door, opened it, and went outside. He did not take the flashlight or turn on the porch light this time, because he was afraid that would scare them off. He went down the porch steps and out through the weeds. The rain was cold on his face and the back of his neck.

"Boys?" he said. "Don't run away. You're not in any trouble."

He could see them, five dark figures standing close together in front of the swing set. One of the swings still wobbled and swayed on its chains. The boys did not move. Even after his eyes adjusted to the darkness, David could not see their faces, but he could feel them staring at him.

"Where do you boys live?" he asked.

They neither responded nor moved.

"How did you get into the yard?"

No reply, no movement.

Then one of them whispered, "He's coming."

"Go!"

"Run!"

"No," David said, "don't—"

They were gone. They had not turned and run away. The boys simply were no longer there. They had disappeared without making a sound.

David's mouth dropped open and he uttered a quiet sound of shock. He looked all around the yard. The boys were gone.

There was a sound behind him—the unmistakable *chitch* of a canned carbonated beverage being popped open. David spun around, mouth still hanging open.

The fat man in the cowboy hat and denim vest and dirty T-shirt stood on the back porch, one shoulder leaning against the wall. "Fuckin' puppies," he said.

"Who are you?" David said, moving quickly toward the porch. The back door stood open right behind the man, and David did not want him going into the house.

The fat man tipped the beer to his mouth and took a few gulps. He sighed and wiped his mouth with the back of his left hand. He pushed away from the wall and shifted his bulk upright. "Let's go down to the basement."

"What?" David said with disbelief as the man came down the steps. David stepped out of his way, but the man stepped aside with him, then into him.

The taste of beer filled David's mouth. He smacked his lips a few times. Not just any beer, but Michelob, even though it was unlikely that David would know that—he drank beer so seldom that most of it tasted the same to him.

Most American pilsners taste pretty much the same, but Michelob has a creaminess the others don't.

It was a thought in David's mind, but it was not his, and he had not thought it—it had been spoken in a mental voice that was foreign to David's mind. Nor was it under his direction that his legs took him up the concrete steps and into the kitchen, where his right hand picked up the Mag-Lite without any help from David while his left closed the back door.

Let's go down to the basement, the fat man said again, but this time the voice came from within David. *I'll show you what to do with them fuckin' puppies.*

The flashlight came on as David started down the narrow staircase to the basement. But the deeper he went, the weaker the Mag-Lite's beam seemed to become.

I'm dreaming again, David thought before he was swallowed up by the darkness.

Miles woke at 3:41 A.M. and sat up in bed. Rain pattered against the windowpanes and branches clawed at the house. His bedroom was dark—too dark. Someone had turned off the desk lamp. But there was something else. Miles did not feel alone in the room. He wondered if the voice had awakened him. He slipped his hand beneath his pillow and closed it on the penlight he kept there.

"You gonna be a good puppy?"

Miles's body froze while his bones seemed to melt with terror deep inside him. It was a low, throaty, gravelly whisper, but it was not the same voice he'd heard on previous nights—there was something different about it, and at the same time, something familiar.

Miles told himself not to scream, not this time—he didn't want to wake his parents and hear his mother talk about horror movies and his dad about nightmares. He realized why it seemed so dark in the room—the door was closed, keeping out the glow of the night-light in the hall. Who would turn off his desk lamp and close the door of his bedroom?

"Be a good puppy and come on over here, now."

Miles brought the small flashlight out from under the pillow and turned it on. As he bounded from the bed and ran for the door, for the light switch on the wall beside it, the flashlight's beam fell on a figure hunkered in front of the shelves, forearms resting on bent knees with hands dangling in between, watching Miles with its head down. But it wasn't the fat man.

"You gonna be a good puppy?"

The figure wore a familiar green sweatshirt and familiar blue sweatpants.

Miles fumbled with the switch, flipped it up, and filled the room with light. He opened the door and spun around. He dropped the flashlight when he saw his dad.

For a second, maybe two, there was something other than Dad squatting there in front of the shelves. Dad's head was craned forward and his lower jaw jutted. His hair was wet and wildly mussed. His brow was gathered into an intense frown, but at the same time, the left half of his mouth was turned up in a malicious grin while the other half curled downward. It was an expression Miles had never before seen on his dad's face, and Dad's eyes were narrowed in a way that was unlike him. Miles knew, in that brief moment, that something else was looking out of his dad at him. He knew it wasn't Dad watching him with that leering grin.

Then the moment passed and Dad fell on his side like

a marionette whose strings had been cut. He got up slowly, looked around with half-closed eyes and a slack jaw. As he rose cautiously to his feet, he said, "Miles?"

Miles said, "Dad?"

He looked around again, as if to double-check his location, then frowned down at Miles. "Did I . . . come in here?" he said groggily. He looked as if he felt sick.

Miles nodded. "You woke me. You were saying what that man usually says."

"What man?" This seemed to startle Dad a little, in a groggy sort of way.

"The man who comes up through my floor."

Dad rubbed his fingertips in slow circles over his temples, eyes closed. He swayed groggily. "And what was I saying that . . . he usually says?"

" 'You gonna be a good puppy? Come on over here and be a good puppy.' Stuff like that."

"Puppies," Dad muttered, his voice thick. He looked away for a moment. "Fuckin' puppies."

Miles could not believe what he thought he'd heard, but he said nothing about it. He sensed that this was one of those times when it was best to say nothing, or as little as possible.

Dad walked over to the doorway and leaned on the doorjamb wearily. "Must've been walking in my sleep. Again. Sorry. Go back to bed. Do me a favor, will you? Keep this just between us, okay?"

"Keep what between us?"

"This. You know, this sleepwalking thing, me coming into your room like this. There's no reason to tell your mom. She'll just . . . worry."

Miles nodded. "Okay."

Dad hugged him, patted him on the back a couple times, and said, "Atta good puppy."

Miles's back stiffened, and he would have taken a step

backward if he weren't momentarily paralyzed by that word—*puppy*. He stood frozen in place as Dad turned and shuffled away, then went out the door. Miles finally thawed enough to take a step forward, then another, until he was standing in the doorway.

Miles watched his dad stagger down the hall to his bedroom. As soon as he closed the door, Miles picked up the little flashlight, turned it off, and put it back under his pillow. Then he turned his light off and went downstairs. He turned on the television, tuned it to The Cartoon Network, and stretched out on the sofa.

CHAPTER TWELVE

Wednesday, 4:02 A.M.

While sleepily watching cartoons, Miles heard a noise from the kitchen, a sound like someone putting the teakettle down on one of the burners. He got up and left the living room, saw the light from the kitchen as he went through the dining room. He found Grandma in the breakfast nook with a cup of something hot and a paperback.

As soon as she saw him, she got up and went down the hallway, and came back several seconds later. She carried her old cardboard checkerboard folded and tucked beneath her right arm. The checkers themselves were in a small net bag. She put the board on the table and took her seat, opened the net bag, and set up the game. Before they started to play, she got up and fixed Miles a cup of instant hot chocolate.

While they played, they spoke in whispers. Miles told her what had happened upstairs earlier. He had promised Dad he wouldn't tell Mom, but he'd said nothing about Grandma. He knew she would keep his secret, and that Mom would never find out. He waited for a response when he was done, but she said nothing.

Miles took a full minute to decide whether or not to say what was on his mind. Grandma had always been very open-minded, but this called for a little something more than that. He wasn't sure how she would react, but he needed to talk about it.

"I think it was the fat man," he said. "I think Dad sleepwalked into my bedroom and the fat man came up out of the floor and right into Dad. I think the fat man was inside him."

"That's crazy talk, Miles," Grandma said. She whispered the response flatly, with a finality that made it clear she wanted to hear no more.

They said nothing for a while and concentrated on the game.

Miles heard the distinct sound of kids laughing outside. He turned to the window and heard it again. His eyes brightened as he turned to Grandma.

"Did you hear that?" he said. "There are kids playing outside."

"No, there aren't."

"There, I heard them again!" He got on his knees on the bench and leaned toward the window.

"Get back down here, Miles, right now," Grandma said, her voice loud and firm.

Miles immediately sat down again, surprised by her harsh tone.

"It's just the rain playing tricks on your ears," she said. "There's no kids out there. I don't hear a thing. It's your move."

He dropped the subject, but as they played, he continued to hear kids laughing outside. Miles decided his bedroom was not the only part of the house where

something very strange was going on. He stopped playing after only a couple games, and returned to the
couch. Grandma went back to reading her book.

The living room was still warm and cozy from the fire
Dad had built the night before. Miles was more comfortable there on the couch, in front of the television,
where all he could hear were the cartoons.

The electrician was a rugged-looking fellow named
Walt, tall with close-cropped black hair streaked with
gray, and wire-framed glasses, somewhere in his forties.
Jenna took his wet jacket at the door. He wore a blue
chambray shirt and faded blue jeans. He carried a black-
and-silver metal toolbox in his left hand.

"I'll take a look around," he said after Jenna explained
the problem, "but this place was completely rewired
about two, maybe three years ago. A friend of mine did
the job, and he knows his stuff, so you can be sure he
did the job right. That wasn't very long ago."

"Just two years?"

"Something like that. I bid on that job myself."

Then you met my father, Jenna thought. For just a moment, she was tempted to ask Walt about him, but decided there would be no point to it.

Walt said, "I'll take a look around for you, see what I
can see."

While Walt was seeing what he could see, the doorbell rang and Jenna found Avril Lauter on the front
porch. She was a stout young woman with short
strawberry-blond hair. She wore a long green coat with
a big red vinyl bag slung over her shoulder. Jenna invited her in, took her coat and umbrella, and hung them
on the wall hooks by the door. Under the coat she wore
a black-and-white sweater and gray jeans. Jenna led

Avril into the living room and told her to take a seat on the couch. "Can I get you some coffee or anything?"

"I can't stay," Avril said. "I've got class soon."

"Let me get my folder, and I'll be right back."

Jenna hurried upstairs to the computer room and removed a thin brown leatherbound folder from a desk drawer. Before she got back to the living room, she heard Martha call "Jenna!" from the kitchen. She turned left at the bottom of the stairs, went down the hall, and entered the kitchen through the back door. Martha was standing in the middle of the kitchen in her robe and slippers, just out of the shower, hair wet, staring at the laundry room.

"What?" Jenna said.

Martha squinted because she wasn't wearing her glasses. "Who's knocking around in the basement?"

"The electrician came while you were in the shower."

"Oh." She leaned against the counter, put both hands over her face, and whispered to herself, "Jeez-Louise, I don't know how much more of this I can take."

"How much more of what, Mom?"

Martha frowned and wagged her hands at Jenna dismissively. "Oh, nothing, nothing."

"I've got a client out in the living room," Jenna said, then hurried back to the living room with her folder.

Avril had her bag unzipped and open on the couch beside her and held a beige folder in her hands. She handed it to Jenna, who opened her brown folder and removed from a pocket a form she'd printed up back in Redding. She wrote down Avril's name on the form, then took the handwritten, paper-clipped pages from the beige folder. The handwriting was neat and clean. She counted the pages—thirty-eight, written on one side only. She wrote that down on the form.

"Are those your sons I saw a few minutes ago?" Avril asked.

Jenna sat up straight and turned to her so suddenly that Avril blinked with surprise, but her smile did not falter. "Sons?"

"The boys who came through here a few—"

"Boys?" Jenna let the folders and pages slide off her lap to the floor as she turned her whole body toward Avril. "You saw boys? In here? Just now?"

Half of Avril's smile fell away. "Um . . . three of them. I—I *thought* they were boys, I didn't see their faces, but they—"

"Three?" Jenna's mind raced with questions, but she did not have time for them. "Where, exactly? Where did you see them?"

"They walked through here, from front to back. I kind of figured they were looking for you."

"What did they look like?"

The urgency in Jenna's voice made Avril scoot away from her on the couch. "I—I don't know, I mean . . . I looked up from my paper and they were passing through, and I looked up again and they were gone."

"A little one—was there a little one?"

"Yes, he came in first, then the other two followed. He had on a jacket with a hood, and the hood was pulled up over—"

"Oh, God, you saw him!" Jenna could only whisper, because for a moment she had no voice. She felt as if her breath had been sucked from her lungs. Tears blurred her vision, and she quickly wiped them away with her knuckles. "My son, Josh, you saw my dead son, you *saw* him. Which way did he go?"

"Are . . . are you all right?"

Jenna smiled and nodded with enthusiasm. "Yes, yes, which way did he go?"

Pointing toward the doorway that led into the dining room, Avril said, "That way."

Jenna stood, reached down, and clutched Avril's elbow and tugged her to her feet. "Come with me."

"Look, I have a class, I can't—"

Jenna put her hands on Avril's shoulders and squeezed. "Please, *please* come with me for just a minute. You saw him once, maybe you'll see him again."

"Did you say . . . your *dead* son?"

Jenna grabbed her hand and pulled her through the living room. "Please, come through the house with me just once."

Avril jerked her hand free and went back to the couch. She bent over and picked up her pages and folder from the floor, put them back in her bag and zipped it up. As she slung the strap over her shoulder, she turned to Jenna. "I—I'm sorry, but I can't, I've really got to—"

"No, please don't take the paper," Jenna said. "I'll do the paper, I'll have it done by tomorrow, if you—"

"Did you say your son was . . . *dead?*"

Jenna sniffled as she nodded. "For three years. We just moved into this house, and I've been seeing him. *You* just saw him. There are no boys in this house. The only boy who lives here is my son Miles, and he's at school."

Avril's eyes slowly widened. "But . . . I *saw* them."

"I know. I have, too. Well . . . I've seen one. I don't understand why you saw three, but the little one, that's my Josh." She moved slowly toward Avril. "Will you help me? Please?"

Avril took a step backward, then another, and a few more. "You're talking about . . . *ghosts?*"

"Whatever you want to call them, I don't really think of it that—"

169

Avril suddenly turned and bolted out of the living room and through the entryway, where she grabbed her coat and nearly tripped on the small throw-rug on her way out the front door. She did not even try to close the door behind her.

Jenna sighed, but it turned into a groan. She went to the door and closed it as Avril started the engine of her car outside.

"Shit," Jenna said, thinking, *That's not the way to introduce yourself to the college community.* As she went down the hall, she muttered, "Don't take your papers to that crazy lady with the haunted house. She'll try to make you talk to ghosts."

"Who are you talking to?" Martha asked as Jenna entered the kitchen.

"Myself."

"Okay, just so I know." She sat in the breakfast nook, still wearing her robe, and returned her attention to her novel.

Walt thumped up the basement stairs and came out of the laundry room with his flashlight in one hand and toolbox in the other. "I'm sorry, Mrs. Kellar, but there's nothing wrong with your wiring. It's clean as a whistle. Are you having problems upstairs, too?"

"No, so far it's just happened down here. One of them was out here on the back porch." Jenna led him out the back door to the bare bulb over the door. She reached inside and flipped the switch, but the light didn't come on. "See? It's out again, and David just put in a brand-new bulb."

Walt reached up and unscrewed the bulb. "Do you have another one?"

"Sure." Jenna hurried inside and got a lightbulb from a shelf in the laundry room, took it from its box.

Walt screwed the new lightbulb in and said, "Okay, try it now."

When Jenna flipped the switch, the light came on.

"Works fine now," Walt said.

"Of course it does," Jenna said. "*You're* here."

Walt laughed. "I know what you mean. Things never break down when you want them to."

"It'll happen again when you're *not* here. Do you have any suggestions?"

"Buy a different brand of lightbulb? Don't know what else to tell you."

"Okay. Come on back inside and my mom'll pay you."

"No charge. I didn't do anything."

"Oh. Well, thank you, I appreciate that. Tell me, while you were down in the basement . . . did you . . . see anything?"

"See anything? Well, you've got a lot of stuff down there in boxes and crates, I noticed that. Is that what you mean?"

"Just wondering." She smiled.

After Walt left, Jenna got Ada's card from her purse. She went upstairs to the bedroom, sat on the bed, and called the number.

"Ada, it's Jenna Kellar, from yesterday."

"The poltergeist, yeah. I was just thinkin' about you this morning. I was gonna call you."

"You were?"

"Yes, but you're calling me. Is there something I can do for you?"

Jenna told her what Avril Lauter had seen, and of her failed attempt to get the young woman to go through the house with her to find out if she would see it again.

"But I don't understand why she saw *three* boys,"

Jenna said. "Josh was there, but there were two other boys with him."

"Like I told you, as long as you got a poltergeist, you can't believe anything you see or hear in your house. But I know somebody might be able to help you."

"Really?"

"A friend of mine in Crescent City. He's retired now, he don't do sittings no more, except once in a while, he'll do one for nothing if somebody really needs help. I talked to him this morning and told him about you. See, he's got experience with poltergeists. He claims he can get rid of 'em. I haven't seen him do it myself, but I know he's a good medium, and he's a good fella. He might be able to help you."

The day's disappointments faded a little. "But you say he's in Crescent City?"

"He's gonna be coming through Eureka this afternoon, honey, and he owes me a favor. He says he'd be willing to come to your place and do a sitting around one, if you don't mind picking him up at the truck stop."

"Truck stop?"

"He's a trucker. He'll be on a schedule, so you might want to fix something for him to eat while he does his sitting. He'll probably eat just about anything you put in front of him."

"He's a . . . trucker?"

"Yeah. What, you think the dead only talk to cranky old women like me?"

"Oh, Ada, I can't thank you enough for this."

"Just keep your poltergeist away from me, honey, that's all I ask."

172

CHAPTER THIRTEEN

Lily. Wednesday, 10:07 A.M.

The teddy bear emerges from the darkness before her. One eye missing, stuffing leaking from holes, filthy and old. The music-box rendition of Brahms's "Lullaby" plays from the stuffed bear, slightly off key, dragging a bit.

"Get over here and be a good puppy," a gravelly voice whispers, filling her with dread. The last two words, "good puppy," echo repeatedly as the teddy bear's head blurs. It is replaced by the head of the brown-haired boy she'd seen screaming in an earlier vision. Names and words fly at her—

Giles styles wiles piles Niles Niles Niles Miles Miles Miles!

—until the correct one lodges in her mind. She feels great fear for Miles, and something else—something that makes her feel as if she's dying inside. Death feelings. They weigh her down, press on her chest and temples.

Then Miles's face is gone and it's just a teddy bear's head again.

The music winds down to a stop as a large, beefy fist clutch-

ing the black handle of a broad-bladed knife swings into view. The glimmering blade of the butcher knife impales the bear's body to the hilt. Dark blood bubbles up around the knife as the bear's head bursts into flames.

The bear disappears as she feels herself falling through darkness. Light comes up from beneath her and she rolls over to see the ground rising rapidly toward her. She sees the same gray house she's seen before, with the swing and slide in the backyard. She slows down as she begins to glide horizontally away from the house, along the gravel drive that cuts through the woods to the open metal gate at the road. She drops suddenly and finds herself beside the mailbox. Gold letters and numbers sit neatly in individual black squares on the side of the mailbox:

2204
The Kellars

A bright red starfish is spread out over the top of the mailbox and throbs with silent ferocity—it looks about to explode. The starfish fills her with a smothering horror as Brahms's "Lullaby" begins to play again, plinking off key. Her dread grows as the music fades, until—

Lily whimpered as she opened her eyes, then fell silent when she saw all the faces looking down at her. There were umbrellas keeping her dry from the rain, but her back was soaking wet. She realized she was lying on the sidewalk. She'd been on her way to get a *Record Search-light* from the vending machine in front of the store, and the smell of bananas and the electric-blue flashing had hit her abruptly, and she'd gone down.

She recognized Evelyn Walsh from the candle shop in the next building over, and Mr. Fitzgerald from the gallery across the street, and Minnie from the Hallmark store a few doors down from there. Lily heard Claudia before she saw her.

"Lily! Oh, no! Did she hurt herself?" Claudia peered down at Lily with one hand flat against the side of her face.

"I'm okay," Lily said, although her left elbow ached, probably from the fall. She hoped she hadn't ruined her green-and-black broomstick skirt. Mr. Fitzgerald took her hand and helped her to her feet. "I just don't feel good," she said.

"You should see a doctor right away, Lily," Minnie from the Hallmark store said. "You look very pale. Has this happened before?"

"I'll be okay. Thanks so much for your help. Really. All of you, I appreciate it. I'm sorry for taking a dive out here." Lily's head throbbed against the backs of her eyeballs and she was sapped by waves of nausea, but she smiled at the small group. They did not go away, though. "Okay, look, I haven't been feeling well, but I'm having it taken care of, and I'm going to be okay. All right?"

"It's nothing serious, is it, Lil?" Evelyn Walsh said.

Irritated, Lily shook her head. "No, no. Now, thank you again, very much, for your help, but frankly, I . . . I just don't feel obligated to explain myself to you any further." She turned and went back into the store.

She went through the store and into her apartment, to the bathroom, where she got a Vicodin from the medicine cabinet. She drank it down with a glass of water, then spent a moment studying her reflection in the mirror. She was pale, and . . . was her face just a tiny bit thinner? She went to her bedroom, took off her clothes, and put on a brown-and-gold muumuu. She opened the notebook in which she was keeping a record of the visions and wrote, "2204, Starfish (red & throbbing), The

Kellars." As she stretched out on the bed, she heard Claudia walk through the kitchen and down the short hall to the bedroom.

"How are you feeling, Lily?" Claudia whispered.

"I've got an awful headache, and I feel sick. Do me a favor?"

"Sure."

"Bring me some saltine crackers from the cupboard over the toaster in the kitchen." The salty crackers sometimes settled Lily's stomach when it was upset.

Claudia returned seconds later with an open package of crackers and handed it to her. Lily nibbled on one of the saltines.

"I, um, I explained to them that you weren't feeling well," Claudia said.

"To who? Out front, you mean? Why do they have to be so nosy?"

"They weren't being nosy, Lily, they were being concerned."

"I don't like people . . . *talking* about me. They do anyway, of course, there's nothing I can do about it, they always have, because I'm just not . . . I don't . . . fit in well with others. But if they're going to talk, they'll have to make *up* things to talk about, because they're not getting anything from *me*. We've never discussed it, Claudia, but I'm sure you've noticed that I'm a very private person."

"But does that mean you have to be rude?"

Lily closed her eyes, rested her forearm across them. "Was I rude?"

"Well . . . yeah."

"But . . . I thought *they* were being rude."

"No, they weren't. They were concerned, that's all. You passed out on the sidewalk in front of your store— they had reason to be concerned."

"And I was rude?"

"Yes, you were. The only reason I'm pointing this out to you is that you told me to. You remember that, don't you?"

Lily smiled. "Yes, I remember. I've never been good at . . . people stuff."

Claudia said, "I'm going back to the register. You rest for a while."

"Thank you, Claudia."

Lily had been living alone for so long, and went out so little, she sometimes lost track of her own behavior when she was around people. She had asked Claudia to point it out to her when she was rude or inappropriate. She would remember to do something nice for Evelyn Walsh and Mr. Fitzgerald and Minnie from the Hallmark store and apologize for her unpleasantness.

But for now, she wanted only to sleep until the headache and nausea went away.

CHAPTER FOURTEEN

Wednesday, 11:39 A.M.

Dwayne Shattuck was a tall, lanky man in his late forties with short black hair shot with gray, and a handlebar mustache. He wore a long-sleeve brown-and-yellow plaid shirt under a tan quilted down jacket, blue jeans, and cowboy boots. He had an easy smile and spoke in a slow, quiet way that reminded Jenna of jazz DJs on late-night radio.

She picked him up at Hansen's Truck Stop in Fortuna and asked him if Subway sandwiches were all right for lunch. When he said the Subway club sandwich was his favorite, she stopped and bought one for him. On the way to the house, she told him everything that had happened lately, right up to Ada's sitting the day before.

"Well, poltergeists are my specialty," Dwayne said. "Ada says you can't get rid of them, they go when they want to go. But I've gotten rid of quite a few."

"How do you do it?"

"I can't really say."

"It's a secret?"

"No, I mean I'm not sure *how* I do it. They seem to listen to me and go away when I tell 'em, is all."

"Ada said you'd retired, but you seem pretty young for that."

"It don't take long to get burnt out on poltergeists. Driving a truck's a hell of a lot more relaxing than dealin' with them buggers, I'll tell ya. So I gave it up. But every once in a while, I'll give somebody a hand. I know how tough it can be tryin' to live with one of them things in the house. But it's real strange that you don't have an adolescent—ten years old is a little young for your son to be drawin' poltergeist action."

Before leaving the house, Jenna had managed to talk Martha into taking a nap. Jenna was relieved to find she was still sleeping when they got to the house. She put the sandwich in the refrigerator for later and took Dwayne to the living room. They stood in the spot where Ada's Ouija board had been set up.

"This is where we had the sitting," Jenna said.

"Okay. I'll need you to be quiet. This may take a little while. If you want, you can go do something else."

Jenna decided to stay.

Dwayne spit on his right palm, then vigorously rubbed his hands together. He raised his arms high, palms out, and closed his eyes. He tilted his head back slightly and said in a clear but quiet voice, "I'm here to communicate with the spirit that has been causing trouble in this house. Do you hear me? Give me some sign that you hear me. I'm here to communicate with you and to tell you it's time to leave this house. Do you hear me? I am telling you it's time to leave this house."

As he spoke, Dwayne slowly rotated in place, like a

satellite dish, arms up, palms out, eyes closed. He turned left, then stopped and moved back to the right again, and continued talking, repeating the same thing a few more times.

Jenna was struck once again by the oddness of her situation. A truck-driving medium standing with his hands in the air in her living room—a month ago, she would have found the whole thing absurdly hilarious. But now she saw no humor in it at all.

"Do you hear me?" Dwayne said. "I've come to tell you it's time to leave this house. Give me some sign that you—"

He stopped speaking and fell still when the room suddenly became cold. Dwayne's eyes opened wide as he quickly looked around. It had taken only a few minutes, and he seemed surprised.

"I sense your presence," he said. "I know you're here, I know you can hear me."

Dwayne's words became a mere hum in the background the moment Jenna saw the toddler in the blue hooded jacket standing in the entryway. His hood was up and his head was bowed. Her right hand flew up to cover her mouth.

Blinking back tears, Jenna slowly turned away from Dwayne and took a cautious step toward the entryway. Then another, and another. "Josh?" she whispered into her palm. "Josh, honey? Look at Mommy. Take off your hood."

As the toddler slowly raised his head, he reached up with pudgy hands and pulled the hood back.

Jenna's hand dropped limply to her side and she took in a sharp breath. The boy standing before her had a freckled face and thick red hair and pale blue eyes. He was not Josh. She had never seen him before in her life.

"Now," Dwayne was saying, "I am telling you once

and for all." He shouted in a clear, booming voice, *"It's time to leave this house!"*

Jenna's attention was still focused on the boy, so she only vaguely noticed the same darkening of the air that had occurred the day before. The room exploded with the sound of shattering glass. Jenna tore her eyes away from the child and spun around in time to see her grandmother's collection of handblown glass animals on the fireplace mantel fall together and shatter into pieces. She turned around again, and when her eyes found the boy, she screamed.

"Stop that!" Dwayne shouted into the air. "Stop that right now! You are to leave this house immed—"

Dwayne doubled over, then fell to the floor on the other side of the recliner.

The boy still stood in the entryway, staring at her, but his clothes were now old and filthy and decayed, and so was he. His nose was gone, his eye sockets empty, and much of his face had rotted away to reveal tiny teeth and jawbone.

The little boy was gone for a few seconds before Jenna realized he had disappeared. Her hand slapped over her mouth again, and she stopped screaming as she spun around to see what had happened to Dwayne. His legs were sticking out from behind the recliner, kicking as he rolled back and forth on the floor.

Then everything was normal again, and the telephone was chirping.

Dwayne lay still behind the recliner. Jenna hurried to his side and gasped when she saw his face. His nose was swollen and crooked, his face bloody, his left eye nearly swollen shut, lower lip open in a fresh cut.

"Oh, my God, Mr. Shattuck. Dwayne, can you hear me?"

The phone continued to chirp.

"Are you okay?" There was a great deal of blood on his face and neck, and Jenna found herself feeling a bit faint. She took a couple deep breaths.

"I'll live," Dwayne said in a strained voice pinched by his broken nose.

"My God, what did it *do* to you? And *how*?"

"It happens." His voice trembled. "Sometimes poltergeists get pretty worked up. 'Cept that was no poltergeist."

Martha came into the living room in a housedress and slippers and looked around. "What the hell is going on in here?" she said. She gasped when she saw Dwayne on the floor. "Who's he? What *happened*?"

"Mom, could you get the phone?"

Martha turned and left the living room.

"That was no poltergeist." Dwayne said again. "You gotta get your family outta this house, Mrs. Kellar. You got somethin' bad in here. Somethin' that's been here awhile, it's settled in."

"I'm going to call an ambulance," Jenna said. "Don't move, stay right there."

"Don't be silly," he said. He slowly got to his feet and leaned on the back of the recliner for a moment. "It knocked me around, but I'm not crippled."

"Your nose is broken."

"It's been broken before."

"Jenna," Martha said as she hurried into the living room. She handed Jenna the cordless phone.

Something about the look on Martha's face worried Jenna. She put the phone to her ear and said, "Hello?"

"Mrs. Kellar? Keith Hollander. I run the garage where your husband works."

Jenna put a hand to her chest and closed it into a fist, as if to hold her heart together. "What's wrong?"

"David had an accident a little while ago, and he hurt

his hand. The ambulance just left with him—they're taking him to St. Joseph."

Jenna's voice was thin as she said, "An ambulance? How bad was he hurt?"

"Well, he lost a lot of blood."

"I'll get down there right away. Thank you for calling." Before she could punch the Off button, the phone slipped from Jenna's trembling hand. She picked it up and handed it to Martha. She heard herself speaking, but her throat felt numb. "David's been hurt. An ambulance has taken him to the hospital." She turned to Dwayne. "I'll take you with me and you can go to the emergency room."

"Would you like me to go with you?" Martha said.

"Somebody has to be here when Miles comes home, Mom."

"Are you sure you should drive? You look pale. Are you all right?"

"I'll be fine." But Jenna was not convinced. She got her purse, and her hands trembled so much, she dropped her keys twice. She stopped a moment in the entryway to take a couple deep breaths. All that was important now was David.

Well, he lost a lot of blood.

Memories of Josh's funeral flashed in Jenna's mind, but with David in the casket instead of their son. She tried to clear her mind and focus on getting to the hospital. She turned to Dwayne as he limped to the front door and took his jacket from the hook on the wall. "Are you going to make it out to the car?" she said.

"I'll be fine. It's you folks I'm worried about. You've gotta leave this house."

Jenna faced him. "Mr. Shattuck, we have no money to go anywhere else. This house is all we have."

"But you've got somethin' bad in this house, Mrs.

Kellar, somethin' . . . sick. And it don't like bein' disturbed."

"Then we won't disturb it. That's the best I can do." She spun around and put on her coat. "Now, I'm really sorry you've been hurt, Mr. Shattuck, and I sure hope you don't plan on charging us for your hospital bills, because there's no way we could possibly pay them. I'm sorry you got dragged into this, but if you don't mind, I'd rather not discuss it anymore." Jenna went out the front door jangling her keys.

They said nothing on the drive to the hospital.

David was in surgery for almost four hours, and Jenna knew nothing until his doctor came out afterward and explained the situation to her. David's left hand had gotten caught on a fan belt. It had been cut between the two middle fingers and down into the palm, almost to the wrist, slicing through several bones and ligaments. The doctor said it was difficult to tell how extensive the damage would be, but he expected David to regain, at the very least, most of the use of his hand. He said David would stay in the hospital overnight, then go home the next day.

When Jenna went in to see him, her knees wobbled with relief when David gave her a groggy smile. But the aftereffects of the anesthesia and the morphine drip made conversation difficult, so she let him sleep. His left hand and forearm lay across his belly, bandaged and in a blue fiberglass cast.

She used the telephone on David's bedstand to call home. She updated Martha on David's condition and talked to Miles for a few minutes to reassure him that everything was okay. She was hanging up the phone when a uniformed police officer walked in, a pudgy man about Jenna's age, bald except for short dark hair around the sides and back, and a tuft just above his forehead.

"Are you Jenna Kellar?" he asked.

"Yes."

"I'm Officer Tom Mayhew of the Eureka Police Department. Could I speak with you a moment, please? Maybe you'd prefer to step outside with me?"

"Okay." They went out into the corridor. "Is there something wrong?"

"Dwayne Shattuck says he was, uh . . . well, he says he was beaten up by a-yuh . . . a spirit. A ghost. In your house."

"I know it sounds crazy, but it's true. He and I were the only two in the room, and *I* certainly didn't do that to him. Did he call you?"

"No, the hospital notified us that someone had been beaten up and—"

"Well, I saw it happen. Look, I didn't believe in this stuff either, okay? But lately . . . well, I've had to take a good hard look at what I believe. It's nothing new to him, though. He's a medium."

Officer Mayhew nodded, frowning. "Yeah, that's what he said. He was pounded pretty hard. I'm just not sure how to write this one up."

"Maybe you shouldn't. No one's complaining, no charges are being pressed."

"The hospital was required by law to make the call, and I answered it. I've got to write something up. Besides, nobody'll believe me if I don't. Would you mind telling me what happened, Mrs. Kellar?" he said, taking a small notebook from his pocket. "I'd like to see if your story matches Mr. Shattuck's."

Leaving out the child in the entryway—Jenna preferred not to think about that yet—she told him what had happened in the living room.

"Does this sort of thing happen in your house a lot?" he asked.

"Is this part of an investigation?"

He smiled. "No, I'm just curious."

"We've had some . . . unusual things happen in the house lately, yes."

"And your address is . . ." He looked down at the open notepad. ". . . 2204 Starfish Drive."

"That's right. But why is that necessary?"

"It's just for the record."

"Okay," Jenna said, but she frowned.

"By the way, Mr. Shattuck's pretty anxious to talk to you. He wanted me to ask you to go see him in ER as soon as you could. He's still there. They've got him bandaged up, but there's some kind of insurance holdup."

"Thank you for the message."

"I hope your husband gets better soon."

She nodded, smiled, and Officer Mayhew turned and walked away.

David was asleep, and Jenna decided to see what Dwayne Shattuck had to say. She felt guilty about his injuries—and at the same time, she was worried about them, wondering if Dwayne was litigious.

He was sitting in the ER waiting room, paging through an issue of *Field & Stream*. Jenna sat down in the chair beside him.

Dwayne had a couple stitches above his right eye and in his lower lip. His face was bruised and lumpy, his nose and eye swollen.

"How are you?" she asked.

"Late with a load, that's all I know," he said. "I'm more worried about you and your family."

"That's the second time you've said that, and I appreciate it, but I told you, I'd rather not—"

"Yeah, I know, but that don't change the fact that

you're livin' with somethin' bad. You'd better keep a close eye on your boy."

Jenna felt as if her lungs had been splashed with ice water. "What?"

"Your son. I don't know what you've got in that house, but I wouldn't let it near my kid if I were you."

"You . . . Wait, do you think it would hurt Miles?"

"You're not hearing me, are you? I've never felt anything like that before—it was scary. I'm tellin' you, you're in danger as long as you're livin' with that thing."

"But I told you, we have nowhere to go. And now that David's been hurt—there's just no way we could leave."

"Then maybe Ada can help you find someone who can get rid of that thing. But it'll have to be somebody who knows what he's doin', 'cause that thing's not leavin' without a fight."

"What *is* it?"

"I don't know. I only know it's about as hostile as a nest of hornets."

"You said it's been there awhile."

"That's the feeling I got. That and . . . something twisted." He shook his head slowly. "It's a sick thing, whatever it is. I don't like usin' the word 'evil.' It's been tossed around too much for too long, and now it doesn't mean so much anymore. But it sure comes to mind here."

"You said it doesn't like to be disturbed. Well, like I told you before, we just won't disturb it."

"No, you don't understand. Somethin's already disturbed it. It's . . . I don't know, it's like it's got somethin' on its mind."

"What should I do?"

Dwayne shrugged, then winced slightly and massaged his neck with his left hand. "I wouldn't mess around with Ouija boards or have any more sittings in there. Not until you've got somebody who's ready to deal with that thing. You're liable to just piss it off, pardon my French. I'll talk to Ada about it and have her call you."

"Would you do that?"

"Sure. I wish I could do more."

Jenna was too confused and frightened to continue the conversation. She stood and said, "Is there anything I can do for you? I feel so bad about all this."

"Please don't, Mrs. Kellar. This kinda thing happens, it's always a possibility. Tell you the truth, this is the main reason I retired. This one's the worst so far, though, I gotta admit. That's because it wasn't a poltergeist, it's somethin' else. But I knew what I was gettin' into when I agreed to try to clean your house. When you deal with the other side, you just never know what's gonna happen."

A woman at the billing window called Dwayne's name. He got up slowly and limped over to the window. He exchanged a few quiet words with the woman, signed a paper, and came away with a copy of his own, which he folded up and slipped into his pocket.

"I'll drive you back to your truck," Jenna said.

"I'd appreciate that."

They said little during the drive. As he got out of the car at the truck stop, Jenna said, "You're not going to get behind the wheel, are you?"

"Not until tomorrow. I made a couple calls at the hospital. I'm gonna spend the night here."

"Are you sure there's nothing I can—"

Dwayne laughed. "You've done enough. And don't you worry, I'm not gonna sue you. Take care of your family, now, 'specially your little boy." He closed the door.

* * *

Jenna brought home chicken in a bucket for dinner. In spite of her reassurances on the phone, Miles looked deeply worried. She explained to him exactly what had happened and assured him that Dad would be home tomorrow.

"But he'll be groggy for a while," she said, "because he'll be taking painkillers. So you'll have to be the man of the house for me, okay?"

"Okay. Can I sleep in your bed tonight?"

Jenna laughed, but it was a tense laugh. Miles's request reminded her of the fat man he claimed to have seen in his bedroom. Jenna wondered if it was connected to the thing Dwayne claimed was sharing the house with them. "We'll see," she said.

After dinner, Jenna did the dishes by hand because she wanted time to think. Her mother had not asked about Dwayne or what had happened that afternoon, although she had cleaned the shattered glass animals off the mantel and the blood from the carpet. But she would bring it up eventually, when they were alone and Miles was out of earshot. Jenna had no idea what she would tell her. She could not imagine Martha keeping a straight face while listening to Jenna's story.

Mrs. Frangiapani says it's nothing to worry about, she thought, *Ada says it's a poltergeist, Kimberly thinks it might be demonic, and Dwayne says it's something sick and evil. Who's right? Whom do I believe?*

It seemed even experts on the supernatural could not agree on much of anything. She regretted not taking Mrs. Frangiapani's advice in the first place, as Kimberly had told her to, and dropping the whole thing. Maybe if she'd ignored it, it would have gotten bored and gone away.

Every time she closed her eyes, she saw the freckled face of the redheaded boy in the blue hooded jacket, the boy she had mistaken for Josh—knowing it had not been her son left a dull ache in her chest—then the boy's round, cherubic face collapsing into the decayed corpse's skull she had seen before he'd disappeared. Something had made the air cold and had destroyed the glass animals on the mantel.

I don't know what you've got in that house, but I wouldn't let it near my kid if I were you.

Martha never mentioned it. She spent the evening watching television with Miles. Jenna made herself busy around the house, did a couple loads of laundry, and called Kimberly on the phone and told her everything that had happened.

"Maybe you should call a . . . I don't know, a minister," Kimberly said.

"You mean, like a priest?"

"Minister, priest, rabbi, take your pick."

"But I don't believe in *that* stuff, either."

"Maybe you should start adjusting what you believe to fit what's happening around you."

Jenna laughed, but it was a sad sound. "All I know is, I wish I hadn't gotten myself started on this stuff."

"Then just focus on what's important, like Mrs. Frangiapani said. Especially now that David's hurt himself. That's awful, Jenna. At least he'll be covered by workmen's comp."

She sighed. "I don't know what we're going to do now that he can't work. I'll have to get a job, there's no way around it."

"I'll help you look. There might even be an opening at the store."

A few minutes after ending her conversation with

Kimberly, she was about to join Miles and Martha in the living room when the phone chirped. She turned around, went back into the kitchen, and answered it.

"Jenna Kellar?" a woman said.

"Yes. Who's this?"

"Donna Lopez, the *Eureka Times-Standard*."

"What?"

"I'm calling about the story of a Dwayne Shattuck who says he was beaten up by a ghost in your house. Is that true?"

"Look, um . . . I'd rather you not write about this."

"I'm sorry?"

"I don't want . . . my family doesn't want this kind of attention. Please don't write about this. It's really not a story, it's—"

"Wanda Bundy, a registered nurse in the ER at St. Joseph Hospital, called the police when Mr. Shattuck showed up badly beaten, and Mr. Shattuck told Officer Tom Mayhew of the Eureka Police Department that he was beaten up by a ghost in your living room. According to the report, Officer Mayhew talked to you, and you corroborated Mr. Shattuck's story. You said, and I quote, 'I saw it happen.' It's a matter of public record, Mrs. Kellar, and I'm writing the story. I'm just calling to see if you have any comment. Do you believe your house is haunted, Mrs. Kellar?"

Jenna stood with her mouth open for a long moment before saying, "No, I have no comment." She returned the phone to its base.

As she stood with her hand on the phone, Jenna's heart hammered. She could not decide what frightened her more—Dwayne's warning about what he said was in the house, or the idea of being identified in the newspaper as "the people with the haunted house." She imagined children picking on Miles at school because of the story. She would have to explain it all to David. Suddenly, Jenna felt exhausted.

When Miles's bedtime came, he asked again if he could sleep in her bed.

"Okay," she said, "but only for tonight."

Relief passed through Miles, and his entire body seemed to relax before her eyes. She told him to go clean up and brush his teeth, and she would be up in a while.

Martha said good night and retreated to her bedroom down the hall.

Jenna went through the house and turned off all the lights. By the time she got upstairs to her bedroom, Miles was already sound asleep.

CHAPTER FIFTEEN

Thursday, 2:42 A.M.

Jenna sat up and listened. Had she been dreaming, or had she heard . . . There it was again: children laughing, boys, in the backyard, and the shriek of the swing's chains. They were back.

She carefully got out of bed without disturbing Miles. She wore a long yellow cotton nightshirt that fell to her knees, with a giant panda on the front. Putting on David's robe, she poked her feet into her slippers, then hurried down the hall. Halfway down the stairs, she faintly heard the music again. She stopped on the stairs and listened a moment to be sure.

It's not Josh, she thought.

The plinking notes of Brahms's "Lullaby" grew louder and clearer as she turned left at the bottom of the stairs and went down the hall. Light fell through the kitchen doorway, and the sound of Martha's radio playing clashed with the delicate tune.

Martha sat in the breakfast nook. She hummed quietly, head low, elbows on the tabletop, and hands pressed over her ears, eyes closed.

As it had the last time she'd heard it, the music came from the laundry room—from behind the basement door.

The laughter sounded just outside the window and the swings screeched. There was no wind blowing tonight.

Jenna went to the back door. She turned on the porch light, picked up the flashlight, and went out on the porch. The flashlight sent a bar of light through the misty yard. After hurrying down the steps, she stalked through the weeds and passed the beam over the slide and the swings, all around the yard, and found no one. The swings swept back and forth on wobbly chains, as if just abandoned. But she could still hear them—their laughter was directly in front of her . . . just behind her . . . to her left, her right. She stood in place and turned all the way around. There was no one there.

In the damp night, Jenna was already cold, but the phantom laughter chilled her bones. She turned and went back toward the house. Before going up the porch steps, she turned around and aimed the flashlight out at the yard one more time.

The laughter stopped and the light passed over empty eye sockets and rows of small teeth exposed by rotting flesh that had peeled back over the cheeks. The image of the group of dead, rotting boys lingered for a moment after they disappeared, like the visual echo of a camera's flash after a snapshot is taken.

In her eagerness to get into the house, Jenna tripped going up the steps and nearly fell through the door. She closed the door and locked the deadbolt. Still holding the shining flashlight, she turned to the laundry room. Brahms's "Lullaby" still played from behind the basement door. She turned and looked at her mother in the breakfast nook at the other end of the kitchen. Martha's head was still low, her hands still covering her ears, eyes closed. Jenna was not even sure if Martha had noticed her yet—it seemed Martha was trying hard to avoid noticing anything.

In the laundry room, Jenna jerked the warped basement door open and shone the flashlight down the stairs. The light shivered ahead of her as her hands trembled, and she could feel her heart throbbing in her throat. She took a few steps down and shot the beam over the rail, down into the basement.

The twinkling music was clear, coming from the filthy old teddy bear lying facedown on the dirt floor. The tarnished key in its back turned slowly.

I shouldn't have been able to hear that from the stairs, she thought. *It's not loud enough to be heard beyond the basement door.*

She moved the beam through the small basement, over the stacked boxes and crates and bags. Jenna half expected to see the little boy with the hooded jacket—

Mommy—

It's not Josh.

—but there was no one down there.

The teddy bear's music gradually slowed to a stop as Jenna's flashlight fell on the bear again. David had said he wanted it to stay in the basement, but Jenna found herself wanting to rescue the poor old toy. It might have been the tune it played—Brahms's "Lullaby" conjured pleasant memories of a gurgling infant Josh. Jenna carefully made her way down the stairs. She heard a small clicking sound and stopped halfway down to listen.

Ticka-ticka-ticka-tick. Ticka-ticka-ticka-tick.

Jenna tipped the flashlight to the right, over the rail, and back and forth through the basement.

Ticka-ticka-ticka-tick. Ticka-ticka-ticka-tick.

It was a tiny, insignificant sound, so she ignored it and continued down the stairs to the basement's dirt floor. She turned right and found the bear with the flashlight. A moment after the beam landed on the bear, it began to play Brahms's "Lullaby" again, clearly and at a faster pace than it had been playing earlier. She watched the key turn slowly in the bear's back. Jenna realized the sound she'd heard on the way down had been the key being wound up.

Her knees bent and she reached down with her left hand to pick up the bear. A large fleshy hand closed on her wrist, cold and powerful, and Jenna sucked in a breath as she reflexively stepped backward, still clutching the teddy bear. As she moved, the light sliced across a fat belly stretching a dirty T-shirt, flanked by an open denim vest, flashed up over a white, forward-tilted cowboy hat. She swung the long, heavy flashlight like a club, but it connected with nothing. The hand on her wrist was gone and there was no one standing in front of her.

"Get outta here," a low, whispered voice said from the darkness to her left. "You got no business down here."

As Jenna hurried clumsily backward to the stairs, the light found him standing among the stacked boxes and crates, but the beam bounced around as she got onto the stairs. There he was again, standing near the foot of the stairs. Each time the flashlight's beam fell on him, he melted away like paper-thin ice in the hot sun.

Still holding the teddy bear in her left hand, she stopped a third of the way up the stairs and passed the light through the basement. He was gone. She continued up. Jenna felt the cold, fat hand close on her bare ankle as the low, gravelly voice said, "Fuckin' women."

She pulled her foot away without effort and ran the rest of the way up the stairs, screaming. She slammed the basement door shut with the weight of her body and dropped the Mag-Lite on the laundry room floor.

You can't believe anything you see or hear in your own house, Ada had said of living with a poltergeist.

That was no poltergeist, Dwayne Shattuck had said. *You've gotta get your family outta this house.*

Martha had heard Jenna scream—she stood in the middle of the kitchen now, jaw slack. Jenna was on the verge of hyperventilating as she embraced Martha. She stood like that for a while and forced herself to calm down. Martha's shoulders hitched, and Jenna realized she was sobbing.

"Mom, what's wrong?" she said as she pulled back.

Martha's lips collapsed into her mouth because she wasn't wearing her dentures. Tears sparkled on her cheeks. "Did you see them?" Martha asked.

"See what?"

"The boys?"

Jenna flinched. "You've seen the boys?"

Words tumbled out of her between sobs, and she leaned heavily against Jenna. "Every night. I can't take it anymore, Jenna. They're in so much pain, they're crying, I can tell, but I can't *hear* them, they don't make any sound. I can only see them in the dark, so I turn the light on, but even then, I still know they're there."

"Mom, calm down. Come back over here and sit down." Jenna led her back to the breakfast nook and they sat down side by side. Jenna put the teddy bear on the table. It still played its song, slow and labored now, nearing its end, while the radio played upbeat big-band music. She stroked Martha's back until the sobs receded. "Who's crying, Mom? Who's in pain?"

"The boys in my room. At night. Hanging on the walls and strapped to chairs. Young boys. Naked and bony, like they've been starved."

Jenna was still calming down from her scare in the basement and needed a moment to process what Martha was saying. She stared with wide eyes at her mother for several seconds. "Why didn't you tell me about this before, Mom?"

"You mean . . . you believe me?"

"Mom, if you only knew the things *I've* been seeing. Why didn't you *tell* me?"

"I was afraid you'd think I was losing my mind and you'd wanna . . . put me in a home." She sobbed again, and Jenna held her close for a while.

"There's no way I'm going to put you in a home, Mother. Do you understand? No *way*. I admit, I thought you were a little confused at first when you saw those kids in the backyard, but it turned out you were right. I'm sorry I doubted you. You should've told me sooner, Mom. I've seen them, too. For a while, I thought I was seeing Josh."

"Oh, no, honey," Martha said, "it's not Josh. I don't know *what* it is, but I see 'em in my room every night when I turn the lights out. So I don't turn the lights out anymore. But tonight the bulbs in my overhead went out and it got so cold in the room all of a sudden, and I could see them struggling and crying even worse than usual, and I had to get out of there."

"You don't have to go back in there. You can sleep on the couch until we figure out some other arrangement. Okay?"

Martha nodded against Jenna's shoulder. "I don't want to go back to bed just yet, though," she said, pulling away. "I think I'll fix a hot drink and do some reading. Would you get my glasses, honey? I don't want to go back in there. And while you're there, grab the glass beside my bed. It's got my teeth in it."

Jenna left the kitchen and went down the hall to Martha's room. She reached for the doorknob, but hesitated when she remembered what Martha had seen in there. She considered going back for the flashlight, which she realized she'd left on the laundry room floor still shining. Instead, she went to the foot of the staircase, flipped the wall switch, and turned on the hall light. An old mirror with a dark walnut frame hung on the wall near Martha's bedroom door, and Jenna paused to look at her reflection. Her eyes were puffy from sleep and she looked tired, but she saw something else in her face—fear.

When she opened the bedroom door, light spilled into the bedroom and over the bed. From the doorway, she could see Martha's glasses, and her teeth in a glass of water on the stand beside the bed.

Jenna entered the room and went to the bedstand, picked up the glasses in one hand, the glass holding the teeth in the other, and turned back. For a fraction of a second, she thought she saw movement on the walls in the darkness, beyond the light cast into the room from the hallway. She stopped and squinted into the dark. All she saw were the still-bare walls of Martha's bedroom. She hurried out and pulled the door closed behind her.

Martha had put the kettle on the stove and was dropping a tea bag into an empty mug when Jenna came back into the kitchen.

"Come here and talk to me, Mom." Jenna went to the breakfast nook and put Martha's things on the table. She went to the laundry room and got the flashlight, turned it off, and put it in its spot beside the back door. She sat down at the table across from Martha, who had taken her usual seat.

Martha took the upper plate from the glass, put it into her mouth, then shook water from her hand. She held a wadded-up paper towel in one hand with which she dabbed her eyes before putting on her glasses.

The radio played "Harlem Nocturne" through patches of static.

"How long have you been seeing this?" Jenna asked.

"Almost since we moved in. It started right after I saw those kids in the backyard."

"Has it been getting . . . worse?"

"Yes. At first, I only got glimpses of them in the dark now and then . . . hanging from the wall, or strapped into that awful high chair. But now, they're always there."

"How old are these boys?"

"It's different boys each time. The youngest are maybe four or five. The oldest are probably Miles's age."

When the kettle began to whistle, Martha got up and made her tea.

"How much do you know about this house, Mom?"

"What makes you think I know *anything* about it?" she said. "All I know is that Leonard was raised here, and he came back to live with his parents after we broke up in Redding. Far as I know, he took care of them until they died, and—"

"I know that part. You don't know anything else?"

Martha returned to the table with her tea. "Honey, I told you before, once Lenny left Redding, I never saw nor heard from him again, and I made no effort to keep in touch. Once every few years, I'd hear from a friend of a friend that he was still living here in his parents' place. To be honest, hon, it wasn't like we were madly in love or anything. He was an exterminator, and we met when he came in at work one night to spray the place for bugs during the graveyard shift. He made me laugh. He made all of us laugh. He was too shy to ask me out, so I asked him. We went out a couple times. We were only . . . *together* . . . once. If you want to know the truth, he wasn't all that good. He was like a little boy, like it was his first time. It might've been, for all I know, but he was a man of forty-something, I expected him to have *some* experience. *I* was the inexperienced one, even as old as I was. I was in my late thirties at the time. Your mother was never popular with men, honey, and the few men I *was* popular with weren't very popular with me, if you get my meaning. I learned that the hard way with a few unpleasant relationships. After those, I stopped trying."

Jenna smiled. "You've never told me this much before."

"Well, you're all grown up now. We haven't talked about this since you were a teenager, and I sure wasn't about to tell you all this stuff *then*."

Jenna found herself laughing quietly. One of the reasons she got along with her mother so well was that Martha could always make her laugh, make her feel better.

The squeal of the swing's chains rose in the stillness outside, and her smile fell away as she turned to the window. Its expanse of blackness reflected Jenna and Martha and the kitchen. When she heard the boys' laughter outside, Jenna saw fear spread over her reflection.

"Do you hear them?" Jenna whispered.

"I hear them every night. Sometimes during the day, too. I don't look out the windows anymore." She turned the radio's volume up a little, then sipped her tea.

Jenna remembered the hideous faces the flashlight had illuminated outside—empty eye sockets and rotting skin. There were no boys playing in the backyard—she knew that. And yet she could hear the swings screeching and the boys laughing. She turned away from the window and tried to ignore the nagging suspicion that the boys were out there staring in at her.

"Who was the man in the living room with the beat-up face?" Martha asked. "Did he have something to do with this?"

She told Martha everything, from the first time she saw the hooded toddler in the upstairs hallway to the incident in the living room with Dwayne Shattuck, and everything that had happened since she'd gotten out of bed twenty minutes earlier.

"Jenna, honey, you should've come to me with this before," Martha said.

Jenna shook her head slowly. "You've always been so practical, so down-to-earth about everything. I didn't think you'd believe something like this."

Martha put her hand on Jenna's arm and whispered, "Look, if getting old has taught me anything, it's that I don't know squat about nothin'. That nightmare in my bedroom . . . it took a few nights for me to convince myself I was really seeing it and wasn't just going batty. Put that together with everything you just told me, and I'd say there's something in this house besides the four of us."

Somethin's already disturbed it, Dwayne Shattuck had said.

Jenna said, "The attorney told us that Leonard never remarried, but do you think he had other children?"

"Not that I know of. Why?"

"Why did he set up playground equipment in the backyard?"

"I don't know. Maybe his parents put them up."

"They're old, but they're not that old."

"Who knows. Why?"

"Just wondering. How do you feel?" Jenna asked.

Martha smiled. "Much better with you here. It's nice to talk."

"You seem so calm. My heart is still beating a mile a minute."

"I've kind of gotten used to it. It's still unnerving, but the shock has worn off. But I've been thinking." Martha leaned back and reached down to the pile of tabloid papers stacked beside her on the cushion. She picked through them until she found the *Global Inquisitor* and opened it on the table. She turned the paper around so Jenna could read it.

The headline read:

**VICTIMS OF DEMONIC FORCE
ENDURED RAPE AND TORTURE!
BLOOD-CURDLING DETAILS OF
HORRIFYING EXORCISM!**

Gooseflesh broke out at the back of Jenna's neck when she heard the laughter from outside again, the sound of boys breaking each other up with fart noises and ass jokes. She wondered again if they were out there watching her.

Martha said, "I heard what you said to that man in the living room, that truck-driving medium. About us not having anyplace to go but here. So I've been thinking, maybe we should call someone who can help us. Arthur and Mavis Bingham have made a career out of this sort of thing. They're experts."

"How could we possibly afford them?"

"I think they make all their money from their books and lectures."

"How would we reach them?" Jenna asked.

"They're on the Internet."

"I can't sit here anymore," Jenna said as she scooted out from behind the table. "Let's go into the living room and start a fire."

"Yeah, I get the feeling they're watching me sometimes, too." Martha turned off her radio and stood. "Would you like me to make you a cup of tea, honey? It's herbal, no caffeine."

"That would be nice, Mom, thanks." Jenna stood and turned to the laundry room, made sure the basement door was still closed. In the living room, she turned on all the lights. Apparently, Miles had brought in some wood and kindling the day before, no doubt at Martha's urging. Jenna used it and some newspaper to make a fire.

Martha came in with a cup in each hand, gave one to Jenna, and sat in her usual spot at the end of the couch. Jenna stood with her back to the fire and they spoke quietly, almost whispering.

Jenna said, "I've got to get some drapes in the windows."

"That would be good," Martha said. "But it wouldn't help, not really. Because it's not really outside. You can put up all the drapes you want, but we've got to do something about what's in here with us."

Jenna frowned. "Are we talking about . . . ghosts?"

"I don't know *what* we're talking about. But I know I can't sleep in that room anymore. I'll take the couch."

"You can have Miles's room, if you think you can take the stairs. He'd love sleeping down here."

"I don't know if I *want* to sleep in Miles's room. He's got a fat man coming up out of the floor every night."

Now that she had seen the fat man herself, Jenna had some idea of how terrified Miles must have been. She wondered if he was ever in any danger, and the possibility made her feel cold in spite of the fire's warmth. She shook her head and said, "We kept insisting it was a nightmare."

"Sometimes we need to listen a little more closely to kids. He knows what's a nightmare and what's not."

"Do you think I should tell Miles that *I've* seen the fat man?" Jenna said.

"I don't know. What do you think?"

Jenna decided she would deal with that later—whatever she told him, or didn't tell him, Miles was not going to be the problem. "David isn't going to buy a word of this," she said.

"Are you sure? Maybe he's seen a few things he hasn't mentioned to you."

"That's possible."

The room became toasty as they sipped their tea in silence. After a while, Jenna put her cup on the lamp table beside David's recliner and curled up in the big chair. Martha stretched out on the couch. As the fire gently crackled, Jenna and Martha fell asleep in the brightly lighted living room.

Jenna slept fitfully, and finally got up, fixed a pot of coffee, and started breakfast. She did not have to go upstairs to wake Miles—he came down dressed and smiling, looking well-rested and better than he'd looked in days. Jenna had not realized, until that moment, how run-down Miles had been looking. Had she been that preoccupied?

Not anymore, she thought. Jenna decided she was going to do exactly what Dwayne Shattuck had told her to do—keep a close eye on Miles.

While Miles and Martha ate breakfast, Jenna called the hospital and spoke with David, who was more alert than he was yesterday, but still groggy from painkillers.

He was eager to come home, but had to wait till his doctor came to see him.

Jenna drove Miles down to the end of the driveway, where he caught the school bus, then she returned to the house, showered, and dressed. A couple guys from the garage were good enough to bring David's pickup truck to the house and park it in the garage while Jenna was getting ready to leave for the hospital. She was on her way out the door when Kimberly called.

"You're in the newspaper," Kimberly said.

"Oh, shit," Jenna said. "I was afraid of that. What does it say?"

Kimberly read the short article to her. It quoted Dwayne's description of what had happened "in the Starfish Drive home of David and Jenna Kellar." Jenna reportedly corroborated his story, but was said to have "refused comment."

"At least they didn't print my address and phone number," Jenna said.

"What are you going to tell David?"

Jenna sighed. "I'm going to have to tell him everything. I'm just not sure how to go about it."

"You could always start by showing him the paper."

A few minutes later, Jenna drove to the hospital to spend the rest of the morning with David. The morning's *Times-Standard* had been left in the room on the bed table, but David had not read it. When Jenna arrived, she took it off the table, put it on the chair, and sat on it. They talked quietly about unimportant things. David sat up in bed and was more animated and alert than he was the day before, but on his face was the same expression he wore when he was experiencing indigestion after a heavy meal—a faint frown, a slight narrowing of his left eye, an uncharming tilt to his mouth. Jenna did not know if it came from pain, or from

David's worries about their future now that he had been injured and would be unable to work indefinitely. It was probably a combination of both.

The doctor came in shortly after noon and talked briefly with David, then said he wanted to see him again in a few days. Shortly after that, David was released and a nurse wheeled him down to the car in a wheelchair. When Jenna left the room, she grabbed the newspaper from the chair and took it home with them.

"I can't believe you brought people like that into this house," David said. Wearing his robe, the left sleeve empty, he sat on the edge of the bed, where he had napped for a couple hours after lunch. He tossed the paper aside and it landed on the bed, open to the article about Dwayne Shattuck.

Jenna stood facing him, fingers stuffed into the back pockets of her blue jeans. "I didn't know what else to do," she said. "After I saw that little boy—"

"I *told* you, Jenna. We're just missing Josh because—"

"I *know* it's not Josh. I know it now, anyway. I saw his face. He's a little red-haired boy with freckles, he looks nothing like Josh. I saw him while Dwayne was trying to contact whatever it is that's—"

"Jenna, are you *hearing* yourself?" He spoke through clenched teeth, trying to keep his voice down, and his right fist was clenched in his lap. He looked away from her a moment, relaxed a little. He slapped his hand down on the newspaper. "Don't you see, Jenna, you gave that guy exactly what he wanted. He's in the paper now. This article's nothing more than a commercial for that guy."

"He's retired."

"Yeah, sure. Not so retired that he couldn't whip up a little publicity."

"David, I *saw* the man. His nose was broken and he was covered with blood."

"Did you see it happen?"

"No. He fell down behind the recliner."

"How do you know he didn't do it himself?"

"For a little article in the lousy *Eureka Times-Standard*?"

"You can't *buy* that kind of publicity. It's how they work. He may get a magazine article out of this, maybe even a book." David sighed as he stood and put his right arm around her. He spoke quietly, gently. "Why didn't you talk to me about this, huh?"

"Whether or not he was a phony has nothing to do with what I saw, David. I haven't been imagining things. There's something in this house. Those boys who keep showing up in the backyard in the middle of the night are part of it." She stepped back, out of his embrace. "You have to admit, David, there's something very weird about those boys, about the way they come and go."

He nodded. "Yes, I admit that. And I've been having some pretty strange dreams lately. Dreams about those boys . . . I think. I've even walked in my sleep."

Jenna frowned. "You've been walking in your—"

His anger flared again as he interrupted. "But that does *not* mean our house is haunted, for crying out loud. I can't believe you'd spend money on some old gypsy woman when we can barely afford the groceries we need."

"Kimberly doesn't expect me to pay her back right away."

"That's even worse—*borrowing* the money. How are we going to pay her back? Especially now that I can't work? I don't understand it, Jenna. You've never been the kind of person to fall for this sort of thing. What were you *thinking?*"

She shook her head. "I didn't know what else to do. There's something in this house with us, and I was trying to find someone who would know how to deal with it."

"There's nothing in this house but *us*, dammit!" he shouted. "But now that we're in the paper, you just wait—every phony-baloney medium and fortune-teller within a hundred-mile radius is going to be knocking on our door. And when they do, we're chasing them off. Do you understand, Jenna? No more of this shit. We can't afford it, and even if we could, it would still be a waste of money, and I won't have con artists in my house milking my goddamned wallet."

Jenna decided to say no more. David was furious, and she knew any further discussion would only anger him more. At the same time, she refused to apologize for doing what she still considered the right thing in the face of something she found frightening and confusing.

"Let's not fight," she said. "Miles is home from school."

"We're not fighting." He sat down on the edge of the bed, shook his head. "I don't understand why you didn't come to me."

"I *tried*. That day in the basement. You didn't want to hear about it, you made that clear. That was when I thought it was Josh. Now I know it's not. But in a way, that's worse, because I don't know *what* it is."

David opened his mouth to speak, but she kept talking.

"Whether you believe it or not, there's *something* in this house." She turned and left the room.

* * *

David tried to calm himself before going downstairs. He was angry that Jenna had borrowed money from Kimberly Gimble. It was bad enough that Martha had been paying for so much, but to borrow from a virtual stranger was embarrassing, and for something so ridiculous. It was so uncharacteristic of Jenna, he wondered if she was okay. Had the loss of Josh been eating at her in a way he had not noticed?

David thought of the boys he'd seen in the backyard. Had he really seen them the last couple times, or had they been part of his dreams? He thought of the fat, cigar-smoking man in his dreams, and of waking up in the basement, and in Miles's bedroom in the middle of the night. But he refused to believe there was anything supernatural involved. He blamed it on his worries about finding work, a good job that would allow him to support his family again. As a boy, he had walked in his sleep whenever he had a lot on his mind—an upcoming test at school, an important football game. There was nothing supernatural about it.

It was so unlike Jenna to do what she had done that David wondered if he should be worried instead of angry.

The chirp of the telephone startled him out of his thoughts, and he picked up the receiver. "Hello."

A second later, he heard Jenna answer downstairs: "Hello."

After a moment of silence at the other end: "Hello, is this the Kellar residence?"

"Yes," David said.

"You don't know me. My name is Lily Rourke. I'm calling from Mt. Shasta." She sounded uncertain of herself and overly pleasant, as if she were trying too hard. "This is going to sound . . . well, it's hard to know how it'll sound to you because I don't know you. I'm a psychic. I've helped the police solve a number of crimes, and I—"

"Hang up, Jenna," David said.

Lily Rourke said, "No, wait, please. I read about you in the paper, and I need to tell you something. It's *very* important. If you'd just—"

"You read about us in the paper?" David said.

"I read about what happened in your house. To the medium. The trucker."

"But that was just in the local paper here in Eureka."

"It was in the *Redding Record Searchlight*," Lily Rourke said. "It seems one of the wire services picked up the story. I got the impression it ran nationwide."

"Oh, shit," David said. "Look, whatever you're selling, we're not interested."

"Mr. Kellar, do you have a swing set in your backyard? And a slide?"

"*What?* Listen to me—do *not* call back, okay? Jenna? Are you still on the line?"

He heard the sharp click of the downstairs connection being severed.

"Good-bye," David said before hitting the Off button with his thumb.

CHAPTER SIXTEEN

Lily. Thursday, 2:19 P.M.

Lily replaced the receiver, not surprised but no less frustrated. She sat at the table in her kitchen. A cup of coffee had gone cold and four slices of Entenmann's apple crumb cake remained untouched on a paper plate. Lily's appetite had been fading, and she did not sleep well at night. The visions left her with a nagging sense of urgency that had preoccupied her to the point of distraction.

She had learned from her previous visions that it was not only the visions themselves that needed her careful scrutiny, but the feelings they left behind, and those they stirred in her waking hours as she thought about them. She had to be open to everything.

She was convinced that the unfamiliar faces she'd seen in her vision were the Kellars—David and Jenna, according to the newspaper article—and that the house she'd seen was theirs. She could not shake the feeling that they were in some kind of peril. But it was the little boy who impressed her as the one in the most danger. From what, she was not sure, but it had something to do with the fat man in the cowboy hat. Even if the Kellars had been willing to listen to her, Lily had no idea what she would have told them.

Claudia had shown her the story in the *Record Searchlight* that morning. As soon as she read "Starfish Drive," Lily remembered the throbbing red starfish on the mailbox in her vision, and knew the address would be 2204.

She'd immediately called Directory Assistance and asked for both the telephone number and street address of the Kellars in Eureka on Starfish Drive. Sure enough, the address had matched. It had taken Lily a few hours to muster the courage to make the call. She had a difficult time dealing with people in normal situations—she had not looked forward to explaining to total strangers on the phone that she was a psychic having visions about them. A small part of her was relieved that Mr. Kellar had solved that problem for her. But she could not stop there.

Lily stood and dumped her coffee into the sink and poured a fresh cup. Flash, her pudgy manx tabby, shot through the kitchen in a gray blur. He made himself scarce most of the time, appeared only long enough to race through a room to get wherever he was going, and stopped only at mealtime to eat, and bedtime, when he curled up beside Lily on the bed and slept.

Phoning the Kellars was not going to work. Lily saw only one other option remaining, and she did not like it, but knew it was inevitable. She sipped her coffee and carried it with her as she left the kitchen and went out front to the store.

There were a couple of browsers—a young man with long dark hair and thick glasses in the Reincarnation section, and a bullet-shaped, middle-aged woman perusing the selection of tarot cards. Claudia was at the front counter, putting a new roll of paper in the register.

Lily joined her behind the counter and leaned close as she spoke in a whisper. "Could you get away for a couple days? Maybe a few?"

"Is this a trick question?"

"I need to go to Eureka, but I can't go alone. So how would you like to get away for a while? I'll pay your regular wages while we're gone, because you'll be doing all the driving, so it'll be like you're working.

"I think I could fit it into my busy social schedule," Claudia said. "What about the store?"

Lily chewed her lower lip a moment as she looked around at all the shelves of books and thought.

Claudia said, "What about Mark Sieber?"

Mark was a local artist who had filled in for Claudia at the store a couple times in the past. Lily remembered him as quiet but efficient, and always pleasant with the customers. She said, "I'll call and see if he's available. If necessary, I'll just close up."

"Did you call the number?"

Lily nodded and told her how the call had gone.

"What makes you think approaching them in person is going to make any difference?" Claudia said.

"I have to try, I don't have a choice. I wish we could leave right now."

"Why?"

Lily took a deep breath and blew it out through puffed cheeks. "I can't get rid of the feeling that I'm running against the clock. I'm not sure why yet, but I'm worried about their little boy."

"Did they say they have one?"

"No, but they do." Lily headed for the back again. "I'll call Mark."

"Hey, are you feeling okay?"

Lily turned to her. "Yeah. Just a little antsy." She went back to her kitchen to make the call.

It took a little over two hours for Lily and Claudia to show Mark Sieber everything he needed to know about opening, closing, and running The Crystal Well for a few days. Lily showed him where to feed Flash and sent Claudia out to stock up on cat food. While she was gone, Lily packed some clothes and toiletries and was ready to go by the time Claudia got back.

Lily opened a can of cat food and Flash hurried into the kitchen a moment later. She dumped the food into Flash's bowl against the back wall of the kitchen and tossed the can into the trash at the end of the counter. While the cat ate, she bent down and picked him up, cradled him to her generous bosom. Flash squirmed, but purred.

"I know, I know," Lily said, "you don't like to be held, but I'm gonna be gone for a while and I want to give you a little lovin' before I go." She stroked the cat. "I'll be gone a few days, and when I come back, you're gonna look at me like you didn't even know I left, aren't you?" She kissed the top of Flash's head, then put him down by his bowl. Flash continued to eat his food with gusto. When she saw Claudia standing in the doorway smiling at her, Lily said, "I love my Flash."

She put her suitcase into the trunk of her silver 1999 Volkswagen Beetle, and Claudia, who had parked her own car in back of the store, got behind the wheel. Lily could not risk driving, because she had no idea when another vision would cause her to black out. They went to

Claudia's house, where she packed some things, then called her mother and asked her to come over and feed her canary and get her mail while she was gone. It was a clear, cold afternoon, and they were traveling south on Interstate 5 by five o'clock.

"We can stop in Redding for something to eat," Lily said, "then we'll get on 299 West."

Claudia said, "Wouldn't it have been better to do this first thing in the morning?"

"I couldn't wait that long."

"It's really bothering you, isn't it?"

"Maybe I'll actually get some sleep tonight, knowing I'm doing something. I've been getting by on two or three hours a night. I'm tired, but at the same time, I've been climbing the walls over this."

Claudia nodded. "I knew it was bothering you, but I didn't know you weren't sleeping. Have you seen your doctor?"

"So he can tell me to get some sleep and lose weight? At the rate I'm going, I just might, because I don't have much of an appetite. In fact, I think I've dropped a few pounds. I can't stop thinking about that boy of theirs."

"Thinking what about him?"

"He's in trouble, that's all I know. I think they *all* are, but especially the boy."

"What are you going to do when we get there?"

"If I knew that," Lily said with a sigh, "I wouldn't have this big soggy lump in my stomach."

Forty-five minutes later, they stopped at a Burger King on their way through Redding and had a dinner of Whoppers with fries and sodas. The restaurant was crowded and noisy. Lily and Claudia ate at a table in the back. Lily forced herself to nibble on her hamburger even though she did not feel hungry. Claudia, on the other hand, took great bites of her Double Whopper and nearly inhaled her large order of fries. She ate more than anyone Lily had ever met before, besides herself, and yet never gained a pound. She was so thin, she didn't have much of a figure at all. But Lily would take that flat chest and ass in a second if given the opportunity, especially if she could go on eating the way Claudia ate.

Claudia had applied for a job at The Crystal Well two years before, after moving back to Mt. Shasta from Sacramento. She'd been attending business school there when she met and fell in love with a young man who asked her to marry him. Claudia had moved in with him and the engagement had lasted a couple years, until she found out he had been cheating on her repeatedly during that time. She'd decided to put the rest of her education on hold and return home for a while, until she decided what to do with her life. She had not yet come to a decision.

"How come you've never asked me about my gift?" Lily said.

"Your gift?" Claudia put her hamburger down and dabbed a paper napkin over her mouth. "You mean . . . your psychic ability?"

"You've never said a word about it. You've never even asked for a reading. I don't even know if you think I'm for real or not."

Claudia smiled. "Why wouldn't I think you're for real?"

"Some people don't believe in that stuff."

"I've heard the way your clients talk about you. I've seen the way they look after their readings. It doesn't matter how many times they come, they always walk out looking like it was the first time and you just knocked their socks off."

"Maybe I'm just a good con artist."

Claudia shook her head. "You're too insecure to be a con artist."

Lily's left eyebrow rose high on her forehead. "Oh. Well. Thank you."

Claudia laughed. "I'm sorry, I didn't mean that in a bad way. I mean, like, when you asked me to tell you when you're not handling people well, when you're being rude—that's not something a con artist would do."

"You've got me there."

"If I thought you were ripping people off, I wouldn't work for you. Really."

"But you've never mentioned it."

Claudia said nothing. She took a bite of her hamburger, bit a few fries in half.

Lily was surprised by the discomfort she sensed from Claudia. She opened herself a bit more, reached out just enough, and discovered beneath Claudia's discomfort a layer of mild fear.

"I'm sorry," Lily said, "I didn't mean to frighten you."

Claudia's eyes widened. "You didn't frighten me."

"Well . . . I made you uncomfortable. I'm sorry. I was just curious."

"You want to know the truth?"

"Of course."

"And you won't be offended?"

"I can't promise that."

"Well, I don't want to offend you."

"Good grief, Claudia, I could probably find out myself in a second, so why don't you just tell me."

The pale freckles on Claudia's forehead huddled together slowly as she frowned. "What do you mean, you could find out yourself?"

"Well, I *might* be able to find out myself. It's probably

right on the surface of your consciousness, because we've been talking about it."

"You mean . . ." Claudia's head bobbed slightly as she swallowed hard. "You can read my mind?"

"See, *that's* what I'm talking about."

"What?"

"You just asked a question about it. That's the first question you've asked in two years. I was just wondering why. Aren't you curious?"

"So . . . *can* you read my mind?"

"Don't be ridiculous." Lily plucked a french fry from the cardboard carton and took a small bite. "I can sense feelings and moods, and I pick up on things that are, say, weighing heavily on people's minds. For example, I can tell when you come to work right after having a fight with your mother. No matter how cheerful you might be, I always know. It's on you like a scent, because it's still foremost on your mind, it's bothering you, and when something's bothering you, or you're ecstatically happy, or furious, it's like a psychic broadcast. And I'm an antenna."

"Then, in a way . . . you *can* read my mind."

"I read mostly emotions, moods. I have no idea what you're thinking right now. If I could read minds, I'd probably have my own TV show. But that doesn't mean I don't pick up information about you."

"Information? What kind of information?" Before Lily could respond, Claudia held up a hand, palm out, and said, "Hold it. Don't answer that. I don't want to know."

"Why not?"

"For the same reason I haven't asked you about your . . . abilities. I'm sorry, Lily, but it gives me the creeps. That's all. I don't *want* to know, because it just gives me the creeps."

Lily washed down the french fry with a drink of soda, then tilted her head back and laughed. "You thought that was going to offend me?"

"It doesn't?"

"Are you kidding? Makes perfect sense to me. Hell, I've been living with it all my life, and sometimes it gives *me* the creeps."

After filling the Beetle's gas tank, they left Redding and headed west on 299. Lily put a Mozart CD into the player, tipped her seat back, and tried to get some sleep. But it was a steep and twisting mountain road, and when she closed her eyes, the motion made her feel nauseated, so she sat up in her seat. She was too preoccupied with the Kellars to sleep anyway.

"Are we going to be coming up on a gas station soon?" Claudia said.

"Not for a while. We just filled up."

"No, it's not that. I shouldn't have had that soda."

"Ah, I see," Lily said. "Well, try to think about something else for a while." Seconds later, her thoughts were interrupted by a clear image of Claudia's mother—Lily had met her once, briefly—and the sound of a dry, hacking cough. It made her chest feel tight, made her feel suddenly tense. She turned to Claudia but did not say anything yet.

She had received impressions from and about Claudia before. Two years earlier, she knew Claudia was going to get a phone call from her ex-boyfriend in Sacramento, and she knew it was going to upset Claudia. Lily considered telling her not to answer her phone that night, but had thought better of it. Since Claudia had never asked Lily about the gift or asked for a reading, Lily felt uncomfortable offering information. She had not told her about the phone call, but had given her the next day off to make up for it. None of the impressions she'd received about Claudia had involved anything important—the phone call from her ex-boyfriend had been the most significant of them all. None of them had involved illness.

"Claudia, has your mother been coughing a lot?" Lily said.

"What? Coughing?" There was a quiet swelling of panic in Claudia's voice. "Yes, she has. I told her she should see a doctor about it."

"Please, don't get upset."

"Lily, when someone like *you* asks if my mother has been *coughing*—"

"I'm not getting any death feelings about her, not at all. But you need to insist that she see her doctor. That's all. Just get her to the doctor, and I'm sure she'll be fine. She doesn't smoke, she's a healthy woman—it could be an allergy. But she needs to see her doctor about it, or it'll get worse. Please don't panic."

"So . . . you're not saying she's seriously ill."

"No, that's not what I'm feeling."

"Okay. As soon as we stop, I'll call her. Maybe if I tell her *you* said so, she'll make an appointment."

"I didn't mean to scare you. But I thought I should say something."

After a moment, Claudia said, "Thank you." They drove in silence for a few minutes before Claudia said, "What are . . . death feelings like?"

"Oh, they're awful. Awful. Before I met Annabelle— I've told you about Annabelle Youngblood before, haven't I?"

"You've mentioned her."

"Well, before I met Annabelle, I had no idea how to manage this gift. Before she taught me how to deal with it, I had this constant flow of information coming at me all the time. It kept me in a pretty steady state of depression for a long time. I didn't know it then, but I understand now that the death feelings were the cause of that depression. They were everywhere. Because we're all dying. It's just a matter of time."

"Can we not get morbid?"

"Sorry, didn't mean to. But when I was a kid, it was pretty—"

It happened quickly—the peripheral flashing, the smell of bananas, then she slipped away.

Two minutes later, Lily sat forward suddenly and put both hands flat on the dashboard as she caught her breath. The screams of a little boy still reverberated in her mind. Her head throbbed, and for a moment she was afraid what little she'd eaten for dinner was going to come back up. She closed her eyes and took a few deep breaths before saying, "We're not moving."

"No. When I noticed something was wrong, I pulled over on this turnout."

"Oh, God," Lily said with a groan. "Something horrible is going to happen in that house if we don't get there in time." The engine idled as passing headlights swept over them. Lily reached behind her seat for her purse and prodded around in it for her pills. She realized she had nothing to drink. "Let's get going. I need to get to that gas station, too."

They stopped briefly at a 76 station. Lily took a pill, and Claudia relieved herself, then called her mother on her cell phone. They arrived in Eureka two hours and forty-five minutes later, bought two different maps of the area and a six-pack of Mountain Dew at a convenience store, then got a room at a Motel 6.

CHAPTER SEVENTEEN

Friday, 3:17 A.M.

Jenna woke to the plinking sound of Brahms's "Lullaby." She rolled over to find David's side of the bed empty, the covers thrown back. His robe lay across the foot of the bed. She sat up and rubbed her eyes with the heels of her hands. The music continued to play. The filthy teddy bear Jenna had rescued from the basement lay faceup at the foot of the bed.

There were two small walk-in closets in the bedroom, each with a chest of drawers. Jenna had put the bear in the bottom drawer of the chest in her closet, along with a few flip-flop sandals and a stack of old sweatshirts. David did not know where she had put it, or even that she had brought it up from the basement.

She reached over and turned on the lamp on her bedstand, squinted against the light. Standing, she took her robe from the chair against the wall and slipped it on, stepped into her slippers. She yawned, still trying to wake up fully. The lullaby began to slow down as she picked up the bear. Across the room in the closet, the bottom drawer of the chest had been pulled almost all the way out.

Jenna took the bear to the closet, put it back in the drawer, and closed it. The muffled music wound down to a few final plunks as she pulled her bowling ball in its black-and-white vinyl bag from the corner beneath her hanging clothes. She and David had last gone bowling the year Josh died. They used to bowl regularly with friends back in Redding. It seemed ages ago now, like another lifetime. Jenna placed the bowling ball in front of the bottom drawer and left it there.

She left the bedroom and went down the hall. Miles's bedroom door was open and light spilled out into the hall. The night before, she'd asked Miles to help her clean up after dinner. While she washed dishes and he dried, she'd told him Grandma would be sleeping on the couch, but if he wanted, he could sleep with the overhead light on in his bedroom, with the door all the way open. It would send the electric bill up, but Jenna planned to start looking for a job right away.

At the foot of the stairs, Jenna turned left and went down the hall. Dim light spilled from the kitchen doorway at the end of the hall. The floor creaked and popped beneath her feet, loud in the silence of the house.

The two fluorescents beneath the cupboards over the counters were the only lights on in the kitchen. Jenna turned on the overhead fluorescent. David was nowhere in sight, but a crumpled plastic grocery bag lay in a heap on the counter beside the sink. The bag bore the 7-Eleven logo. Jenna knew it had not been there when she'd gone to bed—she'd passed the nearby 7-Eleven many times, but had not yet stopped there. Had David gotten in the car and driven down the street to the 7-Eleven to get something? In the living room, she could hear Martha snoring quietly on the couch in the dark. She checked the front door, made sure it was locked.

Back in the kitchen, Jenna wondered if he had gone outside. The Mag-Lite was not standing in its usual position beside the back door, but the door was locked.

Was it possible David had been in the upstairs bathroom and she hadn't noticed on her way to the stairs? She decided she would have heard something—David urinating, the toilet flushing, the faucet running, something, but the house had been dead silent, as it was now. She was about to go back down the hall to the stairs when she heard a muffled thump, then another. It was followed by a murmuring voice, unintelligible but distinct, and it came from—

With the kitchen's overhead light on, Jenna could see into the dark laundry room. The basement door stood open a few inches. She went into the laundry room, turned on the light, and pulled the door open, looked down the stairs and saw light at the bottom. Going down a few steps, she ducked low and peered down into the basement.

David sat on a crate with his back to the stairs, hunched forward over an open cardboard box. He wore old sweatpants, a sweatshirt with the left sleeve empty, and sneakers. The flashlight's long, heavy handle was held between his head and left shoulder, shining the beam into the box. As she watched, he reached into the box with his right hand and pulled out a few magazines, looked them over briefly, then tossed them back into the box. He took the flashlight from the crook of his neck and put it between his legs, shining upward. He reached down and found the can on the ground beside

Ray Garton

him, raised it to his mouth, and tipped his head back slightly, took a few gulps.

Jenna realized he was drinking a beer—she got a glimpse of the gold can in the light and recognized it as a Michelob. Her mind flashed on the image of all those old empty Michelob cans David and Miles had cleaned out of the garage. Her chin dropped when she suddenly realized that David *had* gone to the 7-Eleven in the middle of the night, to get *beer*, of all things—and while he was under the influence of painkillers.

"David?" she said.

He was so startled, he dropped the can of beer as he stood. It hissed as it spilled on the dirt floor. The flashlight stood on end, shining upward as it leaned against the crate on which David had been sitting.

She slowly and carefully started down the stairs. "What are you *doing* down here?" she said. She realized her voice sounded distressed, panicky, but she couldn't help it. Something was wrong, and it wasn't just the fact that David had gone out in the middle of the night to buy beer.

Jenna stopped halfway down the stairs and looked down at David. His left arm, in its cast and sling, was a lump beneath his sweatshirt. He stood with his shoulders back and his hips forward—an odd posture, one that was uncharacteristic of David, who always stood straight. But it was familiar. For a moment, Jenna was chilled by the certainty that she was looking not at David but at the same fat man she had seen in the basement early the previous morning, if only in brief glimpses. David arched his back as if to support a great belly he did not have.

"David?" she said again, but this time the word came out a breathy whisper.

226

He pitched forward suddenly and retched. He dropped to one knee, then the other, leaned his right arm on the floor, elbow locked, and groaned before vomiting onto the dirt.

Jenna hurried the rest of the way down, with both hands on the railing to the right. "David, are you all right?" Her foot kicked a couple of empty beer cans as she hurried to his side, and they clanked together. *How many beers has he had?* she wondered.

He got to his feet and looked around with his mouth open and eyes wide. "Jeez," he said, his voice hoarse, "how long have I been down *here?*"

Jenna's heart skipped a beat. "David . . . have you been asleep?"

He smacked his lips and frowned. "I've been walking in my sleep lately."

Jenna remembered his brief mention of walking in his sleep the day before, but she'd had so much on her mind, she hadn't given it a second thought. "Walking in your *sleep?*" she said.

David shrugged a shoulder. "Don't worry, it'll pass. I used to do this when I was a kid. It's nothing to worry about, it's—"

"David. You drove to 7-Eleven tonight." She bent down and picked up one of the empty cans and held it in the light. "You went out for beer."

He stared at the can as if he'd never seen one before. "Are you sure?"

"Well, *I* didn't go, and Mom doesn't drive, and obviously it wasn't Miles."

"Holy shit," he whispered.

"It's freezing down here," Jenna said, hugging herself against a deep chill. "Can we get out of here, please?"

They went up the stairs and into the kitchen. David

put the Mag-Lite back in its place, then stood and stared at it for a few seconds. Jenna wondered if he was trying to remember picking it up in the first place. She took his hand and led him to the breakfast nook—he stared at the 7-Eleven bag on the counter as he passed it—where they sat facing each other, his right hand beneath both of hers.

"David, you looked very different down there," Jenna whispered.

"What do you mean, different?"

"The way you were standing . . . it wasn't the way you stand. But I recognized it, I recognized the posture. Down in the basement last night, I saw—"

"What were you doing in the basement last night?"

"I heard the music again. It was the teddy bear. I went down there to get it and I saw a man."

David's eyes widened. "You saw *what?* Did you call the police?"

"No, no—he wasn't *really* there. I mean, he kept disappearing every time I shined the flashlight on him. But I *saw* him. He stood exactly the way you were standing when I came down the—"

"God*dammit*, Jenna!" he said as he pulled his hand away from hers and slammed his palm down on the table. "How many times do I have to tell you, I don't even want to *hear* that shit. I don't understand why you're suddenly so wrapped up in this supernatural crap. Is it because of Josh? I mean, I know you miss him, but Jenna, come on, tell me you don't *really* think you're going to contact him with the help of these bullshit mediums and fortune-tellers."

Jenna closed her hands around his again and squeezed as she smiled. "No, honey, I *told* you—I thought I was seeing Josh at first, but it wasn't him, it was another child completely. And there are others, you've seen them—the boys in the backyard who disappear into thin air. And then there's the man I saw down in the—"

"Would you *stop* it!"

"You don't have to believe me, just stick around, you'll see what I mean. There's something in this house with us, David, and when I came down those stairs, I wasn't looking at you—it wasn't you at *all*. Just like it's not you to go out and buy beer in the middle of the night—or any other time of day, for that matter, even when you're awake."

He frowned down at the lump his arm made beneath his sweatshirt but didn't seem to see it. He was thinking about what he had done, and it bothered him, Jenna was certain—the possibilities made fear flash in his eyes as he looked across the table at her again.

"When I went down the stairs, I was looking at you, but you were *completely* different," she said. "Then you vomited. Why, David, what made you sick?"

"Probably the beer."

"You were yourself then."

"When?"

"After you vomited. And you didn't know where you were for a second, did you?"

"Well, no, I'd just woke up."

"Did you wake up, or were you *allowed* to wake up?"

David squinted at her. "What? Jenna, are you having some kind of breakdown?"

The question made Jenna flinch. She slowly pulled her hands away from him and sat back on the bench. She had been trying to ignore the ache deep in her chest—like a tear in her heart that had been there ever since she'd realized she hadn't been seeing Josh after all. It had been buried by her initial fear and concern over

David's injury, and she had put off thinking about it. But now she realized how desperately she had wanted— *needed*, she thought—that hooded child to be Josh. The ache deep in her chest opened like a blossoming rose. Jenna sobbed as tears sprang to her eyes.

"I don't know," she said. "I know how all this stuff sounds, I can hear it coming out of my mouth and I don't believe I'm saying it, but David"—she leaned forward, clutched his right hand with her left—"I'm not imagining any of this."

David shook his head angrily but said nothing for a moment. He had never been able to remain angry about anything when Jenna cried. He came around the table, and she scooted over so he could sit beside her. He put his arm around her shoulders and squeezed her to him.

He said, "I don't understand why you're trying to attach some kind of supernatural significance to this— isn't it enough that I'm walking in my sleep, that I drove around in my damned *sleep*? I mean, what the hell am I supposed to do, tie my ankle to the bed? Wear a bell?"

In spite of her sobs, Jenna smiled because David was trying to make her laugh. It made her feel somewhat normal again, and it was a welcome feeling. She pressed against him, wrapped her arm around him.

"My hand is really throbbing," David said. He sounded groggy. "I'm going to take one of my pills and wait for it to kick in, maybe have a cup of hot chocolate."

"But you've been drinking beer."

"I got rid of the beer in the basement, remember?" He stood. "Why don't you go back to bed, honey. Come on." He tugged on her arm until she stood. He kissed her ear and whispered, "You just let those people get under your skin, honey, that's all. You thought you were seeing Josh and you went to them for help, and they got to you. It's what they do, it's what they're good at. C'mon, let's go upstairs. I'll get my pill and tuck you in."

"You're not coming to bed?"

"In a few minutes, after the pill starts working. My hand is killing me."

They went upstairs together, and David turned on his bedside lamp as she took off her robe and got into bed. David sat on the bed, leaned over, and kissed her. She knew he was hurting badly—she could see the pain in his eyes. Was there something else there, as well? Something he sat up quickly to keep her from seeing?

He took a small plastic orange bottle from his bedstand, shook one of the tiny white pills onto the stand, replaced the lid, and picked up the pill. He stood, turned off the lamp, and said, "You go back to sleep. I'll be up in a while."

After he left, Jenna stared into the dark for a while. She thought again of David's odd posture as he'd stood in the basement, of how unlike himself he had looked. And she thought of the tabloid headlines Martha had shown her the morning before. She decided to look up Arthur and Mavis Bingham on the Internet in the morning. If they had a phone number, she would call them first chance she got. If necessary, she'd go over to Kimberly's house to make the call so David wouldn't overhear her.

He wouldn't like it, but Jenna could not bother thinking about that. Something was very wrong in the house. Dwayne Shattuck's warning weighed heavily on her mind, because she knew he was right—there was something bad in the house with them. She was afraid it had been hunkering inside David down there in the basement, slurping beers and—doing what? What had he been doing down there?

Jenna tried to stay awake and wait for him to come

back, but she drifted off to sleep not long after he left the bedroom.

David went downstairs, got a glass of water from the tap, popped the OxyContin into his mouth and drank it down. Soon, it would make him woozy and tired and he would have to go back to bed. But for the time being, he was pumped full of adrenaline. He filled the kettle with water and put it on a burner—a cup of hot chocolate might help him relax.

"Ghosts, spirits," he muttered angrily as he paced the length of the kitchen a few times. He got a mug and a packet of instant cocoa from the cupboard. He tore the packet open with his teeth, poured the powder into the mug, and tossed the torn packet into the garbage can under the sink. He dropped a spoon into the mug and paced some more. His hand throbbed, and with each throb it felt like it doubled in size.

It had been a stupid, bloody accident. It never would have happened had he been getting enough sleep and had he not been so preoccupied with those damned kids who kept showing up in the yard in the middle of the night, if he hadn't been preoccupied by wondering how they were getting in and out of the locked gate—or if he had been dreaming them. His hand had been cut between his two middle fingers nearly to his wrist. He remembered staring at his own exposed bones and tendons for several dead-silent, paralyzed seconds as blood cascaded down his forearm and spattered onto the concrete floor of the garage's pit beneath a canary-yellow 2000 Chevy Cavalier coupe. He remembered only bits and pieces after that, until he awoke in the recovery room after surgery.

Now the hand buzzed and throbbed with pain. But as

bad as it was, it did not distract him from what was really on his mind—his sleepwalking, his dreams, and what he'd been doing in the basement.

The fact that he'd been walking in his sleep was not much of a surprise given his pattern of sleepwalking in the past. The dreams, on the other hand, were disturbing. He could remember only vague bits and pieces of them, as hard as he'd tried, but they left behind a residue, and the visual echoes of horrifying images. They were images that did not belong inside his head—harshly lit images of young boys, scrawny and naked, posing together in ways that turned David's stomach. The images were repugnant and made him wish he could reach into his head and physically extract them. He did not understand them—they were not memories, because he had never seen such things before, and they were too brutally offensive to him to be anything else. They felt almost as if they had been planted there—as if they were someone else's thoughts.

And the basement—what kept drawing him down to the basement? And what did he do while he was down there?

David stopped pacing and listened for sounds of movement upstairs. He heard nothing and assumed Jenna was still in bed. He took the Mag-Lite from its spot beside the back door, went into the laundry room, and pulled the basement door open. He went down the stairs carefully, determined to figure out what he had been doing down there.

He turned the light on the three empty, toppled beer cans on the dirt floor beside a crate. A few inches away stood the three remaining unopened cans of beer, still in their plastic rings. He thought again of the fact that he'd driven to 7-Eleven while asleep, and it chilled his blood. Next to the crate were a couple of open cardboard boxes. David stepped toward them when he heard the quiet, moist, gravelly voice behind him.

"Y'gotta clean up after yourself. Never know when that bitch upstairs is gonna come snoopin' around."

David gasped as he spun around. The fat man was only inches away and coming closer, and suddenly—

—David was standing before a neat stack of boxes while a scream came from upstairs. He took a step back and bent forward, expecting to vomit because of the wave of nausea that moved through him. But then it was gone, and the shrill screaming continued.

He turned and looked down, found the flashlight lying across the top of the wooden crate shining at the stacked boxes. The two open cardboard boxes were gone, now closed up and stacked neatly with all the others.

David picked up the flashlight, hooked his middle finger through one of the six-packs' plastic rings, and went upstairs. As he closed the basement door, he stopped a moment and looked at the surface bolt on the inside. A stray thought flitted in and out of his head, there and gone in a heartbeat:

Shoulda locked the fuckin' door.

In the kitchen, he replaced the flashlight, then took the shrieking kettle off the burner. He put the beer in the refrigerator. He sat down at the table, put his right elbow on the tabletop and his face in his trembling hand.

When I went down the stairs, Jenna had said, *I was looking at you, but you were* completely *different.*

He scrubbed his face once and his hand scratched over stubble. The pain in his left hand crawled up his arm. He reminded himself he'd just had surgery after experiencing a serious and traumatic accident, and he was under the influence of a powerful narcotic painkiller. Add to that Jenna's ramblings about ghosts and mediums and séances. He shook his head hard again, then got up and poured steaming water into his mug, stirred the instant hot chocolate, then took it back to the table with him.

It was bad enough that Jenna seemed to be reaching out for the kind of crutch David had spent his life trying to avoid. What made it so much worse was the fact that she was starting to make sense.

David had thought the fat man with the gravelly voice only inhabited his dreams. But he had not been dreaming a few minutes ago. Had he? Could the Oxy-Contin be causing him to hallucinate? He looked at the clock and guessed he'd been down there for ten, maybe fifteen minutes. The fat man had been standing directly behind him, then had stepped forward, almost as if he had stepped right *into*—

He laughed into his palm. He refused to take that thought any further. It was a ridiculous thought, and he simply refused to finish it. He laughed a little harder into his palm as a sense of giddiness overwhelmed him. He felt light-headed and suddenly euphoric. It was the painkiller. And so was that thought he'd refused to finish—it was the OxyContin thinking for him, he decided.

I'm not thinking clearly, he thought. *The drugs are messing with me.*

David left his hot chocolate untouched on the table. He went upstairs to bed and was asleep only seconds after putting his head on the pillow.

"Thank you for calling the Phoenix Society of Paranormal Research," a kindly, prerecorded female voice said. "At the tone, please leave your name and telephone number, and a brief description of the paranormal or demonic activity you're reporting. Please speak slowly and clearly so we can understand you. Thank you."

There was a beep, and Jenna opened her mouth, but realized she did not know where to start. She stood alone in the kitchen in jeans and a red sweatshirt, mouth open for several seconds before she said, "I, uh . . . my family and I recently moved, and . . . since we've been in this house, things are happening that I . . ." A sob caught her by surprise, and suddenly she was crying and unable to talk.

After a click on the other end of the line, the same female voice that had been recorded on the answering machine said, "Hello? Are you all right?"

"Oh, I'm so sorry," Jenna said. She quickly looked around to make sure David had not come downstairs. He was still sleeping when she left the bedroom. Martha was taking a shower and Jenna had already driven Miles down to the gate to catch the bus.

"Don't be sorry. I'm Mavis Bingham. What's your name, sweetheart?"

"Juh-Jenna. Jenna Kellar."

"You're having activity of some kind?"

"Oh, God, I don't know *what* we're having."

"Why don't you tell me about it."

A single laugh broke out through Jenna's tears. "I don't know where to begin."

"Just start at the beginning and tell me the whole thing."

She looked around again to make sure she was alone, then told Mavis Bingham everything.

CHAPTER EIGHTEEN

Friday, 8:36 A.M.

Over breakfast at Denny's, Lily opened one of the maps, found Starfish Drive, and worked out the best route there.

"You're just going to knock on their door?" Claudia asked.

"I don't know what else to do. I got the strong sense that Mrs. Kellar was listening very carefully. If I could talk to her alone, I have a feeling she'd be open to it."

"Maybe she'll answer the door," Claudia said.

"We can hope."

It was a gray, misty day, cold and damp. Starfish Drive was flanked by thick forests of pines and firs and birches. Houses were spread out and set well off the road, and several PRIVATE PROPERTY signs were posted on the barbed-wire fences that ran along the road. Mailboxes were clearly numbered, and Claudia slowed as they neared 2204. The mailbox and the numbers and letters neatly arranged on the side looked exactly as they had in Lily's vision. The battered old metal gate stood open. Claudia drove through it and down the gravel road.

When Lily saw the house she had already seen in her visions, she was overwhelmed for a moment by a vertiginous sense of déjà vu. An almond-colored Dodge Durango was parked in front of the closed garage. She knew that behind the house stood a swing set and a slide, and that probably in the house somewhere there was a teddy bear with a winding key sticking out of its back, a bear that played Brahms's "Lullaby" when wound. She had some of the pieces, but was not yet able to put them together.

As Claudia slowed the Beetle to a stop, the front door of the house opened and two women came out. The first was a tall blond woman in jeans and a red sweatshirt whom Lily recognized immediately as Jenna Kellar. The other was a short, plump, busty woman with long dark hair pulled back in a ponytail—Lily had never seen her before and paid little attention to her. Jenna Kellar noticed them first as she and the brunette walked to the front gate, and a worried look darkened her face.

Lily opened the door and got out of the Beetle before Claudia could kill the engine. Her eyes stayed on Jenna Kellar.

"Hello," Lily said as she neared the gate wearing her biggest smile. "You're Mrs. Kellar, right? Jenna Kellar?"

She opened the gate and stepped through, nodding. "Are you from the newspaper? Because I'd rather not—"

"No, my name is Lily Rourke. I called you yesterday, from Mt. Shasta. Your husband, uh . . . he didn't want to talk to me."

"That was you?" Jenna said. She reached out her hand, and Lily shook it gingerly. "I'm sorry about that.

We've been . . . well, things have been very strange around here. This is my friend Kimberly Gimble."

Still smiling, Lily shook Kimberly's hand and said, "Nice to meet you," then turned back to Jenna. "Mrs. Kellar, you have a swing set and a slide in your backyard, don't you?"

Jenna frowned. "Yes, we do. How did you know?"

"I told you, I'm psychic. I've been having visions about you. You have a son. His name is Miles, right?"

Jenna's eyes widened. "Yes. What about him?"

The front door opened and a man came out wearing a baggy gray sweatshirt, blue sweatpants, and slippers. The left sleeve of his sweatshirt dangled at his side, empty. His brown hair was spiky and mussed, and he looked like he'd just gotten out of bed. Jenna glanced over her shoulder when she heard the door shut and saw him coming toward the gate.

"What about my son?" Jenna said, quietly and urgently.

Lily said, "I have a powerful feeling he's in some kind of danger. I think you're all in danger, frankly, but your son most of all. Something in your house—"

"What's up?" the man said as he came through the gate. His weary, puffy eyes moved back and forth between Jenna and Lily, but he faced his wife.

"David, this is Lily Rourke."

He turned to her and frowned. "Lily Rourke?"

Lily sensed a wave of confusion from him—not about her name, but a more general confusion roiling inside him. He was preoccupied, disturbed by something.

"She's the one who called us yesterday," Jenna said. Before he could say anything, she continued quickly. "I think we should listen to her, because she thinks Miles might be in some kind of danger."

"I told you not to call back," David said. "I didn't realize I had to be specific about not dropping by the house."

"Mr. Kellar, if I could just talk with you for a few minutes—"

He turned to Jenna. "Go in the house."

Jenna said, "David, I think we should listen to her."

"We are *not* listening to *any* psychics!" To Lily, he said, "Get back in your car and go. You're not welcome here. If you show up again, I'll call the police."

Kimberly stepped over to Jenna and gave her a brief hug. "I'll call you later today, okay?"

"Okay. Thanks for coming by."

"I mean it," David said, "get out of here now."

"All right, all right," Lily said, taking a few steps back, "I'm not going to argue." She turned to go back to the Beetle as Kimberly walked by her and whispered, "Follow me." Lily walked around the Beetle and smiled at the Kellars, who stood together by the gate. Jenna returned the smile, but David did not. She got into the car as the front door opened and an old woman in a pale green housedress stood in the doorway. Lily wondered if the fat man she had seen lived with them as well. She did not think so—there was something different about him, something very wrong.

"Follow the SUV," Lily said as the Durango backed away from the garage.

Claudia followed the Dodge down the long driveway and turned left onto Starfish, back the way they had come. In town, Kimberly pulled over and parked in front of a small strip mall. Claudia parked beside her as Kimberly got out and came to Lily's side of the Beetle. Lily fingered the button and made the window hum down.

Kimberly said, "I think we should talk."

* * *

David slammed the front door. "You see what's going to happen now?" he said. "We're going to hear from every nut-job psychic and fortune-teller in the country."

Martha had retreated to the kitchen as soon as she heard David shouting. Jenna went into the living room, fingers stuffed into the back pockets of her jeans, and paced. David came in and sat down in the recliner.

"You're making a big mistake, David," she said, fighting to keep her voice low. She was angry too, but she held it in. "We need help, and that woman was offering it. She said we're in danger, that *Miles* is in danger—she knew his *name*. I believe her, because there's something in this house."

"And who told you there was something in the house?" he shouted. "It was one of those damned mediums! They've got you so worked up, you're starting to *believe* their bullshit."

"Before I ever called a medium, I saw things that *made* me believe there's something in this house."

"Look, I'm not in the mood to fight about this. All I'm saying is—no more of this shit. No more psychics or mediums or—"

Jenna put her hands on her hips and took a deep breath before interrupting. "You'll just have to learn to deal with it, David," she said firmly, "because I've already called someone. The Binghams, Arthur and Mavis. They're an older couple. They run the Phoenix Society of Paranormal Research in Arizona. They don't charge anything, not a dime. They're going to be here this weekend to check out the house."

"Check out the— You mean to tell me these people are going to come here all the way from Arizona and they aren't going to want money?"

"Two people have told me, independent of each

other, that there's something in this house, that we're in danger because of it, and that Miles is in danger most of all. You want to ignore that?"

"To ignore it would give it too much significance. I'm going to pretend you never said it and hope all this passes, like a bad mood or something."

"David, I think you know something's wrong, but you won't admit it because it would mean that *you're* wrong, and you just can't stand to be wrong. Am I right? You know *something's* going on in this house."

He averted his eyes a moment, then shook his head and said, "Don't be ridiculous."

"Well, whether you like it or not, the Binghams will be here tomorrow."

"You can call and tell them not to come, or they can make the trip for nothing—it's up to you, but they're *not* coming into this house." He turned and left the living room.

Jenna said to his back, "Well, *I* plan to let them in."

She heard the stairs creak as he went up. Her hands trembled and she noticed she was clenching her teeth. She sat down on the couch and tried to think herself out of being angry, tried to relax. David was in pain, on drugs, and he hadn't slept well—

Because he was out driving around in his sleep *last night!* she thought.

—and on top of that, he was probably boiling with worry inside because he knew it would be a while before he could work again. And David had always resisted anything that smacked of religion or spirituality. It was a racket across the board, as far as he was concerned. It was perfectly natural for him to react so strongly to something like this. But surely it couldn't last. He had to come around, just as she had. She had a feeling he was already having suspicions, but it would take something big to make him admit it—she just hoped that something didn't involve anyone getting hurt, especially Miles.

Martha came into the living room and whispered, "You did the right thing."

Jenna looked up at her mother and appreciated her smile. "You think so?"

Martha nodded. "He'll think so too, eventually." She smiled. "How about I make some corn bread for lunch?"

In a small donut shop in the strip mall, Lily sipped coffee while she listened to Kimberly Gimble.

"Normally, I wouldn't tell you any of this," Kimberly said. "I mean, I don't know you. But Jenna mentioned your call and said she wished she could've talked to you alone. So I think she'd want me to tell you everything, because I don't think David is going to let her."

Kimberly told them everything she knew, paying particular attention to the séance she had attended in Jenna's living room. When Kimberly was finished, Lily said nothing for a long time.

Lily was a psychic, not a medium. While she often received information about the dead, she'd never made any attempt to contact them directly and did not even know if that was possible. She knew, after listening to Kimberly, that these visions were taking her into unfamiliar territory.

"Now that Jenna knows she's not seeing her dead son," Lily said, "what exactly does she think she's seeing?"

"She has no idea. But she's not the only one."

Kimberly told them about the things Martha had

243

seen in her bedroom at night, and that she was now sleeping on the couch, and about the fat man Miles had seen coming out of his bedroom floor.

"Fat man?" Lily said.

"They assumed it was a nightmare, but now she doesn't think so. She lets him sleep with his overhead light on because he says the fat man only comes in the dark."

"Only comes in the dark," Lily muttered. "So there's no fat man living with them."

"No. Did you think there was?"

"I wasn't sure. I've seen a fat man in my visions. In the house. And he's a threat. Especially to the boy."

"Is he . . . well . . . a demon?" Kimberly said.

Lily's instinct was to roll her eyes, but she knew Claudia would disapprove of that, and she didn't want to lose an ally like Kimberly Gimble, so she smiled instead. "This isn't my area of expertise, I'm afraid," she said. "Do you know who lived in the house before the Kellars?"

"Jenna's father. She inherited it from him. She never knew him, though."

"He had other children while he was living in the house?"

"I don't think so, no. Jenna said he lived there with his parents until they died, and then he lived there alone."

"Then why is there playground equipment in the backyard?" Lily said.

"There is?"

"A slide and a swing set."

"How do you—" Kimberly leaned back in her seat and cleared her throat with a small cough. "I'm sorry—never mind."

"Do you know her father's name?"

"No."

"Could you find out?"

"Sure, I guess so."

"If it'll cause trouble for Mrs. Kellar, don't mention that I want to know. Just tell her . . . I don't know, tell her you're curious, that you're wondering if you might have known him when he was alive."

"I can do that."

"Then call Claudia's cell phone." She turned to Claudia and said, "Please give her your number."

Claudia took one of the bookstore's business cards and a pen from her purse and wrote the number on the back. She handed the card to Kimberly.

"Call as soon as you know," Lily said. "And if it's not too much trouble, could you find out right away?"

"Sure." She stood and smiled. "You'll hear from me soon."

While they waited for Kimberly to call, Lily directed Claudia to Eureka's Old Town. Claudia parked the Beetle in a small lot and they strolled the streets, looked into shop windows, and occasionally went inside to browse.

Lily was stroking a beautiful green cashmere scarf in The Irish Shop when Claudia's cell phone chirped. Claudia answered, then handed the phone over to Lily, who stood between the display of scarves and another of sweaters.

"Her father's name was Leonard Baines," Kimberly said. "She knows nothing about him, and her mother doesn't know much more."

"But he lived in the house most of his life."

"Yes, along with his parents, until they died. He killed himself nine months ago."

"Thank you, Kimberly. I'd like to keep in touch, if that's all right with you."

"Sure, if you'd like. But Jenna's already called some-body to come help them with the house. She said David doesn't like it, but she's going to insist. They're coming tomorrow."

Lily closed her eyes a moment. "The Binghams. Arthur and Mavis Bingham."

"Yes, the Binghams. Do you know them?"

"I know of them." Having seen the Binghams in one of her visions, she was not surprised to learn they were involved. But they were only going to make things worse. Lily suspected they were going to find some-thing in the Kellar house for which they were not pre-pared, something much more than the alcoholics and emotional basket cases to which they'd become accus-tomed. "I'm going to hand you back to Claudia so you can give her your phone number."

Claudia quickly dug around in her purse for a pad and pen.

"Thank you for your help," Lily said. She gave the phone to Claudia, then turned back to the scarf she'd been stroking. She turned the name over in her mind: Leonard Baines.

"Okay, I have her number," Claudia said as she put her phone back in her purse.

"Good. Let's go."

"Where are we going now?"

"The police station."

"*Police* station? Why?"

They left The Irish Shop and headed back up the street toward the parking lot where they had left the Beetle, talking as they walked.

"I want to know if the police had any trouble with Leonard Baines while he lived in that house," Lily said.

"What makes you think they'll tell you?"

"I've dealt with the police before. There's a chance they might even have heard of me here."

"Heard of you? Why?"

"Back when I first moved to Mt. Shasta, I helped the police in Redding find a guy who was stabbing young women to death. A few years later, I helped police in Dunsmuir stop a series of rapes that were taking place in the area. That sort of thing has happened a few times over the years. Cops talk, word gets around. Sometimes they've heard of me, sometimes they haven't."

"You've never told me any of this before."

"You've never asked." Lily was getting winded. "Honey, I'm too fat to walk and talk at the same time. Let's wait till we get to the car."

They waited a moment at a corner for the light to turn green before stepping out into the crosswalk. Halfway across the street, Lily smelled bananas. The periphery of her vision began to flash, as if she were flanked by electric-blue strobe lights.

Lily grabbed Claudia's hand and picked up her pace.

"What's wrong?" Claudia said.

Lily stepped up onto the sidewalk on the other side of the street and led Claudia to a bench at a bus stop on the corner. Lily dropped onto the bench, and Claudia perched on the edge of it beside her.

"I can feel one coming on," Lily said. "Please sit with me." She continued to hold Claudia's hand, but her grip loosened as her head fell back and she slipped away.

Eyes still closed a couple minutes later, Lily heard a car horn honk and the sound sent a spike through her skull. She became aware of other sounds around her—traffic, footsteps, voices. The throbbing pain in her head was so bad, she did not want to open her eyes. She felt Claudia's hand still holding hers.

"Has anyone noticed?" she asked quietly before opening her eyes.

"No."

Lily groaned as she sat up on the bench, put a hand to her temple. Her stomach churned and she put her other hand over her mouth and took a couple deep breaths, fighting the urge to vomit.

"You want me to get the car and come pick you up?" Claudia asked.

Lily nodded once and she took off at a run. A couple minutes later, Claudia pulled up at the curb on the corner, reached over, and opened the passenger-side door. Lily wavered a little when she stood, got into the car, and pulled the door closed.

"Do you still want to go to the police station?"

"Take me back to the motel. Quickly." She leaned her head back. "We're running out of time. That boy's in danger."

"Do you know what kind of danger yet?"

"Unless I can intervene somehow, he's going to be killed."

Less than ten minutes later, Lily entered their room at the Motel 6 and went straight to the bathroom to vomit. Afterward, she brushed her teeth, rinsed with mouthwash, then got a pill from her purse and took it with a glass of water. She took her notebook and a pen from her purse and sat on the edge of the bed. In spite of the throbbing pain in her head, she jotted down a few lines of notes about the vision she'd had in town, including two names that had come to her—the names of two little boys whose agonizing cries still remained vivid in her mind: Billy Enders and Jonah Wishman. Then she stretched out on the bed with a groan.

"I don't feel well," she said.

Claudia stood beside Lily's bed. "Is there anything I can do for you?"

Lily patted the mattress and Claudia sat down on the edge of the bed. "Aren't you going to ask me what I saw?" She spoke just above a whisper—to speak any louder made her headache worse.

Claudia shrugged. "I know you'll tell me when you're ready."

"You don't want to know." Lily put both hands over her face and rubbed them up and down, then dropped her arms at her sides and closed her eyes.

"Would you like me to leave you alone for a while? Maybe you should sleep."

"God, no. I'm afraid I'll dream about the vision I had. I'd rather not be alone, if you don't mind sticking around."

Claudia laughed. "Where else am I going to go?"

"You asked me why I've never told you about my experiences with the police. Because they've been mostly unpleasant and I don't like talking about them. The police haven't been unpleasant, but the experiences have."

"How often do they come to you for help?"

"They don't. Well, they have, but I can't really help them when they do. I've tried, but I haven't been much good."

"I don't understand—you . . . can't help them?"

"This gift of mine is very moody. Let's say a woman's missing. The police come to me with some of the woman's personal effects, and they want me to handle them, see if I pick up anything. I'll pick up things, but the chances they'll help them find her are pretty slim.

On the other hand, if I start having a vision about a woman who's, say, locked up in a room somewhere, and I read in a paper that a woman is missing, and she matches the description of the woman in my vision, I can go to the police and give them information that will most likely be helpful. It works when it works."

"Did that really happen? The woman locked in the room?"

"Nine years ago."

"And they found her with your help?"

"Yes. But they don't always turn out that well." Lily took a deep breath, lifted her right arm, and rested her wrist on her forehead. "The year before I met you, an eight-year-old girl went missing in Bend, Oregon. Remember?"

Claudia thought a moment. "Yes, I remember. It was all over the news."

"I kept seeing her in a bathtub in the visions. I went to Oregon and told the police everything I knew. I met the parents. They asked if she was still alive, and I told them I was sure she was because I kept seeing her in a bathtub with bubbles, always smiling every time I saw her. I was sure she was alive." She sighed and dropped her arm. "They found her in a junkyard fifty miles away from the spot where she disappeared. She was lying in an old bathtub wrapped in a plastic tarp. There was snow on her. White snow. Like bubbles in a bubble bath. I couldn't face the parents. I came straight home. I've always felt bad about that, but . . . what could I have said? There was nothing to say."

"I remember that story well," Claudia said. "But I don't remember hearing anything about you. Didn't the police credit finding her to an anonymous tip? Why weren't you given credit?"

"Because I don't *want* credit. It's bad enough that

word gets around among cops. My God, if I showed up in the news once, I'd never have a moment's peace."

"You're probably right."

Lily groaned softly and whispered, "Can you hear my head pounding?"

"You should sleep for a while, let your pill take effect."

Without opening her eyes, Lily whispered, "No, I don't want to waste any time. That boy's in trouble."

"What kind of trouble?"

"I wish I knew. They're very . . . confusing . . . these visions." She hovered on the edge of sleep, thinking about Miles Kellar. "Maybe . . . just until . . . the pill kicks in," Lily muttered just before she drifted off.

Jenna sat on the couch with Martha, watching *Law & Order: Special Victims Unit*, while David snored in the recliner. Miles was upstairs in bed with his overhead light on, sleeping soundly by now, Jenna hoped. The living room was warm from a healthy fire and the only light on was the lamp beside the recliner. The television was the only sound in the house, and even that seemed muted by the smothering atmosphere.

Jenna and David had gone through the usual fights in the early years of their marriage, but none of them had ever lasted long. And none had ever filled the air with as much tension as their disagreement earlier that day. Miles had noticed after getting home from school that afternoon. "Did somebody die?" he'd asked Jenna after being home for only a few minutes. She'd laughed and told him everything was fine, even though they both knew better.

David had spent most of the day in front of the television, where he'd passed in and out of sleep, and spoke only when absolutely necessary.

As she always had whenever she was upset or worried, Martha had baked that afternoon—a batch of black-eyed Susans, David's favorite cookie. But as if he knew Martha had taken Jenna's side, even though Martha had not said a word about anything all day, he'd turned a cold shoulder to the cookies.

Jenna knew a good deal of his behavior was due to the pain in his hand and the powerful painkiller he was taking to fight it off. But she knew just as well that she had made him very angry when she'd told him she intended to let the Binghams in when they arrived the next day.

She was still amazed by how quickly Mavis Bingham had offered to come to Eureka. She had been sweet and friendly on the phone, and Jenna had told her everything—not only about what she'd seen and experienced, but David's strange behavior and everything Martha and Miles had told her as well. Mavis had listened attentively, comforting and calming her when she got upset.

"Listen to me, dear," Mavis had said after Jenna had finished. "I'm going to insist that Arty and I come see you right away."

"Come here?" Jenna had said.

"That's right. You caught us at a perfect time. We just finished an investigation in Georgia—oh, *there's* a story to raise the hair on the back of your neck—and we have nothing on our schedule at the moment. Are you Catholic, dear?"

"No. We're not religious."

"Well, after this, you might feel differently. I can tell that you need help right now, that we shouldn't waste any time—I can feel it."

"You can?"

"I'm clairvoyant, dear, did you know that about me? I'm picking up all kinds of things from you right now, just sitting here on the phone with you. From what you've told me—well, I'm hoping it's not what I *think* it is, but I think we should get out there right away and see what you've got."

"You'd do that?"

"Oh, of course, dear, we do it all the time, it's what we do. We'll catch the first plane out there tomorrow—probably to San Francisco, and then we'll rent a car and come to your house. I will do a reading to see what kind of problem you have. Then we can decide how to deal with it."

"I need to make sure I understand this correctly. I mean, I can't . . . we can't pay you anything for this."

"We wouldn't take it if you could, dear. We don't charge for investigations."

Jenna had given her their address and directions from the airport, and Mavis had said she would call when she knew their schedule. It had been as simple as that.

Mavis had called back an hour later and told Jenna they were scheduled to land in San Francisco at 11:44 A.M. and would show up at the house as soon as they could get there.

Ada had called that afternoon, as well. Fortunately, David had been asleep in his recliner at the time. Jenna told her everything that had happened since Ada had been at the house.

"Dwayne told me whatever you've got beat the hell out of him," Ada had said. "That's typical poltergeist behavior, by the way—the damned things'll knock you silly if you let 'em. But he says it's not a poltergeist." She sounded thoughtful, but at the same time detached. "I wish I could help you, hon. But like I told you before, I don't do that sort of thing anymore. I helped you out 'cause you were nice and, to be honest, I needed the money. But I won't deal with anything violent."

Jenna told her she'd called the Binghams and they would be coming tomorrow.

"Binghams. The name's familiar. But I don't keep up anymore. I don't read the literature. I don't read much of anything anymore—it gives me a headache. Mostly, I just crochet and watch TV. I hope they can help you."

As Jenna hung up the phone, she'd muttered, "Thanks for nothing, Ada."

The television show ended, and Martha stood and said, "I'm going to get ready for bed."

Jenna stood too. "Yeah, I need to get David upstairs." She went to the recliner and gently placed a hand on David's shoulder. "Come on, honey, let's go to bed. Come on."

He grumbled as he sat up, yawned, slowly stood, then went upstairs without a word.

After he was gone, Jenna turned to Martha and whispered, "I'm not looking forward to tomorrow."

"Would you like me to talk to him in the morning?" Martha said. "He might listen to me."

"Maybe. I'll let you know. What am I going to tell Miles?"

"Oh, I think Miles will be a lot more open-minded about this than his daddy."

"Probably. Good night, Mom." She kissed Martha on the cheek.

"Good night, honey. Sleep well. I know I will. I sleep much better out here on the couch."

"I'm glad."

Jenna went into the kitchen and turned out all the lights. On her way down the hall, she paused a moment outside Martha's closed bedroom. When she'd told Mavis Bingham what Martha had seen in there in the dark—*Hanging on the walls and strapped to chairs. Young boys. Naked and bony, like they've been starved*—Mavis had said simply, "Oh, my. Oh, my, my," and her tone had suggested nothing good. But she would say no more about it over the phone.

Jenna slowly climbed the stairs, went down the hallway to the bathroom, and brushed her teeth. In the bedroom, she was relieved to find David asleep.

CHAPTER NINETEEN

Saturday, 1:08 A.M.

Lily woke with a full bladder. The glow of a streetlight outside bled through the closed curtains. Claudia slept in the other bed.

The previous evening, Lily had slept until almost seven, then Claudia had gone out for some take-out Chinese food. Lily had been able to eat only a little wonton soup, while Claudia had eaten everything else. Her head still ached, and she'd taken another Vicodin. By ten o'clock, she'd been back in bed and sound asleep.

It took an effort to get out of bed. Her feet felt like lead weights and her muscles were stiff and achy. She still had a mild headache, and her hands trembled. The visions were steadily sapping her strength. Along with weakness and fatigue, they gave her an increasing sense of urgency. Whatever was going to happen would happen soon.

After emptying her bladder, she left the bathroom

with the light still on and went to the sink just outside the door for a drink of water. She was holding her glass under the tap when she smelled bananas and the flashing began.

"Oh, God," she groaned. "Not again."

She quickly gulped down the water, put the glass down beside the sink, and turned off the tap. She turned to go back to the bed, but felt her strength draining from her quickly. Before blacking out, she managed to say, "Claudia!"

Lily sees through someone else's eyes.

Walking steadily down a dark hallway, then down a staircase, right hand on the banister. Turning left at the bottom into a short, dark hallway. But the eyes are adjusted to the dark and can see the familiar surroundings.

There is throbbing pain in the left hand, which feels enormous. The left arm is in a sling, because to let it hang loose at the side only makes the throbbing worse.

Walking down the hall, pausing for just a moment to look to the left at a mirror on the wall. In the glass, she sees the leering face of the fat man. Small eyes lost in shadow beneath the brim of the forward-tilted cowboy hat. Gray stubble on the lower half of the fat, jowly face and pendulous double-chin.

Walking on down the hall, to the end, turning right, into a dark kitchen. To the refrigerator, opening the door with the right hand. The refrigerator light is blinding in the darkness. Reaching into the refrigerator, jerking a can of Michelob beer from its plastic ring. Putting it on the counter and popping it open as the refrigerator door slowly swings closed on its own. Taking a few swallows of the beer. Turning and leaving the kitchen, walking back down the hall.

A sense of delicious anticipation, of growing sexual excitement—the churning of an insatiable carnal hunger.

Turning to the right and holding the beer under the chin while opening a door. Stepping into a dark room and pausing to close the door again.

Taking a few swallows of the cold beer, then looking around in the dark. It takes a moment for the eyes to adjust to the utter darkness in the room. Then seeing them . . .

Three boys on the wall, arms stretched taut over their heads, naked and terrified. Their terror is exciting, invigorating. A smaller boy with red hair and freckles is strapped into the high chair.

Deep inside and far away, Lily's own consciousness recoils in horror.

Whispering, "Bad puppies. Gotta take care a the bad fuckin' puppies."

The music woke Jenna again. She sat up and found the filthy old teddy bear lying at the foot of the bed playing Brahms's "Lullaby." Standing in the dark nearby were three small figures. She rubbed her eyes, turned to look down at David. He was gone.

Jenna reached over and turned on her bedside lamp. The three figures that had been standing at the foot of the bed disappeared. She looked around the room. The bottom drawer of the chest in her closet was open again. The bowling ball in its bag had been pushed aside.

She thought about David walking in his sleep—*driving* in his sleep—and threw the covers aside and got out of bed. She put on her robe as she hurried out of the bedroom with bare feet.

Miles's bedroom door was open. His overhead light lit up a section of the hallway.

The bathroom was dark and unoccupied.

Jenna went downstairs and turned on the hall light without slowing her pace. She went down the hall and into the kitchen. There were no lights on, so she flipped the switch just inside the door and the rectangular fluorescent overhead flickered on.

The Mag-Lite stood undisturbed beside the locked back door. The laundry room was dark, the basement door closed.

She went through the dining room into the living room, where it was still warm from the remaining embers in the fireplace. Martha was asleep on the couch. Jenna checked the front door, made sure the deadbolt was still locked, then went back through the dining room and kitchen and into the laundry room, where she turned on the light. She opened the door to the garage, reached out, and turned on the light. The pickup and Toyota were both there.

Jenna was wide awake now. Her heart machine-gunned beneath her ribs as she turned off the garage light, closed the door, and left the laundry room. She left the kitchen, intending to go back upstairs and check the computer room, but stopped in the hall when she heard a low, muffled voice, then laughter. She turned back and went to the door of Martha's bedroom, leaned close to it, and listened.

"You gonna be good puppies from now on?" Then deep, throaty laughter.

It did not sound like David, but she knew it had to be. She turned the knob and pushed the door open, but did not step in yet.

Light from the hallway spilled into the bedroom and fell on David. He stood barefoot in his robe with his back to her, a beer in his right hand. The robe's left sleeve hung empty from the shoulder, and the untied belt dangled at his sides.

"David?" she said, her voice hoarse. He turned toward her, and she gasped.

259

Once again, he stood with shoulders back and hips thrust forward. The robe was open in front and he wore nothing underneath. His face had been transformed—forehead creased with a deep frown, a grin peeled back over his teeth.

"What the fuck're you doin' here?" he said, his voice low and throaty. He put the beer on a dresser and walked with a lazy swagger as he came toward her.

Jenna stepped into the room and said loudly, *"David!"*

He stabbed his left elbow into her left shoulder and knocked her aside, saying, "Get outta my help me fucking Jenna way."

Jenna stumbled sideways and fell to the floor in front of Martha's vanity. She lay there motionless for a moment, digesting what she had just heard: *Get outta my help me fucking Jenna way.*

David's bare feet thumped up the stairs.

Jenna thought of Miles sleeping in the bright light of his room. She scrambled to her feet, left the room, and hurried up the stairs as the door of Miles's bedroom slammed shut, darkening the hallway. She was afraid her heart was going to explode. She had never moved so fast before in her life.

Back up the stairs, down the hallway, quickly, quickly. The open door on the left—step inside, turn and close it.

In passing, Lily glimpses the digital clock on the bedstand, shaped like a flying saucer. It reads 1:19.

The boy, Miles Kellar, sits up in bed, eyes wide, mouth forming an O. "Dad?"

The throat laughs as the right hand reaches out for the covers and rips them off the boy.

In Spider-Man pajamas, Miles screams, uses his feet to push himself back against the headboard, hands clutching the crushed pillow.

Climbing onto the bed and laughing as the right hand reaches out for the boy . . .

Jenna burst into Miles's bedroom, shouting, *"David!"*

He was kneeling on the bed, with Miles pressed against the headboard, screaming. Ignoring her, David tore Miles's pajama top open and the buttons scattered through the air, over the rug, chittered on the hardwood floor.

Jenna went to the bed and grabbed David's right arm. "David, stop it!" she shouted. "Leave him alone! Let him go!" She tried to pull his hand away from Miles, but his fist clutched Miles's pajama top. Miles continued to scream, and the sound was filled with fear and confusion. Jenna pounded on David's back with her fists as she shouted for him to let Miles go.

Miles kicked his legs and flailed his arms. His pajama top tore away from him with a sharp ripping sound, and a section of it dangled from David's fist. As he struggled to get off the bed, Miles knocked over his bedstand, and the small lamp and flying-saucer clock went with it. David hooked his right arm around Miles's torso and growled, "Fuckin' puppy." As he pulled Miles back onto the bed, he raised his left arm, bent at the elbow in the sling, out at his side for balance.

Jenna turned to the desk and took a fat hardcover dictionary from the desktop. Hefting the book in both hands, she raised it over her head. She threw herself forward as she brought the dictionary down hard on David's bandaged left hand.

David's scream was high and shrill with agony. He fell off the bed and landed on his back on the floor as his scream collapsed into a growl, then a groan. Then a sickened retch.

The overhead light went out with a *pop* and sparks

rained down in the darkness. The temperature dropped suddenly, and Jenna knew something was in the room with them—the thing that had, a moment before, been inside David. Whatever doubts she'd had were wiped out with the certainty that something had commandeered David's body.

Miles sobbed as Jenna found him in the dark and took him in her arms.

After the explosion of pain, Lily rises up until she is looking down on the Kellars—Jenna on the bed, still holding the book, Miles curled into a ball against the headboard, and David sprawled on the floor.

As the light goes out, Lily begins to sink, lower and lower, until she passes down through the floor into corrupt and filthy darkness and—

Lying facedown on the motel room carpet, Lily opened her eyes. Pain hammered behind her eyes and her stomach was upside-down, but a surge of adrenaline made her roll onto her side and get to her knees. She crawled to the bed, climbed up, and sat on it. "What time is it? How long was I out?"

"Longer than usual," Claudia said. Her voice was shaky and she was pale. "It's one twenty-four. For crying out loud, Lily, I can't take that. I almost called an ambulance. The only reason I didn't was that you kept talking."

"I did?"

"Yeah. You kept saying, 'Real time, real time.'"

Lily nodded once, the heels of her hands placed over her eyes. "That's what it was. I realized it when I saw the clock in the boy's bedroom. It was a real-time vision."

"What do you mean?"

"I was seeing something as it happened. Something in

the Kellar house. And I was seeing it through David Kellar's eyes. Except . . . it wasn't David Kellar." Lily stretched out on the bed and pressed the heels of her hands to her eyes.

Claudia said, "What do you mean?"

"I was seeing through David Kellar's eyes, but I was . . . I was in something—no, some*one* else. There was someone else inside David Kellar. The fat man with the cowboy hat—I was inside *him*, and *he* was inside David Kellar. Does that make sense?"

"You're saying David Kellar was . . . possessed?"

"You could put it that way. I was feeling horrible, *sick* things. But it wasn't David Kellar who was feeling them, it was the fat man with the cowboy hat."

Eyes narrowing, Claudia said, "Who's the fat man with the cowboy hat?"

"Someone who wants Miles Kellar very much." She released a long sigh and said, "We've got to get the Kellars out of that house, especially the boy. And we don't have much time."

Jenna's arms trembled in the dark as she held Miles, who clung to her as if for life. But he had stopped crying— he seemed to be listening for something. David retched on the floor beside the bed.

From downstairs, Martha shouted, "What's wrong?"

Jenna shouted back, "We're okay, Mom. I'll be down in a minute." Then, to Miles: "You're okay, right, honey?"

He nodded and slowly loosened his hold on her, cautiously pulled away.

Jenna's eyes adjusted to the darkness and she saw Miles look around the room. The mattress shifted as David leaned his right arm on it and pulled himself up. Miles made a small, frightened sound in his throat and pulled Jenna with him as he backed away from his dad.

David's voice was a dry croak. "I'm so sorry. I . . . it wasn't . . . I didn't—"

"It wasn't you, David," Jenna said. She turned to Miles. "That wasn't your dad, honey. There is something in this house, some kind of . . . presence. And it was inside your dad. Do you understand? It *made* him do that." To David: "It wasn't *you*, David. When it came out of you, the light blew out and the temperature dropped in the room, just like it did in the living room with Ada and with Dwayne Shattuck."

"The fat man," Miles said.

Jenna nodded. "Yes, the fat man. Honey, I'm so sorry I didn't listen to you. I've seen the fat man, too."

Miles's eyes widened for a moment, but he said nothing.

David slowly got to his feet and closed his robe. Jenna could tell by his posture, straight but weary, that he was himself again. "Did you hear me, David? Do you understand what I'm saying? That wasn't *you*."

David's head drooped as he nodded. "Yes. You're right, Miles, it was the fat man. He wears a cowboy hat, right?"

"Is *that* what's on his head?" Miles said. "I couldn't tell what it was in the dark."

Jenna pulled Miles to her and embraced him again. "You haven't been dreaming. I don't know exactly what he is, but he's real. I'm so sorry we didn't believe you when you told us it wasn't just a nightmare."

"That's okay," Miles said. "I guess if somebody told me a fat man was coming up through the bedroom floor, I probably wouldn't believe it, either."

Jenna kissed his forehead, stood, and faced David. "What are we going to do?"

"We're going to turn on every damned light in this house." He looked down at Miles and said, "Hey, Tiger, how would you like to stay up all night and watch TV?"

They went downstairs to the living room and turned on lights along the way.

David got the fire going again as Miles opened his sleeping bag on the floor in front of the television. He curled up in the bag to watch an old Tarzan movie. Martha sat on the couch and sipped a cup of tea.

Jenna and David sat together in the breakfast nook, where, for about fifteen minutes, David sobbed as she held him.

"Maybe the Binghams can help us," Jenna said once he had calmed down.

David slowly turned his head from side to side. "Maybe they can, but . . . nobody will ever be able to erase what happened tonight. Jenna, it was . . . it was like having a nightmare while I was half awake. The things that went through my mind . . . the horrible, sick thoughts and feelings—"

"They weren't *your* thoughts and feelings. You weren't in control, David. But you had enough presence of mind to ask me for help."

He turned to her with red-rimmed eyes. "You heard me?"

"Yes. It came through, I heard you."

He nodded slowly as he turned away. He told her about his experiences in the house—things that he'd thought, until then, were nothing more than dreams. "These things in my head, these images," he said, "I don't know where they came from. They're . . . sick."

"That's what Dwayne said—whatever is in this house, it's sick."

"What makes you think these people can help? What's their name again?"

"The Binghams." She got up, went around the table, and sat down in Martha's spot. She found the copy of the *Inquisitor* with the article about the Binghams in it. She opened the paper to the article and slid it across the table to David. "The *Inquisitor* covers most of their investigations, according to Mom. She's been reading about them for years. She's read some of their books, too."

"I didn't know your mom believed in this crap," he said as he skimmed the article.

"I was surprised, too."

David looked at her with puffy, red-rimmed eyes. "They sound religious."

"They are. They're Catholic."

"I don't know if I like the idea of a couple religious fanatics coming into the house and spouting their mumbo jumbo."

"I'm not crazy about it either, honey," Jenna said. She reached across the table and put her hand on his. "But what else are we going to do? Do *you* have any ideas? At least they have experience with this sort of thing. It's like with the wiring—we've got to bring in someone who knows what they're doing."

Looking weary and troubled, he nodded. "I guess we don't have much choice."

Jenna made a pot of coffee and they took their cups to the living room. They said little as they sat in the warmth of the fire with the television on, along with every light in the house.

The Binghams, Jenna thought, could not arrive soon enough.

* * *

Chief Oscar Winningham of the Eureka Police Department stood when the desk sergeant escorted them into his office. He was a bearish man in his late fifties, with a voice so deep and booming that Lily could feel it in her chest when he spoke. She felt it behind her eyes, too, where a dull pain steadily throbbed.

Winningham's office was not large, but it was neat—except for his desk, which was cluttered with papers, manila folders and envelopes, a few books. Behind it on an old scuffed credenza was a cluster of framed photographs arranged around a few tall awards from community organizations. A stuffed marlin at least four feet long was mounted on the wall above the credenza and dominated the room.

Lily and Claudia sat in front of Winningham's desk in a couple of metal-framed chairs with dark green vinyl-upholstered seat- and back-cushions.

Winningham's dark hair was cut short and streaked with white. Bushy salt-and-pepper eyebrows rested on the top edge of his wire-framed glasses like exotic caterpillars napping. His nose was bulbous, and when he smiled, his twinkling green eyes nearly disappeared into slits bracketed by crow's-feet. He wore khaki pants and a long-sleeved blue-and-yellow plaid shirt that strained slightly against his barrel-like torso. He lowered himself into his squeaky chair behind the desk and leaned forward toward Lily and Claudia.

"Lily Rourke," he said. "How about that. You're lucky you caught me. I was just on my way out to go fishing. I came in to do a couple things, but didn't plan on staying. In fact, I'm running a little late, but that's okay." He did not stop smiling as he put his forearms on the desk and joined his large hands together. "Would either of you like some coffee?"

"No, thank you," Claudia said.

They'd gone to Denny's again for breakfast and Lily had ordered a bowl of cream of wheat, which she'd hardly touched. She could use some coffee because she'd slept very little the night before, but she still felt mildly nauseated. "Nothing for me, thanks," she said. "I'll try to keep this short."

"Don't worry about the time," Winningham said. "It's my boat, so nobody's going anywhere till I get there. What can I do for you? What brings you to Eureka?"

"I'm here to help a family that may be in some trouble."

"What kind of trouble?"

"I'm not sure yet—that's the problem. I'm afraid I can't give you any kind of explanation other than I . . . well, I *know* this family is in trouble. And I think it has something to do with the house they live in. More specifically, with the person who lived there before them."

Half his smile fell away and the exotic caterpillars sleeping on the top rim of his glasses suddenly rushed together and almost collided above his nose. "If these people are in any kind of danger, you need to tell me so I can—"

"No, it's not a police matter. Not yet, anyway."

"Could you give me some idea of what you're talking about?"

Lily hesitated a moment. "You said you've heard of me?"

He smiled again. "Most of the cops I know have heard of you. The ones in California, anyway. You may not take any public credit for what you do, but cops talk."

"I'm glad. That means I don't have to explain myself.

Sometimes that's difficult. I think the problem this family is dealing with is supernatural."

"Supernatural."

"Yes."

"Is this about the ghost that beat up the medium the other day?"

"It's connected, yes. I hope this doesn't change your mind about talking to me."

"No, no. You're the expert. But as long as no laws are being broken and nobody's in trouble, then why come to me?"

"I need to learn as much as I can about the man who lived in the house prior to this family."

Winningham's eyes narrowed. "Wait a second. That would be—"

"Leonard Baines. He lived on—"

"Lenny Baines on Starfish Drive?" Winningham said.

"Leonard Baines is all I have. It's possible that he went by Lenny."

The chair squeaked as Winningham sat back. "That story about the ghost that beat up the trucker who talks to dead people—that took place in Lenny's old house. I understand his daughter inherited it."

"That's right. So you're familiar with Leonard Baines?"

"Everybody here knew Lenny."

Lily nodded. "I thought that might be the case. What kind of trouble was he in?"

"Trouble? Lenny was never in any trouble. He was a little goofy, I guess, and he liked to drink, but he never got into trouble. It was terrible what happened last year, Lenny taking his own life. A lot of people were real sad about that. But there was no funeral. That's the way Lenny wanted it. No funeral, no memorial, he just wanted to be cremated and his remains disposed of.

Good ol' Lenny Baines. Are you sure we're talking about the same person?" He leaned forward again, no longer smiling.

"If he lived at 2204 Starfish Drive, then yes. Tell me about him."

"Lenny was always helping us out with charitable activities."

"Us?" Lily said.

"Yeah, the department, Eureka PD. He worked hard on the toy drive every Christmas. He played Santa Claus after our regular Santa, Hank Darby, died of a heart attack. And every spring, Lenny put on an Easter egg hunt for a group of handicapped kids. For a few years in a row, he threw the department's summer barbecue for underprivileged kids in his backyard. He set up a slide and swing for the kids. No, Lenny was never in any trouble. Just the opposite. Everybody who knew Lenny liked him. His parents were good folks, too."

"When did all that stop?" Lily asked.

Winningham looked at her a moment wearing a slight smile, impressed that she knew it had stopped. "About nine, ten years ago. It stopped a little at a time. First he quit opening his place up to the kids. Then he pulled out of the toy drive one Christmas. In a couple years, he'd stopped doing everything, and suddenly we realized we hadn't seen Lenny around in months. Months became a year, two years, three. Somebody dropped in on him one day. He was drunk and cranky and alone, and that's exactly what he wanted. So we left him alone. He was never any trouble. As much as he drank, he was never once charged with DWI, didn't even get any speeding tickets. None within the city limits, anyway."

"These charity events—" Lily's voice broke, and she

stopped, cleared her throat. "They always involved children?"

Winningham's eyes narrowed, and he cocked his head. "If you're suggesting something, Miss Rourke, I wish you'd come right out and say it."

Lily felt Winningham's defensiveness and decided to say no more about Leonard Baines for the moment. "No. I'm not suggesting anything. But I do need to ask about children. Have there been an inordinate number of children disappearing in this area?"

"What exactly are you getting at?"

"Chief Winningham, if I knew what I was getting at, I'd get at it. I'm trying to piece together some images I've been seeing, images I don't completely understand. They involve children. Young boys."

"Images? You mean . . . visions?"

"Yes, visions."

Winningham thought about it a moment, shook his head. "No, I can't say we've had any more children disappear around here than in any other town this size. It happens, but there hasn't been an increase in the years I've been in this department, and I've been here forever, it seems. Coming up on thirty-one years."

Lily picked up her purse from the floor and put it on her lap. She removed a pen and a small pad, and wrote down two names: Billy Enders and Jonah Wishman. She tore the page out and handed it across the desk and said, "These are the names of two young boys. I think they might have been from around here."

Winningham frowned at the names. "They don't ring a bell, but I'll have Merry run a search on them."

"Could you do that right away?" Lily said. "I'm sorry if I'm imposing, but it's very important. I think time is a factor in this."

"Merry's not in right now, but she'll be back around noon. Leave a number where one of us can reach you."

"I appreciate that, Chief."

He said, "I'm still very curious as to why you're asking about Lenny Baines."

"You knew him well?" Lily asked.

"Took him out on the boat fishing a few times. Mostly I saw him when he got involved in some department charity. I can't say I knew him well, but I knew him."

"Can you tell me what he looked like?"

"Lenny? Oh, he was a big guy, got pretty fat in his later years, even fatter than me." He turned to the credenza behind his desk. His hand moved in a circle in the air above the framed photographs a few times, then dove like a bird of prey and plucked a single picture out of the group. "This is from one of the Christmas parties." He handed the silver-framed photograph across the desk to Lily.

There were five people in the picture, all in uniform but one. Lily recognized him instantly. The sight of him in a pair of denim overalls and a red-and-black plaid shirt with his white cowboy hat in hand made her feel light-headed for a moment. "That's him, all right," she muttered.

Claudia got up, stood behind Lily, and looked at the picture over her shoulder.

Leonard Baines stood with Winningham and three uniformed officers in front of a Christmas tree. Baines stood in the center and Winningham had an arm around his shoulders. His graying hair was thinning on top, stringy and in need of a cut on the sides and in back. His mouth was askew in a lopsided smile, which revealed a molar with a shiny silver cap.

She handed the photograph back to Winningham and he replaced it on the credenza. "Did anything . . . bad ever happen at Lenny Baines's house?"

"Anything *bad?* What do you mean?"

"I'm not sure. Something you'd remember. Any deaths in the house?"

"Only his mother. She died in her sleep. His dad died in the hospital. And, of course, Lenny."

"Were you ever inside Lenny's house?"

"I was over there several times. But I don't remember if . . ." The creases in the chief's forehead deepened. "You know, now that I think about it, I don't believe I was ever inside Lenny's house. Why do you ask?"

"Again, I'm just curious. I'm groping around for questions as well as answers." Lily turned to Claudia. "Could you give the chief your cell phone number, please?"

Claudia and Winningham exchanged cell phone numbers, each written on the back of a business card.

"How long do you plan to be in town, Miss Rourke?" Winningham said.

"I'm not sure. As long as I need to be. Thank you for your number. I promise not to abuse it."

"Feel free to call me if you need anything. I'll be out on the boat today, but other than that, I'm happy to help in any way I can."

Lily thanked Winningham again for his time, and she and Claudia left his office and the police station.

"My God," she said in the car. "Children. He surrounded himself with children."

Claudia said, "Where do you want to go next?"

"I have to sleep. My head is killing me and I feel like puking. Take me back to the motel. You can go shopping, if you'd like, or do some sight-seeing."

"Okay. The motel it is."

"Would you mind leaving your cell phone with me? I want to know what this Merry comes up with."

"Sure."

Lily leaned her head back and groaned. "I'm worried, Claudia. I can't help them if I can't talk to them."

"Get some sleep first. We can try again this afternoon."

Lily glanced at the small digital clock above the rearview mirror. It was 9:51 A.M. "Yeah. This afternoon."

CHAPTER TWENTY

Saturday, 2:12 P.M.

Mavis Bingham reminded Jenna of Marge Simpson with her tall bouffant of blue-tinted silver hair. Mavis was slender and tall, about five feet ten inches, but the hair made her appear even taller. She was almost regal in bearing, with razor-straight posture. In what was probably an effort to disguise her wrinkles, Mavis wore a bit too much makeup, which only accentuated them. The deep-red lipstick she wore had feathered around the edges of her lips, where she had tiny fine wrinkles on top and bottom. She wore a white blouse under a dark blue blazer and a matching A-line skirt, stockings, and black leather pumps. She had a black leather satchel slung over her shoulder and wore glasses with large amber tortoiseshell frames. The moment she stepped into the house, she stopped and pressed her right hand flat against her abdomen as she looked around, mouth open. "Oh, my," she said.

Arthur Bingham stepped around his wife, grabbed

David's hand, and pumped it with enthusiasm. "Arthur Bingham, but everybody calls me Arty." Arty was about four inches shorter than his wife and looked trim and fit for a man in his late sixties. His movements were quick and birdlike, and he never held still. He wore a dark gray suit with no tie, his light blue shirt open at the neck. His crew-cut hair was white, his features strong, ears prominent, and his crooked smile was warm.

When Arty stopped shaking his hand, David's arm dropped limply to his side. His eyes were only half open, the flesh beneath them puffy and dark. He wore an old Giants sweatshirt he'd had forever and a pair of jeans and sneakers. He hadn't shaved and his jaw was stubbly.

Miles played checkers with his grandma in the kitchen, where Martha had a batch of brownies baking in the oven.

"You people look like you haven't been getting much sleep," Arty said.

Jenna said, "We had an awful night last night."

"I'm getting some pretty strong feelings from this house," Mavis said. She wandered over to the foot of the stairs and stood staring up them for a moment, then turned and came back to her husband's side. "There's something powerful in here."

"We brought two of our students along, Shannon and Willy," Arty said. "They're back at the hotel right now, but they'll join us later. They came to help and observe."

"They're delightful young people," Mavis said.

"Can we sit down and talk before we get started?" Arty said. "I'd like to explain what we're gonna do, let you know what to expect."

"Sure," Jenna said, taking David's hand. She led them to the living room, where the Binghams sat on the couch and David in his recliner. "There's a pot of coffee brewing," she said.

"No coffee for me," Arty said. "But I'd be very grateful for a glass of ice water."

"I take my coffee black," Mavis said.

"I'll be right back," Jenna said. In the kitchen, she got a glass from the cupboard, ice cubes from the freezer, and filled the glass at the tap.

From the breakfast nook, Martha said, "They're here?"

"Yes. Arty doesn't want any and Mavis takes hers black. Will you bring it?"

"Soon as it's ready." Martha had dressed up for the occasion—she wore dark green pants and a yellow blouse. Although she hadn't admitted it, Jenna knew Martha was excited about meeting the Binghams. She had been reading about them in the *Global Inquisitor* for years, and to her, they were celebrities.

Jenna went to the table and kissed the top of Miles's head. "You ready to come out and meet our company, honey?"

David said, "Are they the ghostbusters?"

"Don't call them that," Jenna said. "Be polite."

Martha said, "We'll finish this game later."

Miles went with Jenna to the living room, where she introduced him as she gave Arty the ice water. Arty and Mavis took a moment to fawn over him, told him he was a handsome young man, and Miles smiled and blushed with embarrassment.

Miles sat on the floor beside the recliner and Jenna took the straight-back chair.

Mavis said to Jenna, "Your husband just told us about his terrible accident."

"You're taking painkillers?" Arty said.

David nodded. "OxyContin."

Arty and Mavis exchanged a knowing look. Arty said, "Drugs and alcohol weaken the mind and spirit and leave you open to demonic assault. The first thing we ask people in our investigations is if they use drugs or alcohol, and if there's a problem with substance abuse in the family. Is there?"

David shook his head as Jenna said, "No, we seldom drink and we don't use drugs at all. Except for David's prescription, of course."

To Jenna and David, Arty said, "Has anyone in your family dabbled with the occult? Have you had any tarot cards or Ouija boards in the house?"

Jenna's eyes widened. "I had a medium come in to see if she could deal with . . . well, whatever it is. She conducted what she called a sitting with a Ouija board."

Another knowing look passed between Arty and Mavis.

"There were problems before that?" Mavis asked.

"Yes, that's why I invited her in," Jenna said.

Arty said, "I see. I bet things have gotten worse since then, haven't they?"

"Well . . . yes, they have," Jenna said.

Arty became very solemn. "Ouija boards are extremely dangerous," he said. "Eighty to ninety percent of all our investigations start with a Ouija board in the house. The board opens a doorway to the spirit world that only invites trouble."

Jenna remembered how much the board had frightened Kimberly.

Mavis said, "It's an open invitation to demonic activity. Now, you said you're not Catholic, correct?"

"That's right," Jenna said.

"What religion are you?" Arty asked.

"We aren't religious," David said.

Arty frowned. "You have no religious beliefs at all?"

"No," David said.

"Then I need to make something clear," Arty said. "Mavis and I are devout Catholics. We do this work in the Lord's name. One of the first things we recommend to anyone having negative supernatural activity in their home is that everyone in the household be baptized in the Catholic church. Being baptized gives you the spiritual armor you'll need to stand up to whatever forces you're dealing with."

Jenna glanced at David and saw that he was fidgeting in the recliner. If he decided to send the Binghams on their way, it would be over religion.

David shook his head. "I'm sorry, but we have no interest in being baptized."

Irritated, Arty said, "No *wonder* you're being spiritually assaulted. How can you expect to—"

Mavis patted his knee and said, "Let's wait until we've heard their story, dear." To Jenna and David, she said, "Why don't you tell us what's been happening? Start at the beginning and tell us everything."

Lily had gone to sleep shortly after getting back to the motel that morning, and Claudia had gone out to do some window-shopping and sight-seeing. Lily was in a deep sleep when Claudia's cell phone trilled on the bed-stand at 2:47 in the afternoon. It stopped twenty seconds later without waking her.

Martha had joined them in the living room with four cups of coffee on a tray, and Jenna had introduced her. Once everyone had a cup, Martha put the tray on the coffee table and sat down in her usual spot at the end of the sofa, next to Mavis. Jenna scooted the straight-back chair closer to the recliner and sat in it before she started. She did most of the talking—Martha and Miles spoke up to tell of their own experiences, and finally, David. His words came haltingly, and he often stared down at his lap as he spoke. Other than giving a brief description of the fat man, he said little, only that the thing that had been inside him was horribly sick and twisted.

"What do you know about the house?" Mavis asked.

Jenna said, "Only that my father lived here with his parents until they died, and then alone until he killed himself."

"Suicide generates some very negative vibrations," Mavis said. "It often attracts supernatural activity, sometimes even demonic entities."

"This sounds demonic to me," Arty said. "But we won't know for sure until Mavis does a reading. That's the next step. Mavis will walk through the house. Being clairvoyant, she's highly sensitive to psychic vibrations. You can think of her as a doctor—she's going to examine the house and then give us a diagnosis." He turned to Mavis. "You ready, honey?"

"Yes," she said as she stood. "I like to do the first walk-through alone so I'm not distracted. I hope you don't mind."

"No, I don't mind," Jenna said. She looked at David and saw him press his lips tightly together and frown. She knew he did not like the idea, and normally he would probably voice his objection to a total stranger wandering through their house alone. But he was holding back. His eyes met Jenna's for a moment, and his frown dissolved as one corner of his mouth turned up in a weary smile.

"Yeah, go ahead," David said.

"All right," Mavis said on her way out of the room, "I think I'll start upstairs."

Arty was an animated talker—he sat back, forward,

back, gestured with his hands and arms as he spoke, bobbed his head, tilted it this way, that way. He sounded as if he were talking against the clock.

"We need to talk a little about religion, David," Arty said. "You don't sound like you're even a little bit interested, though."

"I'm just not a believer, that's all," David said.

"Like I said, we do this for the Lord. We're very passionate about our faith, and without it, we couldn't do what we do, Mavis and I. We deal with demons. Fallen angels, Satan's minions. Our faith is our armor, and we can't help you without it. One of the first things we do in our investigations is put a religious icon of some kind in every room in the house. The icons are very powerful, what they stand for is strong, and they will help protect us from the demons."

David said, "You mean, like crosses?"

"Crucifixes, saints, images of Jesus or Mary, anything like that. If you don't have any, we have some you can use."

"What if we don't do that?" David said.

"Then we can't help you. I wouldn't think of dealing with demonic forces without the protection of religious icons. Look, if you don't want to believe in them, that's fine. But we need them for what we do, or we can't do it."

When David looked at her again, Jenna nodded once and smiled. "Okay," he said. "But we're not going to be baptized."

"But that's more armor, David," Arty said. "When you're dealing with demons, you need all the armor you can get, and from what you've told us, I'd guess you've got a demonic infestation here."

"Well, that's not going to happen," David said.

Arty clenched his jaw a few times, rocked back and

forth on the couch, agitated, and a frown crawled over his forehead. "I think it's a mistake. I think if you—"

Mavis's scream brought Arty to his feet. Miles scrambled up off the floor and Jenna and David stood and hurried out of the room with Arty. Jenna had to tug on Miles's shirt to keep him from running ahead of all of them. When they reached the stairs, Mavis was hurrying down them. At the bottom, she stood with her right palm against her chest, which rose and fell with her quick breaths.

"Oh, my God," Mavis said, her voice deep and tremulous. Even with all the makeup, Mavis looked pale, and she swayed unsteadily. Arty rushed to her side and put an arm around her.

"What happened?" he said. "What'd you see?" Mavis leaned on Arty, and for a moment, they made an odd sight—the statuesque woman tilting to lean on the short, fidgety man. Arty said, "Are you all right?"

Mavis turned to look back up the stairs again before walking through the entryway and into the living room. Everyone followed as she went to the coffee table and took a drink of Arty's ice water, then sat down on the couch. Arthur sat down beside her, still concerned. She turned to him and said in a firm, level voice, "There is something in this house."

Jenna asked, "What did you see? The fat man? One of the boys?"

Mavis's mouth hung open for a moment as she looked up at Jenna. Her voice was hoarse as she said, "Yes. The little boy, the toddler. He . . . he came out of the wall, but he was . . . he looked . . ." She took another drink of water and turned to Arthur. "There's something in this house."

"Is it demonic?" Arthur said. "What kind of feelings did you get?"

Still looking at him, she spoke again, firmly. "*Strong* feelings, Arthur. There's *something* in this *house*."

He nodded and looked up at David and Jenna and Martha. "Demonic. That's what I thought."

Mavis finished the ice water, put the glass on the tray, and stood. "Arthur, I need to speak with you privately for a moment."

"Huh-what?" Arthur said as he stood. Mavis took his hand and led him to the entryway, where she whispered to him by the front door.

"Whatever it is," Martha said quietly, "it's sure not trying to hide from anybody." She put a hand on Miles's shoulder and said, "How about some brownies?"

Martha and Miles went to the kitchen. David sat down in the recliner, Jenna in the straight-back chair. After several seconds of whispering back and forth, Arty and Mavis came back into the room. As they went to the couch and sat down, Arty smiled a bit nervously and said, "Mavis and I have a kind of shorthand we've developed over the years. Sometimes we just have to step aside and talk alone for a minute. She says whatever's in this house, it's powerful. And judging by what you've told us, it's obviously malicious, which is why I think it's demonic."

To Mavis, Jenna said, "Do you want to go through the rest of the house?"

Mavis spoke rapidly. "Not right now, no, thank you, dear—that shook me up, and I'd like to wait awhile before I do any more." Her whole face seemed to have collapsed a little, and her hands fumbled with each other.

"I think we should call in Father Malcolm," Arty said.

"For an exorcism?" Jenna said.

"Possibly. But first, this house needs to be blessed." He reached into Mavis's satchel on the floor and removed a cell phone and handed it to Mavis. "Call Father Malcolm, Momma, tell him to catch the next plane here."

"I think he's in San Francisco this weekend. If so, he could be here in hours."

Jenna saw Mavis's hands tremble as she made the call, saw her toss a few uncertain glances at her husband.

Arty said, "We're going to have to invite Jesus Christ into your home, Mr. and Mrs. Kellar. Can you deal with that?"

David sighed as he looked over at Jenna, and they both nodded.

"Good," Arty said solemnly. "You told me you aren't a believer. Well, what happens in the next twenty-four hours or so might change that." He smiled. "And you might even make some money, because if this goes the way I think it's going to go, we'll definitely be doing a book about this investigation. Won't that be nice?"

"Lily? It's almost four o'clock. Did you hear from the police chief?"

Lily opened her eyes. Claudia was sitting on the edge of the bed. Lily's headache had receded, but a dull, faint throb remained. The nausea had passed. She sat up on the edge of the bed, stretched her arms and yawned. "Boy, did I sleep," Lily said.

"No call yet?"

"No. I think the phone would've woke me."

Claudia took the cell phone off the bedstand and checked. "Yes, someone called from the Eureka Police Department."

"They did? Damn. I slept through it."

"You needed the sleep. I'll call the number."

Claudia made the call and handed Lily the cell phone. After four rings, a recorded voice answered and began to recite a menu of options. "Voice mail," Lily said as she took the phone away from her ear and held it in front of her, frowned at it. "I don't feel like dealing with voice mail. How do you hang this thing up?" she asked.

"Press the End button."

Lily pressed the button and handed the phone back to Claudia. "We should try the Kellars again. Do you have their number?"

Claudia flipped the cell phone open again, pushed a couple buttons, and handed it over. "I've already programmed it into the phone."

Lily smiled as she took the phone. "You're terribly efficient."

"Hello?" It was Jenna Kellar.

"Mrs. Kellar, I'm glad you answered. It's Lily Rourke."

"Oh, yes," Jenna said. "Look, I appreciate your concern, but we have a couple investigators here right now. I don't think we'll need—"

"Mrs. Kellar, the Binghams aren't going to help you. If anything, they're only going to make your situation worse. I've been having very strong visions about this, Mrs. Kellar. Something bad is going to happen if they—"

"What have you got against them?" Jenna said.

"I don't know them, but I know *of* them. I know what they do, how they work, and the problem you have is not—"

"I'm sorry, but I can't talk right now. My husband could come in here any second. I barely got him to agree to the Binghams, and he wouldn't be very happy if he knew I was talking to you."

"Wait, it's *extremely* important that we talk. Your son is in danger."

There was a lengthy silence over the line.

Lily said, "I saw what happened in your house last night. I saw your husband attack your son. I think the thing that made him do it—"

"How do you know that?" Jenna said, her voice breathy with surprise.

"I told you, I'm psychic, and I've been having visions about your family."

Jenna sighed. "What do you *want* from me?"

"I want nothing from you but a little of your time. I think I can help you."

"My husband is coming, I have to go."

"I'm staying at the Motel 6 in—"

The call ended with a click. Lily pressed the End button, flipped the phone closed, and dropped it onto the bed. "These people are impossible."

They went to a small diner for a late lunch. Claudia had a corned beef sandwich and Lily a bowl of chicken noodle soup. Halfway through the meal, Claudia's cell phone chirped. She took it from her purse, flipped it open, and looked at the display above the keypad. She handed the phone across the table to Lily and said, "It's the police department. Just press the Send button."

Lily said, "Hello."

"Hello, this is Merry Peebles at the Eureka Police Department. Could I speak to Lily Rourke, please?" Merry Peebles sounded like a teenager.

"This is she."

"Chief Winningham would like to see you right away. He's on his way back to the station now."

"When do you expect him?"

"Any minute."

"Okay. We'll be right there." Lily ended the call and handed the phone back to Claudia, saying, "It looks like we're finished with our lunch."

CHAPTER TWENTY-ONE

Saturday, 3:32 P.M.

Chief Winningham was seated at his desk in his squeaky chair, smiling, when Lily and Claudia entered his office. He stood and said, "Miss Rourke, Miss— I'm sorry, I've forgotten your name."

"Claudia McNeil, but I'm just Claudia."

"And I'm just Lily."

"Well, Just Claudia and Just Lily, why don't you just sit down. Coffee?"

They declined as they sat in the chairs that faced the desk.

Winningham sat down and wheeled the chair up to the desk. He tapped an open folder that held several sheets of paper. "Those two names you gave me— they're both missing. But they're not from around here. Billy Enders, ten years old, disappeared from Crescent City on March 11, 1997, and Jonah Wishman, eight, from Ashland, Oregon, on July 21, 1996. Both are still missing."

Lily nodded. "I suspected as much."

"Now, Lily, if you know something about the where-abouts of these boys, you have to tell me."

"I don't. Not yet."

"Are they related? Can you tell me anything?"

"Nothing I'm certain of yet. And frankly, Chief, I'm not sure you'll want to hear it."

Winningham's smile disappeared altogether and his back stiffened slightly. "It's got something to do with Lenny Baines, doesn't it?"

"Yes, it does."

"Look, Lily, I said I knew the guy, I didn't say I dated him. If you've got something to tell me about Leonard Baines, you have to tell me."

Lily said, "Like I said, I'm not certain of anything yet. I'm still piecing things together. I need to talk to the Kellars—Lenny's daughter and her husband—but Mr. Kellar has made it very clear I'm not welcome. Until I can talk to them and get into that house, I'm still kind of in the dark, so I'm hesitant to tell you anything."

Winningham smiled again and sat forward in his chair, folded his arms on the desk. "I've got this fishing buddy. He's retired now, but he was on the force in Red-ding when you identified the knife being used by that stabber back in—what, 'seventy-eight? He loves telling that story. I've heard some others about you, too."

"All true, I hope."

"Far as I've been able to tell. Nobody knows a damned thing about you, but you've got a reputation, and it's a good one. If you've got information that might lead to the remains of those boys, I want to hear it, even if there's a few holes in it."

A vague, dull ache was all that remained of Lily's once-throbbing headache, but it was enough to irritate her. She rubbed a temple as she said, "I have reason to believe that those two boys were abducted, tortured, and murdered by Leonard Baines. I don't know how or where he disposed of them. But I know they weren't the only ones."

"How many others?" Winningham asked.

"I don't know. But I've got a bad feeling there was a lot of them."

"Damn," he said with a sigh as he leaned back in the chair, rubbed the back of his neck with a beefy hand. "I don't suppose you have the names of any other missing boys, do you?"

"No."

Winningham's bushy eyebrows crept up his forehead. "Is there anything I can do to help?"

Lily was about to tell the chief she'd let him know if she came up with anything, but the electric-blue flashing made her eyes flutter as she inhaled the smell of bananas. She got up and went to the small couch against the wall to her right. She sat in the center of it, then lay down on her left side and said to Claudia, "Another one's coming." She saw Claudia's mouth move but did not hear what she said. Darkness rolled over Lily and engulfed her. Darkness and silence.

Lily regained consciousness but did not open her eyes. Through the pounding of her head, she listened to Claudia and Winningham.

"Can I borrow your garbage can?" Claudia said. "She might vomit when she comes around."

"Sure," Winningham said.

Lily felt nauseated. She'd eaten nothing but a little soup for lunch, but it was threatening to return.

"How long is she usually out?" Winningham asked. He sounded unnerved.

"It varies. Sometimes just a couple minutes, sometimes several."

Lily realized there were tears in her eyes, and her throat felt hot and constricted. Her eyes seemed to press against her closed lids with each throb of her head. She sniffled and whispered, "I'm going to need some water. And some tissue." She slowly sat up on the couch but did not open her eyes.

"Be right back," Winningham said as he left the office.

"You're crying," Claudia said.

"It was awful. Awful."

"What was awful?"

Lily dabbed at her eyes with a knuckle, then folded her arms across her upset stomach and leaned forward as much as her girth allowed. A brown plastic wastecan lined with a white garbage bag stood in front of her legs.

To Claudia, Lily said, "Could you please get a couple pills from my purse?"

Winningham returned with a Styrofoam cup of water in one hand and a box of Kleenex in the other. Lily put the tissues on the couch beside her and drank down two pills with some water. She handed the cup to Claudia, who put it on Winningham's desk. Lily took a couple tissues from the box and noisily blew her nose. She tossed the tissue into the wastecan and said, "Write down these names."

Winningham hurried around his desk and picked up a pen as he dropped into the squeaky chair.

Lily said, "Kenan Miller, Eric Noone, and Martin Pryor. Marty," she whispered. "Everybody called him Marty."

As she spoke their names, Lily saw their faces as she had seen them in the vision, filled with terror and pain.

When she started sobbing, she sounded, at first, like she was laughing. Crying made her head feel worse, which only made her cry harder. She buried her face in her hands as Claudia put an arm around her.

"They suffered so," Lily said once the wracking sobs diminished. "Those poor little boys suffered terribly." She looked up at Winningham. "And you were there. I saw you in my vision—he had children locked in his house while you and other cops were outside with more children. I'm not positive, but I've got the feeling it was those three boys I named—they were in the house while you were there. He . . . he enjoyed that, it excited him, having you there while he had tortured and starving little boys inside his house." One half of Lily's upper lip curled back. "He got off on it."

Winningham left the chair, came around the desk, and perched a hip on its front edge. He rubbed the back of his neck as he cocked his head.

Lily said, "Something I've said bothers you, Chief Winningham. What is it?"

He dropped off the desk and stood up straight before her. "Are you talking about . . . well . . ." He chuckled. "Ghosts?"

"I honestly don't know, Chief. I think there may be some remnant of Leonard Baines in that house, and possibly the remnants of some of his victims. Some lingering presence, or energy. I suppose you could call them ghosts, if you want. I don't like the word myself, because, for one thing, I'm not sure *what* the hell this is yet so I don't know if it applies, and for another, the word 'ghost' comes with too much baggage for it to be of any use to me."

Winningham nodded. "It's useless to me, too, I'm afraid, because 'ghost' doesn't look good in a police report. It doesn't hold up too well in court, either. So, if you have any information that could lead to the where-abouts or remains of any of those boys, I want to hear about it right away. But when it comes to ghosts, or spirits, or whatever you want to call them, I'd rather you just leave me out of it, okay?"

Lily said, "Oh. I see." She stood, took a deep, steadying breath. "I'm sorry if my work offends you, Chief. But this is not something I'm doing out of the goodness of my heart, you know. I'm doing this because if I don't it will drive me insane. I'm doing it because I have to. If I *didn't* have to, I wouldn't be wasting any of your time."

Winningham held up both hands, palms out. "I'm sorry, Lily, I didn't mean to imply that you were wasting my time. But for professional reasons, I'd rather not show up in an article with lurid headlines in the *Global Inquisitor*. That's all."

Lily slowly paced the length of the office with a fore-arm across her belly. "You probably can't *wait* to tell all your buddies about your experience with the weird and mysterious psychic, but suddenly you're worried about becoming a laughingstock. It's that story in the newspaper, isn't it?" Lily said as she turned and looked at him. She nodded her head a couple times. "Yes, the one about the trucker who claimed to have been beaten up by a ghost in the Kellars's house. Ever since that story went national and you started getting calls from the tabloids, you've been wetting your pants because you're afraid of being made a fool of in the media."

Winningham's chin dropped as his eyebrows rose, and he stared openmouthed at her for a moment. He closed his mouth, shifted his weight from foot to foot, and looked like he was about to say something, but he did not.

"Come on, Claudia, let's go," Lily said.

As Claudia stood and picked up her bag, Winningham said, "Wait, I'm sorry, Lily, I didn't mean to offend you. I don't want you to go away angry."

"Don't worry, Chief," Lily said as she opened the door. "I'm angry, but not at you. I'm angry at Leonard Baines, but there's not a damned thing I can do about it." She turned and went out the door and down the corridor.

To Winningham, Claudia said, "Please call us once you've got any information on those boys. Thank you for your help."

"Come on, Claudia," Lily said in the corridor. "I need some chocolate."

In the Beetle, Claudia started the engine. "Did you read his mind?"

Lily released a single humorless laugh. "Are you kidding? I didn't have to. He was broadcasting that like CNN with breaking news."

"Where do you want to go next?"

"We're going to have to go see the Kellars again. But first . . . is there a Marie Calendar's in this town?"

They found one on Broadway in Eureka, and after Lily had squeezed into a booth, she ordered a slice of Chocolate Satin Pie before the waitress could ask what they wanted. Claudia ordered coffee.

"Looks like your stomach is feeling better," Claudia said.

"I need some chocolate. I suppose you think I was terribly rude to Chief Winningham back there."

Claudia shook her head. "I think you were upset."

"I was. I still am. Why do you think I need some chocolate? If I were an alcoholic, we'd be sitting at a bar right now and I'd be knocking back vodka." Lily put her elbows on the tabletop and rested her face in her hands for a moment.

"Are you feeling any better?" Claudia asked. "How's your head?"

Lily sat up straight. "My head feels like a heavy-metal drum solo. My stomach's queasy, but right now my need for chocolate outweighs my desire not to throw up." She rubbed a temple with her fingertips. "I've got to work this out, because I don't know how much longer I can take these visions."

"I imagine they're exhausting, and they're making you sick," Claudia said.

"No, it's not that. Yeah, they make me sick, but I've been through it before, I can take that. No, it's the visions themselves. They're horrible." A moist lump grew in her throat, and Lily took a deep breath and pulled herself together, then began to shed tears.

The waitress came with their orders. Lily took a generous bite of her pie, then sat back and closed her eyes. "Mmm, feel those endorphins," she whispered. After several seconds, she licked her lips and said, "I'm not looking forward to dropping in on the Kellars again. I think we should ask Kimberly to go with us—she might be able to help us get a foot in the door. Why don't you give her a call."

"Kimberly said the Binghams were coming today," Claudia said. "If we deal with the Kellars, we're going to have to deal with them, too."

"I'm not worried about the Binghams. I'm worried about Miles Kellar. Whatever's left of Leonard Baines in that house wants that boy. It wants him bad."

Jenna entered the kitchen and joined Martha at the breakfast nook. Martha was reading a book, but set it aside when Jenna slid onto the bench across from her.

"Mavis called Father Malcolm in San Francisco," Jenna said. "He'll be here this evening."

"You look tired," Martha said. "I just made some fresh coffee. You want some?"

"If I drink any more coffee, my head will explode," Jenna said. "I haven't really *done* anything, but I feel like I've been busy running around all day."

"Well, you didn't get much sleep last night, and you're not used to all this fuss, that's all, honey."

Arty had gone back to the hotel to get some equipment and their two students, Shannon and Willy. Mavis had stayed behind and talked with Jenna and David and Martha as Miles napped on the floor in front of the television. After nodding off a couple times in the recliner, David had excused himself and gone upstairs for a nap.

"While it's just us girls," Mavis had said, "I'd like to talk with you both about my husband, Arty. Even at his advanced age, he's as hyper as a teenage boy. He's very enthusiastic about our work, sometimes to a fault. Don't be surprised if he snaps at you or raises his voice. It doesn't mean he's angry, it's just that he's very excitable."

Jenna had smiled and said quietly, "I hope you won't be offended by anything *my* husband might say. Neither of us has ever been the least bit religious, so this may be a little uncomfortable for us. I think he's going to go ahead with whatever you want to do, but he's not going to enjoy it, so he might make a hostile remark or two."

"In that case, I'll try to keep my Arty on a leash," Mavis had said, smiling. She'd explained that it was important for everyone to stick together at all times once the house was blessed. "After that," she'd said, "the demonic entities in the house will be very angry, and they'll be frantic to make trouble. It will no longer be safe to be alone anywhere in the house."

Jenna had said, "Then we'll stick together."

Smiling, Mavis had said, "Once they get here, our students will move throughout the house with cameras and microphones. Your son will probably enjoy it—most children do. It's an exciting adventure to them."

Jenna had found Mavis Bingham very calming and reassuring, something she needed. She had been preoccupied all day with the phone call she'd received that morning from Lily Rourke.

Your son is in danger, Lily had said. Dwayne Shattuck had said the same thing. Jenna looked over at Miles, asleep on the floor in front of the television. She realized neither of the Binghams had singled out Miles.

Jenna had said, "Mrs. Bingham—"

"Please call me Mavis."

"Okay, Mavis. So far, two people have told me—" She'd glanced at Miles again to make sure he was still asleep, then lowered her voice. "—that Miles is in danger as long as he's in this house. I was wondering if I should get him out of here. I have a friend who might be willing to take him for a while if—"

"Who told you that, dear?" Mavis had said.

"Dwayne Shattuck, the medium who got beaten up here the other day, and a woman who's been calling. She dropped by once. Her name is Lily Rourke. She's a psychic."

"Well, I haven't heard of either of them, and Arty and I are very connected to the paranormal world. The story about your medium appeared in newspapers across the country, and I'm surprised you haven't heard from a lot more of them. You need to understand that there are a lot of opportunistic charlatans in this business, dear. If you have demonic forces in this house"—she'd averted her eyes a moment, sniffed, cleared her throat—"and I think you do, then all of you are in danger, not just your son. Don't worry, dear, we're going to do everything we can."

"Father Malcolm has done this sort of thing before?"

"Many times. If necessary, he'll perform an exorcism."

Jenna had looked at Miles again, sleeping on the floor. As reassuring as she was, Mavis had not made Jenna feel any better.

Somethin's already disturbed it, Dwayne Shattuck had said. *It's . . . I don't know, it's like it's got somethin' on its mind.*

"Well, whatever Father Malcolm does," Jenna had said, "I wish he'd get here and do it soon."

When Arty had returned carrying a cardboard box of religious icons in his arms, he'd brought with him Shannon and Willy, each of whom had a satchel with a shoulder strap. According to Mavis, they regularly attended the Binghams's lectures at the Phoenix Society of Paranormal Research and had accompanied them on a few of the society's field trips to haunted locations. Both were in their early twenties, Shannon a slightly frumpy young woman of medium height with long straight brown hair, Willy a tall, skinny guy with small round eyeglasses, a dark buzz-cut, and a goatee. They put their bags down in the living room, stood close together, and sometimes held hands briefly, stiff and nervous. This was the first time they had assisted in one of the Binghams's investigations, Mavis said, and they appeared nervous. They wore jeans and T-shirts—Willy wore a blue T-shirt that bore the logo for *The X-Files*, Shannon a black one that read *My childhood was supposed to end when?*—and had shed their coats in the entryway. Shannon's eyes had darted all around her as she stood beside Willy, who had eagerly chewed his lower lip. Arty had given them their assignments—first, to move the coffee table out of the way to make more room, and second, to put a religious icon in each room of the house. Jenna had them put the table back in the dining room against the north wall.

Jenna had asked to do the master bedroom because David was resting there and she did not want to disturb him. She'd carried a plastic Virgin Mary upstairs to the bedroom, where she found David sound asleep. She'd put the plastic figure on her vanity and pulled the door closed as she left the room. Then she'd gone back downstairs and into the kitchen to join Martha in the breakfast nook.

Jenna was jarred from her thoughts when Martha said, "Are they going to be sleeping here?"

"I'm not sure. They have hotel rooms. You've read their books, I haven't. Do they usually stay in the houses they work on?"

Martha thought about that a moment, sipped her coffee. "You know, as a matter of fact, I think they do."

"In that case, you and I should go to the store and put a few things in the fridge, don't you think?"

"Well, I suppose if they're going to do this for nothing, we should at least feed them," Martha said.

Arty and Mavis came into the kitchen hesitantly. "Are we interrupting?" Mavis said.

Jenna stood and said, "No, not at all."

Mavis put a small figure of Jesus on the counter. Arty held a crucifix.

"You said you have a basement," Arty said.

"Yes, it's right over here," Jenna said as she led them to the laundry room. She opened the basement door. "You aren't planning to go down there, are you?"

"If there was activity in the basement, we need to

298

place an icon down there," Arty said. "It'll only take me a second."

"There's no light down there," Jenna said. "You'll need the—" She turned around to find Martha standing behind her with the heavy Mag-Lite held in both hands.

Jenna handed it to Arty, who flicked it on. As he stepped through the basement doorway, Mavis moved toward him in a sudden rush, reached out, and clutched his shoulder for a moment.

"Are you sure you want to go down there, Arty?" Mavis said with a slight quaver in her voice.

"Don't worry, Momma, I'll be fine," he said. He smiled at Mavis over his shoulder, then followed the flashlight's beam down the stairs a careful step at a time.

Jenna and Mavis stood at the doorway, peered down the stairs, and watched him. Jenna glanced at Mavis and was surprised by the tension, and even fear, on her face, in her eyes.

After a few seconds, the glow of the flashlight down in the basement went out. Someone said something in a gravelly voice, but the words were muffled. Arty released a throaty, trembling "Oh!"

Mavis's hand flew to her mouth as she gasped and stepped forward. "Arty, are you all right?" she called in a broken voice.

Thunking footsteps hurried up the stairs and Arty emerged from the darkness, mouth open as if he were desperate for air, one hand on the rail, the other clutching his chest, eyes wide. For that moment, Jenna thought Arty Bingham looked like a frightened boy.

Mavis pushed Jenna aside, opened her arms to her ascending husband. "Be careful, Arty, for God's sake, be careful!" She stepped aside and clutched Arty's elbow as he nearly fell through the doorway.

Arty nudged Jenna aside and slammed the basement

door closed, then turned around and leaned his back against it. His chest rose and fell rapidly as he continued to clutch it with one hand. His face had paled.

"Do you need your pills?" Mavis said.

He fumbled in his pocket, pulled out a small tin. He removed a tiny white pill from it and dropped it under his tongue, then closed his eyes and tried to slow his breathing as he returned the tin to his pocket.

Mavis said, "Arty has a slight heart condition. The pills keep it under control."

Finally, Arty said, "There was someone down there."

Jenna nodded. "The fat man. Was he wearing a cowboy hat?"

"I . . . I only got a glimpse of a figure as it came around me from behind. He spoke, but I didn't understand him. Then the light went out and I dropped it. And the crucifix."

"Why don't you come out in the living room and sit down," Jenna said.

"If I try to walk, I'm going to fall," Arty said. "My legs are shaking."

Jenna frowned. Arty Bingham was not behaving the way she expected a professional paranormal investigator to behave. He looked pale and his eyes were still wide with fright. He looked like he'd just seen a ghost— which Jenna had assumed he and Mavis would be accustomed to by now.

Jenna caught a brief but significant look as it passed between Arty and Mavis, and Mavis said to him quietly, "I told you."

"I left the flashlight down there," he said. "Sorry about that, but I don't think I'll go down for it right now, if you don't mind." A nervous laugh escaped him. He turned to Mavis. "We should get Shannon and Willy down there with cameras."

Mavis put an arm around him and said, "Let's get you calmed down first."

During all the commotion, Jenna failed to hear the doorbell ring.

CHAPTER TWENTY-TWO

Saturday, 5:34 P.M.

The second step up on the front porch was the closest Lily had gotten to the Kellars's home. Walking up the path, she'd felt a constriction in her chest that only grew worse the closer she got to the house, as if a giant rubber band were wrapped tightly around her chest and back and getting tighter.

The moment the boy opened the front door, Lily recognized him as Miles Kellar, and she wanted more than anything to sweep him up in her arms and carry him away from that house. He squinted up at them with sleepy eyes, looking like he'd just woke up. Lily and Claudia stood behind Kimberly Gimble.

"Hi, Miles," Kimberly said.

"Hi. Mom's in the kitchen, I think."

"Could you get her for me?"

"You don't want to come in?"

"Um, not yet. Just tell her I'm here."

"Okay." Miles closed the door.

"Remember," Lily said quietly, "get her to step outside. If I can get her to listen to me for a couple minutes—"

"I'll do what I can," Kimberly said. "But if this causes trouble, I'm not going to push it, okay? I mean, I haven't known her long, but she's my friend, and I don't want to stir up any problems between her and her hus—"

The door opened again and Jenna smiled wearily at Kimberly, but her smile faltered when she saw Lily and Claudia. Jenna quickly glanced over her shoulder, then stepped outside and gently closed the door behind her.

"I don't want to make trouble, Jenna," Kimberly said, "but she's been very anxious to talk with you."

"A few minutes, that's all I ask, Mrs. Kellar," Lily said. "I don't want your money, I don't want *anything* from you. I just want to help you and your little boy, your family."

"This is a bad time," Jenna said. "I have a lot of people here, and I—"

"The Binghams," Lily said. "Mrs. Kellar, the Binghams will *not* be able to help you, trust me. They're not prepared to deal with your problem."

"Oh?" Jenna said. "What's my problem?"

"*Terrible* things have happened in your house, Mrs. Kellar," Lily said. "They've left behind a malignant energy—call it a place memory, a ghost, a disembodied personality, whatever—and that energy is lashing out at your family. Particularly your son. It wants Mi—"

The door opened, and Lily stopped speaking when she saw Arthur and Mavis Bingham in the doorway. She recognized them immediately from the pictures she'd seen, but they had aged, and Arthur looked rather pale, perhaps even unwell.

"Who have we here?" Mavis said with a big smile. A speck of red lipstick clung to a front tooth.

Jenna said, "Mavis, this is the woman I told you about."

"The psychic?" Mavis said.

"*Psychic?*" Arthur said with a note of alarm. "*Who's* a psychic?"

Lily forced herself to smile back at Mavis. "If you don't mind, I was having a word with Mrs. Kellar."

"You're the psychic?" Arthur asked.

Lily tipped her head back and looked down her nose at the little man. "As a matter of fact, I am."

Arthur said, "Have you accepted Jesus Christ as your personal Lord and Savior?"

Lily flinched and a single, sharp laugh burst out of her. "I *beg* your pardon?"

"I *said*, have you accepted—"

"I heard you. 'I beg your pardon' was an expression of my utter disbelief."

"Believe it, sister," Arthur said as he stepped out onto the porch. "If you're a psychic who doesn't acknowledge Jesus Christ as the Son of God or credit the Holy Sprit for your gift, then you are Satanic."

Lily tipped her head back again, cocked it to one side. "Sounds to me like you're not taking your medication, Arthur."

Mavis's mouth dropped open and she gasped, and Arthur made an outraged "Bwah!" sound.

"Who are you?" Arthur said as he pointed a stiff finger at her and took another step forward. "Who do you work for? Who hired you to harass us? You're no psychic, you're a couple of those damned Pagans, aren't you? Lesbian witches!"

Mavis put a hand on his shoulder and said, "Be careful, Arty—calm down, please. I don't want you to get sick."

Arty stepped back but looked like a fully flexed muscle. His fists opened and closed at his sides and he moved his feet constantly, looking almost as if he were trying to dance a softshoe on the concrete porch.

Lily spoke firmly when she said, "I am here to see Mrs. Kellar, and that's all."

Mavis said, "First, I'd like to speak with you, if you don't mind, dear." She clutched Lily's upper arm and turned her around. They walked together down the steps and onto the concrete path away from the porch. Mavis spoke quietly, privately. "My husband and I are professional paranormal investigators. The Kellars asked us to deal with their problem, which we are doing."

Lily felt a tingly sensation on her upper arm, just beneath Mavis's hand, as if someone had poured cold, bubbly champagne on her bare skin. Lily stopped walking suddenly as a flood of information gushed and splashed into her mind and vivid images exploded behind her eyes. She blinked hard—once, twice, two more times—against the rapid-fire images and the swirl of emotions as they rushed together in her mind. Jerking her arm from Mavis's hold, Lily turned to face her and saw a look of confusion and suspicion on her heavily made-up face.

"You've been doing this only to play along with your husband," Lily whispered. She frowned, tilted her head slightly. "You've been doing it . . . to keep him sane. To keep him out of an institution. All these years. All those people you've . . . what? Duped? Used?" Lily's words began to come faster. "You knew those families had serious problems you couldn't help them with—

alcoholism, drug addiction, abuse. You could see those things—probably more clearly than you've ever seen a ghost or a demon. But you went along with Arty's obsession until it actually started to bring you some money and fame."

Mavis backed away from her and stood on the grass. She looked as if Lily had just slapped her.

"You saw something in the house," Lily whispered, jerking her head once toward the Kellars's house. "You *know* you can't deal with it, and you tried to tell him that, but . . . but you're doing it anyway, just to play along with Arthur, to keep him happy, because . . . he really believes you *can* deal with it."

Mavis spoke in a trembling, throaty whisper. "I don't know what you're talking about."

"You don't even *think* about them, do you?" Lily said, still whispering, the words tumbling out of her mouth. "The people you prey on—people who need *real* help— you never wonder if your little dog-and-pony show messed them up even more, you don't even—" Lily made a small breathy sound of frustration and threw up her hands. "For crying out loud, why am I wasting my time with you?" She turned and went back to Jenna, leaving Mavis standing slack-jawed on the grass. Standing at the bottom of the porch steps, she said, "I'm going to finish what I have to say to Mrs. Kellar, and we'll let her decide what she's going to do."

Jenna said, "Look, I'm sorry, but . . . well, I've never heard of you, I know absolutely nothing about you. The Binghams at least have a reputation. I don't mean to be rude, but I don't see why I—"

"You don't have to explain yourself to her, Jenna dear," Mavis said as she came back up the walk. She went up on the porch and stood beside her husband. "We have work to do. It will be dark soon."

"Mrs. Kellar," Lily said, "your problem is a real one. These people are not accustomed to dealing with this sort of thing, they're not prepared for it. Something *bad* will happen. My God, I can feel it here, standing outside your door—this house is a psychic boil. You need to—"

"What do *you* know about what we're used to dealing with?" Arthur said.

"I know plenty about you, Mr. Bingham. Even more now that I've had a chance to chat with your wife. You're frauds."

"Bwah!" Arthur said.

"If I don't seem credible enough to you, Mrs. Kellar," Lily said, doing her best to sound as pleasant as possible, "I can fix that, but it'll take a little time. I'll be back later with someone important who can vouch for me." She turned and headed for the gate. "Come on, Claudia," she said, but Claudia was already following along.

In the Beetle, Claudia started the engine. "Where to?" she asked.

Lily took a deep breath. "I'm so angry right now, I could chew nails and shit battleships. Those *people*." She grunted, an angry sound, then said, "Just get us out of here for now. Maybe if the chief of police tells Mrs. Kellar I know what I'm talking about, she'll listen."

"Do you have any idea what you're going to do if you actually get in the house?"

Lily sighed. "None. I won't know till I get in there."

A light sprinkle of rain started to fall as Claudia drove away from the house.

Jenna was exhausted and wanted nothing more than to curl up in bed. But she was pressed on by her desire to get all this over with as soon as possible. As tired as she was, she doubted she'd be able to sleep anyway. If she didn't keep busy and stopped to think much, her mind reeled. Only a week ago, she'd been going about her life as if nothing could ever go wrong. Now it seemed hard to believe they'd ever had a safe or normal moment in the house.

Kimberly had come inside after the psychic and her friend had left. They'd walked through the living room, where the Binghams and their young assistants checked their cameras and tape recorders while Miles watched in fascination and Martha chatted with them. In the kitchen, Jenna paced while Kimberly talked.

"I'm so sorry, Jenna, I didn't mean to cause trouble, but she seemed so sincere, so urgent. I thought you might want to talk to her."

Jenna nodded. "I wish Mavis and Arty hadn't come out on the porch—I would've talked with her longer. I just wanted to keep the peace—that's why I sent her away."

"Are you sure? I've got her number, I can call and tell her to back off. Seriously."

"You have her number? I may give her a call."

Kimberly lowered her voice. "Why? Aren't you happy with the Binghams?"

Jenna stopped pacing and lowered her voice to a whisper. "I don't know. They've got some priest coming in this evening, Father Malcolm. He might exorcise the house. But they don't seem very professional, you know? Whatever Mavis saw upstairs, it shook her up. And down in the basement, Arty saw something that scared him so bad, he had to take a pill for his heart. It's like they've never done this before. I don't know, maybe it's just me. What do I know? But I keep remembering what Lily said about them—that they're frauds. And what she said about this place—'*Terrible* things have happened in your house.' The way she said it, it sounded like she knew a lot she wasn't telling."

"That's what I mean," Kimberly whispered. "I've never heard of her—she can't be *too* famous—but at the same time, she sounded like she knew what she was talking about. Especially about your father."

"My father." Jenna leaned her hip against the edge of the counter. She'd broached the subject once with her mother recently, but had not thought about him since. She wondered if she'd closed her mind to any thoughts about him—if, without even realizing it, she hadn't *wanted* to ask any more questions about him. "Is that why you asked me for his name? You said you wondered if you'd known him."

Kimberly nodded. "I'm sorry, I felt bad lying to you. But like I said, she was very convincing, and I was afraid you wouldn't tell me if you knew she was asking."

"Why did she want to know?"

"She seems to think your father is connected to all this." She narrowed one eye. "How much do you know about him, anyway, Jenna?"

"Nothing. Like I said, I never met the man. But Mom was very honest with me about it. It's not like he left a big hole in my life or anything—Mom did a great job with me by herself."

Neither of them heard Miles enter the kitchen. When he said, "Mom," Kimberly jumped and let out a yelp of surprise.

"You okay?" Jenna said.

Kimberly rolled her eyes as she relaxed. "I'm jumpy. No offense, Jenna, but I'm a little nervous in your house after what happened with Ada."

Miles said, "What are they going to do with those cameras and tape recorders?"

"They're going to try to figure out what's going on in our house, honey," Jenna said. "They're going to try to get rid of the fat man."

Miles nodded once. "Is it okay if I ask them how they're going to do that?"

"Sure. Just don't get in their way, all right?"

As Miles left the kitchen, Kimberly said, "I've got to get home. I haven't started dinner and my boys are going to start worrying soon, I'm sure. Not about me, of course, but about dinner."

Kimberly wrote down Lily Rourke's cell phone number for Jenna, then Jenna walked her out to the porch. As she watched Kimberly get back into her car and drive away, she hated to see her go. She turned and wearily went back into the house.

Lily was brushing her teeth in the motel room when Claudia's cell phone chirped. Claudia was in the shower, so Lily rinsed her mouth and answered it.

"It's Kimberly Gimble."

"Hello, Kimberly," Lily said. "Thank you for meeting us over there. I'm sorry for the little scene that erupted on the porch."

"That's okay, Jenna didn't mind."

"I'm glad."

"In fact, she said she might call you. I gave her your number."

"Really? Why didn't she talk to me while I was there?"

"She was just trying to calm things down. She's had enough stress lately."

"Of course. I understand. Should I call her?"

"No, she'll call if she wants to talk. Were you serious about going back there?"

"Yes. The chief of police is familiar with me and I was going to bring him along to vouch for me, but I haven't been able to reach him. How long are the Binghams supposed to be there?"

"I don't know. The priest is supposed to get there sometime this evening."

Lily's chest began to feel tight again, and she frowned. "Father Malcolm."

"Yes, that's the one."

Lily was not surprised, but an alarm went off in the back of her mind. Something about Father Malcolm going to the Kellars's house bothered her, something beyond the fact that he was just as much a fraud as the Binghams.

He's a defrocked priest, Donald Penner of the South-western Skeptical Society had said. *An embezzler and a pedophile.*

A pedophile.

"Are you still there?" Kimberly said.

"Sorry, my mind wandered. When is Father Malcolm supposed to get there?"

"She said this evening."

"Thank you for your help, Kimberly, I appreciate it. We'll be in touch."

After severing the connection, Lily punched in the number of Chief Winningham's cell phone. She had called the station earlier, but he'd gone and wasn't expected back. She called his cell phone and once again got no answer. She put the phone back in Claudia's purse and sat on the bed.

Lily had a very bad feeling about Father Malcolm showing up at the Kellars's house, but she was still not certain why.

* * *

When Jenna asked Mavis what they would like for dinner, she said, "We're pizza people, so don't bother cooking anything, just order a delivery and we'll be happy." Jenna called Round Table and ordered three large pizzas with different toppings, and soft drinks. David came into the kitchen while she was making the call, and after she hung up, they embraced. She was careful not to press against his injured hand. "How are you feeling?" she whispered.

"Like a zombie. But I'm hungry."

"I've ordered pizzas."

"Like we can afford pizzas."

"Don't worry, Mom will pay for it."

David shook his head. "What exactly are they doing, anyway?"

"Waiting for Father Malcolm."

David sighed. "I can't believe we're going to have a priest in the house."

"I know. But they're here, so we might as well let them do what they do."

David kissed her briefly on the mouth. "I'm sorry for being such a pain in the ass about this."

She smiled. "Thank you. But it doesn't matter now. We're handling it."

Father Malcolm called on Mavis's cell phone a few minutes later and said he was at a Denny's near the freeway in Eureka. Mavis told Jenna where he was and asked for directions to the house.

"I know where he is," Jenna said, "but I honestly don't know how to tell him to get here. We haven't lived here long enough to get to know the area that well. I could go to him and he could follow me back."

Mavis told him they would be there in a few minutes, and Father Malcolm said he would be at the coffee counter. As she put her cell phone back in her purse,

Mavis offered to go with Jenna, who told Martha to take care of the pizzas when they arrived.

"Couldn't we do this tomorrow?" Chief Winningham said over the phone.

"I'm sorry to impose, Chief," Lily said, "but it has to be tonight."

"I'm just sitting down to dinner."

"All right, then, after dinner. Just call me before you leave and we can meet at the Kellars's front gate."

"I wouldn't do this for just anyone, you know. But I suppose you're not just anyone." There was a smile in his voice.

"Thank you so much, Chief."

"I'll call you when I'm finished eating."

Lily pressed the End button and put the phone down on the table. They were back at the diner. Across from Claudia, Lily was squeezed into the same booth by the window they'd occupied before. Claudia was finishing an open-faced turkey sandwich while Lily, still queasy, sipped chicken soup. "The chief will call back soon," she said.

"I'm going to have a slice of pie," Claudia said, pushing her empty plate away. She waved the waitress over and ordered apple pie à la mode.

"There's not much I wouldn't do," Lily said, "to have your metabolism." Her hand holding the spoon stopped halfway to her mouth when the electric-blue flashing started, and the soup's aroma was overwhelmed by the smell of bananas. The spoon splashed into the bowl of soup with a clatter. Before Lily could speak, her head slumped forward and she fell into thick blackness.

Father Malcolm was a round-shouldered, fleshy man in his late fifties with pasty white skin and short, gray hair.

313

His pale blue eyes were set close together above a nose that was prominent and razor-thin. The skin around his dark eyebrows was dry and flaky. He smiled, his lower lip prominent and glistening pink.

When he saw Mavis, Father Malcolm stood, put a few dollars beside his coffee cup on the counter, and went to her, embraced her briefly.

"Good to see you, Mavis," he said.

When Mavis introduced her, Jenna smiled and shook the priest's clammy hand. He put his left hand over hers and said, "I'm glad I was lecturing in San Francisco this weekend so I could come when Mavis called. She says you've been having a difficult time. I want you to know, God has not turned His back on you."

"Come follow us to the house, Father," Lily said.

"Yes, let's go," he said. He stood between them and put a hand on each of their backs as they headed for the entrance. "I've rented a lovely Ford Taurus with the most wonderful sound system. I've been blasting Vivaldi all the way here," he said with a chuckle.

They left the restaurant to go to their cars.

Lily awoke suddenly and her head jerked up with a deep, rough gasp. Across from her, Claudia leaned forward and said, "You okay, Lily?"

Her headache had returned, along with her nausea, but she nodded. She put her purse on the table, ready to leave. "We have to get over there before that priest arrives."

"What? Why?"

"I'm not exactly sure, but there's going to be trouble if we don't."

"What did you see?"

"Nothing good."

"What about the chief?"

"Oh, that's right, the chief." She picked up the phone and punched Redial.

"Winningham."

"Chief, it's Lily Rourke again. I'm sorry to interrupt your dinner, but we've got to get over there right away." She lowered her voice and said, "I've had another vision. I have a . . . a sickening sense of urgency about this."

"It has to be this second? I haven't had dessert yet."

"If you don't come, I'm going over there by myself."

"Look, I don't want you to cause any trouble, Lily. You said you weren't welcome there."

"Something bad is going to happen very soon, Chief."

"All right. I'll eat dessert later."

Lily told him where they were. "We'll wait for you, then we can leave together from here. And could you do one more thing for me, Chief?"

"What's that?"

"Could you wear your uniform? I think it'll give you more of an air of authority, and they might be more likely to listen to you."

Winningham chuckled. "You're a take-charge kinda woman, aren't you?"

"I am? Well, I hope that's not a problem."

"Not at all. Give me ten minutes."

Lily put the phone back on the table and her purse beside her on the booth's cushion. She sipped some more ice water. "I hope he doesn't take long," she whispered. "I don't think we have much time."

On the last stretch of Starfish Drive before reaching the gate, Jenna said, "Mavis, do you think I should get Miles out of the house for the night? I could ask Kimberly to take him."

"If you really feel strongly about it, then you should," Mavis said. "But we encourage families to stick together, particularly if an exorcism is involved. There's a great deal of strength in a family united. It's a powerful force of goodness and can actually help us in what we do. I'm sure Father Malcolm would say the same. By the way, is he still behind us?"

Jenna checked the rearview mirror. "He's there."

She slowed the Toyota, turned right, and drove through the gate. Father Malcolm's headlights swept behind her as he followed. She stopped in front of the house and they got out of the car.

"Should I bring all my things in?" Father Malcolm asked as he got out of his car.

"Just your briefcase for now, Father," Mavis said.

Father Malcolm leaned into the car, came out with a large black briefcase, then closed the door.

Jenna led the way to the front door, then went inside with Mavis and Father Malcolm following a few steps behind.

CHAPTER TWENTY-THREE

Saturday, 7:23 P.M.

It was a chilly, misty evening, but when Jenna and Mavis got back to the house with Father Malcolm, the living room was warm from a fire David had managed to build one-handed, and smelled of pizza. Everyone was sitting around eating off paper plates—Shannon and Willy sat cross-legged on the floor, watching TV with Miles as they ate—except for David, who was stoking the fire. The aroma of the pizzas made Jenna's stomach grumble with hunger, and she went to the kitchen for a couple slices.

She sat in the breakfast nook to eat, and listened as Mavis told their story to Father Malcolm in the living room. In the kitchen, Jenna could not understand what she was saying, but she could hear Mavis's voice and there was a familiar rhythm to it all. She was afraid if she went out there, Mavis would ask her to tell it, and she wasn't up to going through it again. Jenna tried to tune them out and enjoy a little time by herself, but the memory of the terror on Miles's face when David attacked him rose up in her mind. When she closed her eyes, she saw the pain on David's face when she'd hit his injured hand. She remembered why she'd been filling her time with chatter and busywork.

Someone cried out in the living room, a surprised sound, and Jenna got up and hurried out of the kitchen, leaving her pepperoni slices on a paper plate on the table.

In the living room, the lamp beside David's recliner had been knocked off its table and lay on the floor. Everyone in the room—David, Martha, Miles, the Binghams, Shannon and Willy, and Father Malcolm—was on their feet and staring at the lamp, mouths open. The bulb beneath the skewed shade still glowed.

"What happened?" Jenna asked.

Standing beside the recliner, David turned to her and said, "Something knocked the lamp off the table. I didn't touch it, something just . . . it just . . ."

"Miles, come over here," Jenna said. Miles, who stood by Martha in front of the couch, walked over to Jenna. She turned him around and pulled him close, her hands on his chest. Jenna looked at the others.

Shannon and Willy had lost the color in their faces. Shannon's hands were bunched into fists, and Willy held a paper plate with a half-eaten slice of pizza on it in a trembling hand. Arty and Mavis did not look much better—they exchanged a wide-eyed glance, then returned their gaze to the lamp on the floor. Father Malcolm stood a couple feet from the end table at the end of the couch, frowning, mouth open. To Arty and Mavis he said, "What, uh . . . what was . . ."

Mavis stepped over to Father Malcolm and whispered briefly into his ear. Father Malcolm's eyes widened as the wrinkles in his large forehead smoothed out. Mavis looked at David and said, "We, uh . . . we seem to have angered the demonic entities in the house. That, um, that usually happens after we put out the religious icons. Right, Arty?"

Arty cleared his throat and spoke nervously. "Uh, yeah, they don't like the icons. And now we've got a priest in the house, a man of God, and they *really* don't like that."

Jenna waited for one of them to continue, but they stared silently at the lamp. The fire roared softly and crackled in the silence.

"Then what should we do?" Jenna said.

Arty said, "We should, uh . . . we should—"

The lamp at the end of the couch did not fall off its table—it flew off, and slammed into the side of Father Malcolm hard enough to nearly knock him over, then fell heavily to the floor. Its amber glass base broke with a thick *crack* when it hit the floor, but the light inside did not go out. Father Malcolm stumbled forward, away from the lamp.

"God!" Mavis cried as she hurried to Arty's side and clutched his arm.

Shannon screamed and nearly tripped over the lamp on her way across the room toward the entryway. She stopped suddenly and composed herself. She was breathing rapidly when she said, "I'm sorry. That scared me."

"Scared me, too," Willy said as he went to her side.

Arty looked at Shannon and Willy and snapped his fingers a few times. "Get those cameras, start taking pictures!" he said. "Let's not forget why we're here."

They went back to where their bags lay open on the floor in front of the couch. Willy put his plate on the floor, and they got their cameras.

Jenna's heart was beating hard, and gooseflesh spread

319

over her shoulders. But she was not so frightened that she did not notice how flustered Arty and Mavis were.

"Mavis," she said, her voice unsteady. "What do we *do?*"

A cornucopia-shaped Roseville vase flew from the built-in shelving unit in the wall and struck Father Malcolm hard on the left shoulder, then fell to the floor and broke in half. He shouted, "Ah!" and stumbled backward, just in time to miss a heavy pitcher, which flew between Father Malcolm and Martha and landed harmlessly on the couch.

Shannon screamed again and dropped her Polaroid camera as Willy took her in his arms and held her tightly, still clutching a small camcorder in his right hand.

"Oh, my God," Mavis said, adding in a harsh whisper, "Arty, I *told* you."

"Christ," Arty muttered, a hand on his chest.

"Take a pill," Mavis said. "Now."

Arty fished the small tin from his pocket and dropped a pill under his tongue.

David came over and stood beside Jenna, put an arm around her, and Martha followed. The four of them stood close together in front of the large black cabinet that held the entertainment system.

Frowning, David turned to Arty and Mavis and said, "I thought you guys did this all the time."

Jenna remembered something Lily Rourke had said earlier: *These people are not accustomed to dealing with this sort of thing, they're not prepared for it. Something* bad *will happen.* When she saw the lost look on the faces of Arty and Mavis, Jenna wondered if she should have paid more attention to the psychic.

Arty said, "Oh, yes, we do, all the time, but this . . . well, it's a little *early* for this kind of thing to happen.

This is a, uh . . . well, I'd say this demonic infestation has really taken root here. Don't you think, honey?" He turned to Mavis.

"Yes, this is unusual. The fact is, we've seen much worse than this before. This is actually quite tame compared to some of the—"

Jenna started and spun around when she heard a sound on the cabinet behind her. Family photographs stared at her, surrounded by her collection of small ceramic elves. One of the photographs had fallen over. She was afraid to turn her back on the cabinet again. With one arm around Miles, she grabbed David's right elbow and pulled them both back, away from the cabinet. Martha moved with them.

One of the ceramic elves shot off the top of the cabinet like a bullet from a gun and hit Father Malcolm in the neck. He stumbled backward, fell to the floor with a deep grunt, and Mavis hurried toward him with one arm outstretched.

"Mavis, wait!" Jenna said, as an eight-by-ten framed photograph of Miles dressed up as a cowboy for a school play swept off the cabinet. As if it had been thrown with intent, it flew directly at Father Malcolm stretched out on the floor. He cried out in pain when the picture hit his elbow hard and the glass in the frame shattered. The gold-colored frame missed Mavis by inches, and she quickly stepped back to Arty's side.

Shannon screamed until Mavis turned to her and snapped, "*Stop* that!"

"It's trying to hurt Father Malcolm," Jenna said as another ceramic elf missiled straight toward the priest lying in the center of the floor. It shattered against his hip, and he rolled over on his stomach and covered his head protectively with both arms, bent elbows pointing outward.

It must be the fat man, Jenna thought. *Why would the boys do this?*

Jenna moved quickly. She stepped around David and swept her left arm across the top of the cabinet. Ceramic elves and framed photographs clattered harmlessly to the floor in a small pile—glass cracked in the frames and a couple of elves shattered. She looked around to see what else might be fired at Father Malcolm, but her attention was drawn to the broken pile on the floor at the end of the cabinet when it made a small crunching sound. The pile shifted.

A six-inch triangular shard of glass rose up out of the pile and made an arc through the air. It came down and lodged in the upper thigh of Father Malcolm's left leg. Half the piece of glass disappeared through the priest's black pants and into his flesh. Father Malcolm screamed into the carpet as another piece of glass flipped through the air and stabbed into his left buttock.

Arty bellowed, "In the name of Jesus Christ, stop this now!"

Tiny pieces of broken ceramic elves whistled through the air and spattered onto Father Malcolm's back.

Arty shouted louder: "In the name of Jesus Christ, *stop this right now!*"

Father Malcolm lay silent and still, his body stiff. The only sound in the room, in the house, was the huffing and popping of the fire.

After several seconds passed, Arty said hoarsely, "It worked."

Father Malcolm got to his hands and knees, then slowly and carefully stood with his back to the fireplace, arms held out at his sides.

"We must pray," he said with a painful wince.

"You're hurt, Father," Mavis said.

"We must *pray*," he said, insistent and firm. "Together, right where we stand. 'Our Father, who art in heav—' Come on, together! 'Our Father, who art in heaven, hallowed be Thy name. Thy kingdom come. Thy will be done . . .'"

Jenna knew only snatches of the prayer. David's mouth remained closed. Jenna was surprised to see her mother reciting it along with the others.

"Mom?" Miles whispered. "What are they saying?"

Jenna bent down and whispered into his ear. "It's the Lord's Prayer, honey. Don't worry, I don't know the words either. Just be quiet and patient for me, okay?"

Miles nodded, then turned his attention back to Father Malcolm.

Jenna was amazed by Miles's strength—he seemed to be taking all of this so well, without a word of complaint, and with no apparent expression of fear so far. She wished she would hold up as well—she was terrified.

Mavis, Arty, Shannon, Willy, and Martha recited the prayer along with the priest, speaking together in a singsong cadence: "'And lead us not into temptation, but deliver us from evil: For thine is the kingdom—'"

Shannon screamed again and startled Willy so much, he dropped the camcorder.

Mavis made a sound that fell somewhere between a shout and a groan.

Jenna looked at Father Malcolm, and her mouth dropped open as she clutched David's right arm.

Young boys were coming out of the fireplace, one after another—boys Miles's age and younger. Some were clothed, others naked and emaciated. They walked directly into Father Malcolm and disappeared, sometimes as many as three at a time, overlapping like blurred images. The priest screamed and flailed his arms. Some of the boys were little more than shadows, while others were a flickery gray, like old silent-movie images, and others looked as real and solid as Father Malcolm. They silently disappeared as they walked into his back. Jenna lost count of the boys in the commotion.

Shannon ran screaming to the front door, opened it, and fled the house. Willy ran after her and grabbed their coats on the way out, leaving the front door standing halfway open.

Arty muttered, "Oh Jesus, oh Jesus, oh Jesus . . ."

Mavis stood with a hand on each side of her face, mouth open—she looked like she was screaming, but did not make a sound.

Martha walked around behind David to Jenna's side and stood close. Jenna felt Miles tremble as he turned around and hugged her, and she embraced him.

And the boys continued to come silently from the fireplace, oblivious of the hot, smacking flames. Some of them walked slowly, others hurried. None of them smiled. Then they stopped.

Still screaming, his voice cracking, Father Malcolm turned around and faced the fireplace, then dropped to the floor on his hands and knees.

Arty massaged his chest with a fist as his face tightened in a painful grimace. He said, "Oh Jesus, oh Jesus, oh Jesus . . ."

Father Malcolm dropped flat on the floor. His body squirmed, his legs kicked, and his arms flailed as if he were struggling. His screams were interrupted by sobs. The two pieces of glass remained lodged in his fleshy thigh and buttock, and his black slacks glistened with blood.

Arty fell forward and hit the floor hard. He landed with his right arm bent at the elbow, hand between the floor and his chest. He did not move.

Mavis cried out, "Oh, no, Arty!" as she knelt beside him.

Jenna turned to Martha and said, "Take Miles to the kitchen."

Martha put an arm around Miles, and they hurried out of the room.

"Call an ambulance!" Mavis pleaded. "Quickly, call an ambulance, right now!"

Father Malcolm was on his hands and knees again. His screams gave way to blubbering.

Jenna looked around for the cordless phone—she could never find it when she needed it. She hurried into the kitchen, where Miles sat in the breakfast nook, eyes wide. Martha was putting the phone back on its base.

"I called 911," Martha said. "An ambulance is on the way."

"I love you, Mom," Jenna said.

"Is Arty conscious?" Martha asked.

"I don't think so."

Martha's voice trembled as she whispered, "I'm sorry I suggested all this, honey. This is terrible, just terrible."

"Don't be sorry, Mom. Everything's going to be fine. Just keep Miles occupied for me, okay?"

Martha nodded.

On her way back through the dining room, Jenna realized Father Malcolm had stopped screaming and blubbering. Instead, a high keening cry grew louder in the living room.

Shannon and Willy had not come back. The front door still stood open and cold air was creeping into the living room.

Mavis had turned Arty over onto his back. David was on his knees, instructing Mavis as she clumsily performed CPR on Arty with tears rolling down her cheeks—one hand on top of the other over Arty's sternum, pushing, pushing.

The high-pitched wailing sound grew more frenzied, and Jenna realized it was coming from Father Malcolm. His knees were still on the carpet, but he had crawled forward and now his hands were flat on the brick hearth, fingers bent as if clawing the bricks. His head and shoulders were in the fireplace, in flames. The wailing broke and became a gurgling groan.

Jenna screamed as she ran to him. She bent down and grabbed his ankles.

At the same time, David saw him and shouted, "Shit!" He got up, hurried unsteadily to the fireplace, and grabbed Father Malcolm's belt. Jenna and David pulled together and dragged Father Malcolm out of the fire. Flames still covered his head and shoulders. His legs kicked, arms flapped on the floor. The room filled with the smell of burnt hair and cooked flesh as Mavis screamed and sobbed.

Jenna ran to the entryway and grabbed up the throw rug near the front door. She hurried back to Father Malcolm and used the rug to smother the flames.

David and Jenna rolled Father Malcolm over and knelt on either side of him. Great tremors moved through the priest's body as his hands clawed at the carpet and he made a strangled gurgling sound. His hair was gone. Tendrils of smoke rose from his blistered flesh, which was a mixture of dark red and charred black.

Jenna looked over at Mavis as a large man in a policeman's uniform rushed in through the open front door, his gun drawn. He stood in the archway and looked around quickly, taking in everything in the room.

"I heard screaming," he said.

"My husband's not breathing!" Mavis croaked

breathlessly. She bent down, put her mouth over his, and blew.

"What's going on here?" he said.

David stood. "Didn't they tell you? Is the ambulance here yet?"

"Ambulance?" The policeman holstered his weapon as he crossed the room and stood over Father Malcolm. "I'm Police Chief Oscar Winningham," he said. "I came here, uh . . ." He looked around again, concern and confusion on his face. "I came here to talk to you about Lily Rourke."

"Who?" David said. *"What?"*

Jenna saw her then, filling the doorway. A siren became audible as Lily Rourke came into the house and crossed the entryway cautiously. Her redheaded friend appeared in the doorway behind her and followed her inside. Jenna saw Shannon and Willy out on the front porch. They craned their necks to look inside, but came no closer to the front door.

Panting and crying, Mavis said, "Help, somebody please help me, I can't do this anymore, he's not breathing!"

Chief Winningham went to Arty's side, got down on one knee, and felt Arty's neck for a pulse.

The siren grew louder, then stopped. Tires crunched over the gravel outside and the flashing lights of the ambulance throbbed through the open door.

Chief Winningham went over to Lily Rourke. "Did you know about this?"

She shook her head as her eyes met Jenna's. "I only knew something bad was going to happen."

Jenna looked down at Father Malcolm, who had stopped moving. She closed her eyes and put a hand over her mouth as a sob rocked her. David put his arms around her, and she cried against his shoulder.

* * *

Feeling sick, Lily stepped out of the way of the two paramedics who hurried into the house. She was not nauseated—it wasn't that kind of sick feeling. This was deeper. Her bones felt sick—her bones and her mind.

"My God, what happened here?" Claudia said, "Are you okay?"

"No. I'm not."

"Are you going to pass out?"

"No, it's not that. It's . . . this house."

"Do you want to go back outside?"

To Lily, the air in the house felt thick. It wasn't just the awful smell of burning hair and flesh—it was more powerful than that, like a thick black electricity in the air that made the fine hairs on her arms stand up. It penetrated her and hummed in her stomach, buzzed at the edges of her soul. But it was not the directionless electricity that charged the air before a storm—it emanated from a specific source somewhere in the house and had a creeping, malignant intelligence to it, a personality. Lily felt as if she were being watched from all directions, even from inside. She felt naked.

"Yes," she said. "Let's go outside till they're done in here."

The young man and woman Lily and Claudia had passed on the way in were standing on the walkway, arguing quietly. The young man said, "You knew what we were going to be doing, so why did you come?"

"Oh, *please*," the young woman said, arms folded tightly across her breasts. "I didn't believe *any* of that stuff, and neither did you. This was supposed to be for *fun*."

"Hey, I take this very seriously, you know that."

"I didn't realize *how* seriously until now, and I think it's seriously *insane*."

"Why didn't you say something about this sooner?"

"Because I hadn't seen inanimate objects fly across the *room* before!"

"I can't walk out on Arty and Mavis now. I came to—"

"Fine, you stay." She removed a cell phone from the pocket of her down jacket and flipped it open. "I'm calling a cab to take me to the airport. I'm going home."

"Home? C'mon, Shannon, why?"

"All I know is, Willy, this is bullshit. I figured maybe we'd hear a few sounds, see some lights. I didn't know people were going to be hurt."

"I didn't either, but what we saw here tonight, it was incredible. It was—"

"It was scarier than *shit*, William," she said, crying now. "Don't bother to call me when you get home." She punched three buttons, then stepped away from him, saying quietly into the phone, "Eureka? Um, I need a cab. I don't know—try, um, Yellow Cab."

Lily felt a little better outside the house, but not much. There was a dull ache in her head, and she still felt twinges of the presence in the house, but she swept them both aside to focus on her situation. She went down the front steps to Willy and introduced herself.

"Nice to meet you," he said, distracted, still looking at Shannon.

"Could you tell me what happened in there?" Lily asked.

"Uh . . . sure." He didn't take his eyes from Shannon.

"Where are we?" Shannon asked over her shoulder. "What's the address?"

"Two two oh four Starfish Drive," Lily said. To Willy she said, "Please. Tell me."

While Willy told her what had happened in the house, Shannon waited for her cab.

* * *

After all the screaming and wailing, it ended quietly. Jenna was left with a ringing in her ears and the sour smell of Father Malcolm in her nostrils. She and David sat across from Martha in the breakfast nook. Miles had stretched out on the back cushion and dozed off, so they spoke in whispers.

Chief Winningham stood at the table. "You say he did that himself?" he said.

David said, "Yes. He was on all fours, and he crawled into the fire. And he just . . . stayed there. And let himself burn. Jenna and I pulled him out, but . . ." David sighed and scrubbed his face with his hand.

"Why would he do that?" Chief Winningham asked. "Do you have any idea?"

"You wouldn't believe us if we told you," Jenna said.

David shook his head. "No, you wouldn't."

"Something made him do it," Jenna said.

"Something?" Winningham said. "Made him?"

She stood and faced the chief. "Our house is haunted, and yes, *something made* Father Malcolm crawl into the fire."

Winningham nodded, then stared down at the table for a moment, thinking. Finally, he looked at Jenna and said, "Well, they're gone now. The ambulance took them. And that young man drove Mrs. Bingham to the hospital. The young woman left in a cab."

David cleared his throat and said hesitantly, "They're both, uh . . . they died?"

"I'm afraid so. Look, the reason I came here in the first place was not to answer a call. You're outside my jurisdiction. I came over to vouch for Lily Rourke."

"The psychic," Lily said.

"That's right. She's a good one, too. She has an excellent reputation. She's assisted law enforcement on a number of occasions. She's helped find missing people and solve crimes, and she's saved lives doing it. She says you were suspicious of her motives and asked me to come talk to you and reassure you that she's not a fake, and she's not asking for money. When she talks, the police listen. I think you should, too."

Still standing, Jenna looked down at David. He looked pale and tired, but there was a little too much white visible in his eyes. The anger and resistance were gone.

"Let's talk to her," Jenna said.

David nodded without hesitation and said, "Yes."

"I'll get her," Winningham said.

As he left the kitchen, Jenna sat down again. She and David watched Miles sleep while Martha stared at her tea. None of them spoke.

When Winningham returned, he brought with him Lily Rourke and her redheaded friend. Lily saw Miles asleep on the cushion and whispered when she spoke.

She introduced herself and Claudia again, and said, "Mr. and Mrs. Kellar, I'm sorry. I feel partly responsible for what happened here tonight because I didn't put a stop to it. I should've been more insistent, I should've—"

"It's not your fault," Jenna said. "I should have listened to you."

"It's my fault," David said. "*I* should've listened. What do we do now? How do we get rid of this?"

Lily said nothing for a moment. She looked up at the ceiling, around at the cabinets and counters, but she did not seem to see them. She inhaled deeply and seemed to be breathing in the whole room, the house itself. "We'll need help," she said to Jenna. "I'm a psychic, not a medium. I've never dealt with anything like this before. We need someone who has. Kimberly said you talked to some mediums, is that right?"

Jenna nodded. "One of them came here. Ada. But she won't come back."

"Was there another? Someone who didn't seem like a fraud?"

"Mrs. Frangiapani. She claims to be a psychic medium. We were both pretty impressed with her, but I don't know if she—"

"We need her."

"Do you want me to call her?" Jenna said.

"No. Take me to her."

Claudia drove Lily, Jenna, and Miles—Jenna did not want to leave him at home, and Lily agreed—through the rain to Mrs. Frangiapani's house in nearby Ferndale. David and Martha had stayed behind.

"If the slightest thing happens while we're gone," Lily had said, "get out of the house. Go out and sit in your car until we get back."

Lily felt Jenna Kellar's fear and tension—it seemed to fill the cab of the Beetle. Miles remained silent throughout the drive to Ferndale.

"Mrs. Frangiapani is old," Jenna said, leaning forward in the backseat. "She says she's retired, so I don't know if she'll be willing to help us."

"You say she claims to be psychic as well as a medium?" Lily asked.

Jenna said, "Yes."

"Then let me talk to her," Lily said.

Claudia parked on the street in front of Mrs. Frangiapani's white Victorian house. On the porch, Jenna pushed the doorbell. Several seconds later, the door opened and Mrs. Frangiapani smiled out at them.

"Well, hello, angel," she said to Jenna. She unlocked the screen door and pushed it open. "Come in and introduce me to your friends."

Inside, Lily stepped forward and smiled at the old woman. "I'm sorry for coming at such a late hour," she said, holding out her hand. "My name is Lily Rourke, and I've come for your help."

Mrs. Frangiapani shook Lily's hand.

Lily opened up a little, reached out with her mind curiously. She flinched slightly when she realized Mrs. Frangiapani was doing the same thing. Their mouths opened in broad smiles.

"A fellow seer," Mrs. Frangiapani said. "It's so nice to meet you, Lily. Would you like some fudge? I make it with cream cheese and just a little instant coffee, and it melts in your mouth." She looked back and forth between Lily and Claudia and Jenna and Miles. "Or do we not have time for that?"

Lily knew then that Mrs. Frangiapani was going to help them.

CHAPTER TWENTY-FOUR

Saturday, 10:38 P.M.

It was a cold night, and rain fell steadily as Claudia turned the silver Beetle off Starfish Drive and down the long driveway that led to the Kellars's house. The windows glowed brightly—every light in the house was on.

Lily watched Mrs. Frangiapani closely as they entered the house and hung up their coats. The farther into the house they went, the more the old woman seemed to shrink into herself, like a child in anticipation of being struck.

In the living room, Martha was on the couch watching television and David was dozing in the recliner, his feet up. He awoke and sat up when they entered the living room. The smell of freshly baked cookies did little to cover the odor of burnt hair and flesh. Jenna introduced Mrs. Frangiapani to David and Martha.

Mrs. Frangiapani looked frightened and concerned, but she smiled through it and said, "Someone's been baking cookies."

Martha stood and smiled. "Chocolate-chip hazelnut cookies," she said.

"Sounds delicious," Mrs. Frangiapani said.

"I bake a lot. It makes me feel good to feed people happy food."

Mrs. Frangiapani seemed to recover somewhat as she nodded vigorously. "Yes, yes, I know exactly what you mean. I bake all the time. We should trade recipes."

As she led Mrs. Frangiapani out of the living room, Martha said, "I've got recipes up the ying-yang. Come to the kitchen and have some cookies. Would you like a glass of milk to go with them?" She stopped and turned back. "Could I interest you in some cookies, Lily? Claudia?"

Mrs. Frangiapani turned to Lily. "I'd like to walk around a little, get a feel for the place."

"Sure," Lily said. "And no cookies for me, thank you." Her stomach still felt dubious. Claudia politely refused, too.

"I want some," Miles said as he followed Martha and Mrs. Frangiapani.

As he passed Lily, she reached out and gently closed her hand on his upper arm. "Wait, Miles. I'd like to keep an eye on you. Why don't you stay here for now."

"We'd *all* like to keep an eye on you, honey," Jenna said.

The two old women continued to chatter as they passed through the dining room on the way to the kitchen.

Smiling at the boy, Lily released his arm.

Jenna said, "Grandma can bring you some cookies. Why don't you just sit down and watch TV for now, okay? Put in a movie, if you want. Something cheerful and funny."

"You mean something like *Ghostbusters*?" Miles said with a smile.

Lily laughed as Jenna said, "That's not funny, Miles."

He smiled up at Lily, happy that she had appreciated his little joke. He went to the couch, took the remote from the end table, and began flipping through channels.

Lily stepped closer to Jenna and whispered, "There's a dark presence in this house. Something malevolent."

David got up from the recliner and joined them.

Lily continued: "I strongly suspect this presence is some remnant of Leonard Baines."

"My father," Jenna said. "Biologically, anyway."

"Kimberly said you know nothing about him," Lily said. "I don't know how much your mother has told you, but I suspect she found him stranger than she's led you to believe."

"She said he was as clumsy as a child in bed," Jenna said.

"That would make sense." She glanced over at Miles on the couch, absorbed in a Daffy Duck cartoon, then looked at Jenna again and whispered, "He was a pedophile."

David asked Lily, "How do you know all this?"

"Like I said, I'm psychic. I've been having visions about your family. Some involved a man I believe to be Leonard Baines. He was a sexual predator who preyed on little boys. In my visions, I saw him as a tall, fat man in a dirty T-shirt and a denim vest, and he wore a cowboy hat."

"Oh, God," David breathed. "I've seen him. We've all seen him."

"I believe he kidnapped a lot of young boys between the ages of about five and ten, maybe eleven," Lily said. "I don't know how many, or how long he did it. He traveled to other towns, sometimes out of state, to find the boys, and he brought them back here, where he tortured and molested them. He starved them to death—some of them, anyway. Others—I don't know how he disposed of them, I just know he used them up and killed them."

"We've seen the boys," David said. "In the backyard. And in the house."

"At first, I saw only one, a little one," Jenna said. "I thought it was our son, Josh. We lost him a few years ago, and I thought . . ." Jenna was surprised when her voice broke and her throat burned. She sniffled, bent down, and took an unused paper napkin from the plate Willy had left on the floor, wiped her nose with it. "I'm sorry."

"Don't be," Lily said.

Jenna bowed her head. "I guess I was so convinced it was Josh that finding out otherwise was . . . a disappointment. I finally saw his face. He looked nothing like Josh."

"What did he look like?" Lily said.

"Red hair, freckles." Jenna smiled slightly for a moment. "He was adorable. But he wasn't Josh."

"He was a toddler?" Lily asked.

"Yes."

Lily nodded. "I've seen him. He was tortured, as well. In one particular room of this house." She turned and walked away from them slowly, into the entryway.

Jenna and David followed.

Lily walked past the staircase, stopped at the mirror on the wall, and briefly looked at her reflection. It was the same mirror in which she had seen the face of the fat man in the white cowboy hat.

Lily could hear Martha and Mrs. Frangiapani talking down the hall in the kitchen.

Jenna hurried down to the kitchen doorway, leaned

in, and said, "Mom, could you go out and sit with Miles? I don't want him to be alone."

"Sure," Martha said.

As Jenna came back up the hall, Lily walked past the mirror and stopped at the first door on the left.

"In here," she said.

Jenna said, "This is my mother's room. She sleeps on the sofa now because she kept seeing boys hanging from shackles on the wall and toddlers strapped into some kind of perverted high chair."

"I've seen the same thing," Lily said with a nod. "He brought them in here to torture them, to punish them for being . . . bad puppies."

Jenna gasped again and exchanged a look with David.

"Sometimes he'd whip them," Lily said, "and . . . do other things to them, horrible things. Something of those boys is still in this house, too, along with Leonard Baines. I suspect the reason they attacked the priest who was here earlier is that *he* was a pedophile, like your father. Somehow they recognized that and lashed out at him."

"Father Malcolm was a pedophile?" Jenna said.

"I did some research," Lily said. "He was defrocked years ago. He had no business calling himself a priest, just as the Binghams had no business calling themselves paranormal investigators."

Lily reached out, turned the old brass doorknob, and pushed the door open. Light spilled into the dark room, and Lily inhaled sharply through her nose. When she exhaled, she breathed the words "Oh, my God."

She saw them on the wall, in the chair. They were in the dark, but the light from the hall allowed her to see them clearly. They were as solid and real as she. Their wide eyes went to her, took a moment to realize she was not the person they'd expected, then narrowed and pleaded silently for help.

Lily blinked her eyes, and the boys were gone. The walls were bare. They were gone, but they had been there once. *How many?* Lily wondered. *And how long did it go on?* Her visions seldom provided her with all the answers. She reached out with her right hand, swept it over the wall beside the door, and flipped a light switch.

"The lights in here don't work," Jenna said. "We haven't replaced them yet."

"We've been having trouble with our lights," David said. "Bulbs keep blowing out."

Jenna said, "Usually accompanied by a sudden drop in temperature, and sometimes a little destruction."

The sound of conversation continued to come from the kitchen.

"Just a second," Jenna said as she turned and went back down the hall. She stopped in the kitchen doorway and didn't move for a moment. Finally, she turned and beckoned for Lily and David to join her.

Lily went down the hall, and Jenna stepped into the kitchen and out of the way. David went in and stood beside Jenna. Lily stood in the doorway.

Mrs. Frangiapani stood in the middle of the kitchen with her back to them. Her hands were on her thighs and she was bent forward slightly.

"But you're not supposed to be here anymore," Mrs. Frangiapani said to the air in front of her. "Your time here has ended." She said nothing for several seconds, then: "No, angel, you don't understand—you should . . ." Mrs. Frangiapani's head dropped forward for a moment, then she slowly stood up straight, pressed a hand over the base of her spine. She turned around and faced them, spread her arms wide, then let them slap to her sides. "They come, they go. They're just children. They have short attention spans and a fondness for trickery and teasing. Someone kept them here in life, a man. A horrible man."

"Leonard Baines," Lily said.

"They never knew his name. To them, he was just the fat man. He kept them here and did awful things to them. He kept them in the basement. They're so terrified of him, they don't realize their lives have ended. They think they're still under his control."

"Oh, God," Jenna said, turning to David. "He was in Miles's bedroom."

"He wants your son," Lily said, and they turned around to face her. "He's already tried to use you, Mr. Kellar, to get to Miles. That failed, but he'll keep trying." She turned to Mrs. Frangiapani. "Unless you can help us get rid of him."

Mrs. Frangiapani nodded once. "I'll do my best."

As they all gathered in the living room, Jenna went to David and took his hand. He looked sleepy-eyed and moved slowly. She whispered, "How are you feeling?"

"Not so good," he whispered back. "Took another pill and it's starting to kick in."

"Would you like to go upstairs and sleep? I can take care of this."

"No, no. I'll be fine. I'm just a little groggy."

She kissed his cheek. "If you change your mind, I want you to go to bed, okay?"

He nodded as Miles joined them. David put a hand on his shoulder and said, "How's it going, Tiger?"

"Okay, I guess," Miles said. "Is this going to be scary?"

"I don't know, honey," Jenna said. "But you have nothing to be afraid of—you're going to be fine."

Jenna had put the lamps back on their end tables and cleaned up the broken Roseville vase, the shattered ceramic elves, and the pieces of glass from the framed photographs. The pile of broken elves and framed photos remained on the floor beside the black cabinet.

Mrs. Frangiapani said, "I'm going to try to explain to the children in this house that it's time for them to move on. It might take a while, because they aren't very attentive. I suspect that once these children know they can go, they'll leave, and then this terrible fat man will have no reason to stay. Is it all right if I turn off the television? It's distracting."

Jenna quickly turned it off. "No problem," she said.

"I'm not familiar with your work, Mrs. Frangiapani," Lily said, "so feel free to speak up if there's anything else you need us to do."

The old woman smiled. "No, I need nothing else. Just make yourselves comfortable while I do this."

Lily, Martha, and Claudia sat down on the sofa. David lowered himself into the recliner heavily. Jenna sat beside him on the recliner's armrest and Miles sat cross-legged on the floor in front of him. They watched Mrs. Frangiapani, who stood in the center of the room and clasped her hands together before her as if to pray.

"Children," she said. "Boys. I know you're here. Please pay attention to me, boys, I have something important to tell you, something you'll be very happy to hear." She turned to Jenna. "Could you turn the lights down a little?"

Jenna got up and turned off the overhead light and two of the lamps, leaving only the lamp beside the recliner on. She returned to her seat on the armrest.

"Sometimes," Mrs. Frangiapani said, "too much light

keeps them away." She turned away from them again and looked at nothing in particular as she said, "I want to help you, boys. Please come let Mrs. Frangiapani help you."

The room's temperature dropped several degrees. Even with the crackling flames in the fireplace, the living room cooled.

"Boys, you must listen carefully," Mrs. Frangiapani said. "It's time for you to leave this place, children. The fat man no longer has *any* power over you—you can leave anytime you want, just fly away. This is a bad place for you, a horrible place. There's no reason for you to stay here—you should go now, boys, go away together, leave no one behind. There is nothing the fat man can do to you now, you're completely free of—"

The lamp went out. Every light in the house went out and left them in darkness. The soft, dancing orange glow of the fire was the only light in the room.

"Dammit," David said as he got up.

Jenna quickly stood, too. "Where are you going?"

"To get the flashlight," he said as he went into the dining room.

While he was gone, Mrs. Frangiapani continued: "You're free to move on now. You've been here far too long. I understand—"

Mrs. Frangiapani stopped speaking and stared at something in front of her. When Jenna saw it, she inhaled a gulp of air in a quiet gasp.

A small figure stood before the old woman, a shadow in the darkness. Jenna looked closer and realized the boy was as transparent as a faint cloud of dust, the features of his face softly blurred.

"I understand," Mrs. Frangiapani said, "that you've had very bad experiences here and your spirits were

342

broken. You've been confused and hurt by what happened here, so I understand, I really do."

Jenna saw another boy standing near the straight-back chair, another between the chair and the dining room doorway, all part of the dark, melting into it, mere suggestions of shapes. More boys appeared—two, three, four, two of them toddlers.

Jenna hunkered down on the floor beside Miles and put an arm around him. She could feel him shiver as he gawked at the figures in the dark.

"Are those ghosts, Mom?" Miles whispered tremulously.

"Something like that, honey," she said. "But don't be afraid."

"But you have to understand," Mrs. Frangiapani said, "that this isn't a place for you anymore—you can leave. Are you listening to Mrs. Frangiapani?"

"Where's the flashlight?" David said. He stood in the dining room doorway. When he saw the boys, his chin slowly dropped.

Jenna thought about the flashlight and remembered where it was. "I'm sorry, honey—it's in the basement."

"The *basement?*"

They spoke in low tones. The boys did not seem to notice.

Jenna said, "Arty took one of their religious icons down there and something scared him. He dropped the light."

"So he probably left it on. Do we have batteries?"

"On the shelf over the washer and dryer in the laundry room."

David sighed. "So I'm going to have to go down those stairs in the dark," he muttered as he turned to go back through the dining room.

Miles shot to his feet. "Just a second, Dad," he said as he hurried out of the room and through the entryway.

Jenna stood and shouted, "Miles! Come back here!"

"It'll just take a second!" Miles called as he ran up the stairs.

She heard him run down the upstairs hall to his bedroom. A few seconds later, he thumped down the stairs. He went down the hall to the kitchen and appeared beside David in the dining room doorway. He handed David his penlight, already turned on.

"Thanks, Miles," David said, and headed back through the dining room.

Miles followed him.

"Miles, come back in here," Jenna said.

"Okay," he called from the dining room.

"Now, you boys listen to Mrs. Frangiapani," the old woman said. "You need to leave here now. Just let yourself rise up and up and leave this place. The fat man has no power over you, he can't stop you from—"

Faint, whispered voices, terse and frightened—the boys:

"He's coming."

"Let's get out of here."

"Go, go, go!"

"No, don't go away!" Mrs. Frangiapani said. "You have no reason to be afraid!"

The figures in the dark dissolved and the room grew colder.

Instead of going out the kitchen's rear door, down the hall, and back to the living room with Mom, Miles went to the laundry room. He did not feel safe in the dark and wanted his flashlight back. He went to the open basement door and peered down the stairs. He heard Dad's footsteps on the dirt floor below, saw the narrow beam of his penlight moving through the darkness. He decided to wait there for Dad to come back up.

Seconds after the temperature dropped in the living room a second time, something rose up from the floor. It looked to Jenna like a dense swarm of gnats, a cloud of undulating blackness.

Mrs. Frangiapani stumbled backward as the cloud engulfed her. It swirled around her silently, then contracted, moving in close around her. It flexed like a muscle, and Mrs. Frangiapani cried out before collapsing onto the floor.

Lily came up off the couch.

The black cloud dropped slowly, then disappeared into the floor.

Jenna and Lily went to Mrs. Frangiapani. The old woman lay on her back, arms out at her sides.

"Mrs. Frangiapani," Lily said, "can you hear me?"

Jenna picked up Mrs. Frangiapani's right hand and rubbed the back of it. The old woman stirred, whimpered as Lily checked her wrist for a pulse.

"Should we get her on the couch?" Jenna asked.

"No, let's leave her here for the time being," Lily said. "Her pulse is good."

"What do we do now?" Jenna said as they stood.

"To be honest, Mrs. Kellar," Lily said, "I'm not sure."

"Call me Jenna." She turned and looked down at the spot on the floor where Miles had been sitting—he was not there. He had not come back in the room yet. She turned to the entryway, but he was not there, either. Her heart quickened its pace. "Miles! Miles, where are you?"

Miles stepped out of the laundry room and shouted, "I'll be there in a second."

"Come in here right *now*, Miles," she said in the living room.

Dad's footsteps started back up the stairs, and Miles hurried back to the basement door. Dad came up with the penlight in his mouth and the long black Mag-Lite shining in his right hand.

"It still works," Miles said as he stepped back to let Dad into the laundry room.

Using his right hand, Dad clumsily took the penlight from his mouth and handed it over to Miles. "Wait here," he said.

As Dad walked into the kitchen, Miles looked at the penlight and muttered, "It's got spit on it now." He wiped it on his jeans

Dad got something from a drawer, put it in his pocket, then came back to the laundry room. "Come down with me. I need your help."

"Really?" Miles said.

"Come on, you go first."

Miles aimed the penlight straight ahead as he started down the basement stairs. From behind him, Dad's flashlight lit up the narrow staircase.

The light coming from behind Miles disappeared, leaving only the narrow beam of his penlight, which flickered out. Miles turned and looked up the stairs just as Dad pulled the door shut.

Dad faced the door at the top of the stairs, the flashlight tucked beneath his right arm. He threw a bolt lock on the inside of the door, then turned around and came down the stairs. The flashlight's beam hit Miles directly in the eyes and made him glance away, but when he looked again, Dad had removed from his pocket the biggest knife from Mom's knife drawer in the kitchen.

The penlight slipped from Miles's trembling hand, hit one of the stairs, then fell through into the darkness below the staircase.

In a gravelly voice that wasn't quite his, Dad said, "Go on, get down there, you fuckin' puppy."

CHAPTER TWENTY-FIVE

Saturday, 11:26 P.M.

Jenna bumped into one of the chairs at the table as she hurried through the dining room in the dark. "Miles, where are you?" she said as she entered the kitchen. "David?" she said as she looked around the room. "Miles? Where *are* you?" She went into the laundry room and listened at the closed basement door. She heard a low, gravelly voice. The words being spoken were unintelligible, but the voice was enough.

"No!" she screamed as she grabbed the doorknob with both hands and tried to open the door. "Leave him alone! Let him go!" The door would not budge. She pounded on the door while trying to open it. "David! David, can you hear me?"

Footsteps rushed into the kitchen.

"It's locked!" Jenna screamed. "My God, it's *locked!*"

Lily and Claudia came into the laundry room, followed by Martha.

"Let me try," Lily said.

Jenna stepped away from the door. Lily clutched the doorknob with both hands and threw her considerable weight into pulling on it. It would not open.

The basement was cold and damp and so dark that, without Dad's flashlight, Miles would be unable to see anything at all. Miles tried to scream but could not. He made small breathy sounds as his chest rapidly rose and fell. Once off the stairs, he turned to face Dad as he came down the last few steps. The flashlight beneath Dad's arm had tipped downward. Miles backed away from him over the dirt floor.

Dad moved differently as he came toward Miles. Hips forward, torso leaning back slightly, he walked with a lazy swagger. His eyes looked sleepy, but his mouth was curled into a grin that made Miles feel nauseated. The blade of the butcher knife he held in his fist looked enormous. Light from the flashlight held under Dad's right arm flashed on the broad side of the blade.

"Miles?" Mom called in the kitchen. "David?"

Miles gasped at the sound of her voice. Dad did not seem to notice.

"Miles? Where *are* you?"

Miles backed into a stack of boxes. The damp cardboard felt cold through the back of his long-sleeve blue-plaid shirt. As Dad slowly closed in, Miles became paralyzed. Even his lungs seemed to have frozen up, and he did not breathe. His heart was beating so fast, it seemed to hum in his chest rather than pulse.

"You're gonna be a good puppy now," Dad said, his voice low and gravelly and wet. "You're gonna do as I say, or I'm gonna pound on you awhile. Got that, puppy?"

Miles wanted to nod his head "yes" and do whatever he was told, but he could not move.

Dad stopped a couple feet in front of him.

"No!" Mom screamed. She pounded on the basement door, struggled with the knob. "Leave him alone! Let him go! David! David, can you hear me?"

Dad cocked his head a moment, as if to listen.

It's not Dad! Miles's mind screamed within the walls of his skull. *It's not Dad, it's the fat man! Remember that! It's not Dad!*

"You gonna answer me?" Dad said. He hadn't been listening to Mom at all, just waiting for Miles to respond.

Miles opened his mouth, but instead of talking, he began to breathe again, to pant. He nodded his head.

"Get down on the floor," Dad—the fat man—said.

He moved quickly and got down on his hands and knees.

"On your back."

He still could hear Mom's voice on the other side of the door at the top of the stairs. She was talking with someone else and she sounded panicky, but it was just noise to Miles, because the fat man wanted him to lie down on his back in the dark and the only thing Miles could think was *What is he going to do to me with that knife?* His mind was too filled with horrifying possibilities to think about what Mom was saying. He found he was unable to move again.

"I said, *get on your back*." The last four words were not shouted, but the way he said them—teeth clenched, spitting, growling—was worse.

With great effort, Miles forced himself to lie down on his back on the cold, lumpy dirt floor.

Dad towered over Miles, grinned down at him.

Miles remembered what had happened when Mom had hit Dad's injured hand with a dictionary—he had become himself again. Miles could do that. Dad's hand was in such pain already that he wouldn't need a fat dictionary to hurt him, he could use his fist.

Dad knelt down, straddled Miles with his knees—*It's not Dad!*—touched the flat of the blade to Miles's cheek, and chuckled.

"You're gonna be a good puppy now, aren't you?" he said as he slid the knife's large blade beneath Miles's shirt.

"Why is this door locked?" Lily said. The door would not budge.

Jenna spoke rapidly. "I don't know. I didn't even know there was a lock on this door."

"Claudia, call Chief Winningham," Lily said. The feeling of dread she'd experienced in her visions filled her lungs like water and all she could think about was Miles.

Jenna stood in front of the washing machine, wringing her hands and breathing too fast, cheeks wet with tears. Martha was beside her with an arm across her shoulders.

"We're not in his jurisdiction," Jenna whispered, her words trembling. "We're outside the city limits. Call the Sheriff's Department. 911."

Lily turned to Martha. "Would you call 911? Please?"

Martha hurried out of the laundry room.

Lily turned to Claudia and said, "Call the chief. Tell him to get back over here right away."

"Do you think we need him?" Claudia asked. "I mean, with the Sheriff's Dep—"

Lily moved close to Claudia and whispered in her ear, "I want his skeptical ass here to see this."

"Are you kidding?" Claudia said.

"I'm not kidding. I want him here."

"My cell phone's in the living room," Claudia said.

Lily said, "Check on Mrs. Frangiapani while you're there."

Claudia nodded and left the laundry room.

Lily was startled by a hand on her shoulder and spun around to find Jenna standing close.

Jenna spoke too fast in a half-whisper. "Ada said something to me—Ada, that's the medium who came here for a sitting. She said the reason people only need to see her once or twice is that, by then, they've figured out they can talk to the dead themselves. She said anybody could do it. Might not get a response, she said, but it might be worth a try."

"You know what, Jenna? You might have something there." She turned to the basement door again and stood there a moment, thinking. She shouted at the door, "We know your secret, Leonard. Everybody knows. All the people who thought you were such a good guy—they all know now."

Jenna suddenly moved forward a few steps and screamed, "Let go of my little boy, you bastard! Don't hurt him! He's your grandson, your own *grandson*!"

Lily put an arm around Jenna and led her back to the washing machine. She whispered in Jenna's ear, "Please try to calm down, Jenna. Let me do this, okay?"

Jenna rubbed one hand down over her face as she nodded.

Lily went back to the door. "Everybody knows what kind of man you are, Leonard. Chief Winningham, everyone at the Eureka PD—your secret's out."

Martha returned to the laundry room and said, "Are we talking to Leonard?" She moved closer to the door and shouted, "This is Martha, Lenny. Remember me? You were a lousy lay, Lenny. You hear me? Screwing you was like screwing a little boy. Turns out that's what you wanted all along. You're a sick, pathetic coward,

Leonard, and now everybody knows it. It'll be in the paper and people will—"

A horrible sound erupted down in the basement—a growling, gurgling scream—and Jenna moved toward the door, one hand on her hip, the other on top of her head, clawing at her scalp. Her eyes were open to their limit and the corners of her mouth were pulled back in a grin of fear.

And the horrible sound went on.

A whimper escaped Miles when he felt the cold blade against his stomach. Dad cut off the buttons of his shirt one at a time. Miles heard shouting upstairs, but it sounded distant, far away. He stared up at Dad—*It's not Dad!*—and glanced at the lump in his sweatshirt that was his arm in a cast and sling. Miles waited for the right moment. But he didn't know if he could do it. It meant causing Dad a lot of pain—Miles did not want to do that. But maybe it was the pain of being hit that had allowed Dad to separate himself from the fat man. In that case, Miles had no choice.

"Goddamned women," Dad muttered. He grinned down at Miles. "I don't know what I wanna do to you first." He pressed the tip of the blade to Miles's throat. "Mebbe first, I'll make damned good and sure you won't struggle while I have my fun."

Suddenly, a different voice rang out from above, clear and angry: Grandma's.

"This is Martha, Lenny. You remember me? You were a lousy lay, Lenny. You hear me?"

Dad straightened his back and looked up at the door.

"Screwing you was like screwing a little boy."

Hearing Grandma say that made Miles wonder if he was dreaming.

Dad made a sound like a growl as he listened.

Miles realized the moment had come. Dad's attention was on the door. Miles swung his right fist without thinking about it—otherwise he might never have done it. It connected with the back of Dad's left hand.

Dad screamed as he fell back and off of Miles, who crawled backward. Dad dropped the Mag-Lite as he writhed on the floor and cried out in pain. Miles, suddenly on hands and knees, scurried over and grabbed it up. He could use it as a weapon, if necessary.

Dad sat up with his back against one of the wooden support beams beneath the stairs, legs spread, one knee bent. Perspiration glistened on his face. "Miles?"

Miles gasped when he heard his dad's voice, not the fat man's. "Dad?"

"Miles. Run. Get out of here. Now." He sounded hoarse and exhausted, but there was no mistaking the urgency in his voice.

Miles did as he was told. His shirt had already been untucked, and now it hung open in front, its buttons somewhere on the dirt floor. He stepped over Dad's leg on his way to the stairs.

A hand closed on his left ankle and sent him pitching forward. He landed facedown in the dirt.

"Not so fast, puppy."

Claudia returned to the laundry room and whispered to Lily, "He said he's on his way. You should see the living room."

"What? Why?" Lily said.

"She's up and talking again, sitting on the sofa."

"Talking to the boys?"

"Yes. The living room's full of them. I had to go around to get in, because I didn't want to disturb them."

"Okay, let's leave her alone and let her work." Lily was amazed by how well Claudia was holding up. Lily's hands were trembling and her voice was dry and cracked, all from fear. "You're sure handling all this well."

"Are you kidding?" Claudia said. "I'm about to crap my pants."

Lily whispered, "I may join you." She turned to Jenna. Martha stood beside her with an arm around Jenna's shoulders again. Lily said, "Is there a window down there?"

Jenna shook her head. "No, nothing. It's just a hole in the ground with cinder-block walls and a dirt floor. Shouldn't we be *doing* something? There's an ax around here someplace—we should be looking for it."

"Where is it?" Claudia asked. "I'll go. I need to get out of here."

Jenna said, "Behind the garage, where all the wood is stacked, maybe leaning against the wall."

Claudia hurried out as Lily turned to the basement door again. She was tempted to go out through the dining room to see for herself what Mrs. Frangiapani was up to, but she was unable to tear herself away from that door. Hoping to distract him from Miles, if nothing else, she continued talking to Leonard Baines.

Dad rolled Miles over and straddled him again on his knees. He backhanded Miles, hit his cheekbone with the butt of the butcher knife's black handle, which protruded from the bottom of his fist. Miles cried out in pain, and the ground tilted beneath him for a moment.

"What kind of man are you, Leonard?" said a voice on the other side of the door. "You prey on *children*. You're a coward—Martha was right. And she would know, wouldn't she? She told us how childish and pathetic you were in bed."

Dad ignored her. His eyes never left Miles's.

The voice continued, but Miles was too preoccupied to listen.

"You gonna be hit me again a good Miles little puppy?" Dad said.

Miles fought the dizziness, struggled to remain conscious. He wasn't sure he'd heard what he *thought* he'd just heard, but it didn't matter. As if poking Dad with a stick, Miles slammed the head of the heavy Mag-Lite into his left hand.

Again, Dad screamed and fell off him, but this time he dropped the knife. Miles suddenly found himself standing with the flashlight in his left hand, the knife in his right. He swayed with dizziness.

"Get out," Dad said, his voice crushed by pain.

Miles stayed where he was. To get to the stairs, he would have to go around Dad, who was stretched out on the floor, and that would put him within reach of Dad's hand again.

"I said get out," Dad said as he slowly got to his feet.

"*Let* me get out."

Dad hunched forward and let his right arm dangle. For a moment, Miles thought he moved like a mummy from an old horror movie.

"Don't make me hurt you, Dad, please," Miles said. He didn't want to cry, but tears came anyway.

"You're bein' a baaaad puppy," the fat man said. He came toward Miles. "Put that fuckin' knife down now, or I'm gonna make you eat it."

Miles found himself once again backed up against the cold, damp boxes. "Dad, please. I don't want to hurt you."

The fat man laughed. He suddenly stood up straight, swept his right foot out, and knocked Miles's legs out from under him.

Miles was so surprised by the move, his hands let go of the knife and flashlight as he went down.

Claudia came back into the laundry room empty-handed, wet from the rain.

"I'm sorry, I couldn't find it," she said. "But I think the police are here. I heard someone drive up out front."

Lily turned away from the door and said, "The police, or Chief Winningham?"

"I don't know," Claudia said.

"Excuse me," Lily said as she stepped around Claudia and left the laundry room. She went through the kitchen and stopped halfway through the dining room. Orange firelight flickered in the living room. Through the doorway, she saw a dozen boys, maybe more. She could hear Mrs. Frangiapani talking quietly, gently. The boys were nothing more than gossamer outlines of small figures in the dark. Through them, Lily could see Mrs. Frangiapani sitting on the couch, leaning forward, hands folded neatly in her lap. The boys disappeared and reappeared like some kind of fiber-optic illusion—at times it looked like the living room was packed with them, and at others, like there were only a few.

As Lily crossed the dining room, she reached out enough to sense their anger. She was surprised by it—she'd expected pain and fear, but that was gone now. The only thing left was their molten rage. When Lily reached the doorway, the vague figures in the living room began to sink into the floor.

Mrs. Frangiapani stood and smiled at Lily. "I think I convinced them," she said.

* * *

357

Miles was held tightly between Dad's legs. The flash-light was a few feet away from them on the floor, aimed at their feet.

"I told you I was gonna make you eat this fuckin' knife," the fat man said, "and I meant it."

Miles did not wait this time. He pounded Dad's left hand with his fist, then again.

Dad screamed again but did not fall. He leaned back for a moment and became silent. He slowly came forward until he was looking down at Miles. Through clenched teeth, Dad said, "Get . . . out of . . . here."

Miles struggled but could not move. "Get *off* of me!" Miles cried.

Dad's shoulders hitched up and down as he sobbed. "I . . . can't . . . you fuckin' puppy." He smiled, but it was a smile filled with pain—his voice was a groan. "You think you're gonna . . . Miles I . . . stop me from . . . what I . . . love you . . . what I—"

Dad plunged the knife into his own abdomen, all the way to the hilt. His mouth yawned open and he made a grunting sound as blood bubbled up around the hilt and dribbled over the hand that gripped the knife. In the dim light, the blood looked as black as tar. He fell backward and hit the floor hard, knees up.

Miles quickly stood. "Dad? *Dad!*"

Dad's fist still grasped the handle of the knife tightly, but he did not move or make a sound.

Miles picked up the flashlight from the floor and ran up the stairs.

Jenna heard the sound of running foosteps on the basement stairs, and she hurried over to the door. A bolt was thrown on the other side and the door burst open. Miles slammed into her, and she embraced him, squeezed him to her. She was so relieved, she could not speak. Miles sobbed against her and said something. He pushed away from her and said it again as he cried.

"I think Dad's dead! He stabbed himself with the knife!"

Jenna could barely hear him through the sound of her own sobs.

The two sheriff's deputies—a man and a woman, both tall and dark—came into the house with their flashlights held just above their shoulders. Lily led them through the entryway and into the living room.

"This way, quickly," she said. "The basement—do you have something to break down a door with? This way."

As they stepped around her and went ahead into the dining room, the lights came back on.

Lily pointed to the kitchen doorway and said, "In there, to the right." But she did not follow them, because she smelled bananas, and the electric-blue flashes made her blink.

The deputies were gone—in the laundry room, where they belonged.

Lily tried to lie down on the dining room floor but didn't quite make it before blacking out.

The fat man, Leonard Baines, screams—a high, shrill, agonizing sound.

Lily sees him only in brief flashes as the boys attack him. They tear his T-shirt, his vest, his skin. They gouge his eyes and claw at his mouth as his white cowboy hat tumbles away and disappears into the deep darkness, spattered with blood.

She feels their anger and hatred and knows they did not

tear at Leonard Baines's body, but at his soul, at the deepest part of him, and his tormented screams continue.

Darkness swallows her, and the screaming slowly fades to silence.

CHAPTER TWENTY-SIX

Sunday, 8:21 A.M.

Jenna was standing beside David's hospital bed when he opened his eyes to narrow slits. She clasped his right hand in hers and smiled down at him. One corner of his mouth curled into a weak smile. She bent down and whispered, "You're going to be okay." She kissed his forehead. "You were in surgery most of the night, and it was . . . well . . ." She smiled again to keep from crying. "It was a little touchy for a while. But the doctor says you're going to be okay."

David's dry, cracked lips peeled apart and he tried to speak, but he made only a dry croak in his throat before wincing.

"No, honey," Jenna said, "you can talk later. Just rest now, okay?"

He smiled again, that small, weak smile, then closed his eyes and drifted off.

Jenna stepped away from the bed and stretched her arms, her back. She felt stiff and deeply tired, but feared she would never be able to sleep again. She was hungry and decided she would be doing David no good by sitting at his bedside—he had not been out of the recovery room long, and would sleep for a while. She put on her coat, picked her purse up from the floor, and left the room. She stopped just outside the door when she saw Lily and Claudia coming her way.

Lily asked, "How is he, Jenna?"

"He's going to be okay," she said. "The doctor says he's very lucky—he didn't hit any major blood vessels, and he missed his pancreas by a hair. He's still in bad shape, though. He's got a slow recovery ahead of him, and he's going to have to wear a colostomy bag for a while. But he'll live."

Lily said, "What he did was very heroic."

Tears stung Jenna's eyes as she said in a high, unsteady voice, "I know. And Miles knows."

"How is Miles?" Claudia asked.

Jenna wiped her eyes with a knuckle. "He's good. He and Mom are at Kimberly's house. She and Harry are putting us up for a while. Harry's in real estate. He's going to put the house on the market for us and help us find another place. There's no way we can go back there."

"I wish there was something I could do to help you," Lily said.

"How can you say that? You *saved* us, Lily. I'm sorry I didn't listen to you the first time you called."

"Hey, you did what you thought was right at the time. What you've gone through is— Would it be all right if we stepped into your husband's room a moment? I'd feel more comfortable discussing it there. I promise to whisper."

Jenna led them into the room and closed the door.

The room's other bed, next to the window, was empty. She pulled out the cream-colored curtain that separated the two beds, and they stood by the window and spoke in whispers.

"What you've been through is hardly normal," Lily said. "You did what you thought was right. I'm glad I could help."

"Lily, what *did* we go through?"

Lily described to Jenna the vision she'd had after blacking out in the dining room the night before. "Whatever was left in that house of Leonard Baines and his young victims was trapped in a cycle of events. He tortured and killed those boys over and over. Mrs. Frangiapani was able to convince the remnant of those poor boys that they were free to do as they pleased. They chose to attack their attacker."

"You mean, if David had waited just a little longer—"

"Don't think of it that way, Jenna. We don't know exactly what happened down there. Poor Miles was so upset, he didn't tell us everything. David had a knife. He was fighting for control of himself. For all we know, if he'd waited one more second—maybe *half* a second— you might have lost Miles."

Jenna nodded. It made her feel ill to imagine how close they might have come to losing Miles last night. She thought of Josh—

Mommy—

—and how desperate she had been to see him again, even as a specter, a shadow. But she still had Miles. Thanks to Mrs. Frangiapani, and Lily, and especially David, she still had her son. Jenna felt a surge of affection for the large woman before her, and she stepped forward and embraced her. Lily returned the hug awkwardly and patted her on the back.

Lily pulled back and clutched Jenna's shoulders firmly. "Jenna, I'm getting something I think might be significant to you."

"What—"

Lily whispered, "*Mommy—*"

Jenna gasped.

"I feel *real* bad, Mommy, I'm scared. Something's happening to me, something bad. Please hold me, don't let me go."

Jenna's knees gave way, and she sat heavily on the edge of the empty bed. She sobbed, her arms limp at her sides.

Lily sat on the bed beside her. "Does that mean anything to you?"

Jenna lifted a hand to her mouth to suppress her sobs. She nodded. "Yes. Yes, it does. Thank you."

Before coming to the hospital, Lily and Claudia had packed their bags, put them in the trunk of the Beetle, and settled their debt to Motel 6. Now, in the hospital parking lot, they were ready to go home.

"Before we go," Lily said, "I'd like to give Chief Winningham one more call."

Claudia took the cell phone from her purse, opened it, hit a couple buttons, and handed it to Lily.

"Chief Winningham, it's Lily Rourke. We're about to leave town."

"I'm at the Kellars's house," he said. "Why don't you come over before you leave. We've got donuts if you haven't had breakfast yet."

"All right, see you in a few minutes." She handed the cell phone back to Claudia and said, "Let's stop by the Kellar house on our way out."

"But it's not *on* our way out."

"Stop by anyway."

364

* * *

After the ambulance had taken David Kellar away the night before, Lily had insisted that Mrs. Frangiapani go to the emergency room and be examined—after all, she had been attacked. Claudia and Lily had driven her to the hospital and waited while an ER doctor checked her over. Her blood pressure had been alarmingly high, and the doctor had decided to keep her for a few hours of observation. Mrs. Frangiapani had insisted that Lily and Claudia leave and go to bed.

"I have a friend I can call," she had said. "He's up most of the night watching TV anyway. Do you know he asked me to *marry* him last week? Can you believe that? I've been a widow ten months and he wants me to marry him."

"I think you'd be quite a catch, Mrs. Frangiapani," Claudia said.

"That's very kind of you, angel, but I'm through being a wife. He's a good man and I enjoy his company, and he likes to eat my food, which is nice. At my age, that's all he's going to get out of me, so why marry for that?"

Before saying good-bye, Lily had given Mrs. Frangiapani her business card. "If you ever visit Mt. Shasta, come see us. You'll get the psychic medium's discount on anything in the store."

Mrs. Frangiapani had taken the card, smiled, and said, "Maybe I'll bring you some banana-nut bread."

It was a gray, foggy morning, cold and damp. As Claudia drove the Beetle to the end of the driveway, Lily's mouth dropped open. She said, "What the hell?"

Yellow crime-scene tape had been put up all the way around the Cyclone fence that surrounded the house. There were two sheriff's cars parked along the fence, as well as a Eureka Police Department cruiser, most likely Winningham's. The trunk of one of the sheriff's cars was open. As Lily and Claudia got out of the Beetle, Winningham came out of the front door of the house and met them at the gate.

"Since when did this become a crime scene?" Lily said.

"Since Deputy Hooper discovered a very large collection of child pornography in the basement." The chief was unsmiling and grave.

Lily said, "Surely you don't think the Kellars have anything to do with it."

"No, it's obviously been there awhile, and they just moved in."

"They couldn't have known it was there," Claudia said.

"Of course not," Lily said.

Winningham led them up the walk to the door. "There are a lot of magazines, but most of it is homemade, and Lenny Baines is in a lot of the pictures. He even wore his Santa suit in some of them, the son of a bitch."

Winningham and Claudia went inside, but Lily paused at the front door. She opened herself just enough to make sure the house was still clear. She sensed none of the things she had felt the night before. But a feeling of darkness still emanated from the house, left over, she was sure, by the awful things that had happened there over the years. It was a psychic stain that probably would never go away.

Lily went inside, and she and Claudia followed Winningham to the kitchen, which smelled of coffee. Two large pink boxes of donuts had been left open on the breakfast-nook table. There were sounds of activity throughout the house, but Lily saw no one besides the chief.

"The house is being searched," Winningham said. "But I don't think they're going to find anything. Everything was down in the basement, including all of his photography and video equipment, his computer. Even his torture devices. You were right, Lily."

"But we're keeping that between us, right, Chief?" Lily said. She plucked a paper napkin from a stack on the table, used it to pick up a jelly donut, and took a big bite. She picked up another napkin and dabbed at her mouth.

Once she'd gotten back to the motel room the night before, Lily had gotten the first good night's sleep she'd had in a while, uninterrupted by visions and mercifully free of nightmares. She'd awakened feeling famished and had eaten a big breakfast at Denny's. But she still had room for the jelly donut. Her appetite had returned.

"Don't worry," Winningham had said. "I haven't said a word to anyone."

"Bullshit," Lily said. "You've already started telling your story, haven't you?"

Winningham smiled. "Only to cops, Lily, nobody else. You've got a lot of fans in uniform, you know."

"Well, I suppose there's nothing I can do about that." She took another bite of her donut. She said nothing more until she'd finished it and wiped her mouth clean of jelly. She went to the coffeemaker on the counter, beside which stood a couple of short stacks of Styrofoam cups. Taking one, she poured some coffee. There were plastic spoons as well, a container of powdered nondairy creamer, and a box of sweetener. "I hope you're not using the Kellars's coffee," she said.

"Of course not—the deputies brought their own," Winningham said.

Claudia was already eating her second glazed donut.

Winningham walked over to one of the counters and leaned his hips against it, facing Lily with his arms folded across his barrel chest. "I just can't believe it about Lenny," he said, frowning. "I mean, he didn't leave a clue anywhere. He was as clean as a whistle. At least, that's what we thought."

"That's what he wanted you to think," Lily said.

"And he did such a damned good job of it. Then he just kills himself. He must have known someone would find all that stuff eventually."

"But he cleaned it up first," Claudia said. "He put everything in the basement before checking out."

"He didn't destroy it," Lily said, "but he made sure it was all put away."

"I don't know what happened to Lenny the last ten years," Winningham said. "Maybe if I'd checked up on him once in a while . . . maybe I would've seen something. Maybe I could've put a stop to it a lot sooner."

"Maybes and ifs," Lily said as she walked over to the breakfast nook again. "They don't do anyone any good, Chief." She looked out the window at the backyard, at the familiar swing set and the slide inside the tall fence, the ivy growing wild. "I suspect Leonard Baines was haunted by his victims for a long time before finally deciding to put a stop to it himself. The more he killed, the more there were to torment him. When he finally decided to end his life, that began the cycle that was going on in this house ever since."

Standing beside Lily, Claudia said, "I wonder how long it would've gone on if no one had moved in here."

"It might never have ended." Lily turned to Winningham. "I suggest digging up the backyard, Chief. And the land around the house. I don't think he went far to dispose of his victims."

"That's the next step. They start this afternoon. The FBI's been alerted. I don't suppose you have any more information about his victims, do you?"

"I'm afraid not. The visions have stopped." She turned to him. "What's the press being told?"

"Answering an attempted suicide call, Deputy Hooper inadvertently discovered the collection of porn in the basement. As far as the press is concerned, the Sheriff's Department took it from there."

"Well, it's been a pleasure working with you, Chief," Lily said as she went to Winningham and shook his hand, then gave him a business card. "If you're ever in Mt. Shasta, drop by, and I'll give you the police chief's discount."

"That's real nice of you," he said with a smile. "I've enjoyed meeting you, Lily. You, too, Claudia."

"And please, Chief," Lily said, "when you speak of me, be kind." He chuckled as she turned and walked out of the kitchen, saying, "Come on, Claudia, let's go home. We've got a store to run."

At the Gimble house, Jenna found Miles and Martha on the couch in the living room, watching television. Miles was still in his pajamas. His right cheek was swollen and bruised where he'd been hit. He'd become fast friends with Kimberly's youngest, Ronny, who was in the shower. Ronny's two older brothers had already gone out for the day. Kimberly and Harry were in the kitchen having a late breakfast.

Jenna hugged Martha, then Miles, and sat down between them. She put an arm around Miles and said,

"Dad's going to be okay. He was hurt pretty bad, but the doctor operated on him, and he's going to be in the hospital for a few days. But he's going to be okay. Isn't that great?"

"Oh, that's wonderful," Martha said.

Miles said nothing and did not take his eyes off the television.

"Miles, honey," Jenna said, "did you hear me?"

Several seconds passed before he nodded once.

"Look, sweetheart, if you want to talk about what happened last night, or about anything else, please tell me, okay? It doesn't have to be right now, it can be whenever you feel like it, but I want you to know that you can—"

Miles's face suddenly screwed up, and tears sprang to his eyes. He hugged his knees to his chest and curled into a ball.

Jenna quickly embraced him. It was awkward, but she did not let go. "Oh, honey, go ahead and cry. But we're safe now. You, me, Dad, Grandma—we're all safe now."

Miles cried for a while before lowering his knees and putting his arms around Jenna. "I thought he was dead."

"So did I, honey, so did I. But he's not—he's going to be fine."

"Buh-but he did that . . . buh-because of *me*. If I'd gone into the living room when you called me, he wouldn't'a had to do it."

"You can't think that way, Miles," Jenna said. "If you think that way, you'll make yourself sick." She whispered, "Dad hurt himself to keep the fat man from making him hurt you. And now Dad's okay. So everything's fine." She pulled back and smiled.

Miles's eyelashes were clumped with tears and his nose was running. He sniffled a few times to stop the dribbling, but finally gave up and wiped his nose with his pajama sleeve. "Was it God who saved Dad?" he asked. "Like Arty and Mavis said—about God chasing the demons out of the house. Was it God?"

"Well . . ." Jenna had not expected anything quite as heavy as that, and she thought for a few seconds before responding. "Do *you* believe it was God?"

He shrugged. "I don't know."

"I don't know either, honey. But if you believe that, it's okay. Don't be afraid to say that you do. You should never be afraid to say *anything* to me or Dad."

"Or Grandma," Martha said.

"All right?" Jenna said.

Miles nodded.

"Whatever you choose to believe is just fine, Miles." She put a hand on his head and ran her fingers through his curly hair. "You should believe in something. We all should believe in something."

On Monday morning, Lily opened The Crystal Well with a smile on her face. She felt rested and uncharacteristically optomistic. She had gone to bed very early the night before and had slept deeply till morning.

Over a cup of coffee while waiting for Claudia to arrive, Lily looked at the front page of the *Redding Record Searchlight*. The headline read,

MASS GRAVE FOUND IN EUREKA; REMAINS OF 9 BODIES SO FAR

Young bodies, she thought. *Children. Babies.*

According to the article, it would take months to identify the remains and notify the families so proper burials could be planned. The families of missing children throughout California and Oregon were asked to provide authorities with DNA samples for possible matches.

Lily knew it was only the beginning. They would find many more bodies. Once the media made the connections with the death of Arthur Bingham and the story of the truck-driving medium who was beaten up by a ghost in that same house, there would be a wave of rumor and speculation, especially in the tabloids. Reporters would no doubt press Jenna Kellar for interviews. Lily reminded herself to give Jenna a call once in a while to check up on her, and to suggest that she refuse to talk to the press no matter what. Nothing good could come of it. The story would be everywhere. Lily planned to avoid it.

The door opened and a short man in a long charcoal coat came in. He had frizzy gray hair and a large mustache. He came to the counter and smiled at Lily.

"Do you have anything on Bigfoot?" he asked.

Lily returned his smile and said, "Right this way."

☐ **YES!**

Sign me up for the Leisure Horror Book Club and send my FREE BOOKS! If I choose to stay in the club, I will pay only $8.50* each month, a savings of $7.48!

NAME: _____

ADDRESS: _____

TELEPHONE: _____

EMAIL: _____

☐ I want to pay by credit card.

☐ **VISA**   ☐ **MasterCard**   ☐ **DISCOVER**

ACCOUNT #: _____

EXPIRATION DATE: _____

SIGNATURE: _____

Mail this page along with $2.00 shipping and handling to:
Leisure Horror Book Club
PO Box 6640
Wayne, PA 19087
Or fax (must include credit card information) to:
610-995-9274
You can also sign up online at **www.dorchesterpub.com**.
*Plus $2.00 for shipping. Offer open to residents of the U.S. and Canada only.
Canadian residents please call 1-800-481-9191 for pricing information.
If under 18, a parent or guardian must sign. Terms, prices and conditions subject to change. Subscription subject to acceptance. Dorchester Publishing reserves the right to reject any order or cancel any subscription.